The Danger Zone and Other Stories

Lost Classics

ERLE STANLEY GARDNER

Erle Stanley Gardner was not only the creator of classic courtroom dramas about Perry Mason; he was also one of the finest writers of novelettes and short stories for the fiction magazines of the 1920s through the1940s.

Working with the agents for the Gardner estate, Bill Pronzini will edit and Crippen & Landru will publish over the next few years the following books featuring Gardner's pulp characters:

The Danger Zone and Other Stories
The Casebook of Sidney Zoom
The Exploits of the Patent Leather Kid
The Investigations of Small, Weston & Burke
The Adventures of Señor Lobo
The Feats of the Man in the Silver Mask
The Return of Ed Jenkins, Phantom Crook
The Return of Lester Leith

The Danger Zone and Other Stories

by Erle Stanley Gardner 1889-1970

edited by Bill Pronzini

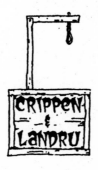

Crippen & Landru Publishers
Norfolk, Virginia
2004

Introduction © 2004 by Bill Pronzini

Cover Artwork by Juha Lindroos

"Lost Classics" cover design by Deborah Miller

Crippen & Landru logo by Eric Greene

ISBN (cloth edition) 1-932009-22-1
ISBN (softcover edition) 1-932009-23-x

FIRST EDITION

Crippen & Landru Publishers
P.O. Box 9315
Norfolk, VA 23505

Contents

Introduction
by Bill Pronzini

Erle Stanley Gardner was among the most prolific mystery writers of all time not only in number of published words — close to 20,000,000 — but in the number of series characters he created over the course of his remarkable fifty–year career. Beginning in the early 1920s he gave birth to no less than 49 unique detectives and adventurers who made two or more appearances in book or magazine form, and to dozens of others who might easily have become series characters if editors, readers, and/or Gardner himself had so desired.

Perry Mason, of course, is by far his most celebrated, fertile, and enduring invention; along with Della Street and Paul Drake, Mason appears in 82 of the 128 novels published by Gardner between 1933 and 1970. The amusing detective team of Donald Lam and Bertha Cool are featured in 29 book–length adventures as by A.A. Fair. Crusading district attorney Doug Selby has the starring role in nine, irrepressible and eccentric Gramps Wiggins and San Francisco attorney and former China service diplomat Terry Clane in two each, and criminologist Sidney Griff and advertising executive cum detective Sam Moraine in one each as by Carleton Kendrake and Charles J. Kenny, respectively.

All of Gardner's other series characters and might–have–beens were created for the magazine markets, both pulp–paper and slick–paper, and appear only in novelettes and short stories. Several hundred of these yarns saw print from the 1920s into the 1950s, the preponderance in a ten–year–span from 1926 to 1936 when Gardner lived up to his billing as "King of the Woodpulps" by producing and selling an average of one million words of fiction annually. *Argosy*, *Black Mask*, and *Detective Fiction Weekly* were his favorite pulp markets, printing nearly 200 stories among them. Series tales and one–shots also ran regularly in *Dime Detective*, *Clues*, *Street & Smith's Detective Story*, *Top–Notch*, *Black Aces*, *All Detective*, *Short Stories* and a host of others. Later, once the Perry Mason novels had begun to achieve widespread popularity, the editors of such slick magazines as *The Saturday Evening Post*, *Country Gentleman*, *Liberty*, *American Magazine*, *Cosmopolitan*, and *This Week* began clamoring for stories, and were obliged with series and prospective series tales. (Gardner even wrote one story on request for the hardboiled digest, *Manhunt* in 1955 — one of his weaker efforts, in part because it is a straight crime story with no series potential.)

Foremost among his amazing array of short–fiction creations are Ed Jenkins, the Phantom Crook, an outlaw and "famous lone wolf" who lives by his wits and solves crimes unjustly pinned on him by the police, many of which have San Francisco Chinatown settings; and Lester Leith, debonair man–about–town, whose "chain lightning mind" allows him to both outfox criminals and outmaneuver his butler, Scuttle, an undercover police spy. Jenkins appears in 72 novelettes published in *Black Mask* between 1925 and 1943, several of which were reprinted in two posthumous collections. Leith can be found in 65 novelettes in *Detective Fiction Weekly* from 1929 to 1943, and in one posthumous collection.

Other series characters with substantial careers include Bob Zane, desert prospector and manhunter, hero of the "Whispering Sands" tales that ran in *Argosy* in the early 30s; Sidney Zoom, master of disguises, who operates outside the law and serves the intelligence departments of three nations; Señor Arnaz de Lobo, Mexican soldier of fortune and revolutionist; the Patent Leather Kid, a wealthy club man with a secret and sinister sideline; Paul Pry, suave "crime juggler," who solves baffling cases by concentrating while banging on his collection of drums; Bob Larkin, adventurer–at–large and juggler whose only weapon is a billiard cue; Ken Corning, a brilliant young attorney and embryonic version of Perry Mason; Speed Dash, the Human Fly; Black Barr, a hardbitten Westerner who believes himself to be an instrument of divine justice; the firm of Small, Weston & Burke, detectives who specialize in macabre and horrific cases; and Sheriff Bill Eldon, good–hearted, aging, and shrewd, a pair of whose investigations comprise the 1947 collection, *Two Clues.*

Some if not all of the above may be familiar to modern readers. Not so the unsung sleuths featured in these pages, none of whom had more than half a dozen outings and several of whom (more's the pity) had only one. Even the most dedicated Gardner aficionado is unlikely to have made a previous acquaintance of:

* Snowy Shane, a tough–minded private eye with a penchant for highly unorthodox detective work.

* Slicker Williams, a felon and ex–convict "so crooked he could hide himself behind a corkscrew," who utilizes the tricks of his trade to help a damsel in distress and astonishes himself by reforming.

* Major Copely Blane, freelance diplomat and adventurer in international politics, who operates in "diplomatic danger zones."

* Key–Clew Clark, consulting criminologist and practitioner of the theory that one major clue dominates any given crime and points to the guilty party.

* Bob Crowder, another freelance detective whose stock–in–trade is the unorthodox and unexpected and who delights in thumbing his nose at the police.

* George Brokay, a wealthy, bored young bachelor whose fondest ambition is to put some excitement in his life by becoming a gentleman burglar, and who gets a great deal more than he bargained for when his wish is granted.

* Gilbert E. Best, as hardboiled and unscrupulous a character as any to come from his creator's typewriter, who is not above such niceties as blackmail and coercion to get results.

* Pete Strickland, big, quiet, philosophical, a deductive–reasoning dick employed by the Manufacturer's Investigating Bureau, who prefers the principles of common sense to those of psychological profiling.

* Barney Killigen, a somewhat flaky criminal attorney in constant money trouble, whose methods are weirdly unpredictable and who has unfailing faith in the power of classified newspaper ads; and his private secretary, Miss Winifred Ilsa "Wiggy" Graham, the narrator of his cases.

* Pete Wennick, law student, former private detective, and undercover operative for a large, highly ethical law firm that sometimes requires unethical investigative methods to best serve its clients.

* Wyoming rancher Howard Kane and his foreman, Buck Doxey, good samaritans and amateur detectives who effectively combine wiles, brawn, and specialized rangeland knowledge.

The eleven stories featuring this disparate assemblage of sleuthing talent contain all the qualities that made Gardner a globally bestselling author: unusual situations, ingenious gimmicks and plot twists, and lightning–paced, no–frills prose. Settings range from large cities to small towns, from San Francisco's Chinatown to a speeding train and the Wyoming grasslands. Some are straight detective tales of various types — ratiocinative, moderately hardboiled, cleverly manipulative. Others feature political intrigue, adventure in the grand pulp manner, rough–and–tumble action, early forensics, points of law and legal trickery. None has been previously collected, nor reprinted in any book or magazine in more than forty years.

Subsequent volumes in this series will showcase the exploits of some of Gardner's long–running but little known pulp series characters — Sidney Zoom, Señor Lobo, The Patent Leather Kid, and Small, Weston & Burke, among others — as well as uncollected tales starring Ed Jenkins and Lester Leith. The first of these volumes, *The Casebook of Sidney Zoom* is scheduled for publication by Crippen & Landru in the spring of 2005.

Petaluma, California
January 2004

Snowy Ducks for Cover

If Molly O'Keefe had been what is known in the vernacular as a "swell looker," Frank Sheridane would never have consulted "Snowy" Shane. For Sheridane was fully as keen a business man as any of the criminal lawyers who handled the big–time murder cases; and it needed no expert in mental arithmetic to reach the conclusion that the more fee for Snowy Shane, the less for Sheridane.

But Sheridane liked to win his cases. A death penalty verdict was as incon–venient for defense counsel as it was fatal for the client. Hence, he consulted the chunky little detective and put his cards on the table. Snowy Shane called the turn with neatness and despatch.

"Bum looker, eh?"

"Not so hot, why?"

"Just wondered. You'd have gone before a jury and trusted to a few tears if she'd been a mamma."

"Yeah, maybe. Anyhow, I'm here. It's up to you."

Snowy Shane had acquired his nickname for a bushy crop of gray hair which silvered his head with a grizzled mane. His eyes matched his hair, steel cold, with the glint which comes from frosted grass when the sun first strikes it. He was a fast worker, and the police would have none of him. He didn't play the game along orthodox lines, but took shortcuts whenever he felt reasonably certain of his ultimate goal.

He picked a pipe from his pocket, regarded the polished bowl lovingly, crammed in moist crumbs of fragrant tobacco and grunted.

"What you want me to do?"

"Get her out, of course."

"Is she guilty?"

The lawyer grinned.

"She tells me she isn't," he confided.

"Humph," grunted the detective. "If she ain't, who is?"

Frank Sheridane knew the ways of the chunky detective, knew just how far he could be trusted. He bit the end from a cigar, struck a match and rotated the tobacco between his fingers as he applied the flame, making certain the cigar would burn evenly.

"Harley Robb, president of the Mutual Morehomes Building & Loan had been dipping into the funds, using them for speculation. He was short something over a million."

Snowy Shane nodded.

"He was exposed by someone, forced to sign a confession. That confession has every earmark of having been written under a great emotional strain. It's all in his handwriting."

The lawyer took a folded paper from his pocket.

"Original?" asked Snowy Shane.

"No. A copy. Here's what it says."

"I, Harley Robb, President of the Mutual Morehomes Building & Loan have been embezzling the funds for speculation. I admit my guilt. I had no accomplices. I alone am to blame. Harry Robb."

"That confession was sent by special messenger to the chairman of the advisory committee. Naturally he went at once to interview Robb. He took a detective with him. They found Robb dead — murdered."

Snowy Shane grunted.

"Sure it wasn't suicide?"

"Yes. He was stabbed. There'd been some sort of a struggle."

"Who was the chairman of the advisory committee?"

"Arthur Sprang."

"Who loses the money Robb took?"

"Lots of people. Sprang for one; my client for another. She will lose all of her savings."

The white–haired detective toyed with a pencil. His cold gray eyes regarded the lawyer contemplatively.

"Clues?" he asked.

"There weren't any."

"Why pick on the jane, then?"

"Because she was the last person to see him alive, so far as the police can find out."

"Tell me about it."

"The murder happened some time around midnight. Robb had been at the office, giving the secretary, Molly O'Keefe, some dictation. He seemed distraught, nervous. She went home shortly before twelve. She says Robb was still in the office.

"The confession reached the chairman of the advisory committee around one o'clock in the morning. A messenger had been summoned over the telephone, ordered to take an envelope that would be found pinned to the office door, and deliver it to the address shown on the envelope.

"That envelope was found pinned to the door, delivered. It contained the confession. Sprang was home and in bed when the message was delivered. He summoned a detective and they went at once to the office of the company, found the door locked, forced it, found the body of Robb.

"There had been a struggle. A chair or two was smashed. Rugs were wrinkled and pitched around into the corners of the waxed floor. Robb had received several stabs. It was a messy job.

"Robb wore a wrist watch. It had been smashed in the struggle. The hands pointed to 11:57. My client caught a street car at 12:15. There was a speck of blood on the outside of the envelope in which the confession was enclosed.

"When they arrested Molly O'Keefe they found a wallet that has been identified as belonging to Robb. It contained something over ten thousand dollars in cash. She had hidden it in the mattress of her bed and then sewed up the mattress where she had slit it to put the wallet in."

The criminal lawyer regarded the tip of his cigar judiciously. Snowy Shane grunted an interruption.

"What's her story — on the wallet?"

"She says Robb dictated to her, seemed very nervous, asked her how much money she had in the company. She told him around fifteen thousand dollars, money she'd been saving for years. He took his wallet from his pocket, told her to keep it in a safe place, if anything happened to her investment to consider the money in the nature of a repayment; but never to let anyone know she had it."

Shane sighed.

"What's the police theory?"

"That Robb told her of his shortage, wrote out the confession. That she asked him about her savings, that he told her they had gone, along with the rest, that she drew a knife, struggled with him, killed him, took the wallet from his body and beat it."

"Find the knife?" asked Snowy Shane.

"No. They can't find it."

"Any stains on her clothes?"

"No. That's a point in her favor."

Shane shrugged his massive shoulders.

"Looks like she could beat the rap before a jury. If they ain't got nothing more than that, it'll be all circumstantial evidence. She could spiel her piece to the jury and raise a reasonable doubt."

The lawyer made a grimace.

"She's got skinny legs," he said, "and a homely face."

"How old?"

"Around forty–three, looks fifty. And — well, the case is young yet. You can't tell what the police will discover later on. I want to get you started now."

"Huh, want me to beat the police to it, eh?"

"Yes."

"And if you're afraid they'll discover something, it's because you've got a hunch your client's guilty."

"Our client."

"Not yet," said Snowy Shane with a grin.

Frank Sheridane twisted the cigar around and around in his mouth.

"She might be, at that," he admitted. "It's funny that Robb would have given her virtually all the cash he had. If he was carrying ten thousand bucks around in his pocket it was getaway money. You know what these looters do as well as I do. They always keep a bunch of cash on them for a quick getaway."

Snowy Shane squinted his eyes in silent thought for a few moments.

"Funny he could have copped that much swag without the advisory committee getting wise."

The lawyer's eyes narrowed.

"If we can get that thought across to the jury, backed by some evidence, we may save our client."

"Your client," said Shane, cupping the hot bowl of his pipe in caressing fingers.

"Maybe if you could find some facts to work on," went on the lawyer, heedless of the comment, "I could pin a theory."

"When was the room janitored?" asked Snowy Shane, interrupting.

"After the office closed."

"Robb was having a night session?"

"So it seems."

"No one else in the room?"

"No."

"If we could show someone else had been in the room, then what?"

The lawyer heaved a sigh.

"Then we'd stand a chance," he said.

"What you want me to do?"

"Give me some facts to work on. I want you to pull some of your fourth degree stuff and give our client a break."

Snowy Shane grinned.

"All right," he conceded, "let's get started and see what we can do for our client."

The attorney chuckled.

"Knew you'd come around," he said.

Shane bristled.

"It was the fourth degree stuff that turned the trick for you," he said.

And Frank Sheridane, criminal attorney, and, therefore, shrewd judge of human nature, suppressed a smile. With Snowy Shane on the job the battle was underway, and he had been saving that fourth degree comment for just the proper time.

The president's private office of the Mutual Morehomes Building & Loan had ceased to be a private sanctorum and had become a chamber of death.

A uniformed officer guarded the door, admitted the lawyer only after careful scrutiny of his pass. The rugs were still rumpled back, the gruesome red splotches discolored the floor. A chalked outline showed where the body had lain. The room reeked of the smell of death and the acrid fumes of flashlight powder where police and newspaper photographers had taken pictures of what had been found in the office.

The outer offices housed hushed groups of wide–eyed women employees who discussed the case in whispers. A detective accompanied Sheridane and Snowy Shane into the death chamber a cigar tilted in his mouth, his eyes weary and watchful.

"Take a look–see," he said, "but don't touch nothin'."

Snowy Shane planted himself in the middle of the room. His eyes went slithering about, steely cold, watchful, alert.

"Fingerprints, Joe?"

The detective shook his head. "Nope."

"Find the knife?"

"Nope."

"What kind of a sticker was it?"

"The surgeon says it was paper knife, or a thin stiletto, the kind a frail would pack."

Snowy Shane grunted.

"Let's go," he said, after a while.

Sheridane followed him to the outer office. There Shane secured the names of the three members of the advisory committee — Arthur Sprang, the chairman; Ernest Bagley and Sidney Symmes. He also secured their addresses.

"Looks sort of gloomy," said the attorney as they descended in the elevator. "I'll go to my office. You let me know if —"

Shane shook his head.

"You'll stay with me. I'm going to see these men. I may want a witness."

The lawyer's eyes lighted.

"Fourth degree?" he asked. "Some of your special kind?"

Shane tamped tobacco into the bowl of his pipe, thrust it into his mouth and gripped the stem with firm teeth.

"Yeah," he remarked, "stick around."

They drove to the home of Arthur Sprang first. That individual was paunchy, red–eyed, pasty–jowled. The shock had left him nervous. He consented to see the pair with the statement that the interview would be brief.

"What time did you get the letter?" asked Shane, his gray eyes gimleting the red–rimmed ones of the heavy man.

"About one o'clock."

"Humph," said Shane and filled his pipe.

The attorney produced a cigar, offered one to the man who let his eyes shift restlessly, from one to the other.

"Thanks," said Sprang, "I have my own pet brand."

He produced a case from his inside pocket, selected a cigar, bit off the end and spat it explosively on the floor. His hand shook slightly.

"Terrific shock," he said.

Snowy Shane leaned forward, jabbed an impressive finger at the bosom of the chairman of the advisory committee.

"How was he lyin' when you busted in the door?"

Sprang repressed a shudder with a visible effort.

"Sprawled out," he said, and shook his shoulders.

"Head toward the door or away from it?"

"Away from it."

Shane grinned triumphantly.

"That," he remarked, crisply, "is exactly what I wanted to know. Come on, Frank."

And he got to his feet, led the puzzled lawyer to the door.

"But you said you wanted to get some very vital information you thought I might have," murmured Arthur Sprang.

"We've got it," said Shane and slammed the door.

In the taxicab, the lawyer regarded him speculatively.

"Really, Snowy, I don't see just what you gained."

"Shut up," said the detective. "I'm thinkin'."

They journeyed in silence to the office of Ernest Bagley. That individual, thin, dour, very nervous, greeted them with a dry, husky voice, shook hands with big, bony fingers that were cold and dry. He was past middle age, abnormally long of arm, high of cheek bone, thick of lip, hollow of cheek.

"You wanted to ask about the murder, you said, over the telephone?"

"Yeah," said Snowy Shane, plunging into the discussion without any polite preliminaries. "How long you known Robb?"

"Ten years."

"Members of the same golf club and all that?"

"No. I don't play golf. Neither did Robb."

Snowy Shane produced his pipe from his pocket, tamped tobacco into the bowl, regarded it ruefully.

"Any pipe tobacco? Mine's run out."

Bagley shook his head.

"I use cigarettes, roll my own. I can give you some of my tobacco I use in them, though."

Shane nodded. Bagley produced a cloth sack, handed it to the detective. Shane filled his pipe.

"Only had half enough for a smoke," he said. "This'll come in handy."

He passed back the sack. Bagley took a packet of brown papers from a vest pocket, rolled a cigarette. His hand shook slightly.

"Ever have any mutual business interests with Robb?" asked Shane, abruptly.

The bony fingers stopped, midway in their task.

"A few," admitted Ernest Bagley, and the cold caution of his guarded tone was apparent to both of his listeners, trained as they were in the subtleties of human prevarications.

"Profitable?" asked Shane.

Bagley looked up from his cigarette.

"That," I think, "is hardly a proper question."

Shane got to his feet.

"All right," he said. "If you won't cooperate with us, we'll have to reach it some other way."

The attorney followed him from the office, his eyes puzzled. Bagley watched them with a face that was utterly void of expression.

"A good poker player," said the attorney, as they got into the taxicab once more.

"Yeah," said Shane. "We'll go see Symmes now."

Sheridane studied the squat, powerful man with the steel–gray eyes and snowy hair.

"Shane, do you know what you're doing, or are you just messing around in the dark?"

The detective regarded him with eyes that were wide with surprise. "Why, of course I know what I'm doing. You said you wanted facts, didn't you? Something you could pin a defense to?"

"Yes," said the attorney, "you give me a peg to hang a defense on, and that's all I want. I'll do the rest."

The detective nodded.

"And you don't see what I'm doing?"

"No. I'm hanged if I do. I presume it's some of your fourth degree stuff, but I don't see it."

"Stick around then," advised Snowy Shane, "and save me a cigar. I'm going to switch from a pipe, after a while."

Sheridane regarded him with thought–filmed eyes.

"You know I've got to have something twelve men can act on," he said.

The detective slumped his head on his shoulders.

"Yeah," he said, and it was apparent that his thoughts were far away. The taxicab lurched over the streets. The two passengers lapsed into utter silence, each occupied with his own thoughts.

Sydney Symmes was a big, broad–shouldered, frank–eyed man whose skin still showed a pale bronze. Undoubtedly, he had lived much of his life in the open. He had just lit a cigarette, and kept it in one corner of his mouth as he shook hands, muttered a conventional greeting.

Snowy Shane regarded him with eyes that held a suggestion of bewilderment.

"How come you're in the building and loan," he asked. "You're an outdoor man."

Sydney Symmes boomed forth a laugh.

"If you're as good a detective on crime as you've just shown yourself to be on occupations, you'll prove an air–tight case on that girl."

Shane shook his head, a fierce, swift, impatient gesture.

"I'm trying to show the girl's innocent."

"Oh," said Symmes, and his manner underwent a subtle change. "I thought you were working for the company."

Snowy Shane let his gray eyes glitter with frosty belligerency.

"You don't want to have this girl convicted unless she's guilty, do you?"

Symmes clamped his jaws in a straight line.

"Miss O'Keefe is guilty," he said.

Snowy Shane grinned.

"Oh well, let's not argue about it. Where did you get your outdoor complexion?"

Sydney Symmes became cordial again. His eyes softened.

"Forest ranger for the government for fifteen years, down in New Mexico and Southern California."

Snowy Shane turned to the lawyer.

"You got any questions?" he asked.

Sheridane frowned.

"I'm listening," he commented.

Shane returned his attention to Symmes.

"Funny you left the service to get into this game."

"No," smiled Symmes, "it wasn't. You see, I was educated as an attorney, but my health gave out and I went into the open. Robb was in my class at college. He often suggested that I should come back to the city. A year or so ago he sold me on the idea. I had a little money. I put it into the building and loan and, through his influence, was placed on the advisory committee."

Snowy Shane rubbed a speculative forefinger along the angle of his jaw.

"The confession must have come as a shock to you."

Symmes squinted his eyes, leaned forward. His fists clenched with visible emotion. His voice quivered.

"That confession is a forgery. The man who says Robb was short in his accounts is a damned liar, and that goes for anyone who says it. See?"

There was no mistaking his belligerency.

Shane got to his feet.

"Sure we see," he remarked, and led the way to the door.

"Wait a minute," invited Symmes. "I meant no particular offense. I was sticking up for my friend, and I got a little hot–headed, I guess."

"Yeah," commented Shane. "You would. That's your outdoor training. See you later, maybe. Good–bye."

Sheridane's brow was corrugated as he settled back in the cushions of the cab.

"That some of the fourth degree stuff?"

Shane nodded casually.

"That's it," he said.

"Well," commented the lawyer in a voice from which he strove to keep his impatience, "it doesn't help any."

Snowy Shane stretched out his chunky arms, yawned.

"Uh huh," he agreed. "Let's go back to the office where the murder was pulled. I want to see something else."

Joe Karg, police detective in charge, regarded their second visit with dour disapproval.

"Didn't you guys see enough the first time?" he asked.

Snowy Shane transfixed him with hostile gaze.

"No," he said.

He took a cloth sack of tobacco from his pocket, held his pipe cupped in his left hand, poured in the tobacco, and some of the grains spilled to the floor. He lit the pipe and broke the match in two pieces, flipped it under the table, bent to examine the floor.

"The old bloodhound," remarked Karg with a grin, "looking for tracks."

"Shut up, Joe," said Snowy Shane.

He puffed placidly at his pipe, his eye, meanwhile, peering along the floor as though taking measurements. Sheridane nervously glanced at his watch, took a cigar from his pocket, bit off the end, spat it explosively.

"Listen, Snowy. I've got to get to my office. I can't just stick around."

Snowy Shane straightened. His eyes were gleaming with frosty enthusiasm.

"Joe," he said, "will you ring up Sprang, Bagley and Symmes and tell 'em to come over here right away. I got the murder solved."

Joe Karg jeered at him.

"Yeah, you're the human bloodhound. Murders are open books to you. You give 'em the once over and —"

Snowy interrupted.

"Of course, if you don't want a promotion."

He let his voice trail off into silence. Joe Karg thought that matter over.

"Would I get the credit?"

"You'd get the credit."

The police detective moved to the telephone.

Sprang was the first to answer the summons. He entered the office, puzzled, awkward, ill at ease. Snowy Shane sat him in a chair, taking pains to make him face the window.

"Sprang," he said, slowly and impressively, "someone was in this room last night. Someone who smoked cigars, and bit off the ends,"

Sprang's glassy eyes stared uncomprehendingly for a moment.

"You mean me?" he asked, a flush suffusing his face.

"I don't know," said Snowy Shane, "but here's the end off a cigar that was on the floor. You smoke your own brand. Let me have one of 'em."

The man handed over a cigar, meekly, questioningly. Snowy Shane extended his hand. "Thanks. That's all."

"You called me over here for this?"

"Yes. That's all. The department will analyze the tobacco in the end of the cigar and the one you gave me."

Sprang lurched to his feet.

"Of all the damned fools!" he snapped, and lunged from the office.

When he had gone Sheridane eyed the detective coldly.

"I presume you are aware," he said, formally, "that I was smoking in here a few minutes ago, and the cigar end you have is one I bit off."

Snowy Shane said nothing. Bagley was entering the room, nervous, furtive, almost cringing in his manner.

"You smoke cigarettes. You roll 'em. Ever spill tobacco?" asked Snowy Shane.

The nervous man blinked his eyes.

"Huh?" he asked.

Snowy Shane pointed to the floor.

"Get down here," he said. "Look here on the floor, grains of tobacco. The same sort that you use to roll your cigarettes. That means somebody was in this room after the janitor cleaned it last night. That somebody smoked same brand of tobacco you do.

"Now suppose that somebody was the murderer. What'd be more natural than for him to roll a cigarette after he'd done the job? And his hand would be shaking, and he'd spill some of the tobacco, and —"

The nervous man interrupted.

"You lie!" he screamed. "I wasn't here. I know nothing about the murder. I can prove it. You're a double–crossing crook. You planted that tobacco here. You came out to my house and saw the kind of tobacco I smoked, and —"

Joe Karg clapped a hand on the man's shoulder.

"Easy, bo," he said, warningly.

Snowy Shane waved a hand toward the door.

"That's all," he said.

Bagley wanted to remain and talk, but Karg escorted him out. They closed the door and waited some five minutes for Symmes. Karg's eyes were singularly unenthusiastic.

"Hope you don't think you're getting anywhere with this stuff, Snowy," he observed.

Snowy Shane shrugged his huge shoulders.

There was an impatient knock at the door. He opened it to admit Symmes. Snowy Shane sat him in the same chair, facing the window, dropped to his knees and pointed to the broken match.

"Symmes," he said, "you were a ranger in the dry southwest. Did you, by any chance, learn to break matches into two pieces before you threw them away?"

Symmes looked at the match, laughed good–naturedly

"Hell no. I've heard of fellows who did that. I never did."

Snowy Shane got to his feet, dusted the knees of his trousers.

"Thanks," he said. "That's all. I guess I pulled a boner, Karg. None of these men had anything to do with it."

Symmes grinned, extended his hand.

"No hard feelings," he said. "You detectives have got to do your duty. Call on me any time."

He left the office. Joe Karg's face showed hostility. "The next time I let a private dick horn in and sell me on a wild theory, you'll know it!" he snapped.

Snowy Shane nodded, gloomily.

"Sorry, Joe."

"And the next time you catch me wasting time on a wild goose chase —" began Sheridane, but Snowy Shane's eye transfixed him with disdainful hostility.

"That'll be about all, Frank. You make mistakes yourself. Come on. You've got one more job."

He led the way to the elevators. Sydney Symmes was standing before the shaft which showed a red light.

"Just in time," he said.

Shane grinned.

"Figured we'd be," he said.

They rode to the Street.

"Come up to my office a minute," invited Shane.

Symmes looked at his watch, frowned.

"Only take a few minutes," said Shane.

Symmes consented with a very apparent lack of enthusiasm. Once in the office, Snowy Shane began to talk.

"I got a theory about this case," he said. "Robb didn't cop that coin without some split. The guy he split with was a friend. And he didn't write that confession when Molly O'Keefe was in the office. Remember, she was a secretary, and he'd been dictating to her. If he'd been goin' to make a confession while she was there he'd have dictated it to her, an' made a long statement.

"That's the way those guys do when they kick through. They write a regular smear. I've seen 'em before. But Robb's confession was awfully brief, too brief. And it put too much stress on the fact that he was the only goat. I have an idea somebody made him write out that confession, put the screws on him somehow.

"Then, after the confession was written, the guy croaked him, telephoned to the messenger service and told them to come and get the envelope for delivery."

Symmes smiled, nodded.

"It's good to see someone who really runs trail on a case," he said. "That's the way we used to do it in the forestry service, just run down trail until we got to where we were headed. But how about the time of the murder? The wrist watch shows that it was right about the time Miss O'Keefe left, doesn't it?"

"Yeah," said Snowy. "The guy that croaked him set the wrist watch back, and then smashed it. That was done after the murder, not before."

He took out a cigarette case from his pocket, extended it to Symmes. Symmes took a cigarette, struck a match, dropped it to the floor, still burning, picked it up and blew it out.

Snowy Shane beckoned to Sheridane.

"I want to see you a minute," he said. "We'll be right back, Symmes. Just wait here."

Sheridane followed Snowy Shane into the corridor.

"What's the idea?" he asked.

Shane grinned at him.

"That cigarette I gave him was awful. It'll just arouse the tobacco appetite, but he can't smoke it. He'll start in smoking one of his own, maybe three or four, if we wait long enough."

"What'll that do?" asked Sheridane.

"Make a smoke screen," said Shane, and grinned.

"You think he's guilty?"

Shane shrugged his shoulders.

"He'll leave if we keep him waiting," protested Sheridane.

"He can't. The door's locked. There's a night latch that's rigged just opposite from most of 'em. It spring–locks a man in, instead of out."

"But I don't get the idea!"

"You said if you could prove some member of the advisory committee was in that room during the night you'd do the rest, didn't you?"

"Yes, and I meant it. That's all the break I want before a jury."

Shane grinned.

"Let's go down and buy some pipe tobacco, I been smokin' odds and ends until my throat tickles."

They went to the tobacco store, took plenty of time. Then Shane almost forcibly restrained Sheridane from returning to the office until another ten minutes had passed.

He opened the door of the private office. Sydney Symmes glowered at them. His face was dark with wrath.

"What the hell's the idea of locking me in here and disconnecting the telephone? I couldn't get out, and —"

Snowy Shane walked past him to the ash tray.

It was littered with cigarette stubs. The detective started fingering through stubs until he found a charred match. It was straight, unbroken. He found other and another, but the third had been broken, then straightened.

"Well?" said Shane.

Symmes laughed nervously.

"To tell you the truth, you got me pretty well flustered up there in that room. I'm going to tell you chaps the truth. I was there last night.

"I got there around eleven fifteen. Miss O'Keefe had been taking dictation, but she'd stepped into the ladies' room to put on a little make–up. Robb told me he was finished dictating. But be seemed all nervous, wrought up over something, so I didn't stay.

"When I heard of the murder I determined to say absolutely nothing about having been there, for fear someone might think I'd come to see him, found out Miss O'Keefe was there, and then gone out, waited for her to go, and then gone on in again."

"As a matter of fact I do break matches. All the rangers in that section of the country do — or used to when I rode it. You flustered me when you dug up that match. I knew I must be careful.

"But you got me shut up here, and I was nervous, and I got to smoking and breaking matches before I thought of it. I straightened 'em again as well as I could. I'd have burnt 'em up, but I knew wood ash is distinctive, and I had an idea you chaps were watching me through some sort of a peep–hole.

"What I'm telling you fellows is the absolute truth, and I want you to believe it."

He looked at them with steady, pleading eyes.

Snowy Shane nodded his head solemnly.

"You've got me sold," he said.

Symmes heaved a sigh.

"I thought you'd see how it was."

Shane nodded again, smiled.

"Glad you explained, Symmes. You can go. I'll have to report to the officer in charge, but there'll be nothing to it. They may ask you a question or two."

Symmes lunged for the door.

"Good–bye Symmes."

"Good–bye!"

The door closed. Sheridane glowered at the detective.

"Of all the damned fools! What if he was telling the truth? We could have browbeat him, called in the police, got the newspaper reporters, got Symmes admitting he had told a false story — Hell, with that much of a break I could give this jane a chance at a hung jury, or a cinch on copping a plea."

Shane smiled.

"Stick around," he said. "We could not browbeat that bozo on suspicion. You wait here. I'm going to run over and see Joe Karg."

And he shot out of the door as a man who is going some place in very much of a hurry. He went at once to the death room, where Joe Karg sneered at him.

"Oh yes," sniffed the officer, sarcastically. "I'll get the credit. I'll get —"

He stopped. Shane was trying to light a cigarette, and his hand shook so that the match simply wouldn't connect with the end of the cigarette until he had steadied it with the other hand.

"Listen, Joe," said Snowy Shane, his voice stuttering with excited eagerness. "It's the b–b–biggest thing in years. I pulled a boner on it!"

"What the hell," asked Karg with interest, "are you talking about?"

"That match. That broken match."

"Hell, you planted all of those smoke clues."

"No, no. That is, Karg, you're right about me planting 'em, but I had a hot tip on Symmes. When he swore he never broke a match I knew he was lying. I got hold of him after he left here and got him up to my office.

"Well, here's what happened. I got him started smoking, and he broke a match before he thought. Then I put it to him, locked the door, rattled the handcuffs, gave him everything I had, and he confessed!"

"What!" yelled the officer.

"Telling you the whole truth, Joe. Honest Injun!"

The officer was suspicious.

"You've lied to us before, Snowy."

"But never unless the lie cleared up a case," protested Shane.

"Well, go on. Then what happened?"

"He thought it over, and retracted his confession and thought up another lie that'd get him out of it. See?"

Something of the detective's trembling excitement communicated itself to Joe Karg.

"What the hell!" he exclaimed. "Why didn't you send for me?"

"Didn't have time. Listen. Here's what happened. He knew Robb was at the office dictating. He hung around until the jane went home. Then he got in and had it out with Robb. He and Robb had been splitting the take. Robb was going to confess. Symmes tried to hold him in line, couldn't. The state examiners were on the tail of the shortage and Robb was panicky.

"So Symmes finally got Robb to promise that Robb would take all the blame in his confession. Robb wrote out that confession. Then Symmes croaked him.

"He set the watch back, smashed it, and dusted. He telephoned the messenger department to come and get the confession and left it pinned to the door. Then he went to bed.

"That was just the way I had it doped. The confession stressed too much about Robb being the only one who was responsible."

Joe Karg's eyes were glistening.

"Never mind what you doped out. What did Symmes himself say?"

"Just what I've told you."

"Then what?"

"Then I told him to write it out. He started, but got cagey, wanted to know if I could guarantee he could cop a plea. Then one thing led to another, and he got the idea he could swear that he'd gone into the building around eleven fifteen to see Robb, that he'd found Miss O'Keefe out powdering her nose, that he'd lit a cigarette, dropped the broken match, and then beat it before Miss O'Keefe came back.

"So that's what he's going to swear to now. He swears he never did confess, that he never was alone with me, that Sheridane was there all the time, and a lot of hooey like that."

Karg took a deep breath.

"If I'd only been there! Then what?"

"Nothing. I let him go. I figured I'd let him think he'd checkmated me. Then you could go to work on him."

Joe Karg bit a cigar clean in two.

"Son of a gun! We'll fix that baby. We'll frame a stoolie to dress up like a janitor and swear he saw him hanging around the building. We wouldn't use the stoolie in court, but we sure can use him to make Symmes cave in again.

"Listen, Snowy, will you do something for me?"

"Anything, Joe."

"Well, just duck out of this case. Leave it all to me. You promised the credit."

Shane was lugubrious.

"I promised Sheridane I'd get the broad free if she was innocent."

"Well, if I get Symmes that's all you want."

Karg looked at the detective anxiously. Snowy Shane thrust forward his hand.

"It's a go," he said.

Sheridane and Snowy Shane sat in a suburban hotel where they had registered under assumed names.

"I still don't get the idea," he said. "You told me you'd give me the low down at breakfast."

Snowy Shane glanced at his watch.

"Well, I started something."

"Fourth degree?"

"Yes. I told Karg that Symmes had confessed, and then I ducked you out of town so they wouldn't start quizzing you and have you throw me down."

The lawyer's jaw sagged.

"You told Joe Karg what?"

"That Symmes had confessed."

"Good heavens! Of all the bone–headed fools! Why, that's criminal defamation of character. What'd you do that for?"

Shane shrugged.

"You see, if Symmes had confessed to us, Karg wouldn't have had much credit. Then again, Symmes would need more third degree stuff than we could give him. But, by letting Karg think, on the q.t. that Symmes had confessed, Karg would start working up a case against Symmes.

"Otherwise they'd never have done anything, because they thought they had the case pinned on the broad."

Sheridane sighed.

"You kept me out of it?"

"Sure, swore you weren't even with me."

The attorney sighed again, this time with some measure of relief.

"You lied to Karg."

Shane nodded easily.

"Sure. A dick's gotta lie occasionally. It's part of the game. We all do. I just tell different kinds of lies from the other guys. You've gotta catch crooks the best way you can, not the way you'd like to catch them."

A uniformed bell boy walked into the dining room.

"You said to notify you if an 'Extra' came out, sir. Here it is."

Snowy Shane reached for the paper. Across the top, in screaming head lines, were the words —

SYMMES CONFESSES ROBB'S MURDER
Detective Joe Karg forces confession after clever deduction traps culprit in mass of lies. Police release Molly O'Keefe.

The attorney glanced with wide eyes, incredulously at the detective.

"Of all the nervy guys in the world, you're it!"

Snowy Shane made a deprecatory gesture.

"No. It's a simple system. All I had to do was to sell the police on the right idea and let 'em go to it. We could never have broken Symmes down. Joe Karg could, and did."

The lawyer reached for checkbook and fountain pen.

"You win, Snowy."

The detective grinned.

"Yeah," he said, "I got by, but only by the skin of my teeth. You hired me because my methods were unusual. Well, they were unusual enough this time. Just make that check payable to bearer. I ducked for cover after pulling that last fast one, and I'm going to stay undercover until Joe gets his promotion."

The Corkscrew Kid

Warden Bogger was a hard man, and he gloried in his hardness. He had no sympathy in his make—up. To him, justice was stern and righteous. His rugged countenance, as grim as granite, betrayed his uncompromising nature.

Slicker Williams stood before the warden. He stood slim and straight. His finely chiseled countenance was a mask.

The warden surveyed him with the grim disapproval which the plodder always feels for the man who has the fire of imagination.

"The trouble with you, Slicker, is that you think you can beat the law."

Slicker took it, erect, silent, outwardly attentive.

He was attired in the conventional prison garb of discharge. The prison tailored clothes, the prison made shoes, the utter newness of every garment betrayed him for what he was, a con who had finished his term and was on his way out of the big house.

The warden made a grimace.

"There's no need for me to talk to you. I could stand here from now until doomsday and preach, and you'd stand there, looking at me, thinking in the back of your mind what a lot of bunk I was handing out, waiting impatiently for me to finish, so you could go out and have another fling at beating the law.

"It ain't as though you were dumb, or couldn't do anything else. You're skilful with your hands. You've mastered every branch of law breaking, and you've done it with an ease that shows how capable you'd be, if you just went straight. But you won't go straight. You're so crooked you could hide behind a corkscrew!"

Slicker said nothing. His hands were at his sides, his eyes level, attentive, and expressionless.

The warden made a gesture of disgust.

"You can go now."

He pressed a button.

Yet, had he only known it, a little sympathy would have cracked through the shell of Slicker's reserve. Slicker was feeling very lonely, very much abused. A kind word or two, a pat on the back, might, perhaps ... But Warden Bogger didn't believe in wasting sympathy on crooks in the first place, and he was temperamentally unfitted to deal it out in the second place.

So Slicker Williams walked out of the penitentiary with murder in his heart, and the feeling that he was as friendless as a stray cat.

Slicker knew how he had happened to "lose out" that last time. It had been because he had been betrayed by a stool pigeon, and Slicker intended to kill that stool pigeon.

He wanted that much of a joke on the law.

He would do it in such a manner that there wouldn't be the slightest clew that would point to him, nothing tangible that the law could lay its hand on, and use as a basis for prosecution. Yet everyone in the underworld, everyone in the inner circle of police, every shivering, cowardly stoolie in the pack, would know that Slicker had had his revenge.

It would be clever. It would be fool—proof, one perfect crime. The warden had told Slicker he could hide behind a corkscrew. Slicker would show them just how easily and completely he could hide behind a corkscrew.

The interurban car jolted him toward the lights which marked the big city. Slicker nursed his thoughts. The corners of his lips played in a smile.

The car stopped at a suburb.

A girl got on. She was sad—eyed, patient—faced. She was tired. The gray of fatigue had tinged her face. The eyes were washed out, lifeless.

There was no vacant seat save the one by Slicker.

The girl sat down. Slicker could hear the sigh as her tired shoulders rested against the back of the seat.

In her hand she carried a brief case. She set it down on the floor, between her feet.

Slicker knew the exact moment her eyes rested upon the newness of his prison garb, on the tell—tale prison shoes. He saw her turn her head away, and interpreted the gesture incorrectly.

The car jolted toward town.

Slicker wished the journey would end. He wanted to get back into the underworld where he could ditch those prison clothes. He wanted to kill that stoolie. He wanted to get away from all contact with these high hat office workers who shuddered away from him because he was a crook.

Then the girl turned back, and Slicker suppressed a start of astonishment. Apparently she hadn't turned away because she was disgusted. She had turned away to hide the tears that came to her gray eyes.

Slicker saw her blink, and then stared incredulously at the hand that rested on his arm.

"I wondered if you wouldn't like to let me make you a cup of chocolate, when we get to the city," she said.

He stared at her unbelievingly.

The eyes were not bold, they weren't commercial. They were pleading and sad, and the voice was vibrant with that quality which had been so singularly absent from the voice of the warden, sympathy.

"You see," she hurried on. "I had a brother who went through the mill up there. And you look so awfully like him that when I saw you were from there ..."

Slicker knew the type now — a sob sister.

Slicker could use fairly good English when occasion required, and he was able to modulate his voice into a semblance of breeding. It always amused him to talk to people who had classified him as a toughie, in a voice that made them start with surprise.

He was polite now, urbane, polished.

He lifted his hat and bowed.

"Madame, I can appreciate your sympathy, and its cause. Unfortunately, however, I have a previous engagement."

That didn't cause her to gasp in surprise.

"You talk just like Phil. He was my brother."

The tears were gone from her eyes, and her voice wasn't so sympathetic now. It was more of a friendly voice, the sort of voice one expects of a friend one has known for a long time.

Much to his own surprise, Slicker Williams continued to talk to her. She didn't mention the chocolate any more, and Slicker was genuinely sorry. He was commencing to like her.

She got out of the seat when the car jolted to a stop out in the district of the cheaper but respectable apartments.

"I'm leaving you here. I hope you ... hope you go straight!"

Slicker surprised himself again. He found himself getting to his feet, bowing, lifting his hat.

"I'll see you as far as your apartment, if you don't mind," he said.

The patient eyes quickened into a smile.

"I'd be delighted."

He got off the car, helped her off, and took her arm as she crossed the street. He felt proud of himself. She wasn't a sob sister at all, just a good pal that knew how a man felt when he was getting out of stir.

Her apartment was about a block and a half from the car line.

Slicker took her hand, bowed over it.

"Give me a ring some time. Ruth Mowbrae, Kenmore Apartments, and ..."

A figure stepped out of the shadows.

Slicker knew the meaning of the broad shoulders, the bull neck, the square–toed heavy–soled shoes. He braced himself. The old formula came to the tip of his tongue: "You ain't got anything on me," he started to say.

But he didn't say it.

The detective's business was with the woman.

"You're Ruth Mowbrae?"

She stared at him.

"Why yes. Why?"

"Work for The Stanwood Construction Company?"

"Yes."

"I want to take a look in that brief case, sister. I'm from headquarters."

And the heavy thumb flipped back the lapel of the coat to show the gleam of the star.

The girl seemed stupefied.

"Why ... why ... I have some home work that Mr. Stanwood wanted me to take with me ..."

Slicker Williams was ignored.

"That's all right, sister," said the detective, reaching over and taking the brief case from the girl's hand. "This is okay with Mr. Stanwood. He's the one that rang us up and told us to get in touch with you ... Hey, Bill!"

Another hulking shadow, similar to the first as two peas from the same pod, came out from the entrance to the apartment house.

"Let's take a look. Got the description of them bonds?"

"Yeah, I got it."

They snapped open the brief case. The flashlight reflected whitely from the interior. One of the men whistled.

"What are these?" he asked.

He fished out a packet of papers, folded, fastened together with elastic. The backs were lithographed in two colors.

"Why," said the girl, "those are the Investment Bonds."

"Yeah," said the detective. "What're they doing here?"

Ruth Mowbrae's hands were white as she clenched them together.

"That's what I don't know."

One of the men took another sheaf of papers from an inside pocket.

"What are these?"

The girl's exclamation was one of dismay

"You got those out of my room!" she said.

"Yeah. That's where they were, eh?"

"Yes. Those are some other bonds. I saw Mr. Neil Stanwood taking those out of the safe and putting them in his desk. I couldn't understand it. I intended to speak to Mr. H. W. Stanwood about it ... I felt there was something wrong, and I took the bonds out of Neil's desk and then telephoned H. W. and told him I must see him at my apartment, and he promised to come, but he was called out of town by a wire ... and so I kept them there. I hid them so no one would find them."

"Yeah," said the detective, and took her arm in a most efficiently business like grasp. "And how did it happen these investment bonds were in your brief case?"

"I don't know. I swear I don't know. Mr. Neil Stanwood might have put them there. He's been drinking pretty heavily lately, and ..."

"Yeah, sure," said the detective.

"Say, listen, guy," interjected Slicker Williams, "this could be a frame—up so easy it wouldn't even be funny. This guy she tells about could have seen her lifting the bonds he'd swiped, and knowing she was going to tell his father."

"His uncle," corrected the girl.

"All right then, his uncle, and —"

One of the detectives stretched out a powerful arm, took Slicker Williams by the shoulder and pulled him around.

"Well, well," he said, "see who's here. Who are you, little buttinsky? And do you want to take a nice little ride in a big black automobile with mesh screen all around the sides?"

Slicker Williams clenched an indignant fist.

The girl's tongue tripped into speech.

"No, no. He's just a man I met on the car. He reminded me of some one I knew, and he was seeing me home, and —"

"Oh," said the detective, "I see!"

And the sneer of his tone told more than the words themselves.

"Let's see," commented the other, amiably, "you got a brother in the pen, ain't you, Miss Mowbrae?"

"He's been discharged!" she snapped.

"Oh yes, that's so. And he wired you for money a little while back, and you sent him two thousand bucks, didn't you? He had to square a little job in Philadelphia, didn't he?"

She drew herself up, regal, dignified, silent.

"Where did you get that two thousand bucks?" asked the officer.

"I got it from my savings."

"Oh yes, and an audit shows that there's been a bunch of securities missing from the company. Ain't that funny! A real funny coincidence, just another one of those sort of things that *will* happen!"

The detective marched over to Slicker Williams, joined the one who had grasped Slicker's shoulder.

"Okay, guy. You got ten seconds to beat it, and don't make any more wise cracks. I have a hunch we'd oughta run you down to headquarters, but we'll give you a break. On your way."

"Say," protested Slicker, "ain't you guys got sense enough to know a frame–up when you see one?"

"She admitted she took the first batch of bonds up to her apartment and hid 'em, didn't she?"

"Yeah. But what does that prove?"

A brawny fist was brandished under Slicker's nose.

"Goin' to get smart, eh? Well, guy, you either make tracks, an' make 'em right now, or you take a ride in the nice black wagon. Which you go'nna do?"

And Slicker knew which he was going to do. With his record, he had just one thing to do.

He looked back over his shoulder at the corner.

The men were taking her away.

Slicker had been able to think circles around the police. Warden Bogger had called the turn. Slicker was one of the boys who wanted to match wits with the law and come out on top. He was the kind of man who could hide behind a corkscrew, and, figuratively speaking, he'd done that very thing, times without number.

He wasn't done yet — not by a long shot.

The sad–eyed girl had given him a break. He'd be a poor excuse not to do as much for her. He'd walked off because he knew he had to, not only because he couldn't keep out of a jam if he'd stayed, but because being in jail would have interfered with the plan he had in mind.

He remembered that the girl had got on at a suburban town. He remembered she was carrying work to do at home. He remembered she worked at The Stanwood Construction Company.

He consulted a telephone directory and looked up the suburban telephones. He found The Stanwood Construction Company, and he found a telephone listed under the name of H. W. Stanwood, "residence"; and one listed under the name of Neil Stanwood, "residence," and both telephones had the same number.

Slicker Williams knew a place in the city where he would be welcome. He went there.

There was a pawnshop downstairs, and a man who sat upstairs, behind a grimy door, in a little room that was littered with old papers and cobwebs. The man was abnormally fat and restless. He had restless eyes, restless hands, restless lips.

Like a spider in a web, Sam Felixburg sat and waited, and his waiting was very, very restless, and very, very productive.

He let his restless eyes slither over Slicker Williams, and his lips mouthed a greeting.

"Whatcha want, Slicker?"

"I want some cash for get–by money, a set of tools, and some soup."

Felix ran an uneasy tongue over flabby lips and raised his head back, washboarding the rolls of fat at the back of his neck.

"What d'yuh want soup for? You never was a soup man. The safe you can't spring with your two hands, ain't a safe, it's an invention."

Slicker shook his head doggedly.

"Do I get 'em?"

"Sure, sure you get 'em. You know what I have, you can have. Ain't we been like brothers?"

"Yeah. I make the profits and take the jolt. You take the profits from me and leave the jolt for me to keep, all for my very own."

The big man waved his restless hands. "Now don't you go talking like that, don't do it I say. I been on the up and up with you. You give old Felix a square deal, and he'll give you one. Whatcha goin' to spring?"

"Nothing you get a percentage on. This is a grudge job. You owe me the stake in return for the stretch."

The humid, brown eyes watched out from under fat brows with expressionless concern, then the head nodded in oily affirmation.

"That's right, that's right, that's right. You always been a square shooter by me. You get the stake."

He turned in a creaky swivel chair that protested unceasingly at the tax that was put upon it. He pawed at a pile of musty old papers, pulled them to one side, fumbled with a section of the wainscoting.

The wainscoting swung back, disclosing a series of well stocked shelves. Felix pulled several articles from the shelves. He opened a wallet and took out money. He paused with the second bill, raised his restless eyes to encounter the steady gaze of Slicker Williams, and hurriedly added two more to the pile. He raised his eyes questioningly once more, shrugged at what he read in Slicker's expression and added a reluctant fifth bill to the pile on the table.

He pushed the pile across.

"When you start workin' for profit, Slicker, you ain't goin' to forget Uncle Felix, are you?"

Slicker shook his head moodily.

"I never forget," he said, and walked out of the door.

When Slicker got to the suburbs he realized why the telephones of Neil Stanwood and his uncle were listed under the same number. The address was a pretentious house that frowned darkly somber from well kept grounds.

Darkly somber, pretentious houses were Slicker's meat.

He vaulted a fence, went to the side of the house, found a trellis and an open window on the second floor. He ascertained there were no burglar alarms, and slid into the warm interior of the house.

He used a flash to guide him to the stairs, went down them, and found a wide window on the ground floor. He opened that window, wide. But first he found and disconnected the burglar alarm that ran along the side of the window.

The ground floor of the house was wired for alarms, and that gave Slicker a thrill of relief. Houses that were wired for burglar alarms usually had something worthwhile in them.

His first plans had been more nebulous. They involved bringing pressure to bear for the getting of what he wanted. But when he saw a highly modern safe in the corner of the library, he changed his plans. He would see what that safe had to offer.

Slicker went about his work with calm deliberation.

He searched the safe for wires, found two and put them out of the running. Then he gave his attention to the locking device.

The manufacturers of that safe doubtless believed that it was reasonably burglar proof. Perhaps they were acquainted with certain idiosyncrasies of the lock, but it is doubtful if they realized in just what manner those little peculiarities could be utilized by expert hands.

Slicker Williams could have delivered a very interesting lecture to the makers of that safe, had he chosen. He did not choose, for obvious reasons.

At the end of fifteen minutes' patient effort, he swung back the door of the safe. Then he commenced a detailed examination of the interior.

There were two compartments, each protected by a locked steel door with a combination. One of those compartments was marked with the initials "H. W. S." The other one bore the name: "Neil."

Slicker Williams made child's play out of those combinations on the interior of the safe. He pulled out drawers, pondering over the contents.

In one of the compartments there was an assortment of jewels that made his mouth water. In another there was a roll of currency. Those were the compartments of the safe reserved for the head of the house. In the nephew's side were several pigeon–holes stuffed with letters.

Slicker read a few of those letters.

Many of them were the usual blah, blah of lovesick girls, falling for an agreeable personality and a background of wealthy parents. But one stack had a far more sinister note. They had to do with blackmail, and the threats were lurid and hardly flattering to the character of Neil Stanwood.

There were other documents which evidenced that Neil Stanwood had been hard pressed for ready cash, and that he had met the demand for that cash by the sale of certain securities.

There was a letter which listed those securities, and there were some of the bonds, negotiable, not as yet sold.

Slicker Williams regarded those documents with great interest. A clock, some—where in the house, chimed the hour of midnight.

Slicker Williams planned his campaign to depend upon what he would find upstairs. He left the safe for the moment, took folding rubber slippers from his pocket, adjusted them over the soles of his shoes, and crept softly up to the bedrooms.

He entered a front room, found a rather heavy man with sagging jowls, sleeping noisily. Slicker presumed this was the head of the house, none other than the great H. W. Stanwood, president of The Stanwood Construction Company. But Slicker Williams never left anything to chance. He made explorations in the pockets of the business suit which hung from a pole in the closet, uncovered a well filled wallet and business cards which confirmed his suspicions.

He left the room, after carefully replacing the wallet.

A side bedroom was the one occupied by Neil Stanwood, the nephew. As might have been expected of a young man whose affairs of the heart were so complex in their nature, Neil Stanwood was out.

Slicker Williams verified these facts.

Then he tiptoed down the stairs again and closed the safe. But he left the inner doors just a bit ajar. He poured soup composed of nitroglycerine around the crevices of the door, and held the soup in place by putting soft soap about the top of the crack, making a little funnel.

Then he piled carpets over the safe. When he had done this, he tipped over a chair and smashed some books to the floor. Then he went on silent feet to the staircase and concealed himself near the head of the stairs.

There were no further sounds of noisy slumber from the other room where the heavy man had sleeping. In place of that, there were the sounds of slippered feet slithering from the bed toward the door.

Slicker Williams glided into another bedroom, half closed the door and waited.

Old Stanwood, looking like an elephant in his gaudy bathrobe, slippety–slopped down the corridor, stood at the head of the stairs, listening. Then he cautiously descended. He held an electric flashlight in his hand.

Slicker Williams went to the head of the stairs, watched the descending figure. He was cool, as a veteran fighter, listening for the sound of the gong.

As Stanwood went into the room and gazed upon the piled up rugs which blanketed the safe, saw the overturned table and chair, the crashed glassware, Slicker Williams could hear the "whoosh" of surprise, the startled exclamation of fear. He heard the slippered feet start on a half run for the stairs once more.

Slicker ducked back out of the way as Stanwood came up the stairs on the run. He saw the flabby face, the joggling jowls, the livid hue of the skin, caught a glint of the panic in the man's eyes.

Then he heard the bedroom door slam, the click of the key in the lock. He heard the sound of a telephone clicking, the quavering voice of Stanwood, summoning the police.

Slicker Williams went softly down the stairs.

He paused at the safe to light the fuse which would set off the nitroglycerine. Then he slipped out of the window and lit a cigarette, waiting patiently.

Ten seconds became fifteen.

There was a deep throated "BOOM" from the safe.

Slicker pinched out the cigarette, nonchalantly climbed back into the room.

The souping had been done in a bungling manner. The whole door of the safe had been ripped away and back. Acrid fumes eddied about the room.

Slicker saw to it that the papers were dribbling out on the floor, and that there was no fire. Then he left the house for the last time and melted into the shadows.

He could see dancing lights from the windows, hear the run of feet, the rattle of voices as the servants became aroused. In the distance, he heard the scream of a siren.

Slicker Williams lit another cigarette when he was a couple of blocks from the house, and casually stepped into the parked automobile he had rented.

He drove back to the city, returned the car, got a room and went to bed.

Twenty–four hours later he read two news items which were of interest to him. One related how a safe cracker, evidently a bungling amateur, had opened the safe at the palatial suburban residence of H. W. Stanwood, head of The Stanwood

Construction Company. The thief, it seemed, had been heard by the master of the house, had been frightened away by the police just as he had the safe open. A check of the contents, made by the police immediately upon their arrival, had disclosed that nothing was missing. The thief had overlooked a large sum of money and missed a valuable collection of gems.

The second item had to do with the fact that one Ruth Mowbrae, arrested under a mistake by the police, had been released upon a dismissal of the charges against her by her employer. The item mentioned that there had been a cash consideration as a settlement of any claims for false arrest.

Slicker Williams laid down the paper and grinned.

It was a year later that he saw Warden Bogger.

Bogger's grim face relaxed somewhat.

"Slicker," he said, "I'm glad to hear that you're married and going straight. Do you know, I did you an injustice? All the time I was giving you that lecture there in the office, I thought you were laughing at me inside. I hadn't any idea you were taking it all in, making a resolve to go straight."

Slicker took the outstretched hand.

"Glad to see you, Warden. You ought to drop in some time and see the kid."

There was one good point about Warden Bogger. When one of his "boys" made good, the warden thrilled with pride, even if he did always insist upon taking a big share of the credit.

"By George," he said, "I will. I always thought you'd stay crooked, Slicker, and I owe you an apology. I figured you could hide behind a corkscrew, and here you are, going straight and making money hand over fist."

"Hang it, man, it's encouraging when you feel that a little interest will make a man see things in a new light. Tell me, Williams, weren't you really a bit impressed by those last few words I gave you, there at the office that day?"

Slicker Williams was a quick thinker. "Warden," he said gravely, "nothing you ever said to me in your life ever made a greater impression."

The Danger Zone

A few blocks to the north of Market Street in San Francisco, Grant Avenue ceases to be a street of high class stores and becomes a part of China.

Major Copely Brane, free lance diplomat, soldier of fortune, knew every inch of this strange section. For Major Brane knew his Chinese as most baseball fans know the strength and weakness of opposing teams.

Not that Major Brane had consciously confined his free lance diplomatic activities to matters pertaining to the Orient. His services were available to various and sundry. He had accepted employment from a patriotic German who wished to ascertain certain information about the French attitude toward reparations; and it was perhaps significant of the Major's absolute fairness, that the fee he had received from the German upon the successful completion of his task was exactly the amount which he had previously charged a French banker for obtaining confidential information from the file of a visiting ambassador as to the exact proposals which the German government was prepared to make as a final offer.

In short, Major Brane worked for various governments and various individuals. Those who had the price could engage his services. There was only one requirement: the task must be within the legitimate field of diplomatic activity. Major Brane was a clearing house of international and political information, and he took pride in doing his work well. Those who employed him could count upon his absolute loyalty upon all matters connected with the employment, could bank upon his subsequent silence; and best of all, they could rest assured that if Major Brane encountered any serious trouble in the discharge of his duties, he would never mention the name of his employer.

Of late, however, the Major's activities had been centered upon the situation in the Orient. This was due in part to the extreme rapidity with which that situation was changing from day to day; and in part to the fact that Major Brane prided himself upon his ability to deliver results. There is no one who appreciates results more, and explanations less, than the native of the Orient.

It was early evening, and the streets of San Francisco's China town were giving forth their strange sounds — the shuffling feet of herded tourists, gazing open—mouthed at the strange life which seethed about them; the slippety of Chinese shoes — skidded along the cement by feet that were lifted only a fraction of an inch; the pounding heels of plain clothes men who always worked in pairs when on China town duty.

Major Brane's ears heard these sounds and interpreted them mechanically. Major Brane was particularly interested to notice the changing window displays of the Chinese stores. The embargo on Japanese products was slowly working a complete change in the merchandise handled by the curio stores, and Major Brane's eyes narrowed as he noticed the fact. Disputes over the murder of a subject can be settled by arbitration, but there can be but one answer to a blow that hits hard at a nation's business.

Major Brane let his mind dwell upon certain angles of the political situation which were unknown to the average man. Would the world powers close their eyes to developments in Manchuria, providing those same developments smashed the five year plan and ...?

His ears, trained to constant watchfulness in the matter of unusual sounds, noticed the change in the tempo of the hurrying feet behind him. He knew that some man was going to accost him, even before he turned appraising eyes upon the other. The man was Chinese, probably Western born, since he wore his Occidental clothes with the air of one who finds in them nothing awkward; and he thudded his feet emphatically upon the sidewalk, slamming his heels hard home with every step.

He had been hurrying and the narrow chest was laboring. The eyes were glittering with some inner emotion of which there was no other external sign, save, perhaps a very slight muscular tenseness about the expressionless mask of the face.

"Major Brane," he said in excellent English, and then stopped to suck in a lungful of air. "I have been to your hotel. You were out. I came here. I saw you, and ran."

Major Brane bowed, and his bow was polite, yet uncordial. Major Brane did not like to have men run after him on the street. Much of his employment entailed very grave dangers, and it was always advisable to keep his connections as secret as possible. Grant Avenue, in the heart of San Francisco's Chinatown, at the hour of eight forty–seven in the evening, was hardly a proper place to discuss matters of business — not when the business of the person accosted was that of interfering with the political situation in the Far East.

"Well?" said Major Brane.

"You must come, sir!"

"Where?"

"To my grandfather."

"And who is your grand father?"

"Wong Sing Lee."

The lad spoke in the Chinese manner, giving the surname first. Major Brane knew that the family of Wong was very powerful and that Chinese venerate age, age being synonymous with wisdom. Therefore, the grandfather of the panting youth must be a man of great importance in the social fabric of Chinatown. Yet Major Brane could recall no prominent member of the Wong family whose given name was Sing Lee. Somehow, the entire name sounded manufactured for the occasion.

Major Brane turned these matters over in his mind rapidly.

"I am afraid I am not at liberty to accept," he said. "Will you convey my very great regrets to your estimable grandparent?"

The lad's hand moved swiftly. His face remained utterly expressionless but the black lacquer of the eyes assumed a red dish glint which would have spoken volumes to those who have studied the psychology of the Oriental.

"You come!" he said fiercely, his voice almost breaking, "or I kill!"

Major Brane squared his shoulders, studied the face intently. "You might get away with it," he said, in a dispassionate voice that was almost impersonal, "but you'd be caught before you'd gone twenty feet — and you'd be hung for it."

The boy's eyes still held their reddish glint. "Without the help which you alone can give," he said, "death is preferable to life!"

And it was only because Major Brane knew his Chinese so well that he determined to accompany the boy, when he heard that burst of impassioned speech. When your Chinese resolves up on murder, he is very, very cool; and very, very wily. Only when a matter of honor is concerned, only when there is a danger of "losing face," does he resolve upon a heedless sacrifice. But when such occasions arise, he considers his own life of but minor moment.

Major Brane nodded. "Remove your hand from the gun," he said. "There is a plain clothes man coming this way. I will go with you."

He reached out, clamped a friendly hand about the arm of the youth, taking hold of the muscles just above the elbow. If the plain clothes officer should accost them, Major Brane wanted to prevent the youth from doing anything rash. And as his fingers clamped about the arm, Major Brane felt the quivering of the flesh, that tremor which comes from taut nerves.

"Steady!" he warned.

There is a popular belief that the Chinese is unemotional. The fallacy of that belief is on a par with the hundreds of fallacies which bar an understanding of the Orient by the Occident. Major Brane realized just how deadly dangerous the present situation was. If the officer should insist upon searching the youth for a weapon ... But the officer was reassured by Major Brane's words.

"If it's real jade," said Major Brane in a loud tone of voice, regarding the bulge in the pocket of the youth's coat, "I'll look at it, but I want a bargain."

The officer veered off. The Chinese glittered his beady eyes at Major Brane and said nothing. A casual observer would have gathered that he was totally oblivious of the danger he had just escaped as well as the ruse by which he had been saved. But the reddish tinge left the surface of the eyes, and the boy took a deep breath.

"M'goy!" he muttered mechanically, which is a Cantonese expression of thanks, and means, "I am not worthy."

Major Brane made the prompt reply which etiquette demanded.

"Hoh wah!" he said, which in turn means, "good talk!"

And the fact that most Westerners would have found the words amusing as well as entirely unrelated to expressions of thanks and welcome is but illustrative of the gulf between the races.

The young Chinese led the way down a side street. Major Brane fell in slightly behind, walked unhesitatingly, his hands swinging free, making no covert effort to reach toward the shoulder holster which was slung beneath his left arm. He had given his word, and his word had been accepted.

They paused before a dark door, which was the center one of a row of dark doors. Apparently these entrances were to separate buildings, huddled closely together in the congestion of poverty; but when the door swung open, Major Brane found himself in a courtyard enclosed by a brick wall. The enclosure was spacious and airy. The other doors had been but dummies set in the brick wall, and were kept locked. Had one opened any one of those other doors, he would have encountered nothing but brick.

Major Brane gave no evidences of surprise. He had been in such places before. The Chinese of wealth always builds his house with a cunning simulation of external poverty. In the Orient one may look in vain for mansions, unless one has the entree to private homes. The street entrances always give the impression of congestion and poverty, and the lines of architecture are carefully carried out so that no glimpse of the mansion itself is visible over the forbidding false front of what appears to be a squalid hovel.

"Quickly!" breathed the Chinese.

His feet pattered over flags, paused at an entrance, to the side of which was an altar and the Chinese characters which signify the presence of Toe Day, the god whose duty it is to frighten away the "homeless ghosts" who would attach themselves to the family, yet will permit free access to the spirits of departed ancestors.

A bell jangled. The door swung open. A huge Chinese servant stood in the doorway.

"The master awaits," he said. The boy pushed his way into the house, through a reception room furnished in conventional dark wood furnishings, into an inner room, the doorway to which was a circle with a high ledge at the entrance, to keep away evil spirits.

Major Brane knew at once that he was dealing with an old family who had retained all the conventions of ten thousand years; knew also that he would be kept with his back to the door if he were received as a prisoner, and given a seat across the room facing the doorway, if he were an honored guest.

His eyes, suddenly grown as hard as polished steel, surveyed the interior of the room. An old man sat on a low stool. A wisp of white beard straggled down from either side of his chin. His face was withered and wrinkled. Most of the hair was gone from the head. The nails of the little fingers were almost three inches long. The left hand waved toward a stool which was at the end of the room facing the door.

"*Cheng nay choh*," he said to Major Brane, and the boy interpreted. "Please sit down," he said.

Major Brane heaved a sigh of relief as he sat down upon the rigidly uncomfortable chair which faced the doorway — the seat of honor.

The servant brought him a cup of tea and a plate of dried melon seeds, which he set down upon a stand of teakwood inlaid with ivory and jade. Major Brane knew that regardless of the urgency of the matter in hand, it would not be broached until he had partaken of the food and drink, so he sipped the scalding tea, took a melon seed between his teeth, cracked it and extracted the meat with a celerity which branded him at once as one who knew his way about. Chopsticks can be mastered with a few lessons, but not so with the technique of melon seeds.

The old man sucked up a bamboo pipe, the bowl of which was of soft metal. It was packed with *sook yen*, the Chinese tobacco which will eat the membranes from an uneducated throat. He gurgled into speech.

There was no doubt in Major Brane's mind but that the young boy would act as interpreter; and he guessed that the lad was quite familiar with the situation, and eager to express himself up on it. Yet such is the veneration for age that the boy kept his eyes upon the old man's face, listening intently, ready to interpret, not what he himself wanted to say, but what the head of the family should utter.

For some three minutes the old man spoke. Major Brane caught a word here and there, and, as his ears conveyed those words to his consciousness, Major Brane sat very rigidly attentive.

The boy interpreted, when the grandfather had finished speaking; and his voice held that absence of tone which comes to one who is repeating but the words of another.

"Jee Kit King has been taken by our enemies. She will be tortured. Even now, they are preparing to start the torture. She will be tortured until she speaks or until she dies, and she will not speak. You are to save her. You must work with speed. And your own life will be in danger."

Major Brane snapped questions. "Who are your enemies?"

"Enemies of China."

"Who are they?"

"We do not know."

"How long has the girl been missing?"

"Less than one hour."

"Why do they torture her?"

"To find out what she did with the evidence."

"What evidence?"

That question brought a period of silence. Then the boy turned to the old man and rattled forth a swift sentence of Cantonese. Major Brane understood enough of that question to know that the youth was asking the old man for permission to give Major Brane the real facts; but even as the old man pursed his puckered lips about the stained mouthpiece of the pipe, Major Brane sensed that the reply would be adverse.

In fact there was no reply at all. The old man smoked placidly, puffing out the oily tobacco smoke, his eyes glittering fixed upon the distance.

The young man whirled back to Mayor Brane, lowered his voice.

"There is, in this city, Mah Bak Heng, who comes from Canton."

Major Brane let his eyes show merely polite interest. He already knew much of Mah Bak Heng, and of his mission, but he kept that knowledge from showing in his eyes.

The boy began to outline certain salient facts.

"Mah Bak Heng has power in Canton. Canton is in revolt against the Nanking government. The Nanking government wishes to unite China to the end that war may be declared upon Japan, over Manchuria. Until the Canton matter is fixed, there can be no war. Canton has money and influence ...

"Mah Bak Heng keeps peace from being made. He cables his men to yield to the Nanking government only upon terms that are impossible. Mah Bak Heng is a traitor. He is accepting pay from enemies of China, to keep the revolution alive. If we could prove that, the people of Canton would no longer listen to the voice of the traitor.

"Jee Kit King is my sister. This man is the grandfather. We talked it over. Jee Kit King has studied in the business schools. She can write down the words of a man as fast as a man can speak, and then she can copy those words upon a typewriter. She is very bright. She agreed that she would trap Mah Bak Heng into employing her as his secretary. Then, when the payment for his treason was delivered, she would get sufficient evidence to prove that payment, and would come to us.

"We know she secured that evidence. She left the place of Mah Bak Heng. But on the way here, two men spoke to her. She accompanied them to a cab. She has not been seen since."

The boy ceased speaking, drew a quivering breath.

The old man puffed placidly upon the last dying embers of the oily tobacco, reached a stained thumb and forefinger into a time–glazed pouch of leather for a fresh portion.

Major Brane squinted his eyes slightly in thought. "Perhaps she went with friends."

"No. They were enemies."

"She had the evidence with her?"

"Apparently not."

"Why do you say that?"

"Because, just before I went to you, three men came hurriedly to her room and made a search."

Major Brane puckered his forehead in thought.

"That means?" he asked.

"That they captured her, searched her but could not find that which they sought, and then went to the room, thinking it was hidden there."

"And not finding it?" asked Major Brane.

"Not finding it, they will torture Jee Kit King." The boy wet his lips with the tip of his tongue, gave a motion that was like a shudder. "They are very cruel," he said. "They can torture well. They remove the clothes, string the body by hands and feet, and build small fires in the middle of the back."

"The girl will not speak?" inquired Major Brane. "Not even under torture?"

"She will not speak."

"How can I save her? There is no time. Even now they will have started the torture," said Major Brane, and he strove to make his tone as kindly as possible.

The boy gave vent to a little scream. His hand flashed out from his pocket. The last vestige of self control left him. He thrust a trembling revolver barrel into the middle of Major Brane's stomach.

"When she dies," he screamed, "you die! You can save her! You alone. You have knowledge in such matters. If she dies, you die. I swear it, by the memory of my ancestors!"

Major Brane glanced sideways at the menace of the cocked revolver, the quivering hand. He knew too well the danger in which he was placed. He looked at the old man, saw that he was lighting a fresh bowl of tobacco and that the clawlike hand which held the flaming match was as steady as a rock. The ebony eyes were still fixed upon distance. He had not so much as turned his head.

Major Brane realized several things. "I will do my best," he soothed, and gently moved backward, as though to get to his feet. The motion pushed the gun a little to one side. "If this girl is your sister," he said, "why is she a Jee, when your grandfather is a Wong?"

"She is not my sister. I love her. I am to marry her! — You must save her. Fast! Quick! Go and do something, and prepare to die if you do not. Here, you can have money, money in plenty!"

The old man, his eyes still fixed upon space, his head never turning, reached his left hand beneath the folds of his robe and tossed a leather bag toward Major Brane. The mouth of the bag was open, and the light glinted upon a great roll of currency.

"Where does the girl have her room?" asked Major Brane, making no move to reach for the money.

The boy was too nervous to speak. He seemed about to faint or to become hysterical. The shaking hand which held the revolver jiggled the weapon about in a half circle.

"Quick!" snapped Major Brane. "If I am to be of help I must know where she lives."

But the boy only writhed his lips.

It was the old man who answered. He removed the stained stem of the pipe from his mouth, and Brane was surprised to hear him speak in excellent English.

"She has a room at Number Thirteen Twenty–Two Stockton Street," he said. "The room maintained in her name."

Major Brane swung his eyes.

"I've seen you somewhere before …" he said, and would have said more. But as though some giant hand had snuffed out the lights, the room became suddenly dark, a pitch black darkness that was as oppressive as a blanket. And the darkness gave forth the rustling sound of bodies, moving with surreptitious swiftness.

Major Brane flung himself to one side. His hand darted beneath the lapel of his coat, clutched the reassuring bulk of the automatic which reposed in the shoulder holster.

Then the lights came on, as abruptly as they had been extinguished. The room was exactly as it had been three or four seconds before, save that Major Brane was the only occupant. The chairs were there. The old man's pipe, the bowl still smoking and the oily tobacco sizzling against the sides of the metal, was even propped against a small table.

But the old Chinese grandfather and the boy himself had disappeared.

A man came shuffling along the flags of the outer room. It was the same servant who had escorted Major Brane into the room.

"What you want here?" he asked.

"I want to see the master."

"Master not home. You go out now."

Major Brane holstered his weapon, smiled affably. "Very well."

The servant slip–slopped to the courtyard, unlocked the door.

"Good–bye," he said.

"Good–bye," observed Major Brane, and stepped out into the street.

A fog was coming in, and its first damp, writhing tendrils were clutching at the dim corners of the mysterious buildings. The sounds of traffic from the main avenues came to him, muffled as though they were the sounds of another world.

Major Brane moved, and as he moved a patch of shadow across the street slipped into furtive motion. A stooped figure hugged the patch of darkness which extended along the front of the dark and silent buildings. Another figure walked casually out of the doorway of a building at the corner, stood in the light, looking up and down the lighted thoroughfare. It might have been waiting for a friend. A bulky figure, padded out with a quilted coat, hands thrust up the sleeves, came from a doorway to the rear and started walking directly toward Major Brane.

Major Brane sighed, turned, and walked rapidly toward the lighted thoroughfare. The fact that the boy had been forced to accost him on the street made it doubly inconvenient. Things which happen upon the streets of Chinatown seldom go unobserved.

Major Brane had no way of knowing who those shadowing figures might be; they might be friends of the people who had employed him, keeping a watch upon him lest he seek to escape the trust which had been thrust upon him, or they might be emissaries of the enemy, seeking to balk him in accomplishing any thing of value.

But one thing was positive. Somewhere in the city a Chinese girl was held in restraint by enemies who were, in all probability, proceeding even now to a slow torture that would either end in speech or death. And another thing was equally positive: unless Major Brane could effect the rescue of that girl, he could count his own life as forfeit. The young man had sworn upon the memory of his ancestors, and such oaths are not to be disregarded. Moreover, there had been the silent acquiescence of the old man.

"Grandfather!" sputtered Major Brane under his breath. "He's no more her grandfather than I am! I've seen him before somewhere, and I'll place him yet!"

But he knew better than to waste any mental energy in jogging a tardy recollection. Major Brane was having his hands full at the moment. He had a task before him which required rare skill, and the price of failure would be death.

He reached back for his tobacco pouch, and his hand touched something which swung in a dangling circle from the skirt of his coat. He pulled the garment around. The thing was the leather pouch which the old man had tossed to him. It was filled with greenbacks of large denomination, rolled tightly together.

That bag must have been pinned to his coat by the old servant as he was leaving the court yard. The knowledge gave Major Brane a feeling of mingled security and uneasiness. That meant that at least one of his shadows must be in the employ of the old man who had posed as the girl's grandfather. That shadow would make certain that Major Brane found the sack of currency, that it did not come loose and roll unheeded into the gutter.

But there were three shadows. What of the other two? And there was the disquieting knowledge that even the friendly shadow would become hostile should Major Brane fail in his undertaking.

The young man had promised that Brane should not outlive the girl; and the promise had been sworn by the sacred memory of the young man's ancestors.

Major Copely Brane walked directly to his room in the hotel, which was almost on the outskirts of Chinatown. That step was, at least, noncommittal, and Major Brane needed time to think. Also, he had a secret method of exit from that room in the hotel.

He opened the door with his key, switched on the lights, bolted the door behind him, and dropped into a chair. He held his arm at an angle so that his wrist watch ticked off the seconds before his eyes.

He knew that it was hopeless to plunge blindly into the case without a plan of campaign. And he knew that it would be fatal to consume too much time in thought. Therefore he allowed himself precisely three minutes of concentration — one hundred and eighty seconds within which to work out some plan which might save the life of the girl, and, incidentally, preserve his own safety.

He thought of Mah Bak Heng. Major Brane had some shrewd suspicions about Mah Bak Heng, but he had no proof. There was a chance that those suspicions could be converted into proof by the burglary of a certain safe. But that burglary would take time. Even with the necessary proof, Major Brane would be no nearer locating those who held the girl captive; and she would be dead long before he could bring sufficient pressure to bear upon the Chinese politician to force a trade or treaty.

Major Brane squirmed uneasily in his chair. Thirty seconds had ticked by. He might trust to blind chance, figure out who would probably be chosen to kidnap a girl who had acquired dangerous information, make a guess as to the location that would be picked upon for torture. But there was only one chance in a hundred that, with all of his shrewd knowledge of things Oriental, he would be able to make a correct guess. Then there would remain the task of effecting a rescue.

No. The girl would have died a slow death long before such a plan could be carried into execution.

Forty–five seconds gone.

Major Brane shifted the position of his legs. His eyes were cold and hard as polished steel.

His jaw was thrust forward. His lips were a thin line of determination. The light illuminated the delicately chiseled lines of his aristocratic face.

He went back to the first principles of deductive reasoning. The girl was a spy. She had evidently secured the thing that would link Mah Bak Heng with interests that were inimical to China. That thing would, if Major Brane read his man right, be in the nature of cash. But cash leaves no trail. Therefore, the thing which the girl had secured was something equivalent to cash, which also indicated the person who had paid the cash. It was a safe bet that this something had been a check.

She had left the place, seeking her friends; and the enemy had known she was a spy — at least that soon, perhaps before. Had the girl been aware that her disguise had been penetrated? That was a question which could only be answered in the light of subsequent events. Those subsequent events proved that the girl had been "taken for a ride" by her enemies. Undoubtedly, she had been searched almost immediately; and the subsequent searching of her rooms would indicate that this search had been fruitless.

So far, then, the enemies were deprived of the evidence which they had sought to take from the girl. The girl had hidden it in some place that was not on her person. Where?

Obviously, those enemies had thought the most likely place was the girl's bedroom. Rightly or wrongly, they had reasoned that the check was hidden there.

It was impossible now to find the girl within the time necessary to save her life; but the people who held her captive would torture her, not for the pleasure of torture, but for the purpose of securing that which they coveted — the check. Therefore, if they secured the check without torture, they would refrain from torture.

That thought lodged in Major Brane's mind, and he immediately seized upon it as being the key to the situation. His eyes stared unwinkingly, his brows deepened into straight lines of thought.

Then, after a few moments, he nodded his head. His eyes snapped to a focus upon the dial of the wrist watch. The time lacked thirteen seconds of the three–minute limit which he had imposed upon himself.

Major Brane crossed to a desk in one corner of his room. That desk contained many curious odds and ends. They were articles which Major Brane had collected against future contingencies, and they dealt with many phases of the Orient. He selected a tinted oblong of paper. It was a check upon a bank that was known for its connections in the Far East. The check was, of course, blank. Major Brane filled it in. .

The name of the payee was Mah Bak Heng. The amount caused Major Brane some deliberation. He finally resolved upon the figure of fifty thousand dollars. He felt that in all probability that amount would be the top price for the final payment, and he knew Mah Bak Heng well enough to believe that he would command the top price for the final payment, assuming that there had been several previous payments.

It was when it came to filling the name of the payer at the bottom of the check that Major Brane pulled his master stroke. There was a slight smile twisting the corners of his lips as he made a very credible forgery of signature. The signature was that of a man who was utterly unknown in the Oriental situation, save by a very select few. But Major Brane had always made it his business to secure knowledge which was not available to the average diplomat.

He blotted the check, folded it once, straightened the fold and folded it again. Then he began to fold it into the smallest possible compass, taking care to iron down each fold with the handle of an ivory paper knife. When he had finished, the check was but a tight wad of paper, folded into an oblong.

Major Brane took the cellophane wrapping from a package of cigarettes carefully wrapping the spurious check in it, and thrusting the tiny package into his pocket.

He left his room by the secret exit: through the connecting door into another room; through another connecting door into a room that had a window that opened on a fire escape platform; out the window to the platform; along the platform to a door; through the door to a back staircase; down the stairs to an alley exit; out the alley to the side street.

He hailed a passing cab and gave the address of the building where Jee Kit King had her residence. As the cab swung into speed, Major Brane looked behind him.

There were two cars, following closely.

Major Brane sighed wearily. It was no surprise; merely what he had expected. He was dealing with men who were very, very capable. He didn't know whether he had shaken off one of the shadows, or whether one of the following cars held two men, the other holding one; but he was inclined to believe all three were following, two in one car, one in the other.

He made an abortive effort to shake off the pursuit. It was an effort that was purposely clumsy. The following cars dropped well to the rear, however, and switched off their lights.

A less experienced man than Major Brane would have believed that the ruse had been a success, and that the shadows were lost. Major Brane merely smiled and sent the cab rushing to the address where the girl had lived.

He found her apartment without difficulty.

It was on a third floor. The lodgings were, for the most part, given over to people of limited means who were neat and cleanly, but economical.

The door of the girl's apartment was locked. Major Brane hesitated over that lock only long enough to get a key that would turn the bolt; and his collection of skeleton keys was sufficiently complete to cut that delay to a period of less than four seconds. He entered the apartment, leaving the door open behind him; not much, just a sufficient crack to insure against a surreptitious bolting from the outer side without his knowledge.

When he had jerked out a few drawers and rumpled a few clothes, Major Brane picked up a jar of cold cream. A frown of annoyance crossed his features as he saw that there was only a small amount of cream in the jar.

But in the bathroom he found a fresh jar, unopened. He unscrewed the top, thrust the cellophane–wrapped check deep down into the greasy mixture. He let it remain there for a few seconds, then fished it out again. In taking it out, he smeared a copious supply of cold cream over the edge of the jar, and wiped his fingers on a convenient towel, leaving the excess cold cream smeared about the edge of the jar, a deep hole in the center of the cream.

Unwrapping the cellophane, he left it on the shelf over the washstand, a transparent oblong of paper smeared with cold cream; left it in such a shape that it was readily apparent it had served as a container for some small object.

Then Major Brane, pocketing the spurious check, wiped his hands carefully to remove all traces of the cream from his fingertips, but was careful to leave a sufficient deposit under the nails of his fingers to be readily detected.

He walked to the door of the apartment, peered out. The hallway seemed deserted. As furtively as a thief in the night, Major Brane tiptoed down this hallway, came to the stairs, took them upon cautious feet, emerged up on the sidewalk.

He motioned to his cab driver.

"Married?" he asked.

The man nodded.

"Children?"

Another nod.

"Remember them, then, if anything happens," said Major Brane. "Your first duty is to them."

"I'll say it is!" agreed the cab driver. "What's the racket?"

"Nothing," commented Major Brane crisply. "I simply wanted to impress that particular thought on your mind. Swing toward Chinatown, and drive fast as you can. Keep to the dark side streets."

"Whereabouts in Chinatown?"

"It doesn't matter. Just in that general direction."

"And drive fast?"

"Take 'em on two wheels!"

"Get in!" snapped the driver.

He slammed the door. The cab started with a jerk. The tires screamed on the first corner, but all four wheels remained on the pavement. The cabbie did better the second corner. Then he nearly tipped over as he cut into a dark side street.

Major Brane gave no sign of nervousness. He was watching the road behind him, and his eyes were cold and hard, frosty in their unwinking stare.

They were midway in the block when a car swung into the cross street. It was a low roadster, powerful, capable of great speed, and it swept down on the taxicab as a hawk swoops upon a sparrow. The head lights were dark, and the car flashed through the night like some sinister beast of prey.

The cab had just turned into the second intersection when the roadster drew alongside. There sounded a swift explosion that might have been a backfire. The taxicab swerved as a rear tire went out. Then it settled to the rim and the *thunkety–thunk–thunk–thunk*, marked the revolutions as the cab skidded to the pavement and stopped.

The cab driver turned a white face to Major Brane, started to say something, then thrust his hands up as high as he could get them, the fingertips jammed into the top of the roof. For he was gazing directly into the business end of a large calibre automatic, held in the hands of one of the figures that had leapt from the roadster. The other figure was holding a sub machine gun pointed directly at Major Brane's stomach.

Both of the men were masked.

"Seem to have tire trouble," said one of the men. He spoke in the peculiar accents of a foreigner whose language is more staccato than musical.

Major Brane kept his hands in sight, but he did not elevate them. "Yes," he said.

The man with the sub machine gun grinned. His flashing teeth were plainly visible below the protection of the mask.

He spoke English with the easy familiarity of one who has spoken no other language since birth. "Better come ride with us," he said. "You seemed to be in a hurry, and it'll take time to repair that tire."

"I'd prefer to wait," said Major Brane, and smiled.

"I'd prefer to have you ride," said the man with the sub machine gun, politely, and the muzzle wavered suggestively in a little arc that took in Major Brane's torso. "You might find it healthier to ride."

"Thanks" said Major Brane. "I'll ride, then."

The man in the roadster snapped a command. "Open the car door for him," he said.

The one who held the automatic stretched back his left hand, worked the catch of the door.

"Okay," said the man in the roadster.

Major Brane stumbled. As he stumbled, he threw forth his hand to catch his balance, and the other hand slipped the folded check from his pocket. He lowered his head, thrust check in his mouth.

The man with the automatic jumped toward him. The man with the sub machine gun laughed sarcastically.

"No you don't," he said. "Get it!"

The last two words were cracked at the man who had held the automatic. That man leapt forward. Stubby fingers, that were evidently well acquainted with the human anatomy, pressed against nerve centers in Major Brane's neck. Brane writhed with pain, and opened his jaw. The folded bit of tinted paper dropped to the pavement. The man swooped down upon it, picked it up with eager hands.

A police whistle trilled through the night.

"In!" crisped the man with the sub machine gun.

Major Brane felt arms about him, felt his automatic whisked from its hoister. Then he was boosted into the roadster. The gears clashed. The car lurched into speed.

Behind him, Major Brane could hear the taxicab driver yelling for the police, so loudly as to send echoes from the sides of the sombre buildings that lined the dark street.

The roadster's lights clicked on. The man who had held the sub machine gun was driving. The other man was crowded close beside Major Brane's neck, the other jabbing the end of the automatic into Major Brane's ribs.

The man at the wheel knew the city, and he knew his car. The machine kept almost entirely to dark side streets and went swiftly. Within five minutes, it had turned to an alley on a steep hill, slid slowly downward, wheels rubbing against brake bands.

A garage door silently opened. The roadster went into the garage. The door closed. The roadster lights were switched off. A door opened from the side of the garage.

"Well?" said a voice.

"We got it. He found it. We grabbed him. He tried to swallow it, but we got it."

"Where was it?" asked the voice from the darkness.

"In a jar of cold cream in her apartment."

The voice made no answer. For several seconds the weight of the dark silence oppressed them. Then the voice gave a crisp command.

"Bring him in."

The man who had driven the car took Major Brane's arm above the elbow. The other man, an arm still around Major Brane's neck, jabbed the gun firmly against his ribs.

"Okay, guy. No funny stuff," said the one who had held the machine gun.

Major Brane groped with his feet, found the floor. The guards were on either side of him, pushing him forward. A door opened, disclosing a glow of diffused light. A flight of stairs led upward.

"Up and at 'em!" said the man on Major Brane's left.

They clumped up the stairs, maintaining their awkward formation of three abreast. There was a landing at the top, then a hallway. Major Brane was taken down the hallway, into a room that was furnished with exquisite care, a room in which massive furniture dwarfed the high ceilings, the wide windows. Those windows were covered with heavy drapes that had been tightly drawn.

Major Brane was pushed into a chair.

"Park yourself, guy."

Major Brane sank into the cushions. His hands were on the arms of the chair. The room was deserted, save for his two guards. The man whose voice had given the orders to the pair was nowhere in evidence.

"May I smoke?" asked Major Brane.

The masked guard grinned. "Brother," he said, "if there's any smoking to be done, I'll do it. You just sit pretty like you were having your picture taken, and don't make no sudden moves. I've got your gat; but they say you're full of tricks, and if I was to see any sudden moves, I'd have to cut you open to see whether you was stuffed with sawdust or tricks. You've got my curiosity aroused."

Major Brane said nothing.

The man who had taken the check walked purposefully toward one of the draped exits, pushed aside the rich hangings and disappeared.

Major Brane eyed the masked figure who remained to guard him. The man grinned.

"Don't bother," he said. "You wouldn't know me, even if it wasn't for the mask."

Major Brane lowered his voice, cautiously. "Are you in this thing for money?" he asked.

The man grinned. "No, no, brother. You got me wrong. I'm in it for my health!" And he laughed gleefully.

Major Brane was earnest. "They've got the check. That's all they're concerned with. There'd be some money in it for you if you let me go."

The eyes glittered through the mask in scornful appraisal. "Think I'm a fool?"

Major Brane leaned forward, very slightly. "They won't hurt me," he said, "and the check's gone already. But there are some other important papers that I don't want them to find. They simply can't find them — mustn't. Those papers are worth a great deal to certain parties, and it would be most unfortunate if they should fall into the hands of these men who were interested in the check. If you would only accept those papers and deliver them to the proper parties, you could get enough money to make you independent for years to come."

The eyes back of the mask were no longer scornful. "Where are these papers?" asked the man.

"You promise you'll deliver them?"

"Yeah. Sure."

"In my cigarette case," said Major Brane. "Get them — quick!"

And he half raised his hands. The masked figure came to him in two swift strides.

"No you don't! Keep your hands down. I'll get the cigarette case. — In your inside pocket, eh? All right, guy; try anything and you'll get bumped!" He held a heavy gun in his left hand, thrust an exploring right hand into Major Brane's inside coat pocket. He extracted the cigarette case, grinned at Major Brane, stepped back.

"I said I'd deliver 'em. That was a promise. The only thing I didn't promise was who I'd deliver 'em to. I'll have to take a look at 'em first. I might be interested myself." And he gloatingly held the cigarette case up, pressed the catch.

That cigarette case had been designed by Major Brane against just such an emergency. The man pressed the catch. The halves flew open, and a spring mechanism shot a stream of ammonia full into the man's eyes.

Major Brane was out of the chair with a flashing spurt of motion which was deadly and swift. His right hand crossed over in the sort of blow which is only given by the trained boxer. It was a perfectly timed blow, the powerful muscles of the body swinging into play as the fist pivoted over and around.

The man with the mask caught the blow on the button of the jaw. Major Brane listened for an instant, but no one seemed to have heard the man's fall. He walked swiftly to the doorway which led into the hall, then down the hall and down the steps to the garage. He opened the garage door, got in the roadster, turned on the ignition, stepped on the starter. The motor throbbed into life.

A light flashed on in the garage. A grotesque figure stumbled out through the door, silhouetted as a black blotch against the light of the garage. The man was waving his arms, shouting.

Major Brane spun the wheel, sent the car skidding around the corner. Behind him, there sounded a single shot; and the bullet whined from the pavement. There were no more shots.

Major Brane stepped on the gas.

He drove three blocks toward the south, headed toward Market Street. He saw a garage that was open, slowed the car, swung the wheel, rolled into the garage.

"Storage," he said.

"Day, week or month?" asked the man in overalls and faded coat who slouched forward.

"Just for an hour or two; may be all night."

The attendant grinned. "Four bits," he said.

Major Brane nodded, handed him half a dollar, received an oblong of pasteboard with a number. He turned, walked out of the garage, paused at the curb and tore the oblong of numbered pasteboard into small bits. Then he started walking, directing his steps over the same route he had traveled in the roadster.

He heard the snarl of a racing motor, the peculiar screaming noise made by protesting tires when a corner is rounded too fast, and he stepped back into a doorway. A touring car shot past. There were three men in it; three grim figures who sat very erect and whose hands were concealed.

When the car had passed, Major Brane stepped out and resumed his rapid walk, back toward the house from which he had escaped.

He walked up the hill. The garage was dark now, but the door was still open.

Major Brane walked cautiously, but kept up his speed. He slipped into the dark garage, waited, advanced, tried the door which opened to the flight of stairs. The door was locked now, from the inside. Major Brane stopped, applied an eye to the keyhole. The key, he saw, was in the lock.

He took out his skeleton keys, also a long, slender–bladed pen knife. With the point of the knife blade he worked the end of the key around, up and down, up and down. Gradually, as he freed the key, the heavier end, containing the flange, had a tendency to drop down. Major Brane manipulated the key until this tendency had ample opportunity to assert itself. Then he pushed with the point of the knife. The key slid out of the lock, thudded to the floor on the other side of the door.

Major Brane inserted a skeleton key, pressed up and around on the key, felt the bolt snap back, and opened the door. The little entranceway with the flight of stairs was before him. Major Brane walked cautiously up those stairs. His eyes were slitted, his body poised for swift action.

He gained the hallway at the top of the stairs, started down is cautiously. He could hear voices from a room at one end of the corridor, voices that were raised in excited conversation. Major Brane avoided that room but slipped into the room which adjoined it. That room was dark; and Major Brane, closing the door behind him, listened for a moment while he stood perfectly still, his every faculty concentrated.

He was standing so, when there sounded the click of a light switch and the room was flooded with light.

A rather tall man with a black beard, and eyes that seemed the shade of dulled silver, was standing by a light switch, holding a huge automatic in a hand that was a mass of bony knuckles, of long fingers and black hair.

"Sit down, Major Brane," said the man.

Major Brane sighed, for the man was he whose name Major Brane had forged to the spurious check.

The man chuckled. "Do you know, Major, I rather expected you back. Clever, aren't you? But after one has dealt with you a few times he learns to anticipate your little schemes."

Major Brane said nothing. He stood rigidly motionless, taking great care not to move his hands. He knew this man, knew the ruthless cruelty of him, the shrewd resourcefulness of his mind, the deadly determination which actuated him.

"Do sit down, Major."

Major Brane crossed to a chair sat down.

The man with the beard let the tips of his white teeth glitter below the gloss of dark hairs which swept his upper lip in smooth regularity. The tip of the pointed beard quivered as the chin muscles twitched. "Yes," he said, "I expected you back."

Major Brane nodded. "I didn't know *you* were here," he observed. "Otherwise I would have been more cautious."

"Thanks for the compliment, Major. Incidentally, my associates here know me by the name of Brinkhoff. It would be most unfortunate if they should learn of my real identity, or of my connections."

"Unfortunate for you?" asked Major Brane meaningly.

The teeth glittered again as the lips swept back in a mirthless and all but noiseless laugh.

"Unfortunate for both of us, Major. Slightly unfortunate for me, but doubly—trebly—unfortunate for you."

Major Brane nodded. "Very well, Mr. Brinkhoff," he said.

The dulled silver eyes regarded him speculatively, morosely. "Rather clever of you to prepare forgery which you could use a red herring to drag across the trail," he said. "That's what comes of trusting subordinates. As soon as they told me how clumsy you were in your attempt to thrust the check into your mouth and swallow it, I knew they had been duped — Fools! They were laughing over your clumsy attempt! Bah!"

Major Brane inclined his head. "Thank you, Brinkhoff."

Ominous lights glinted back of the dulled silver of the eyes. "Well," rasped the man, after a moment, "what did you do with it?"

"The original?"

"Naturally."

Major Brane took a deep breath. "I placed it where you could never find it, of course."

The teeth shone again as the man grinned. "No you didn't, Major. You took advantage of your arrival here to conceal it some place in the room — perhaps in the cushion of the chair. When you escaped, you went in a hurry to draw pursuit. You returned to get the check."

Major Brane shook his head. "No. The check isn't in the house. I placed it where it would be safe. I returned for the girl."

A frown divided the man's forehead. "You hid it?"

Major Brane chose his words carefully. "I feel certain that it is safe from discovery," he said.

The man with the beard rasped out an oath, started toward Major Brane.

"Damn you," he gritted, "I believe you're telling the truth! I told them you'd come back after the girl. That's why I had them carrying on a loud conversation in the next room. I thought you'd try to slip in here and listen, particularly if the room was dark."

Major Brane inclined his head. "Well reasoned," he said. His voice was as impersonally courteous as that of a tennis player who mutters a "well played" to his opponent.

For a long three seconds the two men locked eyes.

"There are ways," said the bearded man, ending that long period of menacing silence, "of making even the stoutest heart weaken, of making even the most stubborn tongue talk."

Major Brane shrugged his shoulders. "Naturally," he said. "I hope you are not so stupid as to think that I would overlook that fact, and not take steps to guard against it."

"Such as?"

"Such as seeing that the check was placed entirely out of my control before I returned."

"Thinking that would make you immune from — persuasion?" asked the bearded man mockingly.

Major Brane nodded his head. "Thinking you would not waste time on torture when it could do you no good, and when your time is so short."

"Time so short, Major?"

"Yes. I rather think there will be many things for you to do, now that that check is to be made public. There will be complete new arrangements to make, and your time is short. The Nanking government and the Canton government will be forced to settle their differences as soon as the knowledge of that check becomes public property."

The bearded man cursed, bitterly, harshly.

Major Brane sat perfectly immobile.

The bearded one raised his voice. "All right. Here he is. Come in."

The door of the room in which the loud conversation had taken place burst open. Four men came tumbling eagerly into the room. They were not masked. Major Brane knew none of them. They stared at him curiously.

The bearded man glowered at them. "He claims he ditched the original check in a safe place," he said. "He's clever enough to have done something that'll be hard to check up on. The check may be in the house. He may have left it in the room where he sat; or he may have picked it up when he came in the second time, and put it some place where we'd never think to look. He's that clever.

"Search him first, and then search the house. Then take up the trail of the car. He wouldn't have taken it far. He was back too soon ... Still, he wouldn't have left it parked on the street. He'd know we'd spot it. He must have left it in the garage that's down ..."

Major Brane interrupted, courteously. "Pardon me, it is in the garage. I left it there and tore up the ticket. I didn't know you were here, at the time, Brinkhoff, or I would have saved myself the trouble."

The bearded man gave a formal inclination of the head. "Thanks. Now, since we understand each other so thoroughly, and since you have shown such a disposition to cooperate, there's a possibility we can simplify matters still further. We can make a trade, we two. I'll trade you the girl for the check."

Major Brane smiled, the patronizing, chiding smile which a parent gives to a precocious child who is trying to obtain some unfair advantage. "No. The check will have to be eliminated from the discussion now."

"We'll get it eventually."

"I hardly think so."

"That which is going to happen to the girl is hardly a pleasant subject to discuss. You see there are very major political issues involved. You, my dear Major, and I, have long since learned not to grow emotional over political matters. Unfortunately, some of my subordinates — perhaps I should refer to them as associates — are still in the emotional stage. If they feel that major political issues have been shaped by the theft of a check, and that this girl is the guilty party ..." He broke off with a suggestive shrug.

Major Brane sighed. The sigh seemed to be almost an incipient yawn. "As you, yourself have so aptly remarked," he said in differently, "*we* have learned not to grow emotional over political matters."

The bearded man sneered. "I thought you came here for the girl?"

"I did."

"You don't seem anxious to save her from an unpleasant experience."

Major Brane made a slight gesture with his shoulders. "I was employed to recover the check. I thought it might be a good plan to throw in a rescue of the girl for good measure."

The bearded man suddenly lost his semblance of poise, his veneer of culture. He took a swift step forward, his beard bristling, the strong white fangs behind it contrasting with the jet black of the beard.

"Damn you! We'll get that check out of you. We'll fry you in hot grease, a bit at a time. We'll pull off the skin and stick burning cigars in the flesh. We'll ..." He choked with the very vehemence of his rage.

This time Major Brane yawned outright. "Come, come!" he said. "I thought we had outgrown these childish displays of emotion! We are playing major politics, we two. If you have lost the check, you have lost the fight. Torturing through vengeance won't help you any."

"It'll make you suffer! It'll eliminate you from any future interference. You've blocked too many of my plans before this!"

Major Brane nodded. It was as though he considered an impersonal problem. "Of course," he muttered politely, "if you look at it that way!"

The man turned his dulled silver eyes morosely upon the others, who had been standing at sullen attention. "Search him. Then the house. Then the streets."

The men came forward. They were thorough about the search and not at all gently. Major Brane assisted them wherever he could. They pulled his pockets inside out, took away all of his personal belongings, searched his shoes, his coat lining, the lapels of his coat, under the collar.

Then they divided into two groups. One searched the house, the other group the street. The man with the beard remained with Major Brane, glowering at him, the nature of his thoughts indicated by the dark of his skin, the closed fists, the level brows.

Major Brane regarded him speculatively. "The girl is here?" he asked.

His answer was a scornful, mocking laugh.

"I merely asked," said Major Brane, "because it is so greatly to your advantage to see that she doesn't come to harm. I telephoned, of course, to friends of hers before I returned to the house."

The bearded man gave a sudden start. Despite himself, he changed color. "Yes?" he asked. "And just what do you expect her friends to do?"

Major Brane pursed his lips. "Probably," he remarked, "they would not be so unwise as to storm the house; but they are well versed in certain matters of indirection. You might have some trouble in leaving the house."

The dulled silver eyes regarded him scornfully. "You lie!" said the man who went under the name of Brinkhoff.

Major Brane made a gesture with the palms of his hands, a deprecating gesture, partially of apology.

"Sometimes," he said, "I despair of you, Brinkhoff. You have a certain shrewdness, yes. But you lack perspective, breadth of vision; and you are unspeakably common!"

That last remark was like the lash of a whip.

"Common!" yelled the infuriated man. "I, who have the blood of three thousand years of royalty in my veins! Common, you scum of the gutter! I'll draw the sight of this gun across your cursed face! Just a taste of what you can expect ..."

He leaped forward, swinging his arm so that the sight of the gun made a sudden, sharp arc. But Major Brane's forehead wasn't there when the gunsight swished through the air. Major Brane had flung himself backwards in the chair; and as he went over, he watched the sweep of the arm, elevated his foot with every bit of strength he could muster. The foot caught the wrist of the enraged man, sent the gun swirling through the air in a lopsided flight. The chair crashed to the floor, Major Brane rolled clear.

Brinkhoff saw his danger and jumped back. His bony, capable hand went to the back of his coat collar, reaching for the hilt of a concealed knife.

He caught the knife, jerked it out and down. The lights glinted from the whirling steel. Major Brane flung his arms out in a football tackle. For a moment it seemed that the downward stroke of the knife would strike squarely between Major Brane's shoulders. But the Major was first to reach his goal, first by that split fraction of a watch tick which seems to be so long when men are fighting for life and death, yet is the smallest unit of measured time.

The Major's weight crashed against the shins of the man with the dulled silver eyes. The impact threw him back. The stroke of the knife swung wild. The two men teetered, crashed. The man with the beard shouted, squirmed.

Outside, the hallway pounded with running feet. There were other voices calling down from an upper floor.

Major Brane swung his fist. Brinkhoff's cries ceased. Instantly, Major Brane was on his feet, as lithely active as a cat. He swooped toward the chair which lay on the floor, lifted it bodily, held it poised for a moment, and then flung it, straight through the glass of the window.

The chair smashed a great jagged hole in the glass. There sounded the crash, the tinkle, of falling glass fragments. Then the chair toppled outward and vanished into the night. There came a thud from the ground below.

Major Brane jumped for a closed door on one side of the room. He flung it open and found that it led, not to an adjoining room as he had hoped, but, into a closet. The closet was well filled with stacks of papers, papers that were arranged in bundles, tied with tape.

Major Brane leaped inside, scrambled atop the bundles, pawed at the door, trying to get it closed. He had but partially succeeded when he heard the door of the room burst open, and the sound of bodies catapulting into the room.

Of a sudden, the sounds ceased. That, reasoned Major Brane, perched precariously atop the slippery pile of documents, would be when the others entered the room and took in the situation, the unconscious form of Brinkhoff sprawled on the floor, the window with its great jagged hole.

"Gone!" a voice croaked, and added a curse.

"Jumped out of the window ..."

"Quick! After him. — No, no, not that way! Close the block! Signal the others! He's got fifty yards the start of us. Turn on the red lights. Hurry!"

Once more, feet pounded in haste. Major Brane could hear excited shouts, comments that were called back and forth.

A small section of the lighted floor of the room showed through the half–open door of the closet. Major Brane watched that section of floor for a full two seconds, to see if there were any moving shadows crossing it. There were no shadows. The room seemed utterly silent.

Major Brane strove to step quietly from his perch, but a packet of documents tilted, slid. Major Brane flung himself back, lost his balance, put out his arms, and crashed through the closet door into the room.

Brinkhoff lay sprawled on the floor. A man was bending over him, and that man had evidently been in the act of going through Brinkhoff's pockets when Major Brane, catapulting from the closet, had frozen him into startled immobility.

He looked at Major Brane, and Major Brane took advantage of his first moment of surprise. He rushed. The man teetered back to his heels, jumped backward in time to escape the momentum of that first rush. Major Brane landed a glancing blow with his left. Then he caught himself, turned, and lashed out with his right.

He realized then that the man with whom he had to deal was one who was trained in jujutsu. Too late he strove to beat down the other's left. It caught his right wrist; a foot shot out; a hand darted down with bone–crunching violence.

Major Brane knew the method of attack well enough to know that there was but one possible defense. To resist would be to have his arm snapped. The hands of the other were in a position to exert a tremendous leverage against the victim's own weight. Major Brane therefore did the only thing that would save him. Even before the last ounce of pressure had been brought to play upon his arms, he flung himself in a whirling somersault, using the momentum of his rush to send him over and around.

He whirled through the air like a pinwheel, crashed to the floor. But even while he was in midair, his brain, trained to instant appreciation of all of the angles of any given situation, remembered the gun which had been kicked from Brinkhoff's hand.

Major Brane whirled, even as the flashing shape of his opponent hurtled at him. His clawing hand groped for and found the automatic. The other pounced, and the automatic jabbed into his ribs.

"I shall pull the trigger," said Major Brane, his words muffled by the weight of the other, "in exactly one and one–half seconds!"

The, words had the desired effect. Major Brane had a reputation for doing exactly whatever he said he would do, and the figure that had been on top of him flung backwards, hands elevated.

Major Brane, still lying on the floor, thrust the gun forward, so that it was plainly visible.

From the yard, outside the window, could be heard the low voices of men who were closing in on the spot where the chair had thudded to the ground.

"Don't move!" said Major Brane.

The man who faced him, twisted back his lips in a silent snarl, then let his face become utterly expressionless.

Major Brane smiled at him. "I wonder," he said, "what you were searching for, my friend?"

The man made no sound.

"Back against the wall," said Major Brane.

The man hesitated, then caught the steely glitter of Major Brane's eye. He backed, slowly. Major Brane raised himself to his knees, then to his feet. His eyes were almost dreamy with concentration.

"You want something," mused Major Brane, "that Brinkhoff is supposed to have on him; but you don't want the rest of the gang to know that you want it. You'd yell, if you were really one of them, and take a chance on my shooting. — The answer is that you're hostile. Probably the others don't even know you're here."

The man who stood against the wall had been breathing heavily. Now, as Major Brane summed up the situation, he held himself rigidly motionless, even the rising and falling of his shoulders ceasing. It was as though he held his breath, the better to check any possible betrayal of his thoughts through some involuntary start of surprise.

Major Brane moved toward the unconscious form of the man who went under the name of Brinkhoff. From outside came a series of cries; rage, surprise, dis–appointment, shouted instructions. — The attackers had found that they had been stalking only a chair that had been thrown from a window.

Major Brane remained as calmly cool as though he had ample time at his disposal.

"Therefore," he said, "the thing to do is to search until I find what you were looking for, and ..."

His prisoner could stand the strain no longer. Already the thud of running feet showed that the others were coming toward the house. The man blurted out in excellent English:

"It's in the wallet, in the inside pocket. It's nothing that concerns you. It relates to another matter. My government wants it. They'll kill me if they find me, and they'll kill you. Let me have the paper, and I'll show you the girl."

Major Brane smiled. "Fair enough," he said. "No, don't move. Not yet!" His hands went to Brinkhoff's inside pocket, scooped out the leather folder, abstracted a document. The man against the wall was breathing heavily, as though he had been running. His hands were clenching and unclenching. A door banged somewhere in the house, feet sounded in the corridor. Brinkhoff stirred and groaned.

Major Brane paused to cast a swift eye over the documents which he had abstracted from the leather folder. He smiled, nodded.

"Okay," he said. "It's a go. Show me the girl."

"This way," said the man, and ran toward a corner of the room. He opened a door, disclosed another closet, pressed a section of the wall. It opened upon a flight of stairs.

Major Brane followed, taking care to close the closet door after him. He could hear the sound of steps dashing down the corridor, the sound of confused voices shouting instructions.

The man led him down a winding staircase, to a cellar stored with various and sundry munitions and supplies. The house was a veritable arsenal, on a small scale. He crossed the storeroom, opened another door; and Major Brane, half expecting that which he was to find, came to an abrupt pause and took a deep breath.

The Chinese girl sat in a chair. Her arms and legs were bound. The clothing had been ripped from her torso, and there were evidences that her captors had been trying to make her talk. But she was staring ahead of her with a face absolutely void of expression, with eyes that glittered like lacquer. She was not gagged, for the room was virtually sound proof.

The girl surveyed them with eyes that remained glitteringly inexpressive, with a face that was like old ivory; but she said nothing.

The man who had guided Major Brane to the room pulled a knife and slit the bonds.

"Devils!" said Major Brane. The man with the knife turned to him. "I have done my share. From now on, it is each man for himself. They have the entire block well guarded. I can't be bothered with the woman. Give me the paper."

Major Brane tossed him the wallet.

The man dashed from the room. "Each man for himself. — Remember!" he said as he left.

Major Brane nodded. He picked up a ragged remnant of the girl's clothing, flung it over her shoulders, looked around for a coat.

From the cellar he heard a voice calling.

"He is down here, with the girl!"

It was the voice of the man who had just guided Major Brane to the torture chamber.

The Major nodded approvingly.

The man had warned him; it was to be each man for himself; and the devil take the hindmost. The one who had guided him to the girl felt that he stood a better chance to escape if he guided the enemy to Major Brane. That would lead to conflict, confusion and a chance for escape. It was the strategy of warfare.

Major Brane heard the men running, coming pell mell down the stairs which led to the room. And the block was surrounded, guarded. They were many, and they were ruthless. Here, in the heart of San Francisco, he had stumbled into a spy's nest, perhaps the headquarters for the lone wolves of diplomacy, the outlaws who ran ahead of the pack, ruthlessly doing things for which no government dared assume even a partial responsibility.

Major Brane stepped out into the cellar. He could see a pair of legs coming down the cellar stairs.

Major Brane observed a can of gasoline. The automatic he had captured barked twice. One shot splintered the stairs, just below the legs of the man who was descending, caused him to come to an abrupt halt. The other shot ripped through the can of gasoline.

The liquid poured out, ran along the cement floor of the cellar, Major Brane tossed a match, stepped back into the room which had been used as a torture chamber, and closed the door.

From the cellar came a loud *poof!* then a roaring, crackling sound.

Immediately, Major Brane dismissed the cellar from his thoughts and turned his attention to the room in which he found himself. The girl had arranged the clothing about her, had found a coat. She regarded him with glittering eyes and silent lips.

Major Brane pursed his lips. There seemed to be no opening from the room; yet he knew the type of mind with which he had to deal, and he sensed that there would be an opening.

The crackling sound was growing louder now. Major Brane could hear the frantic beat of panic stricken feet on the floor above. Then there was an explosion, followed by a series of explosions, coming from the cellar. Those would be cartridges exploding.

Major Brane upset a chest of drawers to examine the wall behind it. He picked up a hammer and pounded the cement of the floor. He cocked a wary eye at the ceiling, studied it.

The girl watched him in silence.

The fire was seething flame now, crackling, roaring. The door of the room in which they found themselves began to warp under the heat.

Major Brane was as calm as though he had been solving a chess problem, over a cigarette and cordial. He moved a box. The box didn't tip as it should. It pivoted instead. An oblong opening showed in the wall as the swinging box moved back a slab of what appeared to be solid concrete.

A fire siren was wailing in the distance. There were no more sounds of running feet above the torture chamber.

An automobile exhaust ripped the night. There were heavier explosions from the seat of the fire; then a terrific explosion that burst in the warped door. An inferno of red, roaring flame showed its hideous maw. Heat transformed the room into an oven. The red flames were bordered with a twisting vortex of black smoke.

Major Brane gave the inferno a casual glance, stood to one side to let the girl join him. She walked steadily to his side, and together, they walked along the passage, climbed a flight of stairs.

They came to what appeared to be a solid wall. Major Brane pushed against it. It was plaster and lath, and doubtless swung on a pivot. Major Brane had no time to locate the catch which controlled the opening; he lashed out with his foot, kicked a hole in the plaster. When he looked through the opening, he was peering into a room, furnished as a bedroom. It was deserted.

His second kick dislodged the spring mechanism which controlled the door. The section of plastered wall swung around. Major Brane led the girl into the room, Brinkhoff's automatic ready at his side. They walked through the room to a passage.

The open door led to the night, revealed a glimpse of the street outside, which was already crowded with curious spectators, showed firemen running with a hose. But Major Brane turned in the other direction.

"This way," he said. "It will avoid explanations."

They ran down the corridor, toward a rear exit. Major Brane recognized the stairs which led to the garage. He piloted the girl toward them.

In the garage she paused, looked about her. There was a wooden jack handle lying on a bench. The girl stopped to pick it up.

Major Brane grinned at her. "You won't need it. They've all ducked for cover," he said.

The girl said nothing, which was as he had expected.

A fireman came running down the alley, motioning calling instructions to other men, who were dragging a hose. He glanced sharply at Major Brane and the girl.

"Get outa here!" he yelled. "You're inside the fire lines. You'll get killed, sticking your noses into danger zones."

Major Brane bowed apologetically. "Is this the danger zone?" he asked, wide-eyed in his innocence.

The fireman snorted.

"It sure is. Get out!"

Major Brane followed instructions. They came to the fire lines at the corner, turned into a dark building entrance. Major Brane peered out, whispered to the girl.

"We don't want to be seen coming out of this district. The thing to do is to wait until they run in that second hose, then slip along the shadows, and ..."

He sensed a surreptitious rustle behind him. He turned, startled, just in time to see the jack handle coming down. He tried to throw up his hand, and was too late. The jack handle crashed on his head. He fought to keep his senses. There were blinding lights before his eyes, a black nausea gripping him. Something seemed to burst in his brain. He realized it was the jack handle making a second blow, and then he knew nothing further, save a vast engulfing wall of blackness that smothered him with a rushing embrace.

When next he knew anything, it was a series of joltings and swayings, inter-spersed with demoniacal screams. The screams grew and receded at regular intervals, split the tortured head of Major Brane as though they had been edged with the teeth of a saw.

Then he identified them. They were the wails of a siren, and he was riding in an ambulance.

A bell clanged. The screams died away. The ambulance stopped, backed. The door opened. Hands slid out the stretcher. Major Brane groaned, tried to sit up, was gripped with faintness and nausea. He became unconscious again.

The next thing he knew, there was a bright light in his eyes, and something soothing on his head. He felt soft hands patting about in the finishing touches of a dressing.

He opened his eyes. A nurse regarded him without pity, without scorn, merely as a receiving hospital nurse regards any minor case.

"You got past the fire line and into the danger zone," she said. "Something fell on your head."

Major Brane had presence of mind enough to heave a sigh of relief that the Chinese girl had taken his automatic with her. To have had that in his possession when he was found would have necessitated explanation.

"A Chinese girl told them about seeing you try to run past the line, when something fell from a building," said the nurse. "Her name's on record, if you want a witness for anything."

Major Brane grinned. "Not at all necessary," he said. "I was simply careless, that's all."

"I'll say you were," said the nurse, helping him to sit up right. "Feel better?"

Major Brane slid his feet over the edge of the surgical table.

"I think I can make it all right, he said.

She helped him to a chair, gave him a stimulant. Fifteen minutes later he was able to call a cab and leave the hospital. He went at once to his hotel.

He brushed past the clerk, who stared at his bandaged head curiously; he took the elevator, went to his own room. He fitted a key, opened the door. The smell of Chinese tobacco assailed his nostrils.

"Do not turn on the light," said a voice, and Major Brane recognized it as that of the old Chinese sage who had started him upon his mission.

Major Brane hesitated, sighed, walked into the room and closed the door.

"I came to give my apologies," said the old man, a huddled figure of dark mystery in the darkened room, illuminated only by such light as came through the transom over the door.

"Don't mention it," said Major Brane. "I was careless."

"But," said the sage, "I want you to understand ..."

Major Brane laughed. "I understood," he said, "as soon as I saw the jack handle coming down on my head. The girl had the check hidden, and she wanted to get it right away. She couldn't be certain that my rescue wasn't merely a ruse on the part of her enemies. I didn't have anything to identify me as having come from her friends. Therefore, it was possible that her enemies, seeing that torture would do no good, had staged a fake rescue, hoping to trap her into taking her supposed rescuer to the place where the check was hidden. I should have anticipated just such a thought on her part."

The old man got to his feet. Major Brane could hear him sigh.

"It is satisfying to deal with one who has understanding," he said.

Major Brane saw him move to the door, open it, saw the hunched figure silhouetted against the oblong of light from the corridor.

"She had dropped the check in the waste basket by the side of her desk when she knew her theft was discovered," said the old man, and closed the door.

Major Brane sat in the darkness for some seconds before he turned on the light. When he did so he saw two articles on the table near which the old man had sat. One was a white jade figure of the Goddess of Mercy, a figure that was carved with infinite cunning and patience, a figure that thrilled the collector's heart of Major Brane. Instantly he knew that it was something that was almost priceless. The second object was a purse, crammed with bills of large denomination.

Major Brane inspected the jade figure with appreciative eyes, touched it with fingertips that were almost reverent for a full ten minutes before he even thought to count the currency in the purse. The amount was ample.

Then Major Brane undressed, crawled into bed. He got up an hour later, took ten grains of aspirin, and drifted off to sleep. He awoke in the morning, jumped from bed and pulled the morning's paper out from under the door.

Headlines announced that representatives of the Cantonese government had consented to consult with Chiang Kai–shek at the international port of Shanghai, the object being to patch up their internal difficulties so that China could present an unbroken front to her external enemies.

Major Brane sighed. It had been a hard night's work, but the results had been speedy.

On his way to breakfast, he encountered the night elevator operator.

"There was an old Chinaman who called on me last night," he said. "What time did he come in?"

The operator stared at him with wide eyes. "There wasn't any Chinaman came in while I was on duty," he said.

Major Brane nodded. "Perhaps," he said. "I was mistaken."

When he came to think of it, the Chinese sage would never have left a back track could be traced to Major Brane.

Doubtless the events of the preceding night had been such that no man and no government wished to be officially identified either with their success or failure.

Major Brane was a lone wolf, prowling through a diplomatic danger zone; but he would not have had it otherwise.

A Logical Ending

The lettering on the door read: *David C. Clark — Consulting Criminologist.* To a few intimate friends he was known as "Dave," and to the profession generally he was known as "Key–Clew Clark," or, sometimes, as "One–Clew Clark."

Across the desk sat Phil Bander, local manager of the Interstate Detective Agency.

"This case has got me stumped, and we're working against time on it. Our men can't seem to get anywhere. We just run around in circles. There isn't a definite lead in the whole case."

David Clark frowned slightly and shook his head.

"There's always a definite lead," he said, "somewhere."

"Yes, I know," said Bander, grinning. "You're going to tell me the old story that somewhere there's one definite, outstanding clew that dominates the entire crime; points to the guilt of the proper party. I'll bet you've told me that a hundred times already."

Clark snapped testily, "Well, apparently I haven't told you often enough."

"Yes, I know," said Bander. "It's usually worked so far, but this is one case where you can't find the one outstanding clew. You can't find anything except a lot of confusion."

"Well," said the criminologist. "I can't find anything until you tell me about the crime itself. What are the clews?"

"There are lots of clews," said Bander, "and they all point to a fellow named Pete Dimmer, who is the chauffeur of the dead man."

"Well," said the criminologist, "if the clews all point to him, why not act on the theory that he is guilty. That's the way you detectives work."

Bander ignored the sarcasm of the tone and made a gesture with his hand.

"Because," he said, "it just happens that Pete Dimmer is the one man in the whole list of possible suspects who has an absolutely perfect, unimpeachable alibi."

"Alibis," said the criminologist, "can be manufactured probably easier than any other form of defensive evidence. In fact, I have solved several cases by suspecting the person who had the most complete alibi."

"Sure, I know all that," groaned Bander. "I've pulled that stuff myself. But this is one case where there's an absolutely perfect alibi that can't be shaken."

"Well," said David Clark, "we are talking around in circles. Suppose you tell me exactly what happened. In the first place, who are you representing?"

"I'm representing the agency, of course, and the agency is representing the insurance company that had the gem insured," said Bander.

"What gem?"

"A huge diamond, known in trade circles as the Clinkoff Diamond."

"It's quite valuable, I take it?"

"Exceedingly valuable. It's worth a perfectly huge sum intact, and it could be cut up into three or four smaller diamonds, each one of which would be worth a very considerable sum."

"And the diamond was stolen?" asked the criminologist.

"Yes. Carson Millright is something of a gem collector. It seems that he'd been after the Clinkoff diamond for some time. A few days ago he had an opportunity to purchase it at what he considered a bargain, and he made the purchase."

"Then what happened?" asked the criminologist.

"The gem was delivered, of course, and Millright decided that he was going to keep it where he could show it to his friends, at least for a few days. He didn't like the idea of getting a stone that was a show—piece and keeping it locked up in a safety deposit vault. He approached the insurance company for the purpose of finding out what the premium would be on a very large sum of insurance."

"I take it," said the criminologist, "the premium was plenty high."

"The premium was plenty high," said the detective, "although, in the light of subsequent events, it wasn't high enough."

"Well, go on," said Clark.

"The gem," said the detective, "cost Millright his life. He was found in the morning by his valet, seated in a deep leather chair in his library, with a bullet hole in the front of his forehead. The gun that shot him, a small caliber affair, was on the table a few feet away. As nearly as we can tell, the shot had been fired from a distance of about five or six feet."

Clark's face was rigid with attention. His deep violet eyes, which seemed to be peculiarly luminous, stared at Bander in concentrated attention.

"No sign of struggle?" he asked.

"No sign of struggle," said Bander.

"What time was the murder committed?"

"About midnight."

"Any visitors received at the house?"

"There'd been one who had been received earlier in the evening. That was Sam Townley, the agent who wrote the insurance policy. That is, he had solicited the business for his company, and Millright had given it to him."

"What time did Townley call?" asked Clark.

"Around ten o'clock. He left about eleven."

"No one else called?"

"No one. That is, we are virtually certain that no one else called. Millright had one iron—clad policy, which was that he would never open the door himself. He was afraid of burglars, and he put chain locks on the door and insisted that his valet answer all rings."

"I take it that there were no rings at the doorbell."

"None. The valet sleeps where he can hear the doorbell."

"Who let Townley in?"

"The valet, a chap named Drake, Bob Drake."

"And Townley left about eleven?"

"That's right. The valet is positive about that."

"How does he fix the time?" asked the criminologist.

"Drake was up in his room, which is directly over the front door," said Bander. "Millright has a private telephone which runs from the library to the valet's room. He rang the telephone and said that Townley was leaving and he wanted the valet to go down and put on the chain lock."

"The valet did so?" asked Clark.

"He did so right away."

"He heard Townley slam the door, going out, and he went downstairs at once and put on the chain lock?"

"No. There was a spring lock on the door in addition to the chain lock. The chain lock was used as a measure of safety."

"All right, that lets Townley out of it apparently. How about the valet?"

"That's just the point," said the detective. "There are several people who come under suspicion. There is Ed Kane, the secretary, Bob Drake, the valet, Edith Mace, the housekeeper, and Ellen Mace, her daughter. Also, if we are going to include everyone who was in the house that night, there is Sam Townley, the insurance man."

"But Millright was alive when Townley left?" asked Clark.

"Apparently so. The valet is positive that he recognized Millright's voice over the telephone. He didn't go into the library after Millright had telephoned, but he is positive that it was Millright's voice on the telephone. He said Millright told him that Townley was leaving and would let himself out, and for the valet to go down and lock the door, and that there was nothing else required for the evening."

"No one heard the shot?" asked the criminologist.

"No one heard the shot. It was a small caliber gun, and the library is a massive room lined with books, and the doors are heavy."

"Isn't it rather unusual for a valet to sleep in a room directly over the front door?" asked Clark.

"I guess so," said Bander, "but Millright was a bachelor who ran his house on peculiar lines. He's a collector of stones and also of rare books. His whole house is really built about the library. That is, the house is centered in the library"

"I see," said the criminologist. "Now, you mentioned that the clews pointed to the chauffeur?"

"Every clew points directly to the chauffeur," said the detective. "In the first place, the gun that killed Millright had been bought by the chauffeur."

"You're sure of that?" asked the criminologist.

"Absolutely certain. We have traced the sale, and the man who made it identifies Dimmer as the man who bought the gun. In fact, while Dimmer tried to deny that it was his gun at first, he finally was forced to admit that he was lying."

"That's a suspicious circumstance," said Clark.

"There are lots of suspicious circumstances," said the detective, "and all of them point toward this man Dimmer. Not only did the gun belong to him, but his fingerprints and his fingerprints alone were on the gun. A suit of clothes belonging to the chauffeur was found in his room, and there are unmistakable blood spots on that suit of clothes. We have traced that suit of clothes, and there can be no question but that it was Dimmer's suit. At the time of his death, in addition to the big gem, Millright was known to have had something over a thousand dollars in currency in his pocket. We found, or rather the police found, almost a thousand dollars, in the pocket of the blood–stained suit, and Dimmer can't explain how it got there or account for having that much money in. his possession."

"I take it," said Clark, "that the police have arrested Dimmer."

"Of course they arrested him," said Bander. "The police thought they had a dead open and shut case until they got to checking on Dimmer's alibi."

"Well, how about the alibi?" said Clark.

"The murder," said the detective, "took place on Thursday night, and Thursday night was Dimmer's night off. Under his arrangement with Millright, Dimmer was to have Thursday night off, and also the privilege of using the car. It seems that Dimmer had a girl in Bridgeport, and he took the car to go and call on his girl. He didn't get in until about three–thirty in the morning. The murder was committed not later than twelve–thirty, probably right around eleven–thirty."

"And I take it Dimmer was in Bridgeport then?" asked Clark.

"He was in Bridgeport then. We find that he has an absolutely iron clad alibi. He took his girl and went to a dance. He was at the dance by eleven o'clock, and he stayed there until one–thirty in the morning. He was with his girl almost every minute of the time, and he was seen by no less than half a dozen reputable people who swear that there can be no mistake. What's more, he was arrested for speeding on his way home at the hour of two–forty in the morning at a point fifty–five miles out of the city."

"What else?" asked the criminologist. "Are there any other clews?"

"Yes, the person who committed the murder had made an attempt to let it appear that he entered and left by a window. The window had been pried open and the lock broken. However, the police have ascertained by the tool marks on the sash that the window was pried open from the inside rather than the outside. Moreover, the chisel that was used in prying open the window had a peculiar nick in the blade, and the police were able to identify the chisel which was used from that nick in the blade. It is a chisel that was in a kit of tools that was in the chauffeur's room."

"The chauffeur's room was over the garage or in the rear of the house?" asked Clark.

"Both," said the detective. "The garage is built into the house, and the chauffeur's room is in the back, right over the garage."

"How about the others?" asked Clark. "Can they give any alibis?"

"Not an alibi in the outfit," said Bander. "Each one of them claims that they were in bed asleep at the time the murder must have happened."

David Clark started drumming upon the edge of his desk with the tips of his fingers.

The detective watched him with an amused twinkle in his eyes, and said, "All right, Clark. Go ahead and pick out your one key clew in this case. You always claim that there's one clew which is a key to the whole thing, that it's bound to be in every case. Now what's your key clew in this case?"

Clark did not turn toward the detective, but kept his face toward the window, his eyes fixed in an intense stare, his cameo–like features making his face seem as keen as the blade of a safety razor, his fingers drumming upon the desk.

Suddenly he chuckled. The chuckle became a low laugh. He turned to the detective, and the tension had relaxed from his face. There was a look of lazy good nature in his eyes.

"Of course there's one key clew in this case," he said, "and it's so perfectly obvious that you can't see it because it's so big."

"The gun?" asked the detective. Clark shook his head.

"The bloody clothes?"

Again Clark shook his head. "The money?"

Clark shook his head once more.

"Well," said Bander, with some show of irritation, "it's a case we've got to work fast on. The insurance on that gem amounts to a huge sum, and it's got to be paid within thirty days unless the gem is recovered. Now, if you know so much about it, suppose you show me just how I can recover the gem?"

The look of lazy good nature left the face of the consulting criminologist, and his eyes once more became keen in their concentration, seeming to radiate rays of deep violet light.

"I've found the key clew," he said, "and I know what happened. The difficult part is to prove it, and it's going to take proof to make a recovery. Tell me, Bander, did this Clinkoff diamond have any particular blemish, and distinguishing marks?"

"No," said the detective, "it's a well–known diamond, however, from the manner in which it's cut, and the color and size. It's described in the insurance policy merely as the Clinkoff diamond."

"You're after the diamond, of course," said the criminologist.

"Of course. But naturally, when I get the diamond I'll have found the murderer, and so I'm cooperating with the police and the police are cooperating with me. We're both working toward the same goal."

Clark reached for his hat.

"Do you suppose you could take me with you and introduce me as a gem expert who had been called in by the insurance company for the purpose of doing some special detective work?"

"Sure," said Bander, his face lighting with relief.

"And," went on the criminologist, "do you suppose that you could manage to keep a straight face, regardless of what I said, and not show surprise, no matter what my remarks consisted of?"

"Well," said Bander, grinning, "I can try. But tell me, what's the one key clew in this case?"

"Not now," said Clark. "I'll tell you later."

"Where do we go and what do we do?" asked the detective.

"First," said the criminologist, "I have got to engage an assistant to run down certain angles of the case. Tell me, Bander, do you know anything about diamonds personally?"

"Not a thing," said the detective.

"Have you ever seen this Clinkoff diamond?"

"No. It was stolen before I was called in on the case."

"Do you know anything about its size and shape?"

"Nothing, except that it's rather a large diamond. But anybody who is an expert jeweler can tell you all about it. It's a diamond that is listed in various catalogues of famous gems."

"I think," said Clark, "that is all I am going to need.

"It's ten o'clock now. Suppose I meet you at three–thirty this afternoon at the Millright residence. I take it that the servants will all be there?"

"They will be unless the police have removed some of them for questioning."

"That's all right. You'd better be there and have the man who wrote the insurance policy there. What did you say his name was?"

"You mean the agent for the insurance company?"

"Yes."

"Sam Townley, a likeable chap, right up on his toes."

The criminologist grinned.

"Yet you included him," he said, "in your list of suspects?"

"Not exactly that," said the detective. "I mentioned that he had been out at the house that evening, and therefore was to be included in the list of suspects."

"Now you say he's a likeable young chap," pursued the criminologist.

Bander grinned and said, "By the time you've been in the game as long as I have, Clark, no matter how likeable they are you'll include them in a list of suspects if they had any opportunity whatever to commit the crime."

"Did Townley have an opportunity?" asked Clark.

"No, but I included him just in order to make it cover everybody who was anywhere around the house that night. You know, as a matter of fact, Townley might have come back and crawled in the window."

"But," said Clark, "the window was jimmied open from the inside."

"Yes, that's right. I'd forgotten about that."

"Therefore, Townley couldn't have done it."

"Well," said the detective, "if you're going to figure that way, you can also figure that Pete Dimmer, the chauffeur, couldn't have done it."

"All right," said Clark. "How about the housekeeper or her daughter?"

"Either or both might have done it," said Bander, "although I'd be inclined to suspect the valet if we were starting out without any clews. It is, of course, obvious that whoever entered that room was someone who had some right to be there. In other words, it wasn't a stranger, either to Millright or to the house. It was someone who walked in to see him about something, and the fact that that person was there didn't arouse Millright's suspicions in the least. He sat calmly and placidly in his chair and faced this person while the person got the gun into position and fired."

"Do you think a woman would have been that cold–blooded?" Clark inquired.

"You can't tell about women," said Bander slowly, "and the daughter of the housekeeper is a very attractive baby. I'm not going to bandy about the name of a woman or besmirch the reputation of a dead man, but there's some servants' gossip to the effect that Millright had taken more than a passive interest in the girl since she had been there with her mother."

"Well," said Clark, "you can't blame him for that. I know what you'd have done under similar circumstances. But anyway, meet me at the house this afternoon and I think I will have some word for you."

Key–Clew Clark didn't engage an assistant of the type that Phil Bander had been led to expect.

The criminologist had the complete record of the lives, histories, and present locations of many criminals. What is more, there were many people, both in the underworld as well as in business along more legitimate lines who were deeply indebted to the criminologist.

Therefore, when the criminologist set about engaging an assistant, he took a taxicab which deposited him in a cheap district on the border of Chinatown. He consulted an address in his notebook, verified a number over the door, and plunged at once into a narrow doorway which opened into a labyrinth of dark, smelly passages.

The criminologist located a flight of stairs and moved upward cautiously. He came to an upper corridor which was better lighted, moved down it to a door, and tapped with his knuckles. As he knocked on the door, he took particular pains to stand well to one side of the doorway.

There were sounds from the interior of the room, and a bolt clicked on the door.

The door swung inward, and an attractive young woman attired in a sable coat stared out at him through uncordial eyes.

"Well?" she asked.

"I am looking," said Clark, "for George McCoy."

"He don't live here," said the girl.

"Do you know him?" insisted the criminologist.

"No!" she said.

"He is more generally known," said the criminologist, "as 'Gorilla George.' "

"I never heard of him," she said, and started to close the door.

The criminologist spoke hastily.

"Tell him that his friend, Key–Clew Clark, is trying to locate him."

There was a rumble of sound from the interior of the room, the noise made by the heavy body crossing the creaking planks, and a hairy hand came out and caught the shoulder of the girl's coat, pushed her to one side, and a grinning gorilla face was framed in the doorway.

"Hell!" said Gorilla George. "I thought I knew that voice, but I couldn't place it for a minute. I figured you were a dick. I was sitting back there with my rod all ready to smoke my way out."

David Clark grinned and extended a tentative hand, which was promptly engulfed in the hairy paw.

"Hell!" said Gorilla George. "Come in! Don't stand there gawking in the doorway. Come in and meet the girl friend. Madge, shake hands with Dave Clark. The boys in the game all call him Key–Clew Clark, and he's a bearcat.

"I've told you about the time they were going to frame me for murder on the Gilmore job, didn't I? Well, this is the fellow that came along and showed where the boys had figured the evidence all wrong, and there was another man who was the murderer. It sure was a break for me, because with my record I would never have dared to get on the witness stand."

The girl extended her hand and gave Clark that glance of the professional moll, a certain demure invitation.

"Hello," she said.

Gorilla George turned her around, spinning her on her heel by twisting her shoulders.

"Look her over, Clark," he said. "Ain't she a peach? She's a cute little trick. She's going steady with me now, ain't you, kid?"

The girl nodded.

"Look at the fur coat," said Gorilla George. "I picked it up the other night, and the beauty of it is, it ain't hot. There's no dick in town has got anything on that fur coat. She can wear it anywhere, could walk right into the office of the Chief of Police with it if she wanted to."

Clark nodded his appreciation of the girl and the coat, and then got down to business.

"Listen, Gorilla," he said, "I want you to pull a daylight stick–up for me."

"Who am I going to stick up, and what do I get?" asked the crook.

"About all you get is the experience and a chance to do me a good turn," said Clark. "On the other hand, you won't be running any risk."

"Do I wear a mask?" inquired Gorilla George.

"No, you don't have to."

"Jeez, guy, my map's pretty well known and pretty easy to identify. They'd have me on the pan inside of three hours."

"No," said the criminologist. "This isn't that kind of a stick up. You're going to stick up a car, and there'll be three men in the car. I will be one of the men, and I will have a big diamond in a plain paste board box packed with cotton. You're supposed to know all about the diamond, and to stick a gun on me and tell me to fork over the sparkler."

"How big's the diamond?" asked Gorilla George.

"Did you ever hear of the Clinkoff Diamond?" inquired the criminologist.

"Jeez, guy, you mean the stone that they croaked Millright over?"

"That's the one."

Gorilla George twisted his face into a grimace.

"Jeez, guy, you're gonna get me on the hot squat before you get done."

"No," said Clark, "on the contrary, I am going to use you to assist the law. I will give you a letter that I have instructed you to hold me up and take the diamond from me, so that it really won't be a stick–up at all, and you can use an empty gun. I'll see to it that there isn't any resistance."

"Well," said Gorilla George, "how about making a good job of it and picking up a little coin on the side? Of course, I wouldn't take any of yours, but suppose some of these other birds would be dough heavy? There wouldn't be any harm in taking up a little collection, would there?"

"No," said the criminologist, "I don't want you to do that. I want you to pull this job so you don't have to wear a mask, and you can grab the gem and get away. I want it to be a piece of fast work. The reason I picked on you is because you look the part well enough so that the other boys will know that you're tough, and won't make it look as though you're an assistant of mine."

"Okay, Chief," said Gorilla George, "what's the dope?"

"The dope," said the criminologist, "is that I am going out to Carson Millright's home at about three o'clock this afternoon. I will leave there at approximately the hour of three thirty, and there will be two other men in the car with me. One of them will be Phil Bander, the manager of the Interstate Detective Agency here, and the other will probably be Sam Townley, who is the agent for the insurance company that underwrote the safety of the Clinkoff Diamond when Millright bought it.

"We'll get in the car and start to travel toward an isolated district which will suit our purpose. I would suggest that I pick a rather deserted road in the suburbs. How would that suit you?"

"That suits me jake, Chief."

"Have you got any suggestions, George? Any place that you're pretty familiar with?"

"Yeah, sure," said George. "Some of the boys have got a still out towards Centerville. Suppose you pick a place out there?"

All right," said Clark. "Do you know where there's a deserted house that sits back on a side road with a well in the front yard and a couple of old pear trees? The place is a little bit dilapidated, and ..."

"Hell, yes," said Gorilla George. "The boys have got the still within half a mile of that place."

"All right," said Clark. "I'll go to that place. It will be just about commencing to get dark then. I'll run in there and pick up the diamond. Then I'll come out to the car, unwrapping the diamond and looking at it. I want you to be waiting so that you can pull the stick–up before I've had a chance to do more than get the car headed back toward town. Just give me a few yards, and then come alongside and pull the stick–up. You can let the air out of the tires, or out of the two front tires, so that we can't follow. Make an artistic job of it, see?"

Gorilla George nodded.

"Okay," he said. "Is there anything else?"

"No," said Clark. "That's all."

"What do I do with this stone after I get it?" inquired Gorilla George.

"Save it for a souvenir," said Clark, and closed one eye in a significant wink.

The criminologist shook hands with Gorilla George and the girl, left the cheap rooming house, and went at once into the manufacturing jewelry district. He hunted up a jeweler who was under even greater obligations to him than was Gorilla George.

"Listen," he told the jeweler, "you're familiar with the Clinkoff Diamond?"

"I know what it looks like, yes."

"All right. I want something that will look like the Clinkoff Diamond when it's in a box packed with cotton around it."

"That's quite a large order, Clark."

"No, it isn't, because the diamond is never going to be taken out of the box. All I want is something that looks like the diamond. You can take a piece of glass and silver the back of it, or fake it any way you want to. I want something that will stand the first blush of inspection in half light when I take the cover off the box and leave it off for just a second or two."

"That," said the jeweler, commencing to grin, "is going to be easy. Are you going to pull a fast one on somebody, Clark?"

"I am going," said the criminologist, with a frosty smile, "to demonstrate to a skeptical detective the value of concentrating on one clew and following that one clew to a logical ending."

The man who came dashing from the residence of Carson Millright gave every evidence of excitement. Key–Clew Clark managed to act the part of one who is flushed with triumph, keenly excited. Phil Bander and Sam Townley were flushed of cheek and eye, and they moved with swift, jerky steps.

"My car's here," said Bander, "and we'll go in it."

"All right," said Clark. "I think I know exactly where the place is. At any rate, I've got complete directions here."

"It's funny that your assistant should have telephoned you to come out there to get the gem," said the detective.

"Oh, I don't think so," Clark reassured him. "You see, I worked on the theory that it takes a crook to catch a crook. You know that a good many of my friends are sprinkled about through the underworld in various and sundry professions. The person who is acting as my assistant in this matter wouldn't want to have anyone suspect the connection. Furthermore, you can understand that the possession of the gem, in and by itself, is almost conclusive evidence of first degree murder until the crime is cleaned up."

"And you haven't any idea who did it?" asked Bander.

"No," said Clark shortly, "and I won't have until after I talk with my assistant."

"Your assistant is going to meet us there?" Bander inquired.

"No, the gem will be there. My assistant is going to meet me at my apartment later on tonight. Then I'll know the identity of the murderer, and with the stone that we have you can go ahead and turn the information over to the police, Bander."

"Hot dog!" exulted the detective. "Won't it be a feather in my cap if I can walk into the office of the insurance company and plunk that diamond down on the table and say, 'Okay, boys, here's your stone. How's that for fast work?' "

He ensconced himself behind the wheel of his automobile.

"You're sure it's the stone?" asked Townley as he slid into the front seat next to the driver.

"Absolutely," said the criminologist, entering the tonneau of the car and slamming the door shut. "Go ahead and step on it, Bander. It's a place out by Centerville, and that's going to take us a little while, even if we smash all the speed records."

"Don't worry," grinned the detective, tooling the car through the gears, "we're going to bust every speed record that's ever been known. Just hold your hats, that's all."

"I still don't understand," said Townley, "just how the gem was recovered."

"You've got nothing on me," the criminologist told him. "I don't myself. I only know that I gave a list of the possible suspects to certain people who make a business of locating valuable properties that have been concealed by their owners. In short, gentlemen, I enlisted the aid of a gang of crooks, figuring that the end would undoubtedly be worth the means."

"Well," said Townley doubtingly, "I don't want to throw any cold water on your enthusiasm, but I'll feel a lot more certain when I have seen the stone."

"Of course," said the criminologist, "we all will. But I have the utmost con-fidence in these people."

Bander pushed the throttle well down to the floorboards.

"Shucks," he said, "there couldn't be any opportunity to mistake that diamond. If the crook says that he's got it located, he's got it located, and that's all there is to it. I'm not so certain about getting the dope on the murderer, particularly if we have to rely on the evidence of crooks, but getting the stone is all I want. The rest of it is up to the police. That's their funeral."

The car swung around the corner, and Clark and Townley both braced themselves.

From that point on, there was little opportunity to engage in conversation. The promise that Bander had made that he would violate all speed regulations was faithfully kept, and his two passengers were forced to exercise all of their strength and agility in hanging on and keeping balanced.

It was dusk when they arrived at the spot which the criminologist designated, out in the vicinity of Centerville. The old house loomed dark and forbidding, with blight–destroyed pear trees in the front yard and a porch that sagged at an angle.

"You chaps wait here," said the criminologist, and, jumping from the car, ran up the weed–choked driveway to the house. He put his shoulder against the front door, pushed it in, and went into the dark interior. He waited for a minute or two, in order to make that which was to follow seem real. Then he came running out with his hands fumbling at a box that had been wrapped in heavy paper and tied with coarse twine.

"Did you get it?" shouted Bander.

"I got it. It was left right where they said it would be," said the criminologist.

"My heavens!" said the detective. "Think of leaving anything as valuable as that out in a place like this, all unguarded."

"Don't worry," said the criminologist. "It wasn't unguarded. Nobody else would have stood any chance of getting up here. You don't know the way these men work, that's all."

His fingers tore off the paper and pulled back the cover of the box.

On the interior was a pillow of white cotton, and in the center of this cotton was a large object which caught the faint light of the dying day and sent it in coruscating brilliance into the dazzled eyes of the spectators.

Solemnly Clark put the cover back on the box and started tying it with string.

"Well," said Townley, "let's have a look at it."

"Not here," said the criminologist, tying the string and pushing the box down deep into his overcoat pocket. "We can't tell just who's around here. The fact that my people gathered out here this afternoon may have led others to follow. We'll stop down the road a few miles and give it a more detailed inspection, but it's the stone all right." He climbed in the car. "Let's get started, Bander," he said.

The detective swung the car around in the road and started shifting the gears. A machine shot out from an abandoned side road, swung into the road directly in front of the detective's car, blocking the entire roadway.

The detective slammed on the brakes, cursed, and reached for his gun. Townley slipped a hand toward the lapel of his coat.

Clark lurched forward from the rear seat and grabbed the shoulders of both men.

"Take it easy, boys," he said, "take it easy. The gem isn't worth getting killed over."

As he spoke, the huge, forbidding form of Gorilla George, a heavy automatic in either hand, swung around from the rear of the other machine.

"Stick 'em up," he yelled.

"My God!" gritted Bander, "I can't lose that gem!"

"Don't be a fool," said the criminologist. "We're on the spot, and there's nothing we can do about it. This is a gang job, and they've probably got machine guns trained on us from the brush on the side of the road."

Gorilla George walked over to the car. "Never mind making any motions," he said, "and there ain't going to be no preliminaries. Just toss out that diamond, and toss it out quick."

There was a flurry of motion from the rear seat, and the box sailed through the air toward Gorilla George.

"There it is," said Clark, and the bandit dropped one of the guns in his pocket, stooped, picked up the case, pried off the cover, looked inside. He pushed the box into his pocket.

All right," he said, "you there in the back seat! Get out of the car and let the air out of the front tires, but before you do it I want to get all of the guns that are in the car."

No one moved.

"I mean what I say," said Gorilla George. "Here, you in the back seat, you take the guns away from them two guys. Go on, now, I'm watching you, and you make a false move and I'll blow the top of your head off."

The other gun had reappeared in the gangster's right hand, and his scarred, evil face seemed suddenly sinister.

"Come on, boys," Clark said. "Pass 'em up here. There's no use in making fools out of yourselves."

He relieved the two men of their guns, tossed them through the open sedan window.

"Now yours," said Gorilla George.

"I haven't got any," said the criminologist.

"Okay," said Gorilla George, "you've acted like a sensible man, and I'll take your word for it."

He walked forward and picked up the two guns from the roadway.

"Now get out," he told the criminologist, "and let the air out of the front tires."

Clark got out, unscrewed the valve stems, and let the air out of the tires.

"Okay," said Gorilla George. "Don't try to follow me, and don't be in too big a hurry to get to a telephone, because if you do it isn't going to be healthy for you. There's other people in the brush here that are watching you. You can start going when you get your tires pumped up, but not before."

He walked forward, got into his car, swung it back into the road, and left.

"Quick!" shouted the criminologist. "Where's the tire pump?"

The detective started to curse.

"Of all the damned cowards I ever saw," he said, "you take the cake."

"Be foolish with your own life if you want to," said the criminologist casually, "but I'm not taking chances with mine. I recovered that gem once, and I can recover it again. If you want to risk your life for an insurance company, that's your prerogative. I make my living with my brains, and I don't propose to have them spattered all over a roadway. Give me a hand with these tires. Maybe we can get started in time to do some good."

The men piled out of the front seat, got out the tools, and started pumping feverishly, taking turns.

"We don't need to get much air in there — just enough so we can steer the car," said Clark.

"All right," gasped Bander, "give me one spell more at the pump and we'll be all right."

He pumped for a few seconds, inspected the tires, and shouted, "Come on! We can get started now. That will keep the wheels together, anyway."

The men ran back to the car, flung the pump helter–skelter in the back, piled in and started traveling.

"There's a service station out where this road runs into the highway," said Clark. "We can telephone froth there."

They jolted into the service station, and while the detective was telephoning a report of the robbery, Clark had the attendant pump up the front tires. Bander came out on the run.

"Let's go!" yelled the criminologist. They started out at high speed toward the city. Clark had taken his position behind the wheel while Bander was in telephoning, and his driving was wild.

They had gone four of five miles when suddenly the motor started to cough, spit, and backfire. Finally the motor quit altogether.

"Now what?" said Clark in an exasperated voice.

"There's a car coming behind us," said Townley. "I can get it and run into the next place and have them send out a tow–car for you."

"Okay," said Clark. "I don't know as we can do any good anyway. We've got the roads all blocked. You go ahead and go into the next town and send out a tow–car. It's probably something wrong with the carburetor. Maybe it's just a loose connection in the gasoline line or the vacuum tank."

Townley hopped to the ground and started waving his hands frantically. A car which was coming behind them slowed down

"We've had a breakdown," shouted Townley. "Can you give me a lift to the nearest garage?"

"Hop in," said the man.

Townley climbed in the car.

As the tail light became indistinct in the distance, Bander stared at the criminologist.

"Now what?" he asked. "You certainly seemed to have done some clever work at the start of this case, and to have made a fool out of yourself on the last of it."

Clark laughed, reached over and pushed in the choke adjustment on the car, stepped on the starting mechanism. The car purred into life.

"You see," he said, "I simply slipped out the cable on the adjusting mechanism so that the carburetor would flood. It's all ready to go now."

"What was the idea?"

"You'll see," said Clark. "We'll pick up that car ahead now."

Within two miles they had picked up the car in which Townley had secured a ride.

"Here's a little town and garage ahead," said Bander. "Townley will stop there."

But Townley did not stop there. The car that carried him went through the town with no diminution of speed.

Mile after mile they followed the speeding car, and Bander's forehead was creased with a perplexed frown.

"Won't he know that we're behind him?" he asked.

"No," said Clark. "He thinks our car is broken down back on the road."

They followed the other car clear into the city, then saw it stop at a taxi cab stand, and Townley got out, shook hands with the driver of the car, entered a taxicab. They had no difficulty in following the taxicab to a little apartment house where Townley discharged the cab and ran in to the house.

"What do we do now?" asked the detective.

"We wait," said Clark, grinning, "but not very long."

They walked to the entrance of the apartment house, stood one on each side of the door, waiting. Within five minutes Townley came running out, and as he ran out, Clark's gun was thrust into his stomach.

"All right," said the criminologist, "get them up, Townley."

The man flashed his hand toward his shoulder, encountered the empty holster, and slowly raised his hands.

"You will find, Bander," said the criminologist, "that Townley has an apartment in this place under an assumed name, and that he used it as a place to hide the gem.

"By making him think that I had discovered the gem, and therefore was in a position to know the identity of the murderer, he naturally wanted to leave us stalled on the road while he rushed in to find out whether or not his stone was safe. Finding it safe, he thought I was mistaken, and he was then going back to send a tow—car for us."

"But how did you ever suspect him?" said the detective.

"Easy enough," chuckled the criminologist. "There was one key clew which pointed to Townley, and to Townley alone. You see, Townley pretended to let himself out of the door. All he did was to slam the door and tiptoe back down the passageway to the chauffeur's room. He stayed there until he thought the house was quiet, put on a suit of the chauffeur's clothes, purloined his gun and then went out and committed the crime."

"Sure, I can see it all now," said the detective. "He thought that he could blame it on the chauffeur. But what I want to know is, what was the one key clew that pointed to Townley?"

The criminologist chuckled.

"Of all the list of suspects," he said, "there was only one who wouldn't have known that it was the chauffeur's night out. Townley was the only one who wouldn't have known that the chauffeur would, in all probability, have a perfect alibi.

Therefore, when he picked the chauffeur to blame the crime on, he showed that he was unfamiliar with the routine of the house.

"Therefore, in order to find the real criminal, I had only to scan the list of suspects to find the one man who was on that list and was unfamiliar with the chauffeur's regular night off. That was the key clew. It only remained for me to follow that one key clew to a logical ending."

Restless Pearls

Bob Crowder tip–toed along the iron platform of the fire escape and tried the window with exploring fingertips.

The window was locked.

Crowder sighed wearily, reached his hand under the lapel of his coat to a leather case which hung suspended from his shoulder, just under the armpit. He took out a curved steel bar, gently placed it under the edge of the window, and pried down.

After a moment, the sash creaked under the strain, then snapped upward, making some noise. Bob Crowder slipped the curved bar back into the leather case, took a flashlight from his pocket, and eased his way over the sill and into the room. He heard a quick gasping intake of breath.

"What's the matter?" he asked casually. "Did I wake you up?"

"Who are you and what do you want?" It was a woman's voice.

"I was inquiring," Crowder told her, "about having disturbed your slumbers."

He switched on the flashlight. The beam disclosed a young woman in silk pajamas, sitting bolt upright in bed, her eyes blinking against the glare of the spotlight.

"Turn that thing away," she said, "and tell me who you are and what you want."

"Right at the moment," said Bob Crowder, "I am looking for a string of matched pearls, reported to be worth some forty–five thousand dollars, although I think the amount has doubtless been exaggerated."

He adjusted a mask about his forehead and calmly pulled down the shades.

"Would you mind switching on that light by the side of your bed?" he asked.

The young woman was in the early twenties. She was blonde, with that peculiar straw color of the hair which shows that artificial means have been used to lighten the hair. She was slender but well–formed, and there was a certain willowy grace about her motions as she flung back the covers and jumped to the floor. She groped with her feet for slippers, then reached out and switched on the light.

She stared at the masked figure.

"Who are you?" she asked again.

"Just a crook," he told her.

"I've got nothing," she said. "I'm a manicurist, and I work for my living."

"Unfortunately," he said, "you don't answer your doorbell."

The eyes stared at him and grew wide, drinking in every detail of his appearance.

"Do you mean to say that you're the one who was pushing the buzzer half an hour or so ago?"

"It wasn't that long," he told her. "Not over ten minutes. It took me a little time to get into the apartment house, and then I found that you had the bolt on the inside of the door, so it became necessary for me to come in via the fire escape."

"There's something phoney about you," she declared. "What are you trying to do?"

"To find that necklace," he said.

"You're crazy," she told him, but her eyes flinched under the steady gaze which beat upon her from behind the black mask.

"You don't seem to be very convincing, somehow or other," Crowder told her, sitting down on the edge of the bed, as though he felt perfectly at home.

She stood staring at him for a moment, then looked down at her thin silk pajamas. "If you'd be so good as to take a chair," she said, "I'd get back into bed."

He shook his head and said, "You'd better get some clothes on."

"Are you crazy?" she asked. "Or drunk?"

"Neither," he said — "Not right at the moment anyway, although I have been troubled with acute symptoms of the latter ailment, if you might call it that. But it happens that right at the present time I'm both sober and sane, and I'm very much in earnest when I tell you that I'm looking for that necklace."

"And I'm equally in earnest," she said, "when I tell you that I'm a manicurist and know nothing whatever about it."

"You're not very convincing," he said. "Why didn't you scream when I came into the room? Why don't you try to make a noise and raise the apartment house? Why don't you make the usual threats to notify the police?"

She fidgeted uneasily.

"Why did you come here?" she asked.

"To be perfectly frank," he told her, "I'm beating the police to it."

Her face showed as suddenly drained of color.

"Just what do you mean?" she asked in a voice that sounded thin and frightened.

"You," he said, "are Miss Trixie Monette, a manicurist. You have been running around with Jim Halmer, who is known sometimes as 'Gentleman Jim,' the slickest gem thief in the country.

"Some thirty days ago, Frank Belman's residence was robbed of some rather valuable jewelry. The most valuable, by far, of all of the loot was the matched pearl necklace which is reputed to be worth from forty–five to fifty thousand dollars. In fact, there's a reward offered of ten thousand dollars for it, and the police naturally are breaking their necks to uncover it.

"At the time, Gentleman Jim was suspected, but they couldn't prove anything. However, they kept him under surveillance and, by accident, managed to trace a diamond ring to him. The diamond ring was part of the loot which was taken at the same time the necklace was stolen. The police arrested Gentleman Jim and gave him pretty much of a third degree. He finally admitted the crime, but said he had given the necklace to a lady friend for safe keeping. He wouldn't divulge her name, but told the police he would make arrangements to have the necklace returned. He wasn't going to get the woman mixed into it.

"Then one of his accomplices hired an attorney, and about the time the police thought they had Gentleman Jim sewed up, the attorney came busting in with a *habeas corpus*, and Gentleman Jim was admitted to bail.

"His liberty was rather short–lived because the police got him on another charge and threw him in. But, in the meantime, Jim had had ample opportunity to consult with his attorney. The betting is better than even that the police never recover the necklace. The attorney is already negotiating directly with Belman to see that the necklace is returned in the event Belman refuses to prosecute.

"That doesn't tell me why you're *here*," she said.

"Oh yes it does," he told her. "You were running around a little bit with Jim Halmer. I started in ahead of the police checking up on Halmer's lady friends, and I'm telling you it was quite a job. However, I finally got you spotted."

"Listen," she told him, suddenly eager, anxious and apprehensive, "nobody knows that I knew Jim."

"Oh yes they do," he told her. "I know it, and the person who tipped me off knows it."

"Who was that person?" she asked.

He shook his head.

"And who are you?"

"Well," he said, "you might call me a crook. You know I'm anxious to recover that necklace, and they say it takes a crook to catch a crook."

"I don't think you're a crook," she told him.

He shrugged his shoulders and laughed lightly.

"Isn't it an irony of fate," he said, "that you're trying to convince me you're honest, and aren't able to do so, and I'm trying to convince you that I'm a crook, and you won't believe me."

"And you say the police are coming here?" she asked.

"Yes," he said, "they'll get hold of the information that I uncovered some time during the next few hours. When they do, they'll come busting in here."

"What will they do?" she asked.

"Turn the place upside down," he told her. "Drag you down to the station house, give you a third degree, turn the newspaper reporters loose on you, have your pictures decorating the front pages of the newspapers, get you fingerprinted, and ..."

"Listen," she told him, "will you believe me if I come through on the square?"

"That," he said, "depends on the impression you make, but you've everything to gain and nothing to lose, so why not try it?"

"Look here," she said. "I don't know who you are, or anything about you, but you seem like a gentleman, and I'm in a jam. I did go around with Jim Halmer. I didn't know he was a crook at the time. It wasn't until after he had taken me out several times that I found out about it, and then I wouldn't go out with him anymore. I'm a manicurist, and I peroxide my hair, but I'm on the level."

"One of these virtuous heroines?" he asked.

"No," she told him bitterly. "But I'm a working girl, and I'm playing the game on the square."

Crowder stared at her with steady, contemplative eyes.

"Well," he said, "what about it?"

"Do you believe me?" she asked.

"I'm thinking it over."

"Well," she told him, "if what you say is true, I think I know where that necklace is. If there's going to be a reward offered for it, I can use some of that money. Now, what I want to know is whether you're really a crook."

Crowder reached up to his forehead, lifted off the black mask, folded it and slipped it into an inside pocket.

"Lady," he said with mock deference, "take a look at my honest pan. Notice my steady honest eyes; notice the straight nose and the firm mouth — features, I may say, which are accepted everywhere as indications of integrity. Notice that my face is clean–shaven; that I am free from dandruff and halitosis. Come closer and observe that I am free from B.O. There is no reason why my friends shouldn't like me. Listerine, Life Buoy Soap, Ipana toothpaste and Absorbine Junior are my daily companions.

"I have neither athelete's foot nor pink tooth brush. I ..."

"You're kidding me," she said savagely.

"Of course I'm kidding you," he told her.

"I don't think you're a crook," she said. "Tell me, if I can show you how to get that necklace will you make a division of the reward?"

"What sort of a division?" he asked.

"Give me two thousand dollars if you get the reward."

Crowder gravely extended a hand.

"Shake, pard," he told her.

She slipped her hand into his, suddenly laughed into his face with a display of pearly teeth.

"You're no crook," she said. "Wait until I get some clothes on."

"Never mind the compliments," he told her, "but tell me what you know."

She pulled her hand from his.

"I'll talk to you," she said, "while I'm dressing."

CHAPTER II
PARDNERS IN CRIME

She ran into a closet. A moment later the silk pajamas were flung out in a flurry of fluttering silk. There followed a barrage of jerky conversation, interrupted from time to time by the sound of snapping elastic or little quick intakes of breath as she struggled into garments.

"He's got a girl," she said ... "I didn't know anything about her ... she certainly is one tough baby. She pulled a gun on me ... I didn't know anything at all about her, but one night when I was getting out of the barber shop where I work there was a coupé at the curb ..."

"Yes, yes, go on," said Crowder. "I'm interested."

"Wait until I get my stockings straight," she said. "Well, this coupé pulled up along the curb, and the door opened. A well–dressed brunette asked me if I wouldn't ride with her. I didn't know her from Eve — she looked like a good scout, and I didn't want to seem to high–hat her. I got in and asked her what she wanted.

"She said she was just driving for recreation and fresh air; that she saw me come out of the barber shop and that I looked tired. She asked me a few questions about myself and said she was going to drive me to my apartment."

"Did she?" asked Crowder.

"Like fun she did," the girl told him. "She drove me down an alley and suddenly stuck a gun in my ribs and told me if I didn't quit playing around her man, she was going to let a load of lead into my guts. She talked something frightful."

"Coarse or threatening?" asked Crowder.

"Both," she said.

"All right; then what?" asked Crowder.

"Then she put me out."

The closet door opened and the girl came out, twisting the belt of her skirt, to get it straight.

"Let's go," she said.

"Wait a minute," Crowder told her. "Let's get the rest of the sketch before we go anywhere."

"Well," she said, "she put me out and made me walk out of the alley. But while I'd been sitting in the car I got a look at the registration certificate in the front of the car. I'd done that as soon as she picked me up, just in case anything went wrong. Her name was Ethel Peters, and the address was 9204 Western."

"Maybe the registration was a frame," said Crowder.

"No, I looked her up. That is, I made it a point to go to that address. There's an apartment house there, and her name is on the mail box."

"I see," said Crowder, interested. "And you think she was a pal of Gentleman Jim, is that right?"

"She most certainly didn't stick a gun in my ribs just because she didn't like my blonde hair," the girl told him.

"And she talked like a moll?"

There was a flare of expression in the young woman's eyes.

"She talked like a — Gee!" she said, "I'd better watch myself or I'll be talking that way too, but you know what I mean."

Crowder grinned.

"Let's go," he said.

The pair stood in front of the apartment house out on Western, and stared at the mail box.

"She won't let us in at this hour," said Trixie Monette.

"I'm not so certain," Crowder told her. "Remember that this girl doesn't live the kind of a life that you do. She's probably accustomed to all sorts and conditions of callers, at all sorts of hours.

He pressed his finger on the button opposite the card which bore the name Ethel Peters, Apartment 48B. Almost immediately the buzzer worked the electric release on the outer door of the apartment.

Bob Crowder grinned and pushed his way into the hallway.

"Look here," he said, "we'd better get a definite plan of campaign."

"If she's got the necklace we can make her give it up," said Trixie Monette determinedly.

"It may not be so easy," Crowder told her. "And, by the way, you don't mind if I call you Trixie, do you, providing you call me Bob?"

"No, Bob," she said.

"All right," he said. "Now we're going up there, and we've got to work out some plan of campaign — before we get there or afterwards."

"I'm game for anything," she told him.

He stared at her steadily.

"Just what would you do for two thousand dollars?" he asked.

"Try me," she said.

His eyes suddenly lost their glint of mocking humor and his face became hard as stone.

"Look here," he said, "it happens that I want that necklace. I'd hate to tell you what I'd do in order to get it. Now, the question is, are you game to back my play?"

She shrugged her shoulders and started for the stairs with a free, swinging stride.

"If you knew the way I felt toward that woman," she said, "you wouldn't waste so damn much time asking questions."

Crowder grinned and followed her up the stairs.

A door on the second floor opened a crack. A young woman with jet–black hair, smoky black eyes, her figure daringly and carelessly displayed beneath a pink negligee, stood in the doorway watching the pair come down the corridor.

"What is it?" she asked.

"Message from Jim," said Crowder in a low tone of voice, keeping his head slightly forward so that the brim of his hat shaded his face.

Ethel Peters hesitated a moment, then stood slightly to one side.

"Come on in," she said.

Crowder stood to one side and pushed Trixie Monette into the room, entered himself. The brunette closed the door of the apartment behind her, snapped a bolt into position.

"Well," she said, "spill it."

"Gentleman Jim got picked up on that Belman job," said Crowder, "and is ..."

He was interrupted by a hissing gasp from Ethel Peters.

"What are *you* doing here?" she blazed.

She pushed her way past Crowder, and walked toward Trixie Monette, her eyes flashing black lightning.

"Now wait a minute," said Crowder. "Keep your shirt on, and ..."

She sprang forward like some tigress and Crowder's arm, dropping down around her chin, caught her by the neck and pulled her back.

"Not so fast, sister," he said.

"Let me at her!" screamed Ethel Peters — "I know who she is; she's the baby-faced little ..."

There followed a string of invectives, words of the gutter which slipped easily and volubly from the red lips of the brunette. Crowder clapped a palm over the lips.

"Hush," he said, "or I'll wash your mouth out with soap and water."

She whirled on him, biting at his hand, thrashing and kicking.

He caught her wrists, held them with one hand, and caught her by the throat with the other.

"Now shut up," he said, "or I'll throttle you."

She lapsed into sullen silence.

"All right," Crowder told her. "We're not mincing words, since you're not. We want that Belman necklace, and we want it quick."

"You cheap heel!" she sneered. "Try and find it. What do you think I am anyway?"

Trixie Monette spoke with dulcet sweetness.

"Oh, we know what you are, dearie," she said.

The brunette whirled on her once more with sudden insensate savagery. She tore herself free from Crowder's grasp, leaving a part of her negligee in his clutching hand. She dashed toward Trixie Monette, suddenly detoured, and made for the table drawer, which was partially open.

"Look out," shouted Crowder, making a dive for her.

The hand came up from the drawer. The light glittered upon blued steel, and then Trixie Monette hurled a paperweight. The paperweight caught the brunette on the temple. She swayed slightly, then slumped to the floor, the gun dropping from her nerveless fingers.

"This," remarked Crowder, surveying the unconscious form at his feet, "is a mess."

"Of course she's a mess," snapped the manicurist. "The dirty little hussy."

Crowder shook his head patiently.

"I didn't mean her," he said, "I meant the situation."

Trixie Monette was breathing heavily, as though she had been running. Suddenly she laughed.

"Well," she said, "you wanted to know how far I'd go; now you've found out."

Crowder used his handkerchief to pick up the gun, careful not to leave any fingerprints. He slipped the magazine from the weapon, then slammed the shell which was in the barrel out into his palm, removed the shells from the magazine and replaced it.

"Well," he said, "let's look around, and do it fast."

They started searching the apartment. "It probably won't be in a likely place," he said. "We've got to look in some of the less likely places."

"We've got to look everywhere," she told him, "until we find it; that's all."

For more than half an hour they moved purposefully about the apartment, searching rapidly, yet thoroughly. They dumped flour into the sink, poured out sugar and salt, emptied every receptacle they could find, raised up the carpets, kneeded the pillows, pulled the bedding from the bed and inspected the mattress. They looked behind pictures, and, in the end, were baffled.

They stared at each other.

"It isn't here," said Trixie Monette.

"Somehow," said Bob Crowder slowly, "I have an idea it is."

He walked over to the woman, picked her up and carried her into the bedroom, where he laid her on the mattress. He felt her pulse and nodded.

"It's still going strong," he said, "just about the way it was. She's out, but I don't think it's dangerous."

"Well," said Trixie Monette, "she was trying to kill us. I don't know what we were supposed to do."

"We were, of course," Crowder reminded her, "entirely outside of our rights in invading the apartment. Furthermore, young lady, let me call your attention to the fact that the police may find out about Ethel Peters and be out here at any moment."

She nodded, her face showing her bitter disappointment.

"Lord," she said, "if you knew how I needed that money, and to think that it's almost in our grasp."

"Maybe," said Crowder, "she's got the gems on her somewhere in this negligee."

Trixie Monette moved forward eagerly.

"I'll step out and you can make a search. Better make a pretty complete search ..."

"She wouldn't mind," said Trixie Monette. "She isn't that kind. You don't need to go out."

"No," said Crowder, "you make the search."

He walked out of the bedroom, stood in the doorway of the living–room, his forehead wrinkled in a perplexed frown. A few minutes later Trixie Monette came to him. There were tears in her eyes.

"We're licked," she said.

Bob Crowder stared about him grimly.

"Not by a long shot we're not licked," he said.

He strode into the bedroom, ripped up a pillowcase into strips about two inches wide.

"What are you doing?" she asked.

"I'm going to fix this young woman so that she'll stay put," he told her. "And then I'm going to find out where that necklace is."

"Where you going to put her?"

"We'll tie and gag her and put her down in my car," Crowder said. "We can run her down the elevator without anyone seeing us at this time of night. There's no one in the lobby."

"What the idea?" she asked.

"Simply going to put her out of circulation for a while," he told her.

"Listen," she said, "I've got an idea that beats that. There's bound to be a vacant apartment on this floor. Suppose we find which one it is, pick the lock, and put her in there?"

"How we going to find out?" he asked.

"I'll go down and take a look at the mail boxes," she said.

Crowder nodded, picked up a bunch of keys which he had taken from the moll's purse, and tossed them to Trixie Monette.

"Better take her keys," he said, "or you might lock yourself out."

While she went down to consult the mail boxes, Crowder moved around the apartment, prowling about, looking for some possible nook or corner which had been overlooked.

Trixie Monette slipped back into the apartment.

"There were two on this floor," she said. "One of them's almost directly across the hall. Can you pick the lock?"

Crowder grinned.

"I'll say I can pick the lock," he said, "but I wish you hadn't flung such a mean paperweight. I'd like to talk with this baby."

"She wouldn't have told you anything; she's hard–boiled."

"You never can tell."

"Well, you can tell about her."

Crowder stepped across the hall, found the vacant apartment, managed to open the door with the second key he tried. He scooped the unconscious form of the girl into his arms, carried her into the apartment.

"Now what are you going to do?" asked the blonde.

"Now," he said, "I'm going to show you some of the fancy technique that gets me places. One of these days it'll probably get me in jail."

"What's the idea?" she asked.

"The underlying idea is," he said, "that crooks read the newspapers."

"I don't get you," she remarked.

He chuckled.

"You won't," he told her.

CHAPTER III
THE HANGING CORPSE

The window of the department store had a display of gowns draped upon the wax dummies; dummies of slender waisted women who stared from basilisk eyes at the passerby on the sidewalk.

Bob Crowder paused in front of the window display, to select just the type that he wanted — a brunette clad in a filmy lingerie.

The department store was one of the smaller department stores; one that had a fair stock of merchandise, yet was not large enough to employ a private watchman. Crowder's job of burglary was remarkably skilful and adroit.

When he had finished, he had left no fingerprints or other clue, and the waxed dummy reposed safely in his automobile. Getting it into the apartment of Ethel Peters was a more difficult matter, but he took a chance on meeting some late incoming tenant on the stairs, and arrived at the door of the apartment.

Trixie Monette stared at the dummy with startled eyes.

"Good heavens!" she said. "You must have gone crazy."

"Find anything?" he asked.

"No," she replied. "I've been over every inch of this apartment. I've gone over everything that we looked in before, just to make certain."

"How's the invalid?"

"She's conscious," she said, "and trying to talk."

"What does she want to say?" asked Crowder.

"You'd better go listen," said the girl.

"No," Crowder told her, "I've got work to do, and it's work of a kind that I don't want you mixed in on. You go in and stay with her. If she starts making too much noise through that gag, throw a pillow over her face, but don't get too hard with her."

Trixie Monette laughed grimly.

"Getting hard with that baby is one of the things I'm the fondest of," she remarked.

"All right," said Crowder. "You go in and take care of her. But use a little judgment. I'm going to start some action. I'll call you when I need your help. I'll need it in about ten minutes, for about two minutes."

"What do you want me to do?" she asked.

"Lower this dummy out of the window," he told her.

"Lower it out of the window?" she asked incredulously

"Yes," he told her. "I've got some rope here."

"But," she pointed out, "someone will be almost certain to see you. There'll be some late motorist coming along the street, or someone who will see you from an adjoining apartment house; somebody who isn't sleeping, or who has come home late or is getting up early in the morning."

"Yes," he told her, "and in order to make certain that there is some witness to what is going to happen, I'll spread it on good and thick."

"You mean you want a witness?"

"I want lots of them," he said.

"What are you trying to do?" she asked.

"Make the front page of the newspapers," he told her, and grinned. "You go on in there and stay with your patient. Be certain that she keeps quiet and doesn't get away"

Trixie Monette slipped across the hall into the vacant apartment where they had placed their prisoner, and Bob Crowder, chuckling to himself, started setting the stage for that which was to follow.

He looped ropes about the shoulders, hips and knees of the wax dummy, then took a string of imitation pearls from his pocket and fastened them about the wax arm of the figure, tying them in such a way that anyone looking at the figure would see first that long string of dangling imitation pearls. When he had things ready to suit his taste, he stepped across the hall and spoke to Trixie.

"Can you leave your patient for a while?" he asked.

"I'll say. I've made a good dog out of her. She thinks I'm going to put acid on her face if she makes any noise."

"My gosh!" Crowder said. "What a little spitfire you are!"

"You haven't seen anything yet," she told him. "What do you want me to do?"

"When I give you a signal," said Crowder, "I want you to lower this dummy out of the window. Just lower away on the rope until I yell 'All right.' Then drop the rope and duck back to the apartment across the hall. Stick in there, no matter what happens, and don't show your face."

"Okay," she said, "but make it snappy. Ethel might get restless, and you know what a sweet disposition she's got."

"All right," Crowder told her. "I'll make it snappy. But be sure and keep your face concealed. Keep your head down so that no one can see your face, do you understand?"

"Sure," she told him. "Let's go."

Crowder ran down the stairs to the street. He parked his automobile, with the motor running, directly under the apartment window.

"Okay," he shouted.

Trixie Monette started lowering the wax dummy out of the window.

"Hold it right there for a minute," Crowder called.

He whipped his gun from its hoister and fired two shots.

"All right," he said, "lower away."

The shots from the automatic arose echoes up and down the quiet street, in the apartment house across the way lights came on, and here and there a figure was silhouetted against the oblongs of illumination. Somewhere a woman screamed.

"Make it snappy," shouted Crowder. "She's got the pearls!"

Trixie Monette continued to let the rope slide over the sill. The wax dummy swayed back and forth.

"Drop those pearls!" yelled Crowder, "or I'll shoot."

Across the way a window slammed open and a woman's shrill voice shouted, "Police! Police! Police!! There's a murder being committed."

"Drop those pearls or I'll shoot!" shouted Crowder.

The figure continued its slow downward descent, swaying slightly back and forth, the cheap imitation string of pearls dangling from the waxen wrist.

Crowder flung up his automatic, took deliberate aim and pulled the trigger.

The bullets *"plumped"* into the wax figure, which jerked spasmodically as each bullet struck it. The street echoed to half a dozen screams. The figure was then some ten or fifteen feet above the sidewalk.

"Drop her!" yelled Crowder. "She's dead."

Trixie Monette flung the rest of the rope over the windowsill. The figure dropped abruptly. The rope twisted and turned like some writhing snake.

Crowder caught the wax dummy in his arms. The rope came spiraling down from above and settled about his head and shoulders. He fought free of the rope, slammed the dummy into the car, jumped to the driver's seat and flung in the clutch.

A police whistle blew somewhere in the side street. The woman who had been screaming for the police raised her voice to an even more shrill pitch and shouted invectives at him.

Crowder threw the car into a skid at the corner, so that the tires would leave black marks and send forth screaming protest.

Behind him, the street was in an uproar.

It was past daylight when Crowder tapped gently with his knuckles on the door of the apartment where Trixie Monette held Ethel Peters a prisoner.

There was no answer.

Twice more he rapped before the door opened a scant half–inch, and the eyes of the manicurist appraised him carefully before opening the door and allowing him to slip into the apartment.

"Well," he asked, "everything all right?"

She indicated the bound form which lay on the bed.

"Everything's all right except Ethel," she said. "I'm certainly having my troubles with that girl."

"Have to pillow her?" he asked.

"I'll tell the world," she said. "My, but that girl's got a disposition."

"What happened in the next apartment? Did the police come?"

"I'll say they came. They went through the apartment and took a lot of photographs. The newspaper men came and shot flashlights. There were people tramping up and down the corridor until it sounded like a small army on the march. After a while they went away."

"How long ago?"

"Just about half an hour."

Crowder took a small gimlet from his pocket and bored a hole in the panel of the apartment door. Then he left the door open, stepped across the corridor and bored a similar hole in the door of Ethel Peter's apartment.

"What's the big idea?" asked Trivia Monette.

"I'm acting on the theory," Crowder told her, "that Ethel had the necklace hid in that apartment; that she had it hid so cleverly we couldn't find it, and the police couldn't find it. But I think there's someone who knows where the necklace was hidden. That man is the partner and accomplice of Gentleman Jim Halmer."

"You mean Ed Conway?" she asked.

He nodded.

"I knew," she said, "that Ed Conway was pretty close to Jim Halmer. I didn't know exactly what it was all about."

"Conway," said Bob Crowder, "is the man who helps him pull most of his jobs. He was mixed in on this Belman necklace business somewhere."

"Well," she said, "what does all that mean when it's translated into English?"

"Just this," he told her. "News travels fast through the underworld. Apparently, someone came to the apartment of Ethel Peters, with a scheme to kidnap her. She was being lowered out of the window. The pearls were dangling from her wrist. The man below ordered her to drop the pearls. When she didn't, he shot her and took her body away in an automobile."

"But," she said, "that doesn't make sense. In the first place, if she had the pearls on her, wouldn't they have taken them from her before lowering her from the window? In the second place, if she was being lowered from the window, and the man was standing below her with a gun, why didn't he wait until she had been lowered to the sidewalk, and then simply take the pearls?"

Crowder nodded.

"That's the nice part of it," he said. "It doesn't make sense. That's why it will get around the underworld and cause all sorts of various conjectures and speculations. No one can figure it out.

"Ed Conway will hear about it and try to figure what the devil happened. There'll be only one way for him to find out."

"You mean," she said, "to come to the apartment?"

He nodded.

"And then again," he told her, "there's another advantage in having it keep from making sense."

"What?" she asked.

"When they get me on the carpet at police headquarters," he told her.

"They're going to do that?"

"Of course."

"What makes you think so?"

"Because they always do."

"Do you pull this kind of stuff often?" she asked.

"Always," he told her.

"You act on the theory that it takes a crook to catch a crook?"

"Partly," he told her, "but partly on the theory that you have got to resort to unorthodox methods if you're going to beat the police to the punch."

"Well," he said, "you know your business. I'm going to along and see what I can shake out of the christmas–tree."

The bound figure on the bed suddenly burst into a volume of noise; inarticular sounds which came from behind the gag. She twisted and turned, fighting against the bonds which held her wrists and ankles.

Trixie Monette said wearily, "There she goes again staging another fit. I've got to go and put a pillow on her face and sit on the pillow."

She picked up a pillow from a chair, moved over toward the bed. The bound woman saw her coming and suddenly became silent and motionless.

"Well," Trixie said, "that's that. She's at least getting so she knows when to quit. After awhile I'll get her educated so she knows enough not to start."

Bob Crowder drew up a chair in front of the closed door of the apartment, lit a cigarette and applied his eye to the peephole he had gimleted in the door.

"Well," he said, "let's hope that Ed Conway has got a pretty good line out of police headquarters, so that he won't have to wait until he reads about the abduction in the newspapers."

Once more, the figure on the bed broke into incoherent noise, and Trixie Monette dove toward it with a pillow. There was a flurry of motion, the sound of struggle, the creaking of bed springs, then silence.

The blonde manicurist straightened with a sigh and grinned at Bob Crowder.

"Never had to do so much work for two thousand bucks in my life," she said.

"And we haven't even got the two thousand," Crowder said with a grin.

"Ah well," she told him, "it's been a great experience anyway."

Crowder finished his cigarette, lit another one. Trixie Monette propped a pillow against her back, closed her eyes and dropped into a half–doze.

Abruptly, Crowder's figure stiffened to attention as he saw a shadowy shape moving in the corridor. There was the sound of a key clicking in the bolt.

Crowder got to his feet, tiptoed across to Trixie Monette, shook her shoulders gently and motioned toward the hallway. The manicurist raised her eyebrows in silent inquiry and Crowder nodded, placed his finger to his lips, and then pointed to the bound figure on the bed.

Trixie Monette nodded, picked up the pillow, and moved silently toward the bound figure of the girl who was now lying with her eyes closed, apparently sleeping. Crowder opened the door of the apartment and slipped into the hallway.

The door of apartment 48B was almost directly opposite him. It was closed. Crowder made sure that the hallway was empty, then dropped to his knees and peered through the peep–hole in the corner of the panel.

He could see into the apartment, could see a figure dragging a chair across the room to one of the windows. The figure was that of a man with powerful shoulders, thick neck, and a bullet head.

As Crowder watched, the man planted the chair in front of the window from which Ethel Peters had been lowered. He climbed to the chair, and Crowder saw that he was reaching for the roller shade at the top of the window. A moment later, and he had disengaged the shade from its fastenings and pulled it down.

As Crowder watched, the man swiftly unscrewed the fastenings on the end of the roller, and tilted the roller slightly, shaking it as he did so.

Crowder saw that the coil spring had been removed from the inside of the curtain roller, and that the place which it had occupied had been used as a receptacle for a long, round object which had been done up in soft cloth.

The man pulled this object from the interior of the roller shade. He slipped it in under his coat, then replaced the cap on the end of the roller shade, and dropped the shade back into position at the top of the window.

Crowder straightened and stood slightly to one side of the door. Three seconds later the bolt clicked softly back, and the shadowy figure stepped back into the hallway.

"Stick 'em up," said Crowder.

The man gave an inarticulate bellow of rage, and swung his fist. Crowder dodged the blow, hesitated for a moment, then dropped the gun and slammed his right fist squarely into the man's body, knocking him back into the apartment, and kicked the door shut. The heavy set man was fumbling with his right hand near his right hip pocket. Crowder managed to land a left, before the man could get the gun from his pocket.

The heavy–set man abandoned his effort to get the gun, lashed out with a vicious kick, then came in with his head down, his arms flailing about.

Crowder took a glancing blow on the head, dodged another, side–stepped, set himself, and whipped up a right upper cut. The uppercut struck squarely on the chin. The man's head rocked back with a sudden jerk, as though a rope had been connected with the top of his head and suddenly pulled.

CHAPTER IV
REWARD

Police Captain Stanwick glared across the desk at Bob Crowder, yet there was a hint of a twinkle in the glaring eyes.

"Crowder," he said, "where the devil did you get that necklace?"

"I got it from Ed Conway," said Crowder. "He was an accomplice of Gentleman Jim Halmer. I knew that they worked together..."

"Nix on that line of hooey," said Stanwick. "What I want to know is how you got it."

"Took it away from him," said Crowder. "I stuck a gun in his ribs and told him to put his hands up, but he wouldn't do it. He went for his gun. Of course, I could have pulled the trigger, but I knew that there would be embarrassing explanations. You see, a private detective can't do the things that a regular detective can, and ..."

"Yes, yes, I know all that," said Captain Stanwick. "The report of the offices gives me all of that stuff. But what I'm particularly anxious to learn is how you happened to catch Conway in the apartment of Ethel Peters."

"Well, you see," said Crowder, "I knew that Ethel Peters had been going with Jim Halmer. She was his woman, although they'd kept the connection pretty secret. It wasn't even whispered around the underworld. You see, Gentleman Jim was one of those cautious individuals who didn't believe in letting his left hand know what his right hand was doing."

"Yes, I know all that," Captain Stanwick said. "But you still haven't told me exactly how it was that you happened to be at the apartment at the psychological moment that Ed Conway entered. You haven't told me how it was that you knew he had the necklace. You haven't told me a single damned thing."

Bob Crowder raised his eyebrows and shrugged his shoulders.

"Well," he said, "I can't tell you anything more than I've told you already."

"You mean you won't tell me anything more than you've told me already."

"No," Crowder said, "I'm perfectly willing to tell you anything within reason that you want to know."

"You get the results — yes — but your methods are going to get you in trouble some day, young man. I'd hate to see your license revoked; particularly after the success you've had. But I just want to tell you you're skating on thin ice."

"But," protested Crowder, "exactly what did I do?"

Captain Stanwick groaned.

"I'll be damned if I know," he said, "and I guess nobody else does. There was a lot of hooey about a young woman being lowered from the apartment where Conway was captured. Some fellow was standing below and apparently using her as a target for a gun. There was a string of pearls dangling from her wrist."

"But why should a man have used the woman as a target?" Crowder asked innocently.

"That's a question I've been asking myself for two or three hours," Captain Stanwick said. "And, do you know, Crowder, I'm commencing to think that I know the answer."

"Indeed?" said Crowder, with courteous interest.

Captain Stanwick sighed wearily.

"Oh hell," he said, "what's the use?"

"Is that all you wanted to see me about?" Crowder asked.

"No," said Stanwick, "that's not all I wanted to see you about. Our men picked up Ethel Peters, the tenant of the apartment at 9204 Western."

"Good work," said Crowder noncommittally.

Captain Stanwick flashed him a searching glance.

"She had a pretty bad bruise on the side of her temple," he said.

"Women of that sort always get beaten up," said Crowder. "That's what I understand. They tell me that she's a typical moll. What was she doing when you picked her up? Trying to escape."

Stanwick nodded.

"Well," asked Crowder, "what's her story?"

"She hasn't got any," said Captain Stanwick. "She's keeping quiet, except when she turned loose to tell the detectives something about their maternal ancestry."

Crowder shook his head lugubriously.

"Isn't it awful," he said, "when a woman talks that way?"

"Well," said Stanwick, "I don't think she's going to give us any great amount of information. In the event she should tell us anything it might mean that she was held as an accessory after the fact, but I was just wondering if you happened to know anything about who the woman could have been that was lowered out of the window in the apartment."

Crowder frowned thoughtfully, after the manner of one who is thinking.

"You say she was shot?" he asked.

"Three or four shots hit her dead center. The witnesses all agree on it. They could see the body jump when the bullets hit."

Bob Crowder said slowly, "That's no way to treat a woman."

Suddenly Captain Stanwick chuckled.

"Well," he said, "that's a new way of looking at it."

There was silence for a period of several seconds, then Captain Stanwick said, "Frank Belman tells me that when he made out the checks for the reward you insisted on having two checks, one of them made out to you, in the sum of five thousand dollars, and one made out to Trixie Monette in the sum of five thousand dollars."

Crowder said, "That's right, Captain," as though praising the police officer for some bit of first-class detective work.

"Why," said Captain Stanwick, "did you have the reward paid in just that way?"

"To be perfectly frank with you," Crowder said, "I did it in order to give a young woman a surprise."

"Ah," said Captain Stanwick, "so there was a woman in the case then?"

"Yes," said Crowder, "there was a woman in the case."

"One of those shrewd little tarts who pick up stuff on the fringes of the underworld?" asked Captain Stanwick.

"No," said Crowder, grinning, "this young woman was very beautiful, and you might say that she was dumb."

"The woman that got the check?" Captain Stanwick asked.

"No," said Crowder, "the woman who assisted me in getting the pearls."

"You mean the woman who was lowered out of the window?"

"I'm not mentioning any names or making any admissions," said Crowder.

"No," Stanwick said, "you wouldn't. But the woman who was lowered out of the window certainly is dumb by this time. The witnesses are positive that she got at least three heavy slugs shot into her body."

Crowder made clucking noises with his tongue against the roof of his mouth.

"Horrible," he said.

"That," Captain Stanwick said, "would be murder unless ..."

"Unless what?" asked Crowder.

"Unless," said Captain Stanwick, looking at him shrewdly, "there should be some connection between the woman who was lowered out of the window, and the report that came in about an hour ago from a department store in the district, that a display dummy had been taken from the show window."

Crowder looked extremely innocent.

"A dummy?" he asked. "Stolen from a window?"

Captain Stanwick nodded.

"Well," said Crowder, "perhaps someone was playing bridge and wanted a fourth for a dummy."

Captain Stanwick's face purpled.

"You," he said, "get the hell out of here!"

Time for Murder

George Brokay latchkeyed the front door of his palatial residence, where he maintained deluxe bachelor quarters. There was a yawn twisting his lips, and complete boredom in his eyes.

The hour was but five minutes after midnight, which was no time for a wealthy, eligible young bachelor to be returning home. And George Brokay was doing it only because he could think of no better place to go.

His hand reached for the light switch and was almost on the point of pushing the button, when he noticed a ribbon of light coming from under the side of a doorway at the end of the hall.

He paused, staring at the ribbon of light.

Grigsby, the butler, should have retired long since. Brokay had left specific orders that his valet was not to wait up for him. There was, therefore, no good reason why anyone should be in the library. Yet, unmistakably, a light was burning in there, and, as Brokay watched the strip of yellow which showed beneath the door, he saw moving shadows cross it.

There was someone in the room; someone who was moving.

Brokay stepped silently into the little den which was at the left of the corridor. He noiselessly opened the drawer of a desk and took out an automatic. Moving as silently as a shadow, he slipped through the dark corridor and paused, with his hand on the knob of the door to the library.

He listened and could hear nothing.

He turned the knob slowly, exerting pressure on the door as he did so, so that the latch would give no audible click. When he felt the knob turn as far as it would go, he pulled on the door, opening it an inch at a time.

The door swung back upon well–oiled hinges. Brokay, the wicked–looking automatic held in his right hand, kept to one side so that he could see through the opening of the door.

The portion of the library which was visible through the partially opened door was the corner which contained the wall safe. The panel which concealed the safe had been swung open. A man was standing in front of it, moving with swiftly silent rapidity.

Brokay watched him with fascination.

The man took a cake of soft yellow laundry soap, kneeded the soap into a cup–shaped container, which he fastened to the door of the safe, just at the point where the door joined the body of the safe. Then, with deft fingers, he pressed the soap along the crack between the door and the safe. The man's fingers moved so swiftly and so capably that Brokay realized he was watching a master workman.

It was when the man bent to a leather satchel on the floor and took out a bottle of thick, slightly yellowish, viscid liquid, and was about to pour a measure of that liquid into the cup–shaped container at the top of the safe, that Brokay announced his presence.

"Don't move," he said.

The man was facing the safe, the bottle held in his right hand. The cork had been removed. As Brokay spoke, the man froze into immobility, without moving so much as a muscle.

Brokay, who had rather expected the man to give a guilty start, to whirl and face him with terror upon a countenance grayed with fear, thought that perhaps the man had not heard him.

"I said don't move," Brokay repeated. "I've got you covered with a gun. I'm rather expert in its use. I most certainly shall drill you right through the back if you make any sudden moves or try to escape."

The man still kept his back turned and spoke over his shoulder.

"Don't ever do that again," he said.

"Don't ever do what?" asked Brokay, puzzled and interested at the well–modulated tone of the man's voice.

"Don't ever interrupt a box–man when he's pouring 'soup' into a box. I was just getting ready to make a jamb–shot, and you came along and pulled that line of yours. Don't you know that there's enough nitroglycerine in this bottle to blow all of us to Kingdom Come? It would wreck the house. If I dropped it, it would probably go off. There wouldn't be two sticks left standing around here. They wouldn't find enough of us to be able to tell what had happened. You couldn't even have a funeral."

"Well," Brokay said, "what of it?"

"I'm just telling you," the man said, "don't ever do that again."

Slowly and deliberately he inserted a cork in the bottle, stooped and put the bottle back in the bag. During all of this time, he had kept his back turned to Brokay.

There was a twinkle of lazy humor in Brokay's eyes. "Be very careful with your hands," he said, "when you take them out of that bag. I'd hate to have to shoot you."

The man straightened, turned toward Brokay, presenting a face that was quick and alert, eyes that were a dark brown, and dancing with excitement.

"Don't worry," he said, "I know when I'm caught. But you haven't got me in the hands of the police yet. I've been in tighter positions than this before."

"Would you mind," Brokay asked with genuine curiosity in his voice, "telling me exactly what you expected to find in that safe?"

"Oh, just a few trinkets," the man said.

"Did you have any specific article in mind?" Brokay inquired.

"No. Why?"

"Nothing," Brokay said, "only, I suppose there's no harm in telling you now, I happen to have a very valuable diamond necklace that I put in that safe yesterday."

"Wouldn't that have been a break for me!" the man said.

"And no one tipped you off?" Brokay inquired.

"Not a soul. That's on the level. I was just on the prowl, and this joint looked easy to me. I figured that a young, good–looking bachelor like you, who had inherited a million and boosted that million to about five million by good business judgment, was pretty likely to have a lot of stuff hanging around the house. In other words, I figured you'd be careless with money.

"It's rather interesting, in case you're at all interested in psychology. A person who has acquired money by scrimping and saving doesn't usually have anything valuable around the house unless he's one of the kind that distrusts the banks and hoards his money. A sap that makes money easily and rapidly gets careless with things. He's very much inclined to get pieces of value and leave them hanging around in safes that don't offer much more protection against a burglar than a bread box."

"Look here," Brokay said suddenly, "you're no ordinary crook!"

"Who said I was?" asked the burglar.

"You're talking, of course," Brokay said, "to gain time. You're simply stalling for a break. You figure that if you can get my interest, you're going to delay my call for the police."

The burglar laughed, and there was genuine amusement in his laugh.

"And," Brokay went on, "you've rather a magnetic personality. You think that if you can engage me in conversation and get me to have a liking for you, I won't be quite so ready to pull the trigger when you rush me."

The smile faded from the man's face. "Listen, brother," he said, "you're too good a mind reader. No wonder you made four or five million bucks in a couple of years."

"Apparently, you've looked up quite a bit of my history," Brokay told him.

"Oh, sure, we always do that. We know the kind of a lay we're running into before we crack the joint."

Brokay suddenly lowered the gun. "Look here," he said, "suppose I'd make a bargain with you?"

"What sort of a bargain?" asked the man, his eyes suddenly hard and appraising.

"A bargain by which you can gain your freedom," Brokay said. "I wouldn't call the police."

The man's eyes studied Brokay's face carefully. "I suppose," he said, "some jane's got some letters of yours. You want me to bust into her apartment and rob the safe, or something of that sort."

"No," George Brokay said, "the thing that I have in mind is something entirely different."

"Well, let's hear it."

"What's your name?" Brokay asked.

"You can call me West — Sam West," said the burglar.

"Is that your name?"

"If you don't like West, you can call me East — William East would be a good name. Or, there's nothing wrong with North — you might call me Carl North."

"I think I'll call you Sam West," Brokay said.

"O. K., chief. Now tell me what's on your mind."

Brokay abruptly tossed the gun to the big library table, crossed the room to an overstuffed leather chair, dropped into it and put his feet on a footstool.

"Sit down, West," he said, "and have a cigarette."

Sam West's eyes slithered across to the gun.

"Listen," he said, "you're taking chances. We're playing opposite sides of this game, you and I, and you haven't put me on my honor, or anything of that sort, so let's not have any misunderstandings."

Brokay gestured toward the gun. "Go ahead and pick it up if you want to," he said. "I'm not going to turn you over to the police, anyway."

Sam West edged slightly further toward the table.

"Go on with your proposition," he said.

"You know about me," Brokay said. "I inherited some money. My uncle, who left me that money, had skimped and slaved all of his life. He left me more than a million dollars, but he lived like a pauper. He didn't get any good out of his money. I took his money and started investing it. I didn't invest it in stocks and bonds, the way my uncle had; I invested it in little business ventures, where I took a chance on my judgment of character and human nature. I made a lot more money. Then there was nothing else to do. I've got more money than I need. I drift around like a butterfly. I go to balls and teas. I dance and talk. I clip coupons, and ride horseback. I travel in the best social circles in the city. And what has it done to me?"

Sam West let his right hand slide over to the top of the table, so that it was within some two feet of the gun. "I'll bite," he said, his eyes hard and glittering. "What has it done?"

"It's made me bored with life," George Brokay said. "It's made me feel like an old man, when I'm not yet thirty. Now, what I want is to get away from the whole damn business. I want to have some adventure; I want to have some fun. I want to have some excitement. That's the reason I'm making this proposition to you."

"What's the proposition?" West asked.

"I want to become a burglar," Brokay said.

Sam West, whose hand had slid across the table until it was less than a foot from the butt of the gun, became rigidly immobile. "You *what?*" he asked.

"I want to become a burglar," Brokay said. "You're getting a great kick out of life; you're living a life of excitement; you're matching your wits against the police; you're taking chances all the time."

"You're taking chances on getting put away for a long, long time in the big house," Sam West said bitterly. "Did you ever stop to think what that would mean? Locked in a stone cell with iron bars staring you in the eyes all the time? No women — no life — no action — no variety — no —"

"That's exactly it," Brokay said. "That's what makes the game so interesting. If there wasn't a big penalty if you lost, there wouldn't be so much fun winning. That's why I can't get a kick out of gambling. No matter how much I lose, I still have plenty left. Money means nothing to me."

"By God!" Sam West said, his eyes staring intently into Brokay's steady, gray eyes, "I believe you mean it!"

"Of course I mean it," George Brokay said.

Sam West abruptly leaned forward and picked up the gun from the table. He snapped the mechanism back far enough to make sure that there was a cartridge in the chamber.

Brokay laughed at him. "Now what are you going to do?" he asked.

Sam West pocketed the gun. His eyes were glittering. "I'm going to ask you a couple of questions," he said.

"Go ahead and ask them."

"Who do you want to rob?"

"Oh, anyone," Brokay said.

"What do you want to do with the stuff?"

"I'd send it back after I'd stolen it," Brokay said carelessly. "Or give it to you, or give it to some poor panhandler I met on the street, and then I'd send the man I'd robbed a check for about twice the value of the stuff I'd taken, so that he wouldn't be losing anything."

"A check would hardly be advisable," Sam West said, a smile twisting the corners of his mouth.

"Well," Brokay told him, "we could leave him the money on his doorstep or send it to him by messenger, or break into the house again and drop it in a bureau drawer. I don't care how he gets it, just so he gets it."

He made an impatient gesture.

"Can't you get the point?" he said. "I'm fed up with life. I'm a good judge of character. I look at you and see in you a man who is living an existence that is outside the law. From a moral stand point, it's probably wicked. You'll probably wind up by being killed, executed or imprisoned. But I can see from the expression on your face that you're enjoying life while you're living, and I'd like to enjoy life with you for a while."

"And," said Sam West, "you don't know one single thing about me, or who I am, or where I come from."

"I have invested a great deal of money during past few years," Brokay said, "because of my ability to judge character. I can see that you're no ordinary crook. I don't know your history and I don't care to. All I want is a partner in excitement."

Sam West suddenly strode across the room, his hand outstretched. "O.K., chief," he said, "you've made a sale."

The two men shook hands.

"And," Brokay said, "I want to start tonight."

Sam West slipped a leather–covered notebook from his pocket, turned the pages, read a notation, then looked up at Brokay and grinned.

"No questions asked?" he inquired.

"No questions asked," Brokay said.

"O. K.," Sam West told him. "Put your hat back on. We're going out."

CHAPTER TWO
Monkey Business

Shadows clung to the vacant house like soft road tar clings to an automobile tire. Crouched in the shadows, George Brokay peered at the dark structure which blotted out the stars.

"And there's no one home?" he asked, in a whisper.

"We're just taking a chance on one person," Sam West said. "Everyone else is accounted for. The servants are out. The chauffeur sleeps out over the garage in an apartment. He couldn't hear a stick of dynamite explode in the house."

"Who's the one person we're taking chances on?" Brokay asked in a low, cautious voice.

"She's a young woman," Sam West said. "You should be interested in her, because she's the same sort that you are — a woman who has more money than she knows what to do with."

"Who is it?" Brokay inquired curiously.

"Her name's Ordway," West told him, "Gladys Ordway. She's about twenty–six — perhaps twenty–seven, and she's easy to look at."

"You've met her?" asked Brokay.

"Never seen her in my life, but I know what she looks like and I've got all the dope on her."

"You've looked this place up?"

"Oh, yes, I look up every place before I go into it."

"Did you know that you were likely to encounter me tonight?"

"No. I knew that you had gone to the Van Dusen's, and I knew that the affair wouldn't be over until two or three o'clock in the morning. I thought I had at least an hour."

"That's what I got for being bored with the party," Brokay said.

"*This* is what you get for being bored with the party," West told him, and chuckled. "Come on, we'll try the window over there on the south side — the one that has the shade tree growing near it."

"You mean we'll climb up in the shade tree?"

"No, we'll take advantage of the shadow. Let's go."

"Suppose the window's locked?" Brokay asked.

"I'll show you all about that," Sam West said.

He led the way across the narrow strip of lawn, to the place where the tree flung an inky shadow against the house. Calmly, methodically, he took a small leather case from beneath his coat, selected a curved steel bar, fitted a telescopic handle to it, placed one end of the curved bar beneath the sill of the window, and pressed downward.

There was a sharp clicking noise, and the window rose for an inch or two, shivering slightly. Sam West casually inserted gloved fingers and raised the sash. "Remember," he said in a whisper, "no matter how inconvenient it is, keep the gloves on your hands. We don't want to leave any fingerprints."

With the lithe grace of an athlete, West swung up from the ground, flung one leg over the window sill and then disappeared in the darkness. "Want a hand?" he whispered.

"No," said Brokay, and slid up and across the sill as easily as West had performed the operation.

From the darkness, the burglar watched him approvingly. "You keep in pretty good condition," he said.

"Fair," Brokay remarked nonchalantly.

"I've got a floor plan of the house," Sam West said. "The safe that we want is in the bedroom, on the second floor. We won't bother with anything else, but we'll go right up there."

"What's in it?" Brokay inquired.

"You can never tell," West said, leading the way to a corridor, where the beam of his spotlight showed a huge winding staircase which stretched upward, into the realm of mysterious darkness above the circle of illumination.

"We take the stairs," said Sam West.

Keeping his feet well to the sides of the stairs, so that no creak would betray him, and motioning to Brokay to do the same, Sam West padded upward. As he traveled, the flashlight sent its beam darting about to the right and left, up and down, dissipating the shadows.

There was not a sound in the dark house. It might have been untenanted, for all the noises that came to Brokay's straining ears.

Sam West found the upper corridor, turned and touched Brokay with his hand, guiding him gently to the left and through a door which was open. West crossed a room, his feet making no noise as they moved across the carpeted floor with a sure—footed caution which would have done credit to a stalking puma. He paused with his hand on the knob of a door.

"Get ready for anything," he whispered. Gently, he disengaged the latch and opened the door.

The room was dark and silent.

"Guess we're O.K.," said West, and pushed the button on the flashlight, which sent the pencil of brilliant illumination darting about the room.

The light showed that the bedroom was that of a woman; that it was handsomely appointed. It showed a dresser on which glittered toilet articles in an orderly array. The beam of the flashlight slithered across the reflecting surface of a mirror, then darted across the bed.

There was something which caught the gleam of the flashlight, a white silent something which caused Brokay to stiffen, caused Sam West to give a quick flick of his wrist, sending the flashlight back so that the beam rested on the bed.

Brokay gave an involuntary exclamation of horror.

The body of a young woman lay upon the bed — a young woman who was clad only in the most filmy of underthings. The body was beautifully formed. Filmy lace rippled over firm, white bosom. The hair was a warm, rich brown, and was spread about in a tangled confusion, contrasting with the deathly pallor of the face. The legs were stockinged, but there were no slippers on the feet.

Clinging to the top of the bed, his tail wrapped around and around the brass of the bedstead, was a monkey which sat perfectly motionless, staring with wide eyes at the flashlight.

"Good God!" said Brokay. "What's that?"

"Steady!" said Sam West, and there was the noise of rustling garments which accompanied swift motion as the burglar reached to his hip pocket and pulled out a revolver.

For a long moment the two men stood silent, staring at the form on the bed, at the monkey which perched motionless on the top of the bed.

"Let's get out of this," said Sam West.

"Wait a minute," Brokay told him, "we've got to find out what's happened. Maybe the woman is unconscious."

"Not me," said Sam West. "We're going to get out. We can't tell what's going to happen here. Remember, we're flirting with the electric chair."

Brokay took two steps toward the bed. As he moved, the monkey screamed with terror. Sam West switched out the light and left the room in darkness.

"Wait a minute," called Brokay. "You can't leave that way, West."

There was no noise from Sam West, who moved with such feline stealth that his footfalls were silent.

Brokay turned and made a lunge toward where he thought the burglar would be. His questing fingers encountered only darkness. He stumbled, lurched against the wall and then groped with his fingers until he found a light switch. He snapped on the light switch.

Sam West was not in the room. The monkey started to chatter with terror a nervous, hysterical chatter that sounded almost like the clicking of castanets. Brokay flung himself toward the door, wrenched it open, looked out into the corridor and caught the gleam of Sam West's spotlight.

"Come back here, West," he said, "or I'm going to shoot."

The flashlight snapped out. The corridor was as dark as pitch.

"I mean it," Brokay said.

"Listen," came Sam West's voice, sounding cold and ominous, "that's a game two can play at. But remember, there's been a murder committed here. You start shooting and you're going to alarm the neighborhood, and if you don't quit making such a confounded racket, you're going to do it anyway. Do you know what it means for us to be caught here?"

"I say come on back," Brokay said. "We're going to see what we can do."

There was a moment of silence, then he heard Sam West sigh. "You," said the burglar, "are just about foolish enough to start making a racket. Come on, if it's going to suit you any better. What do you want to do, hold a *post mortem?*"

"I want to find out something about this business," Brokay said.

He turned and walked back toward the room, conscious of the fact that the burglar was padding noiselessly along just behind him. As Brokay entered the room, he felt something hard prodding into his back.

"I'm just sticking a rod on you," the burglar said, "so that you'll know who's running this show."

Brokay said nothing, but advanced into the bedroom. He stretched forth a cautious hand and touched the bare flesh of the woman's arm, then, muttering an exclamation, he took off his glove.

"Leave that glove on!" Sam West cautioned. "You leave a fingerprint here and it'll mean the electric chair."

Brokay still remained silent, but with his bare fingers felt the flesh of the woman's wrist.

"She's dead," he said, after a moment, "but she hasn't been dead longer than a few minutes. The body is still warm."

"I tell you we've got to get out of here," Sam West said.

The monkey on the bed continued to sit and chatter, but it was no longer motionless. It swayed back and forth rhythmically.

"For God's sake!" said Sam West, "shut up that damned monkey!"

Brokay looked at the little animal. "It's simply terrified to death," he said. He stretched forth his arms and made crooning noises.

The monkey stared at him. After a moment the chattering sounds of terror ceased, the moist brown eyes regarded Brokay speculatively. Then, so suddenly as to startle Brokay into dropping his arms, the monkey unfastened its tail and came through the air in a long, flying leap.

The monkey caught Brokay by the shoulder of the coat, climbed so that he sat huddled against Brokay's neck, and, after a moment, Brokay felt the furry tail wind around his neck. The monkey ceased to chatter.

"Poor little devil, he's shivering as though he'd been in a cold bath," Brokay said.

"Well," Sam West said, "this is your party. What are you going to do now?"

"I want to find out something about how she died," said Brokay, and bent over the form.

"Watch those fingerprints!" the burglar exclaimed. "Get that glove back on if you value your life!"

Brokay paid no attention to him, but held the glove in his left hand while he placed his right hand on the bed and bent over the still figure.

"Expensive lingerie," said Sam West. "Looks as though she was dressing to go out for a party. She had a heavy date of some kind and was going to put on her best clothes."

"Here's the wound," Brokay said in a low voice. "It's a stabbing wound just over the heart."

Sam West turned a practical eye upon the discoloration which blemished the smooth white flesh. "That's where it came out," he said. "It must have gone in the other side."

"You mean from the back?" asked Brokay.

"Uh–huh," said Same West.

Brokay hesitated for a moment then, placing his hand tenderly back of the girl's shoulder, turned the body. As he did so, he stiffened with horror as he saw the red pool which had gathered beneath the left shoulder.

"Told you so," said Sam West.

"Good heavens!" said Brokay.

"Satisfied now?" the burglar inquired.

"Certainly not," Brokay said. "We've got to do something about this. We've got to find out who she is. We've got to notify the police."

"Got to what!" exclaimed the burglar.

"Got to notify the police."

"And just who are you going to say is calling?" asked Sam West.

"We can explain," Brokay said.

Sam West's laugh was scornful. "Explain nothing," he said. "You're simply flirting with the electric chair."

"But I can give them credentials," said Brokay. "I can explain to them that —"

"You might have an hour ago," Sam West said, "but you're a burglar now; don't forget that. You can't explain to them what you were doing in this house. You can't explain how you crawled in through a window that had been jimmied. You can talk until you're black in the face, but you can't make anyone listen to you or believe you."

Brokay was silent as a full realization of his predicament crashed home upon him.

"What's more," said Sam West, "we've got to get out of here. We don't know what's happened. We don't know the motive for the murder. All we know is that the girl has been murdered, and that if anyone catches us here, we're going to have the murder pinned on us, just as sure as —" He broke off.

Clear and distinct through the night air, sounding from some distance down the road, came the low, throbbing wail of a siren.

Brokay stiffened, stared at Sam West, with a sudden realization of his predicament.

The furry tail of the monkey tightened around his neck, and once more, the little animal began to shiver and emit low, chattering sounds of terror.

"Switch out that light," said Sam West. "Someone's heard all that commotion we've been raising. Get started."

Brokay hesitated. The gun jabbed into the small of his back. "I'm running things now," said the burglar. "Get that light off, or the cops will find two stiffs here instead of one."

Brokay switched off the light.

"Walk ahead of me," said Sam West, "and make it snappy. Make for that window we came out of. I'll give you the light."

He snapped on the flashlight, showing the carpeted floor. The gun jabbed into Brokay's back. Brokay walked rapidly across the corridor.

"Faster," said Sam West, and jabbed with the gun.

Brokay went down the stairs at a fast run, turned down the corridor.

"First door to the left, and step on it," Sam West said. "We've got to hurry!"

Brokay pushed his way through the door. The window was still open, as they had left it.

"You first," the burglar said, "and there'll be no more flashlight."

He clicked out the flashlight, and Brokay jumped out into the darkness, lighting with a thud on the ground. The siren wailed again, this time measurably nearer, and Brokay could hear the sound of a rapidly racing motor.

The burglar thudded to the ground directly behind Brokay, kept the gun pushing into his ribs. "Run for it!" he said. "Never mind being seen, run for it!"

Brokay started sprinting across the lawn, not bothering to hug the shadows, but taking the most direct route toward the place where they had left their automobile. As he ran, the monkey chattered and thrust its tiny paws up under the brim of Brokay's hat, holding on to Brokay's hair, chattering its shrill sound of terror.

Brokay's hat, thus dislodged, fell back across his shoulders and hit the ground. He slowed and swerved, but Sam West jabbed him with the gun.

"I'll shoot," he said. "I mean it. Keep going."

Brokay speeded up once more.

Headlights from the police machine swept across the grounds. The red glow of a spotlight, with crimson glass in it, shed ruddy rays over the lawn. The car slid in close to the curb and stopped.

"Step on it!" yelled West.

Brokay gave one final spurt, jumped into the light roadster which the burglar had been driving. A split second later Sam West leaped to the running board. The burglar's leap pulled down the springs of the automobile, causing the car to creak and sway. Then Sam West slid into the seat and pressed his foot on the starter.

The blood—red shaft of light from the police car caught them squarely, held them for a moment. Then there was the sound of a hail and once more the sound of the siren, this time a piercing scream.

The motor roared into life. Sam West snapped the light car into gear, and the wheels churned for a moment as they bit into the road. Then the car lurched forward.

There was the sound of a shot, the sharp *ping* of a bullet as it struck the body of the car. Then the light roadster leaped forward into a tree—lined roadway, where trees and shrubbery prevented the police spotlight from holding them in its brilliance.

"This is a driveway that comes into the garage," Sam West said. "They'll have to go around the block to get to it. It gives us that much head start. Hang on."

The car skidded along the gravel as the burglar whipped it into a turn, then straightened and roared along the pavement. West fought the wheel around. The tires screamed into the turn as the machine skidded, straightened, then skidded once more, straightened into speed on the straightaway. The night behind them echoed with the shrill, menacing scream of the siren.

Sam West pushed the throttle down to the floorboards. The needle of the speedometer climbed steadily upward. Street intersections flashed past. The sound of the siren grew indistinct in the distance.

"I believe we've made it," West said, and slowed the car slightly and swung wide. "Watch out," he said, "we're taking another turn."

He swung the car to the left, ran four blocks and swung to the right again, then to the left. He slowed. There was no sound of the siren.

Sam West heaved a sigh. He reached forward and turned a key in a radio, which illuminated a dial. "We'll tune in on the police broadcast," he said.

He slowed the car, and, after a moment, a mechanical voice said: "Calling all cars ... calling all cars ... calling all cars. Car Thirty—two answered a telephone call to the residence of John C. Ordway. As the police car approached the residence, two men were seen to run across the lawn and jump into a light roadster. When police hailed them, they refused to stop. A shot was fired which apparently hit the roadster. Both men are young, probably under thirty. They are of medium height, and run as though they had received athletic training at some time in their lives. One of the men wore a gray business suit, and the other wore a tuxedo. The taller of the two men, who is approximately five feet ten and one—half inches high, weight about one hundred and eighty pounds, had a monkey which was swinging to his neck as he ran.

"It is not yet known whether these men were burglars or were merely prowling about the house when they were disturbed, but they evidently are avoiding the police, and should be picked up for questioning at all costs. Car Thirty—two is continuing to search the neighborhood in which the roadster was lost. Car Sixty—four will swing in toward Thirty–fourth and Central. Car Eighty–two will run down Central until it comes to Thirty–fourth. Car Seventy–six will run down Forty–fifth to Grand Avenue, turn on Grand Avenue until it comes to Thirty–fourth and then meet the other cars. All other cars will keep a watch for a light roadster. Car Ninety–one will divert from its beat, to go to the residence of John C. Ordway, at Five–seven–nine Riverview, and make a report on what is found, after a complete investigation. That is all."

Sam West turned to stare at George Brokay. "That damned monkey!" he said, and slammed his foot on the brake. "Put him out," he told Brokay, as the car skidded in close to the curb.

"The poor little devil, he's frightened," Brokay said, "and —"

The gun in Sam West's left hand jabbed meaningly and savagely into Brokay's ribs. "Listen," said Sam West, "this is no time to run a debating society. I should have known better than to take on a damned amateur. Either get that monkey out of here, or I'll blow you wide open."

Brokay disengaged the monkey's tail from around his throat. The monkey, sensing his purpose, chattered and screamed, hanging on to Brokay's arm.

"Get back," said Sam West suddenly. "I'll blow the damn little brute's head off."

"You know what will happen if you shoot here," Brokay told him.

West cursed. "Throw him out, then, and make it snappy," he said. "Break his damn neck! Beat his head against the side of the car!"

Brokay managed to unprison the little animal's arms and legs.

"Get ready to go," he said, "I'm going to toss him out."

Sam West snapped the car into gear.

Brokay tossed the animal to the pavement. The animal screamed shrill rage. The car veered sharply from the curb and jumped into immediate speed.

"You wanted excitement," Sam West said, "and you're going to get it. We've got to find some place to hide — and what I mean is, we've got to take it on the lam. Every radio car in the city will be looking for us, and three of them are converging on this district."

"You know the routes they're coming, so you can avoid them," Brokay pointed out.

"We know where three of them are coming, but how about the others?"

"I'll tell you what I'll do," Brokay said. "You got into this thing partially because of me. I'll give you a break. We can go to my place and we'll hole up there. The police certainly won't think of searching my house. I'm a respected member of society, and —"

"And don't ever kid yourself that this isn't a society murder," said the burglar. "That woman, lying almost naked on the bed, was killed by someone that's accustomed to evening clothes, and all the fine things of life, don't ever forget it. It's a society killing. We sure as hell chose a great time to bust into that place."

"You're the one who picked the time," Brokay reminded him.

"Yeah," said Sam West, "so you could get a thrill — and a hell of a time I picked — a time for murder!"

"Nevertheless," Brokay said, "you can't think of any place that's better to hide than my place."

"O.K.," Sam West said, and swung the wheel to the right. "It's just a case of any port in a storm."

The men rode in silence for half a dozen blocks, and then the burglar turned the car into Brokay's driveway. The car purred smoothly up to the garage and then stopped as the burglar applied the brakes. Brokay reached from the car, pressed an electric button on an upright post by the side of the driveway. The doors of the garage slid smoothly back. The roadster slipped through the doors and came to rest in the spacious garage. Sam West sighed and shut off the motor. Brokay opened the door and stepped to the cement floor.

"Well," he said, "we'd better look the thing over for bullet marks. They probably hit us. We'd better find if we can disguise it so it doesn't look so much like a bullet mark."

He walked to the rear of the car.

There was a glad cry, the sound of a shrill chattering, and the monkey leapt from the spare tire directly to Brokay's shoulder, where it cuddled up against his cheek, wrapping its tail around Brokay's neck.

"Where the devil did that beast come from?" said Sam West.

"He rode the spare tire," Brokay said. "Poor little devil, he's shivering so he can hardly hang on."

Sam West grimly drew his revolver.

There was an angry glint in Brokay's eyes. His right hand slid to his own hip pocket. "No you don't!" he said.

The burglar looked at Brokay's concealed hand. "Why don't I?" he inquired ominously, his eyes glinting.

"Don't forget one thing, West," Brokay told him. "Before we get done, we may have to solve this murder to prove that we didn't do it, and this monkey may be the only clue that we've got and the police haven't."

The glitter faded from Sam West's eyes. He frowned thoughtfully. Slowly, he lowered his gun. "You may be right, at that," he said slowly.

CHAPTER THREE
Cover for a Crook

Morning newspapers carried headlines which screamed the news of the murder to the world. Gladys Ordway, a beautiful society girl, had been found nude on the bed of her bedroom. She had been stabbed in the back, with some long slender instrument which had penetrated the heart, and the point of which had even pierced the skin of the left breast. Death had been instantaneous.

The chauffeur, asleep in the garage, happening to glance out of his window, had seen lights flickering in the Ordway residence, a light which led him to believe that someone was using a flashlight in the house. He had called police headquarters and the call had been relayed to the radio cars. Car 32 had gone to investigate and had surprised two men running away from the house. The officers claimed to have seen a monkey clinging to the shoulder of one of the men, but subsequent investigation had shown that none of the servants in the house knew anything at all about a monkey.

John C. Ordway had been attending an important conference. The servants had either retired, or, as in the case of the butler, had been spending the night away from the house. The chauffeur had had the evening off, but had returned at about eleven o'clock; he had been restless and had not slept well; he was awakened by some sound. He thought it might have been a scream, but could not be certain. He looked toward the house, saw the reflections of the flashlight, and notified the police. Gladys Ordway was supposed to have attended a masquerade ball. The costume which she was to have worn had been found in the closet of her room. No one knew whether she had actually attended the ball and returned to meet her death, or whether she had not gone to the masquerade. The police were making a check–up for the purpose of ascertaining. They had failed to find a weapon.

Sam West, clad in a pair of brocaded silk pajamas, sat up in bed, read the papers and made a wry face at Brokay. "Well," he said, "you wanted excitement."

Brokay, fresh from the shower, with the tingle of youth and health on his cheeks, his hair still wet at the temples, grinned reassuringly. "I've got some more news for you," he said.

West yawned. "What is it?" he asked. "And when do we eat?"

"You notice that the newspaper mentions that the police have some clues that they are running down."

"Yes," said Sam West, "it always mentions those things. Those don't amount to anything. That's just a sop that the newspaper guys hand to the police."

"In this case it may not be?" Brokay said.

"How do you mean?" West inquired.

"When we started to run," Brokay said, "the monkey jittered around on my shoulder; he reached up and grabbed my hair. In doing that he dislodged my hat, and it fell off. I was going to stop to pick it up, but you jabbed the gun into my ribs and I didn't have a chance to explain."

Sam West sat bolt upright in bed, staring at George Brokay with wide, startled eyes. "Your hat?" he asked. Brokay nodded.

"Now," said Sam West, "go ahead and pour it on, hand it to me right on the chin. Tell me that your hat has got your initials in it."

Brokay nodded. "And more than that," he said, "it has the name of my hatter. The police can trace that hat and can identify it, just as sure as I'm standing here."

The covers flung back as Sam West's bare feet hit the floor. He started peeling off the pajamas, reaching for underwear.

"We can't run away from them," Brokay said. "We've got to face the music."

"The hell we can't," Sam West told him. "You don't know what you're up against, brother. If the police trace that hat here, and start asking you questions, what are you going to tell them?"

"If necessary, I can tell them the truth," Brokay said.

"Oh no you can't, brother. We went into that last night. You can't explain what you were doing in the house."

"I might say that I was driving by and saw someone jimmying the window; that I tried to stop him and he ran away."

"And then, instead of calling the police to help you, you ran when the police came up," sneered Sam West. "Moreover, they go out in the garage and open the garage door and find my roadster in there, with a neat little bullet hole in the rear of the body. Try and explain that away."

Brokay nodded. "Get your clothes on," he said, his jaw pushed forward, his mouth a firm thin line. "We're going to beat the police to it."

Sam West paused in the middle of his dressing to regard Brokay critically. "If you've got any shabby clothes," he said, "you'd better put 'em on. Hiding with you wasn't so hot. If we can get out of here ahead of the police, you're going to hide with me. The cops won't think of looking for a burglar prowling around with a society guy, and they sure as hell won't think of looking for a society guy prowling around with a burglar. Let's get started."

"The monkey?" asked Brokay as they started to leave the place.

"Ditch him," said West.

"Oh no you don't," Brokay told him. "The monkey has got to come with us. He's our clue. What's more, we don't dare to let the police find it here."

Sam West made a gesture of irritation. "What a boob I was," he said, "when I picked this house for a burglary. And what a bigger boob I was, when I didn't let you turn me over to the police. Why the devil did I have to get bats in my belfry and take on a dude apprentice?"

Brokay held out his arms to the monkey. The little animal, chattering delightedly, leapt to Brokay's shoulder. "Come on, crook," said Brokay grinning. "Let's go out and find some more excitement."

The burglar groaned.

Sam West swept his arm about in an inclusive gesture, indicating the room with its twin beds, the grimy window, the cheap pictures on the wall. "O. K.," he said. "This is home."

"Are we safe here?" Brokay asked.

"Safe as we can be."

"But, I don't get the sketch," Brokay said.

"It's a rooming house that's run by crooks. Did you notice the girl at the desk? That's Thelma Grebe. She's a moll. Whenever anyone wants to hole up, they simply tell Thelma that they're on the lam. Thelma gives them a room and if any smart dicks come around and ask any questions, Thelma gives them a run around."

"What did you tell her about me?" Brokay asked.

"I told her you were on the lam from Chi. You're supposed to be a red–hot. You can keep in the room as much as you want to."

Brokay opened the wicker basket in which he had, carried the monkey. "Come on out, Jocko," he said.

The monkey, curled up inside the basket in a neat little nest of rags, climbed up to Brokay's shoulder, made little patting gestures of affection with his paws on Brokay's cheeks and hair.

"That little devil sure likes you," West said, "but you want to keep him out of sight. We'd better fix a place for him in the closet."

"What I want to do," said Brokay, "is to find out something about this murder. I want to get more information about it."

"I've got most of the dope on that," Sam West said. "When I was talking with Thelma, she gave me the low–down on the thing. The job was pulled by a girl named Rhoda Koline. Anyway, that's what the police figure."

"Who's Rhoda Koline?" Brokay asked.

"She was employed as a social secretary by John Ordway. She kept his house–hold accounts and handled his social engagements. You see, the police figure that Gladys Ordway was undressed at the time she was stuck with the knife. Now, she wouldn't have undressed in front of a man unless it was somebody she was playing around with and she was a nice kid. The police figure that it was a question of some woman being in the room with her and sticking her with the knife after she'd got her clothes off. They started in on the maid, but didn't get anywhere because the maid had an alibi. Then they started looking around for Rhoda, and when Rhoda found out about it, she took it on the lam."

"They don't know where she is now?"

"No."

"Then," said Brokay, "they're not going to suspect us?"

"Only as being mixed up in it with Rhode somehow," Sam West told him. "If we keep under cover, the thing may straighten out all right."

"How many other people are in this rooming house?" Brokay inquired.

"You can't ever tell," West told him. "Thelma Grebe keeps her own confidences. That's why she's on the job. If it wasn't for that, she'd be found in an alley some night with her throat slit."

"You didn't get a paper, did you?" Brokay asked.

"Not the late edition."

"I want to get one."

"O.K., but be careful how much prowling around you do. You're safe as long as you're here in the house. There's a room in the front of the house — Number Ten. It's used as a kind of lobby and sitting room. They keep newspapers in there. There's also some magazines, and if any of the folks here get to feeling lonesome they go in and sit around for a chat. You can talk to anyone you see there, and you won't need to introduce yourself. Monikers are considered nobody's business, except to the guys that own them. Don't ask anybody's moniker and nobody's going to ask yours."

Brokay put the monkey in the closet, left the room, found the door with the number "10" over it, and pushed the door open.

There was a table in the center of the room. Sunshine streamed through windows on the south. The rumble of traffic came up through windows on the west. There were half a dozen chairs in the room; the table was littered with magazines and newspapers.

A young woman of perhaps twenty–five years of age was standing at the table reading one of the newspapers. She caught Brokay's eye as he came in the room, and half turned away, as though trying to hide her interest in the newspaper, then she caught her breath, turned back to Brokay and smiled.

"Hello," she said.

"Hello," Brokay told her. "You staying here?"

"Yes," she said smiling, "temporarily. And you?"

"Temporarily also," he told her.

They both smiled. Brokay started looking through the newspapers on the table.

"I've got the latest edition here," she said.

"Take your time," Brokay told her.

"You might," she said smiling, "like to look over my shoulder."

"Thanks," Brokay told her, "if I may." He moved so that he could see over her shoulder.

"I don't know just what you're interested in," said the girl, "but I'm interested in this." Her forefinger swept across the front page of the paper.

Brokay, following her forefinger, saw that she was indicating the account of the Ordway murder. "You interested in that?" he asked.

"Yes," she said. "Are you?"

"Just as a matter of news," he told her. She laughed lightly. There was something almost of mockery in her laugh, and yet there was an undertone of nervousness; a certain throaty catch of the voice.

Brokay stared at her curiously, catching a part of her, profile, the curve of her cheek, the long sweep of her eyelashes. It was impossible for him to place her as a crook. He would, ordinarily, have unhesitatingly branded her as a young woman of beauty and refinement. To find her in this crook's hide–out came as a distinct shock and surprise.

She evidently felt his eyes upon her, for she suddenly turned to face him. "I thought," she said, "you were interested in the newspaper." This time there could be no mistaking the mockery in her voice. "As a matter of casual news, of course," she said.

Brokay devoted his attention to the newspaper account.

There was nothing in the paper which represented any startling developments in the case. For the most part, it merely elaborated what Brokay had already learned from the burglar.

As Brokay finished reading, the girl suddenly turned toward him and gave him a searching glance. "Do you think," she said, "that the two men with the monkey had anything to do with it?"

"I'm sure I don't know," Brokay said, "I try not to think about matters which don't concern me. I have enough that does."

"Well," she said, "I think that those men are the guilty ones. They can say all they want to about some woman being mixed up in it. I think it was a man who killed her. You notice the newspaper account says that the window on the lower floor had been pried open with a jimmy. That doesn't look very much as though a woman had done it. Does it?"

"That, of course, is an interesting fact," Brokay said.

"There's no reason on earth why the woman couldn't have been killed, when she was undressed, by two men."

"Would she have turned her back to two men?" asked Brokay.

"She could most certainly have turned her back to one of them," said the young woman. "If the men had separated, she'd have had rather a difficult time facing in two directions at once."

Brokay made a little gesture of dismissal. "Well," he said, "it's something that I can't concern myself with. You said you were staying here?"

"Yes," she said, "I have Room Twenty–one."

Mindful of what the burglar had told him, Brokay made no effort to inquire her name, but for the life of him, could not keep from staring at her, and wondering how she could be interested in a life of crime, or why such a refined young woman could be, as the burglar had expressed it, "on the lam."

"I wish you wouldn't stare at me like that," she said abruptly.

"I beg your pardon," Brokay said, "I didn't realize that I was staring, I was just ... er ... thinking."

She met his gaze frankly. "Wondering just what brand of crime I was mixed up in, that necessitated my enforced stay in this house?" she asked.

He felt himself flush. "Not at all, not at all," he said. "Please don't think that I'm prying into something that's none of my business."

"It's quite all right," she said. "To be perfectly frank, I was looking at you and wondering the same thing about you."

He caught his breath, started to make an indignant comment, then suddenly remembered that he *was* on the lam. "Oh well," he said, "circumstances are frequently peculiar and account for many strange things."

She nodded, placed a swiftly impulsive hand upon his arm. "Please forgive me," she said. "I know the rules of the house. I know that it is quite all right to chat with anyone met here in Room Ten, but, I know that I mustn't ask any questions. I hope you'll forgive me."

"Certainly," he said, "there's nothing to forgive." She flashed him a smile, turned and left the room. He heard the quick pound of her steps in the corridor and after a moment, the slamming of a door.

He sat down and studied the paper at length. There was nothing in it which gave him any particular clue, and, frowning thoughtfully, he refolded the paper, placed it on the table, and once more sought the companionship of Sam West, the burglar.

"What did you find out?" asked West when Brokay had seated himself and lit a cigarette.

"Nothing very much," Brokay said, "just more of the same stuff you've given me."

The monkey in the closet, hearing Brokay's voice, made shrill chattering noises.

"He's got to cut that out," West said.

"He's just glad that I'm back," Brokay said. "I'll open the door for a moment." He opened the closet door. The monkey came out in a long, flying leap, jumped to his shoulder, and made crooning noise of endearment.

Brokay was stroking the monkey when suddenly the knob of the door turned and the door pushed open. "Ditch that monkey," said Sam West, speaking out of one side of his mouth, while his hand slid swiftly to the holstered weapon which hung from his hip.

Brokay disengaged the monkey, literally flung it into the closet and stood with his back to the door. The door from the corridor swung open, and Thelma Grebe, the young woman who had assigned them their rooms, stood in the doorway. She saw the tense attitude of Sam West, saw the right hand which had dropped to the hip and suddenly caught her breath.

"Good heavens!" she said. "I came in without knocking, and letting you know who I was."

Sam West sighed, an his hand came away from his revolver. "You're going to get yourself drilled, doing that trick some day, Thelma," he said.

"I know it," she said. "I usually wait until the corridors are clear, and then I slip in, and sometimes I forget to knock, because I'm in a hurry." She closed the door.

"What is it you want, Thelma?" asked Sam West.

"Frank Compton's downstairs," she said.

"The fence?" he asked.

"The fence," she answered.

"What does he want?"

"He wants to see you about pulling a job."

"How does he know I'm here?"

"I don't know how he knows you're here. It's some hunch that he's got I think. He says he's simply got to see you; that he has a job you can make some money on."

"You didn't tell him I was here?" Sam West asked with sudden suspicion.

"Don't be silly," she said. "Of course, I didn't tell him you were here."

"What did you tell him?"

"I told him that you weren't here, that I didn't have any idea you were coming in, but, that if you did, and wanted to get in touch with him, I'd have you give him a ring."

Sam West frowned thoughtfully. "Compton's all right," he said. "He's a good fence. He's put me out on a couple of jobs that I've made money on. If he wants to see me, I have an idea it's about something that would put some cash in my pocket, and I may need some money right now. I may have to get out of the country. Tell him it's O.K."

"Do you want to telephone him?"

"No, you telephone him and tell him to come on up, right away."

The young woman turned toward the door. As she turned, Brokay stepped a little away from the closet door; almost immediately there was the sound of scurrying motion. He turned, but it was too late. The monkey made a long flying leap from the closet, grabbed the tail of his coat, and ran up the garments until he had nestled up close to Brokay's cheek, where he sat, with his furry tail wrapped around Brokay's neck, his hands caressing the short hairs over Brokay's temple.

"Good God!" said Thelma Grebe. She stood staring from Brokay to the monkey.

Sam West, his face snarling, pulled the revolver from his hip pocket, pointed it toward the monkey.

Brokay turned so that his head and neck were between the monkey and the burglar. "Take it easy, Sam," he said.

"I've told you to keep that damn beast in the closet," Sam West said.

"All right," Brokay told him, "take it easy. Thelma's all right. She knows that we're here, so it won't make much difference about the other."

Sam West stared at Brokay with a mouth that was clamped in a firm, thin line. His nostrils were dilated and there was murder in his eyes. "I should have killed that damn monkey the first time I saw him," he said.

"Shut up," Brokay said.

Thelma Grebe laughed lightly. "My God!" she said, "the monk gave me a start. I couldn't imagine what it was. What the hell, boys, there's nothing wrong about having a monkey, is there? I just didn't know you had one. There's no rule against pets in the house."

Sam West turned to her. "I don't want any misunderstanding about this, Thelma," he said. "You keep your mouth shut about that monkey. Do you understand?"

"Of course," she said. "I keep my mouth shut about everything."

"And a damn good thing you do, too," he said. "Go ahead and get Compton on the telephone and tell him to come up here."

Thelma Grebe slipped through the door, closed it behind her. When the latch had clicked into place, Sam West turned to Brokay and his face was white with rage.

"Damn it," he said, "that's what I get for mixing up with an amateur. You've bungled everything so far. I should have killed that monkey and taken it on the lam in the first place."

"You're crazy as hell," Brokay told him. "That monkey represents the best clue we've got. He's going to lead to a solution of the mystery one of these days." He reached up his hand and patted the monkey's head.

"I'm warning you right now," Sam West said, "that we're finished. We're going to dissolve partnership."

"O.K. by me," Brokay said. "Personally, I'm going to clean this crime up. I might say, that it served me right for teaming up with a burglar that didn't know his business."

"What the hell do you mean, I didn't know my business?" West flared, irritated at the aspersion cast on his professional ability.

Brokay laughed. "I was just kidding," he said, "so that you could see how it felt. Come on, old man and snap out of it. We're in this thing together; we've got to see it through together. Now the question is, do you want me in here when the fence comes to call on you, or not?"

"I most certainly do not," West said. "You get out of here and stay out for ten minutes, then you can come back. When you come back, knock on the door. If I'm still busy, I'll tell you to keep out; if you don't hear anything from me, you can come in. And put that monkey in the closet and leave him there."

"I want you to promise me," Brokay said, "that you're not going to do anything to that monkey. You're not going to try to get it out of the way."

"Oh, it's all right now," the burglar said. "The damage has been done. I didn't want Thelma to know why we were on the lam."

"Do you think she knows now?" Brokay asked.

The burglar laughed scornfully. "You think she's a fool?" he inquired.

"Well, we can trust her discretion, can't we?" Brokay asked.

"A woman doesn't have any discretion," the burglar said. "But get the hell out of here and let me see what this fence wants. Probably he's got some pretty good job staked out. If he has, I'll take a whirl at it, and make enough money to get out with, if I have to take a plane to Mexico City or some place."

CHAPTER FOUR
The Fence

Brokay once more put the monkey back in the closet, closed the door tightly, found a key that fitted it, locked the door and slipped the key in his pocket. Then he left the room and returned to the lounging room.

He had hoped that the young woman who had attracted his attention a few moments earlier, would be back in the room, but he had it all to himself. He dropped into an overstuffed chair, relaxed, yawned, picked up a magazine and turned the pages idly. After he had glanced through the magazine he tossed it back on the table and looked down at the traffic in the street below.

The rooming house was in a cheap district and there were numerous wholesale houses on the streets, through which trucks rumbled and clattered. Brokay watched the traffic for several minutes in idle speculation, then figuring that his time was up he got to his feet, walked back down the corridor and knocked at the door of his room.

There was no answer. He turned the knob and opened the door, stepping into the room.

Sam West was lying on the bed on his side. From the closet came a shrill chattering noise of simian terror. Brokay stood staring at the form of Sam West with wide-eyed incredulity.

The burglar was in his shirt sleeves. His eyes were wide open and glazed in an expression of terrific futility. His legs were spread apart. The left arm was flung up on the pillow; the right arm clutched at his breast. There was a stain of red on the bed spread, and a slight stain of red on the front of the burglar's shirt.

Brokay gained the man's side in two swift strides, and felt for his wrist.

The burglar was quite dead.

The monkey in the closet continued to moan and chatter. The closet door was locked, as Brokay had left it. There was no sign that anyone else had been in the room during Brokay's absence.

Brokay inserted his hand beneath the shoulder of the dead burglar and lifted. He could then see the nature of the wound. There could be no doubt but that the burglar had been stabbed in the back, just as the partially clothed woman had been stabbed in the back. The body of the burglar was in a position which was almost identical with the position of Gladys Ordway's body, when the two men had found her lying there in the bedroom of the Ordway mansion.

Brokay moved toward the door, having no definite plan in mind, but intending to notify Thelma Grebe of what had happened. Halfway to the door, he heard the shrill panic-stricken scream of the monkey, and knew that the little animal was terrified lest Brokay should leave the room without opening the closet door.

He moved to the closet door, unlocked it and gathered the monkey to his arms. The monkey took a look at the body which lay on the bed and then, shivering with terror, buried his head in the collar of Brokay's Coat, jabbering and chattering, keeping up a constant stream of low-voiced, terrified protest.

Brokay once more turned toward the door.

As he did so, the knob turned, the door opened and a man entered the room. The man was of middle age, with exceedingly broad shoulders. His head had been thrust forward until it gave to his neck and shoulders the appearance of a crouch. His eyes were small and bright, like the eyes of a bird, and he stared at Brokay with quick suspicion.

"Who are you?" he said. "I came to see Sam West."

Brokay started to speak, but before he could formulate the words, the man's eyes had turned to the body which lay on the bed. "That's Sam," he said. "Why — why — why, my God he's dead!"

The man jumped back and stared at Brokay with eyes that widened with horror. "He's dead!" he said. "Do you hear me? The man's dead!"

Brokay retorted calmly: "Yes, I heard you."

The man moved toward the body; stared down at it; touched it. "Murdered!" he said and stared accusingly at Brokay.

"Are you Frank Compton?" asked Brokay.

"Yes."

"The fence?"

"What do you mean, a fence? I make an honest living, my friend. I never touched anything stolen in my life. What do you mean, a fence? What are you talking about? I should sue you for slander or libel, talking to me that way. And who are you, in here with the body of the man who has been murdered? You, a murderer, should talk to me about being a fence."

He whirled and started for the doorway.

"Just a minute," said Brokay, "I want to talk with you."

Compton's hand sought the knob of the door. "I don't talk with murderers," he said.

Brokay took two swift strides, reached out with his hand and caught Compton by the collar of the coat, jerking him backward. "Just a minute," he said, "you can't pull that stuff."

Compton whirled and lashed out savagely. Brokay blocked the punch, pushed the fence around to one side, slammed his right fist to the man's jaw. The impact sent Compton staggering backward.

The monkey jumped from Brokay's shoulder to the foot of the bed, where he sat chattering and jabbering. Compton, a powerful man, regained his balance, gave a bellow of inarticulate rage and charged with his fists swinging wildly.

Brokay, moving with the swift precision of a trained boxer, side–stepped, held himself perfectly balanced, snapped across a well–timed blow, which caught the fence squarely on the point of the chin.

This time the man went down. He swayed slightly on his knees, then crashed to the floor.

Brokay heard swift steps, the sound of the knob turning, then the door opened and the girl he had met in the social hall stood staring at him with wide, startled eyes. "What is it?" she asked. "I heard the commotion. It sounded as though a horse were trying to kick out the side of the building."

Brokay motioned back toward the hall. "Please go out," he said. "This isn't anything for a woman to see."

She turned swiftly toward the still form which lay on the bed, then gave a partially suppressed scream. Her eyes bulged as they stared at the dead burglar. "Good heavens!" she said, "he's dead." Then, as the full significance of the scene registered upon her senses, she said: "Dead, just as Gladys Ordway died ... and there's the monkey."

Brokay crossed behind her, closed and locked the door. "All right," he said, "you're in it. Now you've got to see it through."

She turned her eyes to his, and he could see the startled fear in their depths. "Tell me," she asked, "is this the man who ran away from the place; the one who had the monkey?"

Brokay faced her steadily. "No," he said. "I am the man who ran away from the place. This is my monkey." He held his arms out to the monkey and the little animal gave a flying leap, cuddled up close to Brokay's cheek.

The fence on the floor stirred, moaned and sat up. He was still punch–groggy. Brokay surveyed him for a moment, then turned to the girl. "Now," he said, "I'm going to find out about you. I know I'm not supposed to ask questions, but you were interested in this murder, and I want to know —"

"Who I am?" asked the girl.

"Yes," he said.

"I," she told him, "am Rhoda Koline."

Brokay felt his own eyes growing wide.

"Yes," she said, speaking hastily, as though it were a relief to get the words out, now that she had started, "I'm Rhoda Koline. I was the social secretary for John Ordway. I'm the one that the police are looking for. I came here, because I understood it would be a safe place to hide, until the police could get the mystery solved."

"How did you come here?" Brokay asked. "How did it happen that you knew of this place?"

"Thelma Grebe," she said, "brought me here."

"You knew Thelma Grebe before, then?"

"Yes."

"How did it happen that she —"

Frank Compton moaned, tried to get to his feet, and finally was successful. He stood swaying and holding on to the foot of the bed.

Brokay turned to him. "Look here," he said, "you've got some explaining to do. You were supposed to have entered this room some little time ago. What detained you?"

"None of your business," said Compton thickly. "You're a murderer; I'm going to see that you don't pin this crime on me."

"I thought so," Brokay said. "You're trying to make excuses before there's even been an accusation. I didn't accuse you of murdering him."

"Of course you didn't," Compton said, his eyes commencing to lose some of their dazed appearance. "I'm the one that accused you of murdering him. How could I have murdered him? You were here in the room when I came in. You were the one who murdered him."

"I'm not so certain about this business," Brokay said. "You were supposed to have entered the room some time ago. You could have come in and killed him then walked out, and returned, pretending that you were just entering the room."

The fence laughed sarcastically. "Sure, sure," he said, "I could have gone ahead and killed him and then come back so that you could catch me. And what could you have done, my friend, while you were here in the room? You were the one that shared the room with this man. You have either got to show who did the murder, or else you're going to be held responsible for it."

"I left the room," Brokay said. "I left the room because you were coming in and Sam West wanted to talk with you where there wouldn't be any witnesses to overhear the conversation."

"Baloney!" said Compton. He started for the door.

"You're not leaving just yet," Brokay said.

"The hell I'm not!" Compton blazed at him.

"When I'm ready to notify the police," Brokay said, "I'll notify them."

"Police? Police? Who's talking about the police?" said the fence. "You aren't in a place now where you can call the police, my friend. Nobody calls the police here."

"There's been a murder committed," Brokay pointed out.

"That doesn't make any difference," Compton said. "The body isn't going to be found here. The police aren't going to be notified. What will happen will be that the body will be put in an automobile and taken somewhere tonight. It'll be dumped by the side of a road somewhere in the country and the police will find him in the morning. But in the meantime, my friend you are responsible. You have got to answer to the people here in the house — not to the police. This man has friends; I am his friend; he had other friends. You have got to explain to those friends. This is something that's different from the police, you understand. This is something that is handled as a matter of friendship."

"And you're going to try and hold me responsible?" Brokay asked.

"You are responsible," said the fence. "You know it."

"And where are you going now?" Brokay asked with ominous softness.

"I'm going to report to Thelma Grebe. She'll make arrangements to dispose of the body, but you are going to be held responsible, my friend, don't you forget that. You have to —"

His hand once more groped for the knob of the door, and once more Brokay grabbed him by the collar of the coat, jerked him back.

"Listen," he said, "you're not going to leave this room until —"

The fence jerked up his knee in a vicious kick to the groin. Brokay managed to block it. His left fist lashed out. Compton's apelike arms dropped about Brokay's back. The two men swayed in a struggle. The monkey, once more jumping to the bed, screamed and chattered.

Compton was a man of great strength. With Brokay in his arms, he was more than a match for the lithe activity of the millionaire clubman, but Brokay managed to get his head down so that the top of it was pushing against Compton's chin. He arched his back, straining the muscles, gradually pushed Compton away. He freed his own arms, sent a short jabbing left and right to the ribs.

Compton groaned, released his hold and swayed, and, as he staggered groggily, Brokay stepped in and snapped over a businesslike right which clicked on the side of Compton's jaw.

As the fence went limp, Brokay stepped in and held the slumping body in his arms.

He turned to Rhoda Koline. "Please," he said, "stand by me. Let's get out of this thing together."

"What do you want me to do?" she asked.

"Tear up that pillow slip into strips," he said. "I'm going to tie this man and gag him."

She did not hesitate even for a moment, but stepped quickly to the bed, pulled the slip from one of the pillows and ripped it into strips. Brokay tied and gagged the fence, and Rhoda Koline held the door of the closet open while Brokay pushed the man into the dark interior, closed and locked the door.

He turned to Rhoda Koline. "Now," he said, "let's get clown to brass tacks."

"How do you mean?" she asked.

"I want your story," he told her.

"There isn't any," she said. "I had some friends there at the house. I wasn't supposed to be home; I was supposed to be out somewhere. Then we heard a commotion. There was the sound of a siren, the noise of a shot, and automobiles speeding away. We went to see what the trouble was and we found Gladys Ordway."

"Who do you mean by 'we'?" asked Brokay.

"Thelma Grebe and myself," she said.

"You're friendly with Thelma Grebe?"

"Yes."

"How long have you known her?"

"Not very long. I got acquainted with her in rather a peculiar manner. Thelma, I think, has clung to me. She wanted to get away from this life. I guess I'm the only friend that she has who isn't connected in some way with crooks or gangsters."

"And she suggested that you come here?" Brokay asked.

"Yes. Just as soon as she saw the body, she knew that there was going to be trouble. You see, I wasn't supposed to be at the house at all."

"Were there any men in the party?" asked Brokay.

"No," she said, "just Thelma and myself."

"What I can't understand," Brokay said, "is why you didn't stay and explain the situation to the police."

"I couldn't very well," she said.

"Why?"

She met his gaze squarely. "Because of Thelma," she said. "Don't you understand? Thelma was there with me. Thelma was a known moll. She was the companion of crooks. I was supposed to be out, yet the police would have found that I was in the house; would have found that I had this woman with me. You can see what would have happened."

Brokay nodded slowly. "Yes," he said, "I can see complications. But it would still seem to me that —"

"Thelma told me," she said, "that the case was bound to be cleared up within a short time; that if I would go with her, she could promise me sanctuary until everything had been explained."

"It sounds to me," Brokay said bluntly, "like damn poor advice."

She stared steadily at him and smiled slightly. "Well," she said, "now I'll hear your story."

CHAPTER FIVE
Time for Murder

Brokay told her his story; told it without embellishment, without any elaborate explanations, giving her merely an outline of what happened. She stood staring at him steadily.

"What's the matter?" asked Brokay.

"I think," she said, "that you at least owe me a certain amount of frankness. I have been frank with you; you should be frank with me."

"But I have been frank with you."

"The story that you have told me," she said, "is probably the most improbable yarn I have ever heard."

Brokay realized, then, the utter hopelessness of expecting the police to believe his story. "I'm sorry," he said stiffly, "if you don't believe me. It's the only story I can offer."

She stood staring at him for several seconds. Finally she said: "I'm going to believe you, Mr. Brokay. My reason tells me I shouldn't, but there's something about you that makes me believe you in spite of myself."

"Thank you," he said, still with that stiff formality.

"But," she went on, "you could never tell that to the police."

"I know it," he said.

"What are you going to do?" she asked.

Brokay turned to the monkey. "That," he said, "is the only clue. Apparently the monkey didn't belong to Gladys Ordway."

"No," she said, "the monkey didn't belong to Gladys Ordway, I know that, because I was in the house with her. I saw her just a few hours before she was killed. She didn't have any such pet as this."

"Then," said Brokay, "it stands to reason that the monkey was introduced into the house by the murderer."

"But why on earth would a murderer bring a monkey to the house?"

"I don't know."

"And why would the monkey remain after the murder had been committed?"

"I think," Brokay said, "I can give you some explanation of that. Monkeys are really sensitive animals, although many times people don't realize it. When I entered the room, the monkey was sitting on the head of the bed, chattering in blind terror. What's more, the murder had been committed but a few minutes before I entered the room. That means that the murderer must have been in the room when we entered the house; perhaps heard us on the stairs, or saw the beam of our flashlight as we came toward the room. He had to make his escape."

"And you mean he was trying to catch the monkey?"

"Yes, the monkey had become terrified when he committed the crime. It had run from him. He had tried to recapture the animal, and then he heard us. He had to escape and leave the monkey there."

"That," she said, "sounds reasonable. But I still can't understand why the murderer should have taken the monkey with him, or who the murderer was, or what the motive for the murder was."

Brokay's eyes glinted. "Well," he said, "I'm going to do some detective work of my own. There's one thing that's a cinch, I'm in this thing up to my necktie and I've got to get out. The only way I can do it is by finding out what actually did happen."

He crossed to the telephone which set on the table by the window.

"Take the classified index, Miss Koline," he said, "and read down through the pet stores. I'm going to call them up one at a time. You give me the numbers."

"What's the idea?" she asked.

"The idea is," he said, "that this monkey must originally have come from a pet store. I don't think that the murderer had owned the monkey very long; certainly not long enough to have won the confidence of the little animal; not long enough to have learned very much about him. I'm acting on the theory that the monkey was sold recently."

"I can't understand just how you can figure that," she said. "I see that there's something to be said in favor of it, but —"

"Nevertheless," he interrupted, "that's the only theory we've got to work on, and we're going to work on it."

She opened the telephone book, ran her finger down the classified directory, and said: "All right, here's the first one — Drexel Four–o–six–two."

He dialed the number, and, when a voice answered, said: "I am trying to get some information about a monkey that was sold from your store within the last week. Have you a record of such sales?"

"We haven't sold any monkey during the past week," the man said. "It's been a month since we made a sale of a monkey. You understand that at this particular season of the year the demand isn't brisk, and we very seldom sell monkeys. Usually we handle them on order."

"Thank you," said Brokay, and hung up.

Rhoda Koline gave him the next number. Brokay called it. The result was the same. The third store had sold a monkey within the last week. Brokay got a description of the monkey and of the person who had bought it, together with the address. The fourth store yielded a blank. The fifth store had sold a monkey. The clerk couldn't tell the name or address of the people who had purchased it.

"There was a man," he said, "who had a slight scar on the left side of his forehead, a little star–shaped scar. He was carrying a cane. He wore a tuxedo — a man about forty–four or forty–five, I should judge. He was broad across the shoulders, but not fat. He was accompanied by a girl in a leopard–skin coat. The girl was ten or fifteen years younger than he was. They had been looking at this monkey that we kept in the window, and decided they wanted to purchase it. They had both been drinking. We gave them some instructions on the care of the monkey and delivered the monkey to them."

"Can you describe the woman?" asked Brokay.

"Not much more than that she wore the leopard–skin coat, and, as I remember it, had black hair and black eyes. It was the man I was interested in mostly. He was rather a remarkable individual, although I couldn't tell just how he gave the impression of being remarkable. It was something in his manner; something in his character."

"Tell me something more about the monkey," Brokay said. "Give me a description of it."

The man gave a technical description of breed, species, place of origin, and so on.

When he had finished Brokay said: "Can you tell me that in less technical terms? I want to know exactly what the monkey looked like."

The man gave him a description which tallied exactly with that of the monkey which was at the moment clinging to Brokay's shoulder.

"Thank you," Brokay said, when he had noted the points of the description.

"You said you were with the police?" asked the man in the pet store.

"I didn't say so," Brokay answered, "but you can draw your own conclusions."

He slid the receiver back into place and turned to Rhoda Koline.

"Miss Koline," he said, "I think we're on the trail. You've got to do something and do it right away."

"What is it?"

"Find out if Thelma Grebe has a leopard–skin coat."

"Oh yes," she said, "I know that she has. She wore it one night when she was out with me. In fact, she had it on the night she came to call on me there at the Ordway residence."

Brokay stood staring at the dead body on the bed. "There's one funny thing about these murders," he said.

"What's that?" she asked.

"There's a single stabbing wound, made with a long, narrow–bladed weapon. It's too long and thin to be an ordinary type of knife. Moreover, the murderer has always had to work fast. He's had to thrust and then run. I am wondering if he is absolutely certain that his victim is dead when he leaves the room."

"What difference would it make?" Rhoda Koline asked.

"I'm going to show you," he said. "This is going to be a little gruesome, but it's got to be done."

He walked to the bed, picked up the body of the dead burglar, dragged it half from the bed, so that it lay partially on the bed and partially on the floor. Then he took a pencil from his pocket, a piece of paper, and wrote in a rude scrawl —

"Thelma is mixed up in it. She notified ..."

At this point Brokay let the pencil trail across the paper. He placed the paper directly beneath the left hand of the corpse, pushed the pencil into the fingers of the right hand, and then arranged the arms so that it looked as though the burglar had tried to scrawl some message just as he was dying."

"But," she said, "I don't see what you're getting at."

Brokay nodded toward Sam West. "That man," he said, "was killed because he knew too much."

"What did he know?" she asked, with a frown.

"It wasn't what he knew, so much as what they thought he knew," Brokay said. "Now I'm in exactly the position that he occupied, only I really know what they could only surmise that Sam West knew."

"In other words," she said, her face suddenly changing color, "you mean that —"

Brokay consulted his wristwatch. "I mean," he said, "that it is going to take three murders to make the chain complete. There was the murder of Gladys Ordway. We don't know yet what the motive was. There was the murder of Sam West. He was murdered because he knew too much about the Ordway murder. The next murder will be when I am stabbed in the back with some long, thin weapon."

"But when?" she asked. "Will they attempt —"

"Almost immediately," he said. "I think we can count on the attempt within the next hour." He turned and smiled at her, but his smile was grim and without mirth.

"What time is it now?" she inquired.

The smile remained fixed upon his lips. "Time for murder," he said in an undertone as the knob on the door turned quietly. The latch clicked back. The lock held the door in place.

"Unlock the door," said Brokay.

Rhoda Koline turned the key in the lock. The door opened and Thelma Grebe crossed the threshold. "There's a message," she said, "for Frank Compton. Someone wants him at once, and —"

She broke off with a quick scream as she stood, apparently rigid with terror and startled surprise, staring at the figure which lay half off the bed, with the tell–tale red pool which had seeped through the covers telling its own grim story.

"Good God!" she said, "it's Sam! What's happened?"

"I'm sure I couldn't tell you," Brokay said. "I was talking with this young lady in the social hall. I came in to see Sam. I found him like this."

"There was a man who came to see him," she said quickly. "A man by the name of Compton, a fence. Where is he?"

Brokay shrugged his shoulders.

"Then," said Thelma Grebe, "he's the one that did it. He's the one that's responsible. We've got to find him."

"Probably," Brokay said, "that means Compton was at least the last one to see him alive. The police will want him as a material witness."

"The police?" exclaimed Thelma Grebe. "Who said anything about the police?"

"Don't you notify the police?" asked Brokay.

"Certainly not," she snapped. "This is a place where we can't have the police prowling around. We'll have to handle the matter in such a way that the place will never be mixed up in it. But that isn't going to prevent Sam West's friends from getting vengeance."

She turned and stared at Rhoda Koline. "When did you get in here?" she asked.

"You heard what the gentleman said, Thelma," Rhoda Koline remarked.

Brokay entered the conversation once more. "We had just this minute entered the door," he said. "We saw the body and turned the key in the lock of the door. We didn't want to be disturbed until we could find out what it was all about. Then you twisted the knob on the door. I decided that it might be better to let you in, because I didn't know who you were, and I was afraid you might make a racket if you found the door locked and got no response."

Rhoda Koline, playing her part as though she had been carefully schooled in it by several rehearsals, moved toward the body, then recoiled.

"Look!" she said, "there's something in his hand! Something that he was writing on — a paper or something."

Thelma Grebe moved swiftly forward.

"I'll take it," she said.

"Just a moment," Brokay said, and moved quickly, so that he was standing shoulder to shoulder with her as they bent over the figure and stared at the paper.

Brokay read, then looked accusingly at Thelma Grebe.

"Are you the Thelma that he referred to?" he asked. "That's your name, I believe."

"Certainly not," she said. "It's some other Thelma. What's more, that doesn't look like Sam West's writing. I don't believe Sam West could possibly have written anything after he received that stab wound in the back. That must have been instantaneous. This is some kind of a frame–up."

Brokay shrugged his shoulders. "At any rate," he said, "the paper is evidence."

"No it isn't!" she said and swooped for it.

Brokay bent swiftly, caught her wrist with his hand, pulled her back and picked up the paper. He folded it and slipped it in his pocket. "Oh yes," he said, smiling frostily, "it's evidence."

She stepped back, stared at him with blazing eyes. "You can't get away with that sort of stuff," she said. "Who the hell do you think you are?"

Brokay shrugged his shoulders again. "I am," he said, "a friend of Sam West — that is, I was a friend of his."

"You're a great friend!" she blazed. "You were left here alone in the room with him, and he was murdered. That may be what you call friendship."

"I was down at the end of the hall," he said, "in the social room — Room Ten."

"You're a liar!" she said. "You weren't there at all."

"Oh yes I was, and this young lady was with me."

"This young lady talked with you a moment and then went back to her room," said Thelma Grebe. "You can't pull that stuff on me. You're dealing with somebody that's not a greenhorn, you know. I wasn't born yesterday."

She suddenly whirled and stormed from the room, slamming the door behind her.

"Quick, Miss Koline," Brokay said, "I think you'd better get back to your room."

"No," she said, her lips white. "We've got to get out of here. Don't you understand what's going to happen?"

"I understand perfectly" he said, "but I'm on my guard."

"No, no," she told him, "let's go. We can notify the police. Certainly they can trace down the clue of this monkey. I believe that the dealer would be able to identify the people. You could tell your story, and —"

"And it wouldn't be believed," he said, interrupting her. "You know your reaction to the story."

"But it's different now," she said. "Please come. We can leave here, and —"

"No," he said, "you've got to go to your room, and keep out of this. Go to your room and promise me that you'll keep the door locked." He took her by the arm, gently pushed her across the corridor to her room.

"And you're going to stay here alone?" she asked.

He nodded. "It's my only chance," he said, "to get the thing cleared up. It's got to be done for your sake, as well as mine."

"But that doesn't mean that you should take any risks," she said.

Brokay gently but firmly pushed her across the corridor and into her room. "Stay there and don't come out," he said curtly.

He pulled the door shut with a bang, walked back across the corridor to the room where the dead burglar lay sprawled on the bed, and waited.

After a while, he thought he heard steps on the stairs. He braced himself and watched the handle of the door.

Nothing happened.

He frowned and looked at his watch.

More than fifteen minutes had elapsed since Thelma Grebe had left the room. Brokay couldn't believe that she would summon the police; neither could he believe that she had intended simply to run away and leave the place. He kept thinking of those steps on the stairs; there had been something furtive about them, something —

Suddenly he gave a convulsive start. He strode to the door, jerked it open, crossed the corridor, twisted the knob of Rhoda Koline's room and opened the door.

Thelma Grebe was standing just within the doorway. Standing beside her was a heavily built man, with a small star–shaped scar on the left side of his forehead. The man was carrying a cane in his right hand; his left hand held his hat and gloves.

"But surely, my dear young lady," he was saying, "you can't —" They turned as the door opened.

"Here he is now," said Rhoda Koline with a quick catch in her voice.

The man faced Brokay. "Ah!" he said. "I was going to see you in a moment, my friend. I'm on special duty with the police. I am very friendly to Thelma Grebe, but I understand there has been a serious crime committed here."

"There's been a murder, if that's what you mean," George Brokay said, watching him closely.

"Where?" asked the man.

"In the room across the hall," Brokay said.

The man bowed. "Kindly lead the way," he said. "That is what I was trying to find out. Miss Grebe was rather indefinite about the entire affair. She wanted to get the thing hushed up in some way. I explained to her that it was impossible to hush up a murder." He gestured toward the door.

Brokay turned his back to the than, put his hand on the knob of the door.

Several things happened almost at once. Rhoda Koline screamed. George Brokay flung himself down in a quick duck. Something hissed through the air above his head, and struck the panels of the door with an ominous *thunk*.

The man behind Brokay had lunged forward with the cane. The covering of the cane, which, apparently, was wood, had slipped back from a long, thin blade of keen steel, and the blade had embedded itself in the door.

Thelma Grebe, realizing what had happened, flung up her arm, and sunlight glinted upon blued steel as she pointed an automatic at Brokay. Brokay, still crouching under the blade which had pushed itself into the doorway, went forward in a long, low tackle, catching the legs of the man with the scarred forehead.

Thelma Grebe fired. The shot crashed through the panels of the door, missing Brokay by not more than an inch. Rhoda Koline flung herself upon Thelma Grebe, struggling for the gun. The man with the scarred forehead crashed down under the impact of Brokay's rushing tackle. They squirmed about on the floor together. Brokay felt the man's hand pushing its way under his coat lapel. He grabbed the arm with his left hand. The man lurched and twisted. Brokay caught a brief glimpse of a gun. He flung himself to one side, smashed his right fist over and across.

Another shot rang out, the gun so close to Brokay's ear that the report was deafening. There was a shower of powdered plaster as the bullet struck the ceiling. The two women were struggling and twisting, Rhoda Koline hanging onto Thelma Grebe's arm with the grim tenacity of a fighting bulldog.

The man with the scarred forehead gave a lurch, got to his hands and knees, flung up the weapon once more. Brokay pushed the weapon aside, sent everything he had in a terrific right which crashed through, full to the other's face. As the man staggered backward and rolled inertly to the floor, Brokay grabbed the weapon from the man's limp fingers. At that moment Rhoda Koline staggered backward. Thelma Grebe raised the gun once more, this time not at Brokay, but straight at Rhoda Koline's breast.

Brokay lunged forward. His left hand caught the woman's arm, pulled it down and to one side as she fired. Then he wrested the gun from her, backed to the door and stood with the guns covering the pair. "Call the police, Rhoda," he said.

CHAPTER SIX
Brokay Entertains the Law

Grigsby, the butler, coughed apologetically as George Brokay latchkeyed the front door of his residence. "I beg your pardon, sir," he said, "but —"

A gruff voice from the shadows of the corridor interrupted. "Stow that stuff," said the voice, "we'll do our own talking."

Two men stepped forward.

"You're Brokay?" asked one of the men.

"Yes," said George Brokay.

"We've got some questions to ask you."

"All right," said Brokay, "I'll be glad to answer them."

"How does it happen that there was a roadster in your garage with a bullet hole in the back of the body? How does it happen that your hat was found in the grounds of the John C. Ordway residence? How does it happen that you were running away from the police last night, when the police radio car tried to stop you? How does it happen that there was a monkey clinging to your neck, and fingerprints that have been developed in the room where Gladys Ordway was murdered show that there had been a monkey sitting on the head of the bed?"

Brokay nodded.

"Gentlemen," he said, "come in. Sit down and have a drink. It happens that you gentlemen are just a little bit behind the times. I can explain those points very readily, but, before I do so, you might be interested in learning something about the murder of Miss Gladys Ordway."

"Yes," said one of the men, "we'd be interested in learning a lot about it."

They followed Brokay into the library.

"Highballs, Grigsby," said Brokay.

"Go ahead and talk, guy," one of the men said.

"It happens," said Brokay, "that Gladys Ordway had been blackmailed by a man named Charles Giddings. She had been rather indiscreet. Some of the high-powered stuff, that is indulged in at times by the younger set. There were photographs, and, altogether, it would have made a nasty scandal. Giddings had been blackmailing her; she finally decided that she was going to report to the police; she told Giddings that she was finished and that she was going to tell everything.

"Giddings had an accomplice, a Thelma Grebe. They tried to keep Gladys Ordway from telling her father, or reporting to the police. She had reached her decision, however, and the decision was final as far as she was concerned. Thelma Grebe had been cultivating Rhoda Koline, the social secretary of Glady's Ordway's father. Giddings had a cane, the lower portion of which was rubber made to represent wood. There was a steel blade inside of the cane. While Thelma Grebe was talking with Rhoda Koline, Giddings entered Gladys Ordway's bedroom and stabbed her in the back, simply reaching out and stabbing her with the cane.

"He had been drinking some that night, and, acting upon impulse, had purchased a pet monkey. The monkey was clinging to his shoulder. When the monkey saw the blood, and saw what had happened, it became terrified.

"Rhoda Koline didn't know that Thelma Grebe had been accompanied by a man. Thelma had entered the house, using Rhoda's latchkey which Rhoda had given her, because Thelma Grebe said she didn't want to face the servants. Thelma Grebe was a moll, and professed an interest in Rhoda, saying she wanted Rhoda to take here away from the life of crime she was leading."

"Rather a slick story," said one of the men. "How about a little proof for it?"

"Plenty of proof for it," Brokay said. "It seems that there was a burglar by the name of Sam West, who got a clue to what had happened. Giddings was acquainted with West. He entered West's room, shook hands with him and when West turned his back, Giddings ran him through the back and deposited the body on the bed. He was assisted by Thelma Grebe.

"I had a pretty good idea of what had happened. Giddings tried the same stunt with me. It didn't work."

"And your proof of all this?" asked one of the detectives.

"The fact that the police just a few minutes ago took Thelma Grebe and Giddings into custody, and that Thelma Grebe is making a complete confession, in order to save her own neck."

The men looked at each other.

"Call headquarters," said one of the men.

As one of the detectives went to the telephone to call headquarters, the other stared at George Brokay. "The thing that you still haven't explained," he said, "is how it happens that you were mixed into this and were running around through the night with a monkey clinging to your shoulders."

Brokay smiled at him. "That," he said, "is unfortunately one of the things that I can't explain. That is, if I did explain it you wouldn't believe me, and since it isn't any of your damn business in the first place, and doesn't have any bearing on the murder in the second place I don't think I'll try."

"Yeah?" said the detective. "Well, buddy, you may have another think coming about that."

Brokay shook his head.

"Oh, no," he said, "I think I'm in the clear in the matter."

"Then how about this car that was in your garage. What was it doing there?"

"Staying there," said Brokay.

"And how about this monkey?"

Brokay shrugged his shoulders. "The monkey," he said, "is a different story. It's really too bad that you're never going to learn the inside story about that monkey."

"Listen," asked the man, "how did you get wise to all this?"

"I got wise to it," Brokay said slowly, facing the man with steady, belligerent eyes, "by doing a little thinking that the police might well have done for themselves. I got wise to it by realizing that Sam West, the burglar, had been murdered because he knew too much, and that I could expect Giddings to try to murder me, because I knew too much. I baited a trap. I used myself as human bait. I knew that it was time for a murder, and that I was to be the victim. Does that answer your question?"

The other detective rushed from the outer corridor into the library. "It's true," he said, "every damn word of it. He's caught the pair and turned them over to the homicide squad. They're at headquarters now. The woman is spilling her guts."

Brokay smiled. "And now, gentlemen," he said, "if you will excuse me, I want to shave and change my clothes. You see, I have a date for dinner with a very estimable young lady, who, because of some very poor advice which was given her by Thelma Grebe, was taking it on the lam. You see, Thelma Grebe wanted to have a goat, a fall guy for the police, so she persuaded this young lady to, as they so quaintly express it in underworld circles, 'take it on the lam'."

"You mean, Rhoda Koline, the social secretary?" asked the detective.

Brokay nodded.

"That's another thing you haven't told us about," the detective said. "Tell us some more about this Rhoda Koline."

Brokay smiled at them. "Gentlemen," he said, "your murder case is solved. The murderers are making a complete confession. Rhoda Koline is exonerated. I am exonerated. We don't have to answer any more of your questions. Frankly, I don't know very much about Rhoda Koline and that's why I'm taking her to dinner. I want to find out."

Hard as Nails

Gilbert E. Best was as full of dynamic energy as a busy coffee percolator. He started out of the elevator before the door was more than half open, pounded his way down the flagged floor of the skyscraper hallway, not as a man who is in a frantic rush, but as one who is so filled with surplus energy that he finds an outlet in pounding the floor with his feet.

He walked past six doors marked, each with the legend on the square of frosted glass which fronted the hallway, *Frank C. Dillon — Attorney At Law — Private.* The seventh door was lettered, *Frank C. Dillon — Attorney At Law — Office Hours 10:00 to 12:00 — 2:00 to 4:30 — Entrance.*

Best's broad shoulders swung in a pivot from the waist. He used enough force in opening the office door to have moved the steel door of a vault, and came to a stop before a reception desk.

A pair of blue eyes that looked up with listless boredom from behind a telephone switchboard on which was a brass sign marked, *Information*, suddenly sparkled to life. "Hello, Gil."

"Hello, Norma. What does Dillon want?"

"I don't know, Gil. He's in an awful sweat about something. He told me to rush that call through to you. I wanted to listen in, but the board got busy and I couldn't. What did he want?"

"Wanted me to come over right now."

"Did he sound apologetic?"

"As apologetic as he ever sounds," Best said. "He wanted to bury the hatchet. That means he's in a jam and he needs me. Is he alone in there?"

"No, there's a woman with him."

She ran her finger down the page of a day book and marked a name with the pointed tip of a crimson fingernail. "Ellen Hanley, her name is. She's plaintiff in a case against the Airline Stageways."

"Personal—injury suit?"

"Yeah."

"How long's he had it?"

"A couple of months, I think. The case is at issue and ready to be set for trial. Maybe it's set for trial. I've forgotten. Gee whiz, Gil, after that last scene you had, I didn't think he'd ever send for you again!"

"And I didn't think I'd ever come," Gilbert retorted. "But I guess he needs a real detective agency, and I need the dough — if there's enough of it."

"Stick him plenty," said Norma Pelton with sudden vindictiveness. "He just gave me a ten—dollar cut."

"What's the idea?"

"I don't know. He said business was rotten, and —"

A door of veneered mahogany, which bore in gilt letters the one word, *Private*, opened with explosive force. A big man whose paunch was buttoned tightly inside a cream–colored vest rumbled into irascible speech before the glittering, avaricious eyes had fully focused on the office.

"Where the devil's that detective? Put through a call and —"

He broke off as his eyes rested on Best standing by the window.

"Hello, Dillon," said Best.

The lawyer didn't reply to the salutation directly, but there was a relieved note to his voice as he rasped out: "Why the devil didn't you let me know you were here? I told you this was an emergency. If I hadn't busted out here, you'd have been talking to Norma for another ten minutes yet. Come in."

"What is it?" asked Best, crowding past the bulging vest as the lawyer held the door open for him.

"I'm in a jam."

"Again?"

"Don't be funny."

"What sort of a jam?"

"I'm going to lose about ten thousand bucks."

"That's a lot of money," Best said, "even if you haven't got it to lose."

Dillon snorted, grasped the detective's elbow with fingers that were surprisingly strong, for all of their coating of fat, pushed him through a law library and into an office fitted with massive furniture that matched the huge bulk of the lawyer.

A woman, who seemed as pathetically small as a boy in a man's overcoat, raised hopeless eyes to survey the broad–shouldered detective.

"This is Ellen Hanley," said Dillon. And, turning to Ellen Hanley, said: "This is the detective I told you about — Gilbert Best."

Best tossed his hat to the big desk, smiled reassuringly at Ellen Hanley. Her eyes were bleached with suffering. Her lips twisted into a smile, but there was no hope in her eyes.

Dillon squeezed himself past the corner of his desk. Springs in the swivel chair squeaked protest as he adjusted his weight.

"Ellen Hanley," he said, "has a swell case against the Airline Stageways. That is," he amended hastily, "she did have."

"What happened to it?" Best asked.

"She didn't follow instructions," said Dillon, with an accusing glare at the woman.

She started to say something, but raised a handkerchief to her lips and coughed with hacking monotony.

Best looked at the lawyer inquiringly.

"Accident happened five months ago," said Dillon. "It was night. The stage was coming around a corner too fast to get over on its side of the road. The driver was fighting the steering wheel. He couldn't turn off the spotlight. It glared into Miss Hanley's eyes. She was crowded off the road, smashed into a stump, wrecked her car, smashed some ribs. Gave her some serious lung injuries."

"Was the stage injured?" asked Best. "No, she never touched the stage. The stage crowded her off the road and into a stump."

"And kept right on going?" asked Best.

"It would have, but one of the passengers heard the crash, looked back and saw what happened. He made the driver stop. The driver pretended he didn't know anything about it. The passenger was sore. Miss Hanley was unconscious. They stopped a passing motorist and had him take her to the hospital. The driver then admitted to the passenger that he was going pretty fast and didn't have a chance to turn off the spotlight when he saw the car coming."

"That," said the detective, watching Dillon shrewdly, "should make a pretty good case."

"It should have!" snorted the lawyer. "I sued the Airline Stageways, and Walter Manning. He was the driver. You know, his statement wouldn't be admissible against the stage company because it wasn't a part of what we call the *res gestae*. But, on the theory that both the stage company and the driver were responsible for the accident, I sued the driver, as well as the stage company. Then I could have introduced the admission as against the driver. The jury would have considered it as against the stage company, in spite of the judge's instructions."

"Well?" asked the detective.

Dillon snorted. "Sam Wigmore," he, said, "is the most unscrupulous shyster that ever represented a corporation! Do you know what he did?"

"What did he do?"

"He got Manning to make a default. I've got judgment against Manning for fifty thousand dollars. That judgment isn't worth fifty cents, but now that I've got judgment against Manning I can't introduce the statement that he made, as a declaration against him. That means the only thing I can do is to put him on the stand as a witness and ask him questions. If he denies the statement he made, I can impeach him."

"I still don't see anything to worry about," Best said.

"I can't find Manning. They've spirited him out of the country."

"Like that, eh?"

"Like that."

"Why didn't you have me get in touch with him five months ago?" Best inquired.

"The action was only put in my hands three months ago, and I thought it was a cinch case. I thought they would settle, until Wigmore pulled that fast one on me and spirited Manning out of the country."

"You still could have reached me thirty days ago," Best said.

"Yes, but, damn it, you had to go and get temperamental and wouldn't work for me any more!"

Best laughed. "You were the one that got temperamental," he said, "and swore you'd never call me again. What do you want me to do — find Manning?"

"We've got to find Manning."

"How about the passenger?" Best suggested. "He should make a good witness for you."

"He's a swell witness to the statement that Manning made, but he can't be a witness to the accident. He was dozing at the time. It was the crash that woke him up. He looked through the back of the stage and saw the car rolling over, had a glimpse of Miss Hanley being pitched out."

"I see," the detective remarked.

"You don't see anything yet," grumbled Dillon, pulling a handkerchief from the side pocket of his coat and mopping his perspiring brow. "Wigmore pulled a fast one."

"Another one?"

"Yes, another one."

"What did he do?"

"Miss Hanley hasn't any money," Dillon said. "She hasn't any money to even pay her ordinary living expenses. She had to get some form of work. A woman who must have been in the employ of the stage company told her about some employment she could get if she'd write to a certain address. She made it appear that the applicant would have to show she was in good health."

The lawyer broke off, to stare at the frail form of the woman as though she had been some particularly obnoxious insect.

"Do you know what she did, Gil? The little fool went ahead and answered a questionnaire that was sent her — a questionnaire that said the position was open only to applicants enjoying good health, and containing a lot of inquiries about whether she'd ever been in an accident, and if so, whether she'd had a complete recovery, and a lot of that stuff. It was a printed questionnaire. It looked innocent enough. It wouldn't have fooled me if she'd told me about it. But she didn't tell me about it until afterwards. She filled it in, stating that she'd been in a minor accident, but that she'd had a perfect recovery; that she was enjoying good health."

Dillon glared at his client. Ellen Hanley had another fit of coughing. Best's eyes showed sympathy. "How did you find out about it?" he asked the lawyer.

"When Wigmore quit his talk of compromise and decided he was going to trial. I had him almost worked up to a twenty–thousand–dollar settlement."

"Twenty thousand dollars is a lot of money," said Best.

"There's some bad injuries in this case," Dillon said, and tapped his lungs.

Best frowned. "Then," he said, "as I see it, aside from the fact that you can't prove your case against the stage company, in the first place, and can't show any serious injuries, in the second place, there's nothing much wrong with your lawsuit."

"That's it," groaned Dillon. "Of course, I could put Ellen Hanley on the witness stand and get a doctor to support her testimony concerning the injuries, but you know how juries are. They see so many people who fake injuries against transportation companies that as soon as Wigmore flashes her written statement on 'em that she'd had a complete recovery and is in good health, I'd stand no chance of collecting anything, except maybe a few hundred dollars for doctor and hospital bills."

Best frowned for a moment, then stared at Dillon. "It's going to take money," he said.

Dillon's face instantly became a cold, hard mask. "I can advance you," he said, "a hundred dollars, and pay you twenty dollars a day."

Best shook his head. "I said money," he remarked.

Dillon's face mottled. His voice grew high–pitched with emotion. "What the hell do you think I am?" he asked. "Santy Claus? Do you think money grows on bushes? This whole thing is contingency with me, except costs. I got a retainer to cover costs, and that's all."

"How much of a retainer?" asked Best.

It was the woman who answered the question. "All I had," she said. "A hundred and eighteen dollars."

Best picked up his hat. "So long, Dillon," he said, and strode from the office.

The lawyer tugged at the edge of the desk, heaved his bulk out of the chair. "Now wait a minute, Gil," he said. "You can't —"

Best slammed the door of the private office behind him, walked through the law library, pushed open the door into the outer office, shook his head at Norma Pelton.

"No go?" she asked.

"No go," he told her. "I can't stand your boss. He makes me seasick. The big stuffed shirt."

"Huh," she said, "you should be working for him."

"Took all she had," said Best in a voice that was edged with disgust, "and then kicks her all around the office because she tried to go to work and make some money to support herself — over a hundred dollars for 'costs.' Hell, it didn't cost him over fifteen dollars to file the suit and serve the papers, and then he was too damn stingy to get a detective to sew the case up for him, but pocketed the rest of the retainer and tried to club the stage company into a settlement. It serves him right."

Best pounded his way across the office, slammed the door to the corridor and started toward the elevator.

A key clicked in a lock, a knob turned. One of the doors marked, *Frank C. Dillon — Attorney at Law — Private*, opened. Dillon's faun–colored vest blocked the opening. His face wore an ingratiating smile.

"All right, Gil, old kid," he said, "I wouldn't hold out on you. I'll put up the money."

The detective remained in the hallway. His face did not smile. "I meant money," he said, "not for myself, but to keep that woman going until we can get a settlement for her, or bring the case to trial. And I need money for some help in this thing, and I don't want any questions asked about what I do with it. You know the way Wigmore and his detectives strong–arm a case as well as I do. They've had five months' head–start on me. I've got to pull a fast one."

Dillon sighed, stood to one side and wheezed: "Come on in, Best. We can fix all that up."

"And," said Best, "I want the address that she wrote to get the employment."

Dillon's reply was a snort of contempt. After a moment he said: "That's what burns me up, Best. That damn shyster, Wigmore, had the crust to put on there the address of Five Hundred and Three, Transportation Building. That's the claim department of the Airline Stageways."

Best pushed his way into the office, took a notebook from his pocket, handed it to Ellen Hanley, smiled reassuringly.

"Sign your name on that page," he said, "just the way you signed it on that questionnaire."

"What are you going to do?" asked Dillon, peering over Best's shoulder, his wheezing breath sounding in the detective's ear.

"Give me some money," Best said, "and shut up. The less you know about this, the better."

CHAPTER TWO
Hard as Nails

Gilbert Best completed his canvass of the city directory. He had four Ellen Hanleys listed. Two of them were housewives; one was a milliner; the other was a stenographer. He also had three Miss Hanleys whose first names were not given, but were indicated only by initials and whose first initials were "E."

They were, respectively, E. L. Hanley, E. M. Hanley, and E. A. Hanley.

Best selected the Ellen Hanley who was a stenographer as being his best bet. She resided in an apartment on Ninety–first Street. He made note of the address, climbed into his light, fast car, found the apartment without difficulty, jabbed his finger against the bell, and, within a second or two, heard the buzz of the electric door release. He pushed the door open, barged up a flight of stairs, and found an apartment door half open on the second floor, the figure of a young woman silhouetted against the light which came from the apartment.

"Miss Hanley?" asked Best.

"Yes, what is it ?"

"I want to talk with you."

She seemed dubious, but Best smiled amiably and pushed past her into a modest, one–room apartment.

"Nice place," said Best.

"Thank you," she said in tones of rather frigid formality. "Don't you think you're taking in quite a bit of territory?"

"What do you do for a living?" asked Best.

"Work — when I can get it."

"What are you doing now?"

"Looking for work."

"I've got it."

"Got what?"

"Work."

She stood by a soft wood table that had been stained to make it resemble mahogany. "Go on," she said, "what's the catch?"

"You're a stenographer?"

"Yes."

"Out of work?"

"Yes."

"Any relatives or dependants?"

"No, not here. I've been supporting my mother, when I had anything to send her. She's in Denver."

"That's a break," Best said.

"Why?"

"Because you're going to Denver."

"Listen, big boy, I wasn't born yesterday. If you'll come down to earth and tell me exactly what it is you're fishing for, we'll get along a lot better."

Best looked professionally serious. "I've got a job for you," he said. "It's a job I've got to send someone on personally. I want a stenographer who can take down shorthand so she can make a complete report. I'm working on a case. It doesn't matter to you what sort of a case it is. I want you to go to Denver. I want you to cover all of the hotels in Denver. I want you to look for a man named Walter Manning. If you find him, I want you to get acquainted with him. Find out what he's doing in Denver, who sent him there and who's paying his expenses. Then report to me."

Best took a card from his pocket, handed it to her.

"Oh," she said with quick interest in her voice, "a detective, huh?"

"Some people say I am."

Quick hope glean in her face. "Then it's on the square."

"What is?"

"The job."

"Of course."

Best opened a wallet, pulled out bills. "Here's money for the trip to Denver," he said. "Better take a plane. Stay at the Brown Palace Hotel. Register under your own name — Ellen Hanley. When you've finished covering the hotel registers, wire me what you find."

"But suppose he's there and not registered under his own name?"

"That won't make any difference. You just ask the question."

"When do I leave?"

"Quick as you can pick up a bag. And," said Best casually, "you'd better leave me the keys to this apartment."

"Why?"

"Because I want to use it."

"Use my apartment?"

"We might say," Best remarked, still holding open his wallet, "that I'm going to rent it."

She leaned against the table. "Listen," she said, "I've had nothing on my stomach except coffee and doughnuts for so long I'd hate to tell you about it. There's two month's rent due on the apartment. If you want it, you've got to pay that rent. If you're going to talk turkey with me, you've got to do it over a table in the restaurant downstairs, after you've advanced me enough for a sirloin steak and some longbranch potatoes. Now when do we start?"

Best grinned at her. "Now," he said.

Evelyn Rane sat in Gil Best's private office and shoved a fountain pen rapidly over a pad of legal foolscap. From the tip of the fountain pen flowed smooth signatures, each one that of Ellen Hanley, and each one matched with a surprising accuracy the signature of Ellen Hanley which that individual had signed in Dillon's private office the day before.

Best nodded approvingly. "You got it down now," he said. "Try and develop a little more speed, Evelyn."

She nodded, increased the swing of her forearm.

"A nice, smooth job," Best remarked approvingly. "I can believe that story now about the way you forged a pardon when you were sent up."

She looked up at him, a face that was neither unsophisticated, nor yet hard. Her eyes were wide, dark and mysterious. When she spoke, her voice had a soft, cooing quality.

"Gil," she, said, "please don't talk that way about me. I know it's just a joke, but someone might hear you and not know you were joking. I told you I got my gift with a pen from studying penmanship when I was a little girl. I had one of those old–fashioned professors — a relic of the gay nineties. He used to make me draw beautiful doves with flourishes of the pen. You should have seen his business cards, Gil, they were written by hand with more flourishes to the square inch than —"

Best laughed, opened the drawer of his desk, took out a printed dodger with its conventional front and profile views, its smear of fingerprints.

The photographs were those of Evelyn Rane, photographs which had been taken some five years earlier when her face held a look of cherubic innocence.

Evelyn Rane stared at the dodger. She scraped her chair back from the table, got to her feet, slid her tongue along the line of her lips.

"Gil," she said in a harsh, strained voice, "where did you get that?"

"I dug it up," he told her. "I always figured there was something fishy about that story of the old–fashioned penmanship teacher. I got you to press your hands against the glass top on the desk a month or so ago. There was a fine coating of oil on the glass. I got your fingerprint classification, and —"

"You dirty two–timing crook! You cheap tin–star, gumshoe, stool pigeon!" she blazed. "You damn blackmailing rat! What do you want? Go ahead and spill it, you've got me. What is it? What's the price?"

Gil laughed, motioned to the chair. "Sit down, Evelyn," he said, "I just wanted you to understand that we understood each other."

Her nostrils were wide now. She was breathing heavily.

"It makes such a hell of a lot of difference," the detective said, "if two people have confidence in each other. I always like to have operatives that I know I can trust. So many of them give a detective a double–cross. Now you know that you can trust me, and if anything should happen that I couldn't trust you, it would be — well, it would be too bad, that's all, because I like to trust people."

"So that's it," she said.

"That's it."

She picked up the pen again, tried to sign the name, but her hand trembled so that she could hardly hold the pen.

"Damn you," she said softly, and looked up at him, once more, with eyes that had lost their hard glitter, and were dark pools of mysterious invitation.

"You're hard, Gil," she said softly.

"I have to be," he told her, without the slightest change of expression.

He took a key ring from his pocket, slipped off a key, tossed it to her. "Take some suitcases," he said, "and move into that apartment on Ninety–first Street, the one that I gave you to use as a residence."

She stared at the key with surprised eyes. "Then that's not a phony address?" she asked.

"No," he said, "it's a real address."

"You want me to live there?"

"Yes."

"Under the name of Ellen Hanley?"

"Yes."

"Then," she said, "you think people are going to call on me."

"Right."

"But listen you boob, they'll check up on how long I've been living there."

Gil laughed. "When they do," he said, "they'll find out that Ellen Hanley has lived in that apartment for more than three months."

"Gil," she said, "you do some of the damndest things!"

He nodded and smiled. "It's my artistic temperament," he said. "I like to do everything artistically, and I hate to leave a back trail that anyone could follow."

She picked up the key, twisted it about with long, sensitive fingers. "Gil," she said, "you're hard. Just as hard as nails. You've got a polite exterior, but underneath you're ruthless as hell."

The detective grinned at her. "Let's talk about me," he said, "after you get your work done. You know what you're to do?"

"Yes."

"O.K., then. Get started."

CHAPTER THREE
Alias Ellen Henley

Evelyn Rane, with a look of suffering innocence on her wide, black eyes, stared at the frosted glass of the door for a moment, standing in such a position that her indecision would be apparent to anyone in the office who might be glancing at the ground glass panel on the door.

After a moment she knocked timidly with her gloved knuckles.

A typewriter ceased clacking. There was a period of silence during which Evelyn Rane knocked again.

There was the sound of steps back of the door. It opened, and a woman of about thirty–five surveyed Evelyn Rane with skeptical eyes.

"What is it?" she asked.

"This is Five Hundred and Three, Transportation Building?" asked Evelyn Rane.

"Yes."

"I'm Ellen Hanley."

"I don't understand."

"I sent a questionnaire here," Evelyn Rane said. "It was an application for employment. I didn't hear anything about it, so I thought I'd call in person."

The older woman frowned. "I see," she said at length. There was pity in her glance.

"I don't think you'll get any employment here," she said in a low voice.

"Oh, but I've got to see the person who received the questionnaire," Evelyn Rane said. "I can't leave a stone unturned. I thought I had answered the questions very well indeed. I must see the man who has charge of the employment, and —"

A door from an inner office jerked open. A man who wore spectacles as though they were in some way a badge of scholarship, whose face held a cherubic look of beaming good–fellowship, said: "What is it, Gertie?"

The older woman sighed, made a gesture of resignation, indicated Evelyn Rane with a wave of her hand.

"Ellen Hanley," she said.

The man in the doorway frowned. "Hanley?" he said. "Hanley ... Ellen Hanley? It seems to me that —"

The woman interrupted quickly. "Ellen Hanley," she said, "submitted a questionnaire, Mr. Wigmore. You may remember sending out a questionnaire in response to Miss Hanley's application for employment."

The man in the doorway still looked blank.

"It was a questionnaire," his secretary prompted, "to determine the qualifications of applicants for a position, and in particular, their state of health."

Sudden light dawned upon Wigmore's face. His manner became fairly beaming. He rubbed his hands together, bowed and smiled.

"Yes, yes, yes," he said. "Yes, indeed. Come right in, Miss Hanley. I remember you perfectly now. Come right into my office. Now let's see, Miss Hanley, you said, as I remember it, that you were in excellent health, did you not?"

Evelyn Rane nodded.

Wigmore's hand rested on her shoulder, slid down her arm to her elbow. With a gentle pressure he guided her toward the inner office.

"Yes, yes, yes," he said with the purring satisfaction of a cat that has just chanced upon a saucer of thick cream. "I remember you perfectly. I was very much impressed by the answers you gave me in the questionnaire. Very much impressed, indeed. Do come right in."

The tired–eyed secretary returned to the typewriter at which she had been working. Her eyes watched the door of the private office as it slammed shut. It was a good two minutes before she sighed and returned to the task of pounding the typewriter.

In the inner office, Sam Wigmore fairly oozed solicitous hospitality. He placed Evelyn Rane in a chair, nodded his head in beaming satisfaction.

"I am so glad you called," he said. "I was going to write you and ask you to call, but I kept putting it off. Now tell me, Miss Hanley, you were in an accident I believe you said. I am, of course, very much concerned about the personal health of the applicants for employment. I am afraid that an accident would incapacitate you from the rather exacting work that I require."

"I'm strong enough to stand up to anything," said Evelyn Rane.

The beaming eyes of the chief counsel for the Airline Stageways surveyed her approvingly.

"I'm quite sure you are, my dear, but would you mind standing up, flexing the elbows and knees ... Ah, that's it ... that's fine. No inhibition of motion whatever. Complete use of the limbs. And how about the lungs, my dear? Can you take a deep breath? Let's see the chest expansion ... Ah, yes, very fine, but by the way, Miss Hanley, suppose we make a good job of this while we're at it. Just be seated again, please."

Wigmore's finger jabbed down on a pearl push–button. The door to the outer office opened and his secretary surveyed the pair with eyes that held no expression, a face that was a mask.

"Ask Doctor Carr to step in here, please," said Wigmore. "Tell him that it's very important."

The secretary nodded. The door slammed.

Wigmore went on with purring complacency: "You understand that our most important positions," he said, "require women who are in good health. Of course, we wouldn't submit you to a detailed examination, my dear Miss Hanley, unless we felt that your other qualifications were quite satisfactory. In fact, I may go so far as to say that the question of your health is all that stands between you and a very remunerative situation. As I said, I was on the point of asking you to drop in, and —"

The door to the private office opened, a tall, bald–headed individual in a white coat, from the pocket of which protruded the ear pieces of a stethoscope, stepped into the office.

Wigmore got to his feet. "Bob," he said, "this is Ellen Hanley. You may remember the name. Ellen Hanley. I need only to call your attention to the fact that Miss Hanley signed a questionnaire and submitted it to us for the purpose of securing employment.

"And Miss Hanley, this is Doctor Bob Carr, one of my associates. He would like to ask you a few questions, would like to look you over. Would you mind stepping into his office with him? It will be just a superficial examination, nothing that will cause you the slightest embarrassment."

Evelyn Rane looked a trifle dazed, permitted herself to be escorted from the office. Ten minutes later the telephone rang and Bob Carr's cautious voice came over the wire to Wigmore's receptive ear.

"Listen, Sam, there's something phony about this."

"How do you mean?"

"That girl's as sound as a nut. She's *too* good. Are you sure she's the one?"

"Sure," said Wigmore enthusiastically. "We had an operative contact the woman who had been in the smash, talk it over with her and all that stuff, and the operative saw her write the letter asking for the questionnaire."

"Well, if this woman's ever been in an accident, she doesn't show it."

"Sure she doesn't, just another one of those cases, although we figured there were some pretty serious injuries. A rib punctured a lung, and the results have been pretty bad."

"Well," Doctor Carr said, "this woman's rib never punctured her lung."

Wigmore frowned thoughtfully. "Just in order to make sure," he said, "I'll send in that questionnaire. You get her to sign her name and see if the signatures check up. Find out where she's living now and I'll check back on her to make sure she's not a phony."

Wigmore hung up the telephone, pressed the buzzer for his secretary, and said: "Get that Ellen Hanley questionnaire into Doctor Carr's office right away."

Evelyn Rane, attired in the most filmy of negligees, lounged in the Ninety–first Street apartment smoking a cigarette. From time to time she looked at the watch on her left wrist, and frowned. Once she stood up, examined herself approvingly in front of the mirror, stood between the mirror and the window so that the light from the window, filtering through the thin silk, showed in frank outline the curved contours of her body.

She was smoking her third cigarette when the buzzer exploded into sound.

She promptly pressed the electric door release, gave herself one last look in the mirror, pinched out the cigarette, and when she heard a tap on the panels of the door, opened it a bare three inches.

"Why, Gil Best!" she exclaimed, "you're not due here for half an hour. I wasn't expecting you until I got some clothes on."

"I'm half an hour late," the detective said.

"Why it can't be. My watch must have stopped."

He frowned. "Come on, Bright Eyes, quit stalling and let me in."

"But I'm not dressed."

"You've got something on, haven't you?"

"Yes, but I wasn't exactly dressed to receive company."

Best muttered an exclamation, pushed the door open, walked in and sat down.

"I just this minute got out of a bath," Evelyn Rane said.

Best walked across to the davenport, sat down, stared approvingly at Evelyn Rane, then shifted his eyes from the steady insistence of her frank gaze.

"How did you come out?" he asked.

"Like I told you over the telephone. O.K."

"Did they fall for it?"

"Hook, line and sinker."

"What happened?"

"I met the guy who looks like a motion–picture parson."

"That's Wigmore."

"Yes."

"What did he do?"

"Had me kick and stretch and flex my joints. Then he called a doctor."

"A guy named Carr?"

"Yes."

"He's their regular stand–by. What did Carr do?"

She tittered and said: "He led up to it by degrees. He was interested. I was just an unsophisticated little girl. He and his office nurse went over me with a fine tooth comb, then he got suspicious and telephoned Wigmore. Wigmore sent in the questionnaire. They asked me to sign my name and write some stuff about my history, then finally the doctor came out and asked me if I'd been in an automobile accident. I told him no, that the only accident I'd referred to in the questionnaire was a street car accident where I'd received a slight strain to the ankle, but no broken bones. That was what you told me to say, wasn't it?"

"Yes. Did they fall for it?"

"It made a commotion."

"What happened?"

"The office was turned upside down. They were as busy as bees in a hive. They made me sign my name at least a dozen times, and watched me to see that I wasn't slipping anything over on them. I sold them on the idea that they'd got the questionnaire from the wrong woman. Wigmore was so mad that he damn near died. I heard him get on the telephone and fire the woman investigator who had tricked Ellen Hanley into submitting the questionnaire."

"So then what?"

"So then after the commotion had died down, I pretended to become very indignant and threatened to sue the whole outfit for damages because they had tricked me and trifled with me. I told them I saw it all now, that it was all a plant, and I accused Doctor Carr of faking the whole examination so that he could get my clothes off and paw me over. You should have seen his face when I pulled that one. It was as red as a boiled beet."

"So then what?"

"So then they offered me a job at a hundred dollars a month. I laughed at them. They offered me a job at a hundred and fifty.

"I demanded five hundred for a cash settlement, and then I pulled a fast one."

"What was it?"

Evelyn Rane glanced coyly at the eager detective as she continued. "I reached out and picked up the questionnaire off Doctor Carr's desk and stuck it in my purse. I told them I was going to save it for evidence."

"Good girl."

"I could see," she went on, "that the thing that bothered the doctor the most, was the talk about professional intimacies. I spread it on thick."

"Did they make a settlement?"

"No, they wouldn't make a cash settlement. They offered me a job."

Best held out his hand. "Where's the questionnaire?" he said.

She crossed to the table, opened her purse, took out a folded paper, handed it to the detective.

Best read it over. As he read, he shook his head lugubriously.

"The damn little fool," he said.

He shoved the questionnaire into his pocket. "They got your address?"

"Yes."

"They'll be checking up on you."

"I know it."

"Think you can bluff it out all right?"

"Sure."

"Don't let them get your fingerprints."

"Think I was born yesterday? They're frightened now — afraid that they're going to run into a damage suit."

"They may have been for awhile," Best said, and grinned, "but when Wigmore gets to figuring out that the net result of all this business was that he lost the questionnaire which was his biggest piece of evidence against Ellen Hanley, he'll smell a pretty big rat. They'll come around and check you up. If they find you're not Ellen Hanley, they'll probably talk about arresting you for larceny of the paper."

"Larceny my eye," she said, "I folded it up right in front of their noses, and I've still got that charge of unprofessional conduct against Doctor Carr."

"That bothered them?" Best asked.

"That bothers them."

Best got to his feet, reached for his hat.

"Aw stick around awhile, Gil, you're not going."

Gil Best pointed to the ashtray with the two cigarette stubs, the third half–smoked cigarette. "Next time," he said, "that you just get out of a bath, don't smoke two and a half cigarettes while you're waiting for the bell to ring."

He moved toward the door.

Evelyn Rane came after him like a tiger. The silk negligee flowed out behind her, her face white, her eyes dark with rage.

"Damn you, Gil Best," she said, "what are you insinuating? What kind of a girl do you think I am? I don't have to put up with your dirty cracks just because —"

He opened the door, turned back to look at her, and smiled approvingly. "A damn good line," he said. "Save it for the boys from the Airline Stageways."

When he had closed the door, she stood staring at it for several seconds, then ran to the davenport, flung herself down on her face and sobbed, long–drawn, convulsive sobs that shook every inch of her frame.

CHAPTER FOUR
Shyster Trap

Gilbert Best's secretary imitated the cooingly sweet notes of the telephone operator.

"Long–distance call for Mr. Samuel C. Wigmore," she said. "Is Mr. Wigmore there?"

"Yes," said a feminine voice. "Who's calling?"

"A party named Manning. Will you put Mr. Wigmore on the line?"

"Is Mr. Manning on?"

"Yes."

"Very well. Hold the line."

A moment later, Wigmore's voice said cautiously: "Hello, what is it?"

Best, seated on the edge of his desk, with a French telephone held to his ear, said in a strained voice: "You know who this is, Mr. Wigmore."

"Who is it?"

"I don't like to mention names but you know, I'm the driver of the stage."

There was still silence over the wire. "You know — Walter Manning," Best blurted.

"What is it you want?" Wigmore asked.

"Listen," Best said, letting his voice rattle in the swift utterance of one who is excited and afraid, "there's a couple of process servers snooping around. They have found out where I am. In some way, there's been a leak somewhere. I'm going to go someplace away from here and make it snappy. Can you tell me where to go?"

"You're sure they're after you?"

"Yes, I'm sure. I can't tell you everything over the telephone. You tell me some place to go, and then I'll report from there."

"Can you get away O.K.?"

"Yes, I think so."

There was a period of silence, during which the wire buzzed with faint static noises. Then there was the rustle of paper.

"You can get a train out of there at three five. Go to Big Springs and register at the Palace Hotel."

"Do you think I'd better use the same name?" asked Best.

"No. Register under the name of Pete Freeman, from San Francisco."

"O.K. You'll have to send me some money."

The voice at the other end of the wire rasped into harsh impatience. "Money, hell!" said Wigmore. "We've been doing nothing but sending you money! What the hell do you think you're pulling?"

"Listen," Best said, putting a whining note into his voice, "you haven't sent me so much, and it's expensive, being on the dodge this way. And that ain't all. A guy told me the other day that claimed to know, that you folks figured to string me along with a lot of promises and keep me out of the way until after the trial, and then you were going to tie a can to me and turn me loose."

"That's all baloney. You know we're standing back of you. We don't blame you."

"I know, but it makes me nervous just the same, and I've got to travel. I had a little bad luck yesterday. You know, sitting around here without anything to do gets monotonous. I got in a poker game and lost some — not much — but some. I've got to have some money if I'm going to travel."

Wigmore's voice was fairly quivering with rage. "You keep out of poker games!" he said. "What you're trying to do is stick us up. You think we're afraid of your testimony, and you can stick us. Now, you try anything like that and you're likely to wind up in jail. And don't think I'm kidding, either!"

"I'm not trying anything like that, but a guy's got to have expense money, hasn't he?"

"I'll send you a check for a hundred dollars and that's got to last you for a week."

"Gee, that Big Springs place is expensive. Ain't that kind of a resort?"

"Not at this season of the year. You get down there and there'll be a check for a hundred dollars in the mail."

"Now listen," Best said, "that's a strange place. I'll get my mail under the name of Pete Freeman, but if I go to the bank to cash a check, it's got to be under the name of Walter Manning, because that's the way my driving license is made out and all of my credentials."

"Sure," Wigmore said, "I understand that. You catch that train and keep out of poker games. What's more, you'd better have some confidence in the company and not listen to all this line of hooey that's handed you."

He banged the receiver back on the line, and Gilbert Best dropped his own receiver, signaled to his secretary to sever the connection.

He grinned at the secretary. "Get me," he said, "time tables of all lines that run into Big Springs. Check back on the trains in all directions and segregate those that have station stops at five minutes past three in the afternoon. Get a description of Walter Manning from the application for driver's license on file in the Motor Vehicle Department. Send an operative to any of the places where trains that run to Big Springs stop at five minutes past three in the afternoon. Cover the hotels until you find a man answering the description of Walter Manning. He'll be registered under an assumed name. He'll be a man who's hanging around the hotel, more or less. He could be contacted in the lobby of the hotel. Get an operative who can contact him and build up an acquaintanceship. Manning will be hungry for companionship."

His secretary nodded efficiently. "Anything else?"

"Yes, take a wire to Ellen Hanley at the Brown Palace Hotel, Denver, Colorado, tell her to go by plane to Big Springs at once and register under her own name at the Palace Hotel there. Tell her to await further instructions. Get me some cash and my traveling bag."

"Where are you going?"

"The Palace Hotel at Big Springs," he said. "If you want me, you can reach me under the name of Pete Freeman. That's the name that I'll be registered under. I'm going down there to work on a case."

The Big Springs resort was favorably known among vacationists. During the height of the summer season every available accommodation would be taken. Now the Palace Hotel was operating at approximately one quarter of its normal capacity.

Gilbert Best registered at the hotel under the name of Pete Freeman.

"Mail?" he asked.

The clerk thumbed through a pile of letters, took out a long envelope which bore no more definite information as to the identity of the sender than the fact that it came from Room 503 in the Transportation Building.

Best took the letter to his room, slit the envelope and took out the letter addressed to Pete Freeman at the Palace Hotel at Big Springs.

The letter was written in a slightly more conciliatory tone than had marked Wigmore's conversation. It enclosed a check of Airline Stageways, Inc., payable to the order of Walter Manning, in the sum of one hundred dollars. It went on to assure the addressee that his cooperation was being keenly appreciated; that the company would endeavor to reciprocate in the future; that it would not much longer be necessary for Mr. Freeman to remain "in seclusion," and that the writer appreciated the strain of inactivity, but went on to mention the importance of retaining good employment in these days of almost universal unemployment.

It was a cordial, friendly letter, one that was well designed to appeal to both friendship and loyalty.

It was signed with the scrawling signature of Sam C. Wigmore.

Best placed the letter in his inside coat pocket, reached for his telephone, and, when he heard the voice of the operator on the wire, said: "I'm expecting a young woman by the name of Hanley to register at the hotel. When she does, please notify me at once."

He then took off his shoes, coat and vest, tossed pillows up on his bed, stretched out at luxurious ease and proceeded to read a magazine.

Toward evening, Best telephoned his office, learned that operatives had contacted a man who answered the description of Walter Manning, who was registered at the Cosmopolitan Hotel at Pleasantville under the name of Charles Allen. The operatives had already established a contact. Allen was lonely and anxious for human companionship.

Best gave terse instructions. "Send a wire," he said, "to Charles Allen at the Cosmopolitan Hotel at Pleasantville that will say, simply: 'Unforeseen developments necessitate your immediate departure. Go Palace Hotel Big Springs, register under name of Pete Freeman and await further instructions.' Sign the telegram — 'Sam Wigmore'."

He hung up the telephone, switched on the lights and had finished bathing and dressing when he received word that Ellen Hanley had arrived and was in Room 309.

Best grinned into the telephone. "An unexpected change in my plans," he said, "is going to necessitate my departure this evening. Will you arrange to have my bill ready, please."

Then Best walked down the corridor and tapped on the door of 309.

After an interval, the door opened and Ellen Hanley's face broke into a smile of welcome.

"Come in," she said. "I had a great trip. Gee, it's swell, riding around in planes. I never got so much kick out of anything in my life! I thought I'd be frightened, but I wasn't. It's simply swell. And they tell me that it's just as safe as traveling by automobile."

Gilbert Best entered her room, sat down on the edge of the bed, lit a cigarette.

"Sometime tomorrow," he said, "a man's going to register here by the name of Freeman. I want you to get acquainted with him and then start going out with him."

"Do I try to find out anything from him?"

"No, just be friendly with him. Keep playing around with him. Go places and string him along."

"And don't try to find out anything?"

"Not a thing."

"Anything else?"

"Just wait for instructions."

"This," she observed, "is the swellest job I ever had in my life."

"Get a kick out of it, sister," he told her, "because it ain't going to last long."

He returned to his own room, to find the telephone ringing. His office was on the line. His secretary said: "Mr. Dillon, the lawyer, rang up and said that you could discontinue work on that Airline Stageway case because he already had the matter well in hand."

The detective's laugh was scornful. "You ring up Dillon," he said, "and tell him that he hasn't got anything in hand and that if he compromises that case before he sees me tomorrow, he's going to be the sorriest mortal in the world."

He hung up the receiver, crossed to the desk, took out some of the hotel stationery and scrawled a note addressed to Sam C. Wigmore at 503 Transportation Building.

> Dear sir: — You may not know it, but Ellen Hanley is registered at this hotel. She's the real Ellen Hanley that you want, and if you want to know where she is, you'll find her playing around with a man who's registered here as Pete Freeman. I don't mind seeing that you are double-crossed, but I hate to see you paying for the privilege. If you don't believe what I say, send one of your men down here to make a check or telephone the house detective. Never mind who I am. I'm just a friend who likes to see fair play.

Best sealed the letter in an addressed envelope, took it to the desk.

'Will this go out tonight?" he asked. "No, not until tomorrow morning," the clerk told him.

Best grinned and dropped the letter into the mail box.

CHAPTER FIVE
Compromise

Gilbert Best shoved his way through the door marked *Frank C. Dillon — Attorney At Law — Office Hours 10:00 to 12:00 — 2:00 to 4:30 — Entrance.* Norma Pelton's teeth flashed in a smile.

"How's the girl?" asked Best.

"Fine as silk, Gil. What's the good word?"

"Oh, so–so. What's Dillon doing? Is he busy?"

"He's been having a lot of telephone calls from Wigmore. He's virtually got that case compromised."

"Yeah?"

"Yeah. He's sore at you."

"Why?"

"He thinks that you got him when he was pretty low and stuck him for a bunch of money to handle a case that was a cinch anyway."

"Yeah," Best said. "Tell him that I'm going in."

"You mean that you're here in the office?"

"No, that I'm going in."

"He won't like that."

"You mean he'd like to keep me waiting for ten or fifteen minutes."

The eyes twinkled. "Well, I didn't say exactly that."

Best snorted. "Tell him," he said, "that I'm on my way in."

He strode across the office, pushed open the door marked, *Private*, crossed the law library and heard Dillon's voice registering protest in the telephone transmitter before he was halfway across the office.

Best timed his entrance to the private office to coincide with the banging of the receiver back on its hook.

"You've got a crust, busting in on me when I'm busy," said Dillon.

"Oh, were you busy?"

"Of course I'm busy. I'm busy trying to make up some of that money you swindled me out of."

"Meaning what?" asked Best, his eyes cold.

"Meaning that I had a cinch case against the Airline Stageways, and you went ahead and threw a scare into me and made me put up a lot of money to pay you for doing a bunch of stuff that was unnecessary. And, worse than that, you made me kick through to support that Hanley woman in idleness."

"She's got a cough," Best said. "She should go down to Arizona or some place for awhile."

"Well, I've got a compromise through for her. She can go to Arizona or any place."

"Oh, you've got a compromise through?"

"Yes."

"How much?"

"Well," said Dillon, "I don't know as it's any of your particular affair, because I haven't seen that you've done anything very wonderful on the case, but, just between us, it's a compromise of twenty thousand dollars."

"How much is your fee?" asked the detective.

"That," said Dillon in tones of positive finality, "is none of your damn business."

Best grinned, and said: "When you wanted me in on the case, you mentioned you had lost ten thousand dollars on a compromise that was figured at twenty thousand. That leads me to believe you've got her sewed up for a fifty–percent fee."

"What if I have?" Dillon demanded. "Best, I'm getting damn tired of the way you do things. You could be a good detective if you'd follow instructions and confine yourself to doing the things you're told to do. But you take in too much territory. You want to tell me how I am going to try my cases, how I am going to deal with my clients. You want to bust in here unannounced. You want to be the big shot in this business, and you can't make it stick."

"Oh, can't I?"

"No, you can't."

"And you've compromised for twenty thousand?"

"Yes."

"Didn't you get my message telling you not to?"

"It happens," said the lawyer with paunchy dignity, "that I am responsible to my clients for handling matters to their satisfaction and protecting their interests. When I start taking orders from a private detective, I want to know it."

"So you didn't think you needed me?"

"No, I didn't."

"Don't think I did you any good?"

"Not a damn bit. I know you didn't. Wigmore said he had intended to compromise all along for twenty thousand, but that the matter had slipped his mind because the file had been misplaced in his office. He said he was satisfied there was a real injury there and that he wanted my client to have sufficient money to restore her to health."

The detective sighed. "Just when I thought," he said, "I was doing you some good."

"You weren't," Dillon said. "You should pay me back the money that I advanced to you."

Best looked at the floor with a woebegone expression.

Dillon elaborated upon the idea he had expressed and warmed to his task as he grew more indignant.

"You stuck me for a bunch of money for my client and for seven hundred and fifty dollars as a retainer for your services. It was out of all reason. You didn't do a thing for the money. I probably could have you jailed for obtaining money under false representations. As a detective, you're a frost — a pain in the neck. You had some luck in a couple of cases you handled for me, and like a fool, I thought it was due to your ability. The amount of money you stuck me on this thing was simply outrageous, and I'm telling you frankly, Best, I want it back."

"Aw, gee, you wouldn't make trouble for me over a lousy seven hundred and fifty bucks, would you?"

"It isn't the seven hundred and fifty dollars so much, as it is the principle of the thing," Dillon declared. "I want that money back."

Best hesitated, pulled out his wallet. "It will leave me cleaned," he said.

Dillon laughed sarcastically. "Just as I thought," he said. "You pocketed the whole money and haven't even spent a cent of it on expenses."

Best said nothing, counted out seven hundred and fifty dollars in cash from his wallet, then opened the wallet to show the lawyer the interior.

"Just three one–dollar bills left," he said.

Dillon held out his clammy hand for the money.

"Wait a minute," Best said. "If you're going to deal that way, I'm going to have a receipt for this money, and a complete release of any claim for what I've done in that case."

Dillon nodded, jammed his finger on the button which summoned his secretary. When Norma Pelton entered the office, Dillon said: "Make out a receipt right away to Gilbert Best, for seven hundred and fifty dollars, show that the receipt is by way of complete settlement of any claim I may have against him for an overcharge, or obtaining money under false representation."

Norma Pelton looked surprised.

"Also put in there," Best said, "that by accepting the money, Dillon waives any benefit that might accrue to him from my services, and I agree not to make any charge against him for anything I've done."

Norma Pelton's blue eyes regarded Gilbert Best with thoughtful speculation. The detective's right eye drooped in a slow, significant wink.

Norma Pelton suddenly turned away. "Very well," she said.

She left the door open to the outer office. The men glowered at each other in silence while her typewriter exploded into clack noise, then she jerked the paper from the typewriter, brought it to the inner office.

Dillon read it and nodded. He took out his fountain pen. "Seven hundred and fifty bucks, Best," he said.

Best passed the money across, as Dillon signed the receipt; he pocketed the paper and got up to go.

"I'm sorry," Best said, "that you feel I didn't do anything. I thought I did a lot."

"I don't know what you could have done," Dillon said, "the compromise was concluded along the original lines that I'd discussed with Wigmore."

"Well," Best said drawlingly, "you'd always claimed that Wigmore cut corners and pulled shyster tactics in his cases. You wanted to get some dope on him, but you'd never been able to do it. I've got some proof that he spirited away this witness, Manning. I've got a letter signed by Wigmore and a check for a hundred dollars made out by the Airline Stageways, and charged on the stub to legal expense, a check that is referred to in Wigmore's letter, and show that it was sent to this witness, Manning, in order to keep him out of sight, and intimates that he's to suborn perjury if he has to, in order to keep his job. Then I've found Walter Manning and had a subpoena served on him so that he'll have to appear and testify, and managed to make Wigmore think Manning had double–crossed him so that he won't have anything to do with Manning anymore and is shivering in his boots for fear the whole thing is going before the grand jury."

Frank Dillon heaved his paunchy figure from the chair, his mouth was sagging open, his eyes were bugged out in startled surprise.

"You've got *what?*" he yelled.

"Sure," Best said, pulling the papers from his pocket, holding them in his hand. "There's Wigmore's signature on the letter, there's the original uncashed check payable to Walter Manning, here's the questionnaire that they tricked Ellen Hanley into signing, with her signature on it.

"They may have reached a compromise, but a compromise isn't binding until the releases have been signed, and the money paid over. They can back out of a compromise anytime they want to."

"What do you mean?" Dillon demanded. "What are you intending to do?"

"Why," Best said, "I'm going over to the Airline Stage of course, and see how much Wigmore will pay to get this questionnaire back. That's the plaintiff's signature on it all right, and she says in there plain as day that she received only superficial injuries in the accident, and has had a complete recovery. And then, of course, Wigmore should pay something to get that letter back that he wrote to Walter Manning. He wrote that sort of hastily, and it might look kind of bad for him if it was taken up before the Bar Association."

"Good God!" said Dillon. He tried to talk, but could only make pawing motions with his hands. He dropped back into his chair, and finally found words.

"Get Wigmore on the telephone, Norma," he said. "Get him right away. Tell him that my client simply refuses to consider a twenty–thousand–dollar compromise. Tell him that we won't settle for a cent less than a hundred thousand dollars ... No, you get him on the line. I'll talk to him myself. Put through the call right away. Good God, to think that I almost lost forty thousand dollars. Why, I'd have settled for twenty. As it is now, he'll pay a hundred. He'll have to pay in order to get that stuff back."

Best stretched and yawned. "I wouldn't turn down that twenty–thousand–dollar compromise, Dillon," he said.

The lawyer snorted. "That shows," he said, "what a dumb boob you are. You certainly are lucky, that's all. Damned if I know how you do it. It's just luck, it can't be brains. Why you poor boob, Wigmore has got to give almost anything I ask to get that letter back."

"Yeah," said Best, "I understand that, but what I meant was that you ain't got the letter, and when Wigmore gets that letter back, and the questionnaire signed by Ellen Hanley, he won't even compromise for twenty thousand bucks. He won't pay you a damn cent. That's why I didn't think it would be wise for you to turn down that twenty–thousand compromise."

The detective pulled open the door of the law library, and at that moment the telephone on Dillon's desk exploded into noise.

Dillon made clawing motions at the air, as though trying to pull the detective back with his right hand, his left reached for the telephone.

"Hello ... For God's sake, Best don't go! ... Hello, yes Wigmore ... Hold the line. For God's sake, Best listen! ... No, no, Wigmore, I can't tell you ... Yes, I asked my secretary to get you, but ... For God's sake, Best! ... Best! ... Best! ..."

The detective by that time had crossed the outer office. He tipped Norma Pelton a wink. "The big stuffed shirt," he said.

There was the sound of running steps. The paunchy lawyer waddled into the room, his face the color of ashes.

"For God's sake, Gil, old kid," he said, "don't treat me like this. Don't turn me down. I'll give you anything you want."

"No," Best said, "our business relations are at an end. The work I did on the case wasn't done for you, it was freelance work. I can sell it to the highest bidder."

"But I'll bid for it," Dillon said. "My God, I'll give you five thousand dollars."

"Wigmore," said Best, "would probably give me fifty. It would get him out of a jam personally, and enable him to get rid of that Hanley case without paying out anything by way of compromise."

"No, no, no, you don't understand —"

Best turned to face Dillon.

"Listen," he said, "you big stuffed shirt, I know you like a book. You four—flushing, loud—mouthed, grandstander, now here's once you're going to talk turkey. If you want that letter from Wigmore and that questionnaire, you're going to agree that you won't charge Ellen Manley more than twenty percent of whatever amount you receive, and you're going to pay me twenty percent. The rest of the money is to go to her."

Norma Pelton looked up from the switchboard. "Mr. Wigmore is still on the line," she said. "He's sputtering —"

Dillon danced up and down in an ecstasy of rage. "You damn robber!" he shouted. "You damn —"

Best started for the door. Dillon lunged for him, flung his arms around the detective's shoulders, looked imploringly at Norma Pelton.

"For God's sake, Norma," he said, "tell him to wait."

The flabby hands tugged at the detective's shoulders.

"Come on in, Gil old kid," he said. "I'll play ball with you. Come on in."

Best turned, vanished through the door marked, *Private*, with the lawyer pushing along behind him.

It was fifteen minutes later when Best emerged from the office.

"How's tricks?" asked Norma Pelton.

Best grinned at her. "Pretty good. I told Dillon that I heard he'd been reducing wages because business was bad. I told him I thought business was picking up with him."

She grinned. "What did he say?"

"You listened in on the conversation with Wigmore?"

"Yes. It was the funniest thing I ever heard in my life."

"Well," Best said, "to make a long story short, that ten—percent cut becomes a twenty—percent increase."

"I could kiss you," she said, "if I weren't afraid you'd take it seriously."

Gilbert Best strode toward the desk.

The switchboard buzzed into activity and Norma Pelton started to plug a line into Dillon's phone.

"The boss wants me," she said.

Best leaned over, jerked the plug out of her fingers, tilted her face to his. "Let him wait," he said. "The stuffed shirt."

Complete Designs

Peter B. Strickland looked like a typical salesman as he barged toward the desk marked "INFORMATION." That was because John Du Nord had insisted the employees were not to know a detective had been consulted.

"Mr. Du Nord," he said.

The blue eyes behind the telephone switchboard grew slightly scornful as they drifted over Pete Strickland's massive frame, and rested momentarily on the battered, leather sample case.

"Mr. Jocelyn does all the buying," she said, "and his hours are two to three-thirty."

Strickland sighed wearily, the sigh of one who has learned not to expect too much of his fellow men. It would, after all, be just in the nature of things that Du Nord should go to all the trouble to impress upon the agency that the detective they sent, to cover the case, must keep his identity sufficiently concealed to fool the employees, and then make no arrangements by which the man could be received, without disclosing his errand and the nature of his business.

Yet there was no rancor in Pete Strickland's manner, just a great weariness, a resignation to mediocrity.

He fished a leather card case from his pocket, took out a card, held it so the girl at the desk couldn't see it.

"An envelope?" he asked.

She hesitated a moment, then with curiosity in her eyes, handed him an envelope. "We can take your card in," she said, "but it won't do any good."

Strickland pushed the card into the envelope, carefully sealed the flap into place.

"Take that," he said, "to Mr. Du Nord. Tell him I've got a special proposition to make him."

"Mr. Jocelyn," she began, "is —"

"Mr. John C. Du Nord," Strickland interrupted, and there was something in the impact of his eyes upon hers which led her to press a button without further comment. A sluggish office boy lounged into view from around the corner.

"Mr. Du Nord," she snapped at him and thrust the sealed envelope into the boy's hand.

The boy flashed Strickland a glance filled with the insolence that only youth can muster, and listlessly vanished around the corridor.

Ten seconds later there was a swirl of motion. A short, paunchy individual with the manner of one who is restlessly pushing time before him, as the bow of a steamer pushes up water, propelled his bulging stomach toward Strickland with piston–like strides of short, active legs.

"I hope I didn't keep you waiting," he said. "Come right in. Come right in."

Strickland's voice held a note of warning.

"Got some fine price bargains," he said, as he stooped for his worn, leather sample case.

Du Nord looked puzzled for a moment, then nodded his head in vehement assent.

"Oh yes. Yes, of course," he bubbled with too much emphasis and too much cordiality. "Of course, of course, come right in, Strickland. Come right in."

The blue eyes of the girl back of the telephone board turned to the baffled countenance of the office boy. She pursed her lips in a silent whistle and said "Gee," in an awed undertone.

From which it was to be inferred that John Du Nord reserved such effusive courtesy only for bank presidents and the buyers of the largest customers.

Du Nord bustled down a corridor, flung open a door and said, "Step right inside, Strickland."

Pete Strickland looked around him at the big desk, the thick oriental rugs, the massive leather chairs. His eye spotted the envelope in which his card had been enclosed, and on it, the card itself.

He fished a leather card case from his pocket.

"Hope you don't mind," he said to Mr. Du Nord, picking up the card and replacing it in the card case. "The agency makes us pay for our cards out of our own pockets, and I'm Scotch."

Du Nord laughed nervously, adjusted himself in a big, swivel chair, motioned Strickland to a seat.

"I take it," he said, "the agency manager has told you why you are here. We've got four of the highest priced garment designers in the business. They work in a room which is isolated. Each one of the four is above suspicion. Their finished designs go into our vault. Aside from Mrs. Carver and myself, three employees have access to those vaults. There is a very definite leak in our proposed designs. I happen to know that in at least two instances they've been in the hands of our competitors within twenty–four hours of their approval by us."

Du Nord's glasses quivered with indignation.

The president of the Du Nord Sincere Service Stores could consider a leak in his organization as a major catastrophe. To Pete Strickland it was just another case.

"Who's this Mrs. Carver?" he asked.

Du Nord's eye beamed.

"A most wonderful woman," he said, "a psychologist. She has charge of our personnel and placement. It's surprising what she can tell about you just from looking at you. Most of your work on the case will be with her. In fact, I've got to leave within half an hour. My son arrives from Paris. He's taking a trip to the Orient. He arrives on the *President Coolidge*."

Pete Strickland made polite conversation.

"Going to be here for awhile before he starts for the Orient?" he asked.

"No, he sails on the same boat," Du Nord cleared his throat, and went on hastily, "He's young, impressionable. I want him to take the tour to get perspective. There was a woman in Paris — wanted his money, of course. It was serious — Dane intended to marry her."

Du Nord jammed a suddenly savage thumb against a bell button.

Almost immediately a swinging door was pushed open by a woman, a pair of granite hard eyes surveyed Pete Strickland in swift appraisal, a pair of hands that seemed about ten years older than the face, made swiftly fluttering gestures, a voice that rattled effortlessly from between two layers of even, glistening teeth, struck Strickland's ears with the rapid fire rattle of a boy running a stick along the pickets of a fence.

"Don't tell me who you are; I know. I can tell from the slow appraisal of your eyes. I can tell from the cynical twist at the corner of your lips, and yet you're not the type I expected at all. I would think a detective would be more the deductive type. Your training was acquired. You didn't take up the profession because of a natural aptitude. It shows in a hundred unconscious mannerisms. You're a big man, physically strong. You hold your hands awkwardly, as though you didn't know what to do with them. That's merely the external manifestation of a subconscious condition. You have learned to make a livelihood by deductive reasoning. You are naturally fitted to engage in a business calling for more physical activity. Therefore, your mind finds your body in the way. It's too big, too strong — that's the reason you hold your hands the way you do."

She stopped, stepped back, tilted her head from side to side, as a canary might appraise a dish of bird seed, nodded her head and smiled in self–satisfied triumph.

"See that!" exclaimed Du Nord triumphantly. "Isn't that wonderful? Give her one of your cards, Strickland, and see how much she can tell about you from your business card."

Strickland took a card from his card case, handed it to her. Mrs. Carver pounced upon it, held it in her bony–fingered, blue–veined hand.

"Ha," she said. "Scotch — economical — this card has been used several times — very loyal to your employers — self effacing — that's apparent from the modest manner in which you have the name, 'Peter B. Strickland,' down in the left hand corner, while the words 'MANUFACTURER'S INVESTIGATING BUREAU' are prominently displayed."

Strickland nodded, reached for the card, took it from her hand and replaced it in his case.

"Oh," she beamed, "I was just joking about the Scotch part; that's an old joke."

"It ain't a joke with me, ma'am," Strickland said, "the agency makes us pay for our own cards."

She laughed, flashed a glance at Du Nord.

"And tell me, Mr. Strickland," she said, "do *you* go in for the study of applied psychology?"

"Not the way you do," he said, "mine's sort of a rule of thumb business. The man on the street didn't know what psychology was when I was getting my education."

She graciously indicated a chair, snapped her left elbow into a position to consult her wristwatch, rattled on with swift efficiency. "Sit down, Mr. Strickland. Mr. Du Nord, your boat docks in exactly twenty–seven minutes. I have instructed your chauffeur to be in readiness at the Market Street entrance, and —"

She broke off abruptly, glanced through the glass partitions of the office to a corridor where a young woman with very blue eyes, an impertinent nose, and a chin that was tilted aggressively forward, was walking with quick purposeful steps.

"Quick," she said, "look at her, Mr. Strickland, that's the one. That's Anita Lyle. Note the characteristics of the clenched hands as she walks. That shows a furtive disposition. That shape of the nose indicates one who wants the good things of life and doesn't care how she gets them. She's the one you've got to convict. She's the one that did it."

Du Nord frowned as the swiftly walking figure vanished beyond the edge of the glass partition.

"She's got her hat on. What's she doing going out? I wanted her to be here so Mr. Strickland could observe her habits, and arrange a plan of campaign."

"We can't help it," Mrs. Carver said. "It's not her afternoon off under our new schedule of hours, but she had traded with one of the other girls. She said she wanted to get off particularly this afternoon, and I couldn't have upset the arrangement with out making her suspicious."

Both of them looked at Strickland. Strickland said nothing.

"You tell him, Mrs. Carver," Du Nord said.

Mrs. Carver needed no second invitation; her voice rattled on Strickland's eardrums.

"There are three of the trusted employees," she said, "who have access to the vaults. Anita Lyle, Nell Brent and Mabel Walker — those are the only three. We know that one of them must be dishonest. I made a test of their honesty. I left rings in the wash–room, a purse on the sidewalk. I slipped an extra twenty dollar bill in Anita Lyle's cash drawer, so that her cash would be twenty dollars over at night. All of them responded satisfactorily to the honesty test except Anita. She didn't report an overage in cash. Therefore, she was dishonest and kept the money. To my mind, the evidence is conclusive. It's up to you now to catch her red handed."

"If you know who it is," Strickland said, "why not fire her?"

"We can't; she's under contract. She'd sue us. We've got to have something specific."

"Maybe it's a leak from the designing room," Strickland suggested.

"It can't be. The designers are well paid and above suspicion. They work at a long table under the constant supervision of a foreman. Even the wastebaskets are not emptied into the general hopper, but the contents are collected and burnt. Jacqueline — that s my own daughter — has charge of the room; I mean keeping it clean and so forth. After the designs are created, they're submitted to us for approval. Those we approve are placed in the vault.

"No, Mr. Strickland, unfortunately there can't be the slightest doubt about the identity of the culprit. The habit of walking with clenched hands shows a furtive, secretive disposition. If she had been honest she would have reported the cash overage. My applied psychology has definitely picked out the criminal for you. It's up to you to get the evidence to convict her."

"Maybe someone slipped the twenty out of the cash drawer before she made up the cash," Strickland suggested.

Mrs. Carver's significant, scornful silence branded the remark as being puerile.

"If you'll step this way," she said, "I'll show you the room where the designers work ... Ah, there's my daughter now. *Jacqueline!* Jacqueline, come here please. Yes, step right in this way."

A slender girl with a flat chest, her mother's eyes, and a quick restlessness of manner, which had also been inherited, opened the door just far enough to enable her slender body to slip into the private office.

"Jacqueline," said Mrs. Carver, "this is —" She broke off, as an office boy carrying a file of papers entered through another door. She frowned at the office boy, paused for words, then had a sudden inspiration.

"Show her your card," she said to Strickland.

Strickland sighed once more, took a card from his card case, and handed it to the young woman.

Jacqueline Carver studied the card. Her face showed sudden comprehension.

"Oh," she said, and nodded, then set the card down on a corner of Du Nord's desk.

"I understand," she said.

Strickland leaned forward, retrieved the card, started to put it back in the card case, then frowned as he saw a black, grease–like smear on the back of the card. He ran his thumb over it in frowning contemplation, sighed, and dropped the card into the wastebasket.

Mrs. Carver tittered.

"So sorry," she said, "it only did its duty twice, didn't it, Mr. Strickland?"

"Three times," he corrected her. "I sent it in to Mr. Du Nord — and I guess I hadn't better leave it around in the wastebasket either."

He leaned forward, picked up the card, and pushed it carelessly into his side pocket. Jacqueline Carver inspected her right hand, frowned, and scrubbed at the fingers with a handkerchief, wiping a black smudge from her right thumb.

"I'm so sorry," she said. "I've been greasing my typewriter."

"I want you to show Mr. Strickland the designing room," said Mrs. Carver. "Make it snappy, Jacqueline, because Mr. Du Nord is going to the boat to meet his son. I think it might be well for Mr. Strickland to ride down as far as the dock in

Mr. Du Nord's car. They can talk during the trip. You see," she explained to Strickland, "Mr. Du Nord has an important appointment at four o'clock, and that won't leave him much time to see Dane and get back from the boat."

Strickland nodded, permitted himself to be led like some big Newfoundland dog, along a glass enclosed passageway, to a room, the door of which was locked. Jacqueline Carver selected a key, unlocked the door. Four men seated at a long table looked up.

The table, covered with green imitation leather, held taut by wooden strips screwed along the side, was illuminated by huge drop–lights. In front of each of the men was a sheet of paper, fastened to the table by thumb tacks. The table itself was littered with pages clipped from fashion magazines with photographs of smart women.

"You see," said Jacqueline, "they work in absolute privacy. The best points of all the styles are combined and then submitted to Mr. Du Nord himself for approval. It's all very confidential."

Strickland nodded, turned away from the door.

"Yeah," he said, and looked at his wristwatch.

"Don't worry," said Jacqueline, with the quick efficiency so characteristic of her mother, "I am watching the time. You will have plenty of time for your conference with Mr. Du Nord. And there goes Nell Brent. She's another of the possible suspects, only mother says she responded okay to the honesty test."

Strickland looked through the partition window at a tall woman who, suddenly becoming conscious of his appraisal, flushed a bright scarlet.

"Looks like she knows who I am," he said, "and why I'm here."

Jacqueline Carver tittered. "Mother says you can't disguise a detective — she does look guilty, doesn't she?"

Strickland grunted.

Du Nord grew confidential as the huge limousine purred down Market Street.

"Part of the credit for this," he said, "should go to Mrs. Carver, but personally, I think it's a fine scheme. It's rather a clever trap —"

"Listen," Strickland said, "I'm a rule of thumb detective. I don't judge people by the fact that they walk with their hands closed, or the shape of their noses. I like to get evidence before I accuse anybody of crime. There is a crook somewhere in your organization. Those dishonesty tests don't mean a thing — particularly that one you tried on the girl you suspect. The real crook must be smart enough to know what's going on in the joint. She could have taken the twenty bucks out of the cash drawer before cash was made up in the evening."

Du Nord nodded, leaned forward.

"To some extent," he said, "I agree with you."

"What I'm trying to tell you," Strickland blurted, "is that I sympathize with that Anita girl."

"No, no," Du Nord said, "you mustn't do that. She's beautiful, magnetic, attractive. You mustn't be influenced by that."

"I'm not influenced by that, I'm influenced by the fact you're all picking on her without giving her a chance to defend herself."

"Well," Du Nord said, "I've thought up an idea of my own. It's so confidential that I'm not even telling Mrs. Carver about it, and she knows everything that I do."

"What's the idea?" Strickland inquired.

"A crook," said Du Nord, "is dishonest. A crook is after money. A crook who would sell me out to my competitors here, would be that much more eager to sell out information to a foreign competitor. I have some very valuable process secrets that are in my vault. I have decided to get a clever man to impersonate a foreign buyer. I am going to arrange things so that Anita Lyle will be called back to work tonight. She will actually catch this man rifling the vault. If she is dishonest, she will make him a proposition to share in his profits if she turns him loose; otherwise, she will report him. That generally is my scheme. The point is, do you speak a foreign language, Strickland?"

Strickland sighed.

"I don't speak a foreign language," he said. "In fact, I don't even speak *your* language."

Du Nord frowned.

"That," he said, with an edge to his voice, "makes you unavailable. I shall have to get someone else. Good heavens — my son! I can use Dane. No one will know him. He has foreign labels on his baggage and speaks French like a native."

Strickland sighed.

"While you're doing all that," he said, "would you mind getting me a screw driver?"

"A screw driver? You mean now?"

"No," said Strickland, "when we get back to the plant."

The big liner nosed its way into the dock, a blunt–nosed tug pushing at the bow to overcome the effect of the swirling tide at the stern. Men and women waved arms, handkerchiefs and hats.

Du Nord gripped Strickland's arm, waved frantically.

"There he is," he said, "up on the boat deck, with the binoculars. He's looking the crowd over — looking for us. Hi, there, Dane! Here I am, Dane — down here. Hello — hellooo!"

Strickland nodded.

"Good looking boy," he said.

The lenses of the binoculars swung down, fastened upon them in appraisal. The young man took off his hat, waved it frantically. The father dislodged his glasses, juggled his paunch as he waved his arms in almost hysterical violence.

The detective watched the thin figure of the young man as the binoculars were lowered, listened to the shouted greetings lost in the hoarse bellow of a roaring steam whistle. Then, as the boat edged in closer to the dock, as lines thudded to the pier and winches started warping the ship through the last few feet of water, to snug it up against the pier, Strickland saw the lenses of Dane Du Nord's binoculars swinging about in the casual appraisal of a curious tourist anxious to be home, curious to look over the faces of his fellow countrymen, in search, not so much of a familiar face, as to feast upon the general familiarity of all faces — the kinship of a country.

Abruptly, the lenses fastened in rigid, steady appraisal. There was a swirl of motion in the back of the crowd. Pete Strickland saw a young woman, with firmly clenched, defiant little fists, slipping rapidly through the open door, to the interior of the huge shed. She was almost running.

The detective's finger started to tap Du Nord on the shoulder then was arrested mid—motion. Slowly, the huge, awkward hand dropped back to his side.

"When we get back to the plant," he said, "don't forget that screw driver."

Pete Strickland groped, with his big, awkward hand, for the ringing telephone. The instrument was cold to his touch. He pressed the receiver to his ear and said in a thick voice. "Yeah?"

The voice of the manager of the detective agency smote his eardrum in a metallic rattle. Strickland was advised to get out of bed and down to the main office of the Du Nord Sincere Service Stores. Hell, it seemed, had broken loose. Burglar alarms were ringing. The police were rushing reserves down, and Du Nord, himself, was hysterical.

Strickland made tasting noises with his mouth.

"Okay, chief," he said. "God, I got an acid stomach! Yeah, I'll get down there right away. I got the flivver in the garage. G'bye."

He groped for and found the light, got into his clothes in the wearily philosophical manner of one who is accustomed to midnight emergency calls, flivvered through the fog—swept streets to the side entrance of the Du Nord Sincere Service Stores.

A police radio car was at the curb. A watchman at the door scrutinized Strickland's badge and moved to one side. Strickland's big feet pounded down an echoing corridor, the midnight silence contrasting to the humming activity of the daylight hours. Lights blazed in an office on the mezzanine floor. Strickland wearily climbed the stairs.

Du Nord was standing in front of a safe door. Lights shone upon a glistening array of nickeled knobs, shining wheels. To one side was the grimly disapproving countenance of Mrs. Carver, her blue eyes staring reproachfully at the excitement—distorted features of the president of the company.

Strickland arrived in the middle of Du Nord's impassioned explanation.

"... my own son! He just arrived on the boat today. He's spent the last year in France. I left orders that the vault wasn't to be locked tonight and arranged that the party we suspected was to be sent to the store by Mrs. Carver on an errand. I didn't take Mrs. Carver fully into my confidence as to the scheme. My son was to be caught by this person in the vaults, apparently having mastered the combination. And now they're both in there — shut in!"

"What is it?" asked the radio officer. "A time lock?"

"No, no, no," Du Nord explained hastily. "There's a time lock on the outer door, but it's open. See? We can open it."

He pulled back the massive doors.

"It's the inner sealed doors. There's an inner and an outer lock, so that a person in the vault couldn't be surprised by thieves. It's locked from the inside. Can't you see what's happened? She's killing him or something. She won't come out."

Du Nord ran to the door and banged on the metal with his fists. One of the officers pounded with a night stick.

"She's trapped him in there! Killed him!" Du Lord screamed. "Break the doors down! Do something!"

One of the officers inspected the doors.

"Had this vault made to order?" he asked.

"Yes."

"Better get a representative of the manufacturer and see if an acetylene torch will cut through them."

He banged once more on the doors with the point of his night stick.

"You're trapped!" he shouted. "We'll cut through the doors with a torch if we have to. If you're alive, come out!"

Mrs. Carver gave a gasp.

"Perhaps," she said, "it's murder and suicide."

She had hardly spoken when there was the sound of a rasping bolt. The doors swung open. Those who had been prepared to see the evidences of murder stood dumbfounded before the pair who stood in the entrance to the vault. Dane Du Nord, his eyes beaming with a strange, misty happiness, stood with his arm around Anita Lyle, whose lips were half parted, revealing the tips of her teeth. Her shoulders heaved with her breathing, as though she had been running.

"Damn it, Dad!" said Dane Du Nord. "You took her away from me once — you can't do it again! Let us out of here! We're looking for a preacher."

"Stop!" Du Nord cried. "She's a thief! We have the proof."

Pete Strickland pushed his way forward.

"Can I say something?" he asked in a voice that was strangely without emotion.

Perhaps it was the very lack of emotion in his voice which compelled attention. They turned to him.

"That little stunt of mine," he said, "about the cards, is something I always use on a job to get fingerprints. The cards are coated with stuff that gives me the prints of the people who handle them. I always seem to give the same card out two or three times. I don't — I put it back in my case and give out another one. You take on a job of this kind, people like Mrs. Carver and Mr. Du Nord would resent it if I asked for their fingerprints. So I use the card trick. Of course, I don't get a complete set of ten fingerprints, but I get enough to get a pretty general classification of the kind of prints, loops, arches, whorls or composites.

"You folks figured the designs had been stolen after they got in the vault. I wasn't so certain; particularly after I handed one of my cards to Jacqueline Carver, and when she handed it back there was a smear on the back that was oily to the touch — something like graphite. I pretended to think it wasn't of any importance, but I knew right away it came from a very soft carbon paper that had smeared on her thumb.

"So I got a screw driver, and when I got an opportunity, after we came back from the boat and the designers had gone home, slipped into the room, unscrewed the strips that held the imitation leather cover in place on the designing table and found just what I'd expected — a whole bunch of soft carbon paper underneath.

"There were fingerprints on the carbon paper. They all came from the same person — Jacqueline Carver."

"What?" screamed Du Nord.

Strickland nodded gloomily.

"Fact," he said.

"Why didn't you tell me?" Du Nord asked. "Why didn't you report immediately?"

"Because," Strickland said, "I wanted to find out whether she was working alone," and he glanced meaningly toward Mrs. Carver. "Of course, we can probably get it out of her by using a little — persuasion, but if you hadn't forced my hand I'd have been able to give you a complete report tomorrow. I'm telling you now because of Miss Lyle.

"And you'd better be sort of careful how you treat her, because she'd have a suit against you for defamation of character if you went too far.

"Personally, I don't go for this fancy psychological stuff. Maybe people clench their hands when they're trying to conceal something, but they also clench them when they're mad or when they're getting a rotten deal, or when they're determined to do something.

"Now maybe this Anita Lyle knew that the father of the man she loved disapproved of her, and she decided she'd get a job in his company and work so hard that he'd have to respect her. And all that time, the man's son was chasing around Paris, trying to find what had happened to the woman he loved, and then when the son finally did show up to report to his father, the girl got some time off and sneaked down to steal just one heart–hungry glance at him.

"You see, it hadn't been easy going for her. She tried to make the man's father respect her, but there had been a psychological expert in charge of the personnel, who hadn't liked the way this girl had made herself almost invaluable in the business, and this psychological expert had a daughter. And that's why the poor kid walked around with her fists clenched."

Strickland ceased speaking, raised his arms above his head and sucked in a prodigious lungful of breath as he yawned. "So," he said wearily, "I guess I can go back and get the rest of my sleep. God, but my stomach's sour! You can't get jerked out of bed and —"

Mrs. Carver, who had been glowering at him with speechless indignation, shrilled into high-voiced accusation.

"It's all some kind of frame-up! You and this creature framed —"

Strickland's big forefinger, rigidly extended, stabbed at her chest.

"Look out, sister," he said, "you've got your hands clenched. That's a sign of secretiveness, you know."

Barney Killigen

Charlotte Ray came into my office, and her eyes looked as though she'd been crying. "I swear," she said, "I don't know what's going to become of that man, Miss Graham."

She dropped into a chair and slammed the big office checkbook down on the desk.

"Overdrawn again?" I asked.

"Overdrawn!" she exclaimed. "Overdrawn is no name for it! Last month we took in five thousand two hundred and sixty–four dollars and nineteen cents. We should have had a balance of two thousand six hundred and four dollars and thirty–two cents, and the bank's sent me a notice that we're overdrawn three hundred and forty–two dollars and seven cents."

"Banks are so heartless," I said sympathetically.

Charlotte Ray took life seriously, and she took our bank account more seriously than life. Frosty haired, tight lipped, austere, she acknowledged forty–seven summers, and I had a shrewd suspicion that she was passing up about fifty percent of the winters. However, she could certainly keep books, and she could handle the income tax as well as anybody could with Killigen's finances.

Killigen came in while Miss Ray was still sitting there.

"Hello, everybody," he said, cheerfully tossing his hat at the hatrack in the corner, and pausing with his hand on the knob of the mahogany door marked *Mr. Killigen, Private.* "Cheer up, Miss Ray; it's only the twenty–fifth of the month. There won't be any bills to pay for another six days." He grinned at me.

"I suppose," she said acidly, "it wouldn't interest you to know that you have absolutely nothing with which to pay any bills."

"Not in the least," he told her, grinning.

"Moreover, I've just received a notice from the bank that you're overdrawn again."

"Fine," he said. "Some people have a checkerboard career. I have checkerboard finances — all black and red."

She couldn't take his kidding. She turned away, blinking back tears.

"Why *can't* you be sensible?" she pleaded. "When you want to draw money, why don't you let me check it out of the account? In that way we can at least keep the account balanced."

Killigen seemed to be giving the idea grave consideration. "How would that help?" he asked.

"Can't you see?" she said. "I'm trying to keep the books of this business. You sign checks and scatter them around like confetti at New Year's. I think we have money in the bank, and it turns out we're broke. You might at least tell me when you draw a check. Then we wouldn't have overdrafts."

"How much are we overdrawn?" Killigen asked.

"Three hundred and forty–two dollars and seven cents."

"Now then, let's see," Barney said. "Under your system, we wouldn't be overdrawn, isn't that right?"

"Yes, that's right."

"In other words, when I wanted money, I'd come to you and get it."

A ray of hope showed in her face. "That's right."

"And under those circumstances, you'd have stopped me drawing out that last three hundred and forty–two dollars and seven cents?"

"Exactly," she said.

"In that event," Killigen said, "I'd have been poorer by three hundred and forty–two dollars and seven cents, or looking at it the other way, the bank would have had that much more money, and I'd have had that much less. Therefore, Miss Ray, it seems to me you should be working for the bank instead of me. Under the circumstances, *I* think our system is excellent."

He walked on into his private office, and left us sitting there, Miss Ray looking as though she were on the verge of hysterics.

"I swear," she said, "I never saw a man like that in my life. Of all the irresponsible, scatterbrained individuals, he's the worst."

"Well," I said, "there's one satisfaction. He doesn't have a huge pay roll to meet."

"Well, he has us two," she said. "I don't know how you feel about your salary, but I want mine on the first, and — and there isn't anything to pay it with — there never is."

"Cheer up," I told her. "We always get it before the tenth. He'll turn up something. He always does."

She found that I wasn't going to sympathize with her so she picked up her checkbook and went back to the outer office. A few minutes later, she rang my phone and announced that a Mrs. Frank Whiting was waiting in the outer office to see Mr. Killigen on a matter of the greatest importance.

I put on my best office manner and went out to see if Mrs. Frank Whiting offered any possibilities of ready money.

One look at her and I knew the answer was negative.

Her hands were the hands of a woman who has worked all her life. Her face had the drab expression of one who has forgotten how to laugh; her eyes looked at me with pathetic resignation. I've seen the same expression in the eyes of a dog that had been whipped too much, by too many different people.

"Good morning," I said. "I'm Miss Graham, Mr. Killigen's private secretary. You wanted to see him?"

She didn't have any objections to telling me her business, which was another sign she didn't represent ready money. People who intend to pay a reasonable retainer always at least go through the motions of refusing to talk to a secretary.

"Yes," she said, "I wanted to see Mr. Killigen. They say he is very sympathetic and understanding."

"He's all of that," I told her. "What did you want to see him about?"

"My daughter."

"What about your daughter?"

"She's been arrested, charged with burglary — and my daughter's honest. She *couldn't* be guilty. Of course, she's living in a different age from what I did when I was a girl, and things are different, but —"

"Just a moment," I said. "I'll tell Mr. Killigen you're here, and see if he wishes to talk with you."

"Oh, thank you *so much*," she said.

Charlotte Ray caught my eye, and made a wry grimace, as though she'd bit into a lemon.

That's a funny thing about the bookkeeping complex. It never occurs to a bookkeeper that clients are human, and that fees represent one phase or another of human misery. All a bookkeeper can see is figures, marching in columns down ledger pages.

I walked past her, through my office, and into Killigen's. He was seated, tilted back in his swivel chair, his feet up on the desk. He looked up at me over the sporting page of the morning newspaper, and said:

"Hi, Wiggy. Want to bet on the ball game?"

When I first started to work for Barney Killigen, I'd put the dictating marks on his letters, "BK:wig," the "Wig" standing for Winifred Ilsa Graham; and so Killigen started calling me "Wig." Later on he made it "Wiggy." I'd become so accustomed to it, I considered it my real name.

"No takers," I told him.

"This is a swell bet."

"Not for me, it isn't," I said.

"You're getting too conservative," he told me. "I think it's association with Miss Ray that's made you that way."

"I came to tell you there's a client in the outer office."

He grinned. "I hope that cheered Miss Ray up, Wiggy."

"You should be more considerate," I said. "She's more loyal to you than you are to her."

"Quite possibly," he admitted, "that's true, but she worries too damn much. I don't like to worry. It would make me lose my spontaneity, and that wouldn't be so good for my business."

"But," I said, "you *could* be more considerate. Charlotte Ray deals in figures; they're her life. Your casual offhand manner in regard to money is bad enough, but when you throw her balance all out, that's worse. I suppose you've been gambling."

"Gambling?" he said, arching his eyebrows. "Why, no."

"I gather," I said, "that outside of your regular expenses, you've written some twenty–five hundred dollars' worth of checks in the last thirty days."

"I suppose so," he admitted casually, as though dismissing a minor matter, unworthy of serious consideration.

"That," I told him, "sounds like gambling to me."

"It isn't," he protested. "Mostly it was charity."

"Charity?" I asked.

"Uh–huh. I got interested in some of the boys who were laid off when the sash and box mill closed down."

"How in the world did you get interested in *them?*" I asked.

"I don't know," he said; "just dropped in on a meeting — natural curiosity, I guess. They're awfully nice people. You know, Wiggy, we make a mistake looking on laborers as laborers and businessmen as capitalists. We forget that we're all human beings and, down underneath, all American citizens."

"Well," I said, "the first of the month is rapidly approaching, and a Mrs. Frank Whiting is waiting in the outer office. Mrs. Whiting has neither looks nor per–sonality. Moreover, she has no cash, connections, or sex appeal. Her daughter has been arrested for burglary. Mrs. Whiting doesn't look as though she could be the least bit of financial help to you in connection with your overdraft. However, I have on occasion seen you perform startling feats of financial legerdemain with the juice of a turnip. The point I'm getting at, however, is that Mrs. Whiting's troubles are very, very serious to Mrs. Whiting."

"Naturally," he said, "they would be. What does she look like?"

"Late forties," I told him. "She looks as though she'd been taking in washing ever since she was twenty. The world has kicked her around, this way and that. She quit fighting back at least ten years ago."

"Look as though she had any friends who had money?" Barney Killigen asked.

"No. She probably had to hock something to raise the carfare to come downtown."

"I'll see her," Killigen said.

He folded the sporting page of the newspaper, opened the right–hand top drawer of his desk, and dropped the sheet in.

"That," I protested, "is your important drawer. It contains correspondence I've been weeding out for the last two weeks. Things which really require your immediate answer."

"You wouldn't expect anything to be more important than the sporting page, would you?" he asked, in surprise.

I quit arguing with him. What was the use?

I went out and brought Mrs. Whiting in. Then I eased out of Killigen's private office and gently closed the door behind me.

If the woman had had money and the ability to take life in her stride, I don't think Barney Killigen would even have wasted time talking with her. As it was, I could hear the rumble of his voice, from time to time, and the thin, reedy notes of hers. I couldn't distinguish words; all I could get was tones and the mutter of conversation through the door.

I could have told her one thing: if Barney Killigen took her case, he'd get results. Heaven knows how he'd get them, or what they'd be. He does things in a weirdly unconventional manner. No one can ever predict what he's going to do next, least of all Killigen. He has an instinct for the dramatic, an uncanny ability to make his buildups seem convincing, and an unfailing faith in the power of classified advertising in the newspapers. I never could figure whether he delighted in ac— complishing a logical result by utterly illogical means or whether the means really were logical, and it was simply the unconventional inhibitions of my mind which made them seem utterly ridiculous at the time.

Of late, I'd begun to suspect the latter as being the case, because, on occasion, I could see some real underlying reason for some of the things Barney Killigen was doing, when Charlotte Ray would feel the man should be committed to an institution.

II.

Barney Killigen called for me to come in and take notes when Mrs. Whiting had been closeted with him for about fifteen minutes.

"Wiggy," he said, "I'm accepting employment from Mrs. Frank Whiting to represent her daughter Estelle. Estelle Whiting is accused of first degree burglary. Now, Mrs. Whiting, I'm going to dictate some notes to my secretary. I want you to listen carefully, and if anything I say is incorrect, correct me."

She nodded and Barney Killigen started to dictate:

"Mrs. Dwight Chester–Smith's son, Dwight Chester–Smith, II., was married Monday night at the Chester–Smith home. It was also the bride's birthday. Wedding and birthday presents were in a room on the second floor and were guarded by Robert Lame, a private detective. Sometime, shortly after midnight, a man pushed a ladder against the building and noiselessly climbed to the window of the room in which the wedding presents had been placed. Lame, the detective, was just finishing a midnight lunch he had brought with him — sandwiches and coffee from a Thermos bottle. The robber pushed his head over the sill, smashed in the glass of the window with the muzzle of a revolver, commanded Lame to stick them up. Lame had no chance to go for his gun. The man reached through the broken windowpane, unlocked the window, raised it, entered the room, and cracked Lame over the head with a blackjack. Lame fell to the floor, unconscious.

"It is, of course, assumed that the burglar collected his loot while Lame was unconscious. It just happened that one of the guests heard the crash of glass and started an investigation. The burglar evidently heard people approaching the room and hurriedly grabbed up some of the more valuable presents and thrust them in his coat pocket. Then he climbed out of the window and down the ladder. An accomplice was waiting for him at the bottom of the ladder. Lame regained consciousness before the robber and his accomplice had reached the car. He staggered to his feet, pulled his gun, lurched to the window, and saw a man and a woman running, carrying a ladder with them. He opened fire with his revolver. The couple jumped in a car and made their escape. Lame reports he was able to make out the first four characters on the license plate. They were 'IVI3 —'

"Estelle Whiting, Mrs. Whiting's daughter, spent the evening in company with James Grayson, the young man with whom she has been going. She says, and Grayson says, that he took her home about midnight. Mrs. Whiting didn't hear her come in, doesn't know what time she arrived. Estelle got up Tuesday morning and went to work as usual at Cutter & Baggs Department Store. She says that Jimmy Grayson called on her about ten Tuesday morning, very much excited, and presented her with a beautiful engagement ring, a large white diamond surrounded by emeralds. He told her a man to whom he'd loaned some money years ago had struck it rich and had given him this ring in payment. Police arrested Estelle about two hours ago, and claim she was the young woman who held the ladder and assisted Jimmy Grayson in perpetrating the robbery."

Barney Killigen paused, and I caught up on the last few words, held my pencil poised, and glanced up at Mrs. Whiting to see if she had any comments to offer.

"That's right," she said, "but you've forgotten about the burglar having a hole in his pocket, haven't you?"

"That's right, I did," Killigen said. "Make a note of this, Wiggy. It's a peculiarly suspicious circumstance. The police are acting on the theory that the burglar, rattled by the sound of persons approaching, hurriedly pushed the gems into his coat pocket. That pocket had a hole. The gems spilled out as he and his accomplice ran, carrying a ladder."

Mrs. Whiting said, in the voice of woman who has suffered so many of life's vicissitudes that she has learned to take grief as a matter of daily routine: "I guess that's all. That's everything I've been able to find out from the newspapers, talking with the detective, and the few minutes' visit they gave me with Estelle."

"And she's being held in jail?"

"Yes. They fixed her bail at fifteen thousand dollars."

"Now then, do you know exactly what's missing?" Killigen asked.

"No, I don't. I know there's ten thousand dollars in cash and this ring, and they found some stuff there in the driveway which the man dropped when he was running to the car."

"There was ten thousand in cash?" Barney Killigen asked.

"That's what they tell me. A rich uncle gave one hundred hundred—dollar bills — that makes ten thousand dollars."

Barney Killigen frowned and said musingly: "That's the irony of fate. Had the burglar been affluent, he would have worn a coat which didn't have a hole in the pocket; but, because of the very poverty which forced him to resort to burglary, he was deprived of the property he'd taken. What does Jimmy Grayson say about that hole in the pocket of his coat?"

"I don't know what he says; I haven't talked with *him.*"

"Do you know if he has a lawyer?"

"No, I don't."

"Well," Killigen said, "I'll do what I can for your daughter. Don't worry about her."

"I suppose," she said, picking up the purse which lay on her lap, "you'll want a retainer. I've been saving some money — not much, but putting away a little here and there."

She started counting out one dollar bills. Giving her roll a hasty appraisal, I figured there couldn't have been over thirty or forty dollars in it.

Barney Killigen brushed her offer aside with a gesture. "Don't worry about fees," he said; "not right now, anyway. How did you happen to consult me?"

"I heard you helped people out when they were in trouble and sort of fixed your fees according to what a body had. Now, I haven't much except what I can take in from my washing, and I don't know about Estelle's job. I'm afraid even if you prove she didn't do it, she won't have any job left because —"

Barney Killigen swung out of the office chair, crossed over to pat her reassuringly on the shoulder.

"That's all right, Mrs. Whiting," he said. "Just quit worrying. I'll take care of your daughter. Anything which can humanly be done, I'll do."

"Don't forget the hearing comes up day after tomorrow," she said, "and they're going to put on a lot of testimony —"

"I won't forget it," he assured her, as he escorted her through the door. And his confidence was so contagious that he had her smiling before the door closed. He turned back to me and danced a little jig on the carpeted floor. "Tell Charlotte Ray the good news," he said. "Tell her to wipe the grim, tight lipped expression off her face. Tell her to sweep the gloom bugs into the wastebasket. Tell her to ring up the bank and notify it —"

"That you've accepted a case from a woman who hasn't to exceed thirty—five dollars in the world?" I asked dryly.

"Now, Wiggy," he said reproachfully. "That's not like you. You're more of *my* type. That caustic, sarcastic, cynical crack would have been more becoming to Miss Ray than you. Good heavens, girl, it's six days until the first of the month, and here we are plunged right into the middle of a case which is attracting all sorts of public attention! A burglary in the Four Hundred — people who are reeking with wealth have lost some of their dough — a girl is snatched from behind the counter of a department store and dragged down to jail, because her sweetheart gave her an engagement ring! Think of the human interest! Think of the sob sister stories! Think of the —"

"But just *how* do you expect to make any coin out of the case?" I interrupted.

He looked at me in surprise. "How should I know? I'm not a prophet. I'm just an opportunist. Don't worry. A way will open up. How about you and me having a little drink in celebration?"

"O.K. by me," I surrendered, "but don't make it too heavy because it's early in the morning, and I have to transcribe these notes."

"Bless your soul," he said. "You don't have to transcribe those notes. I just dictated them for the moral effect. It helps to reassure a client if he feels you're taking down all the facts for future reference and study. How about four fingers of Scotch?"

"Two," I said firmly.

"We'll compromise on three," he said.

Charlotte Ray came in on us as we were just getting ready to drink. Barney Killigen raised his glass.

"What ho!" he said. "Success! Prosperity! Wealth is just around the corner! Quit worrying about your bank account. Quit bothering about your books. Within the next forty–eight hours — as the police love to express it — I shall pour wealth into our coffers. You can walk down to the bank and make a deposit so big —"

She looked at me in stern disapproval. Charlotte Ray knew her office conventions. The idea of a secretary drinking with the boss at eleven o'clock in the morning was more than a violation of the conventions. It was sheer sacrilege. "In the meantime," she said dryly, "the cashier of the bank has telephoned and requests me to advise him just what we expect to do about this overdraft."

"What we expect to do with it?" Barney Killigen echoed. "Why, we expect to pay it — of course."

"I believe he'll be quite relieved to hear that," she said. "He'll probably ask when."

"Tell him," Barney Killigen said, "that I have a five thousand dollar retainer fee I'm bringing down to deposit within a day or two, that I'm too busy to get down to the bank now."

I saw her face flush with pleasure. "A five thousand dollar retainer?" she said. Killigen nodded.

"Give it to me," she said, "and I'll deposit it right away and —"

"Not so fast," he told her, "not so fast. I always like to carry a little pocket money with me; and then it's good discipline for the banks to wait. Tell them we'll make a deposit on Thursday, or Friday, but tell them in the meantime please not to bother us with trivial matters. Tell them I've had much larger overdrafts than this."

She said: "The overdraft has been increased by two hundred dollars. Another check came through this morning. The cashier says unless we can give him satisfactory assurances, he won't cash any more checks, and, furthermore, he says this is absolutely the last overdraft the bank will ever tolerate."

"He's said that before," Barney Killigen said, tossing off the last of his whisky. "It does seem to me he'd find something new to say. He's like the police — completely lacking in originality.

"And now, Miss Ray, you'll pardon me for finishing this drink without offering you one? I've just had one with Wiggy. Do you feel I should have one with you?"

"A drink!" she exclaimed. "At this time in the morning!"

"Why, certainly," Barney Killigen said, "or, if you think it's too early, we can wait for five minutes — well, five minutes is perhaps too long. We could wait, say, two minutes, Miss Ray."

She turned and started for the outer office, her chin up in the air.

"Don't let a mere overdraft interfere with your carousal," she said acidly.

When the door had slammed, Barney Killigen looked at me and sighed. "That," he said, "is the way with conventional people. They have no sense of adaptability. All right. Wiggy, get your nose powdered and your lipstick distributed evenly and regularly because you and I are going out and look things over."

"You need me with you?" I asked.

"Of course," he said. "I simply can't concentrate without having you along to talk to. I think out loud better than I just think — just thinking is so damned unsociable, you know, and I crave society and companionship for my cerebrations."

"Shall I put a shorthand notebook in my purse?"

"Have you got room for that whisky?" he asked.

I looked at the flask and shook my head.

"Well, then," he said resignedly, "make it a shorthand notebook."

III.

On occasion, Barney Killigen could be as plausible as a politician explaining a broken election promise, and to the butler at Mrs. Dwight Chester–Smith's home, he was disarmingly polite. "I suppose," he said, "Mrs. Chester–Smith has left orders that she is not to be disturbed in connection with the unfortunate affair of a few nights ago."

"Quite right," the butler said frostily.

"Under those circumstances," Killigen observed, "you may show us around. You look like a man of more than average intelligence, and I don't think it will be necessary for us to disturb Mrs. Chester–Smith. In fact, I promise you that I won't do so except upon a matter of the greatest importance."

"What did you wish to see?" the butler asked.

"First," Killigen said, "we'll take a look at the place where the jewels, which were recovered, were found. We'll take a look at the place where the ladder was placed against the side of the house, and then we'll take a look at the room itself."

The butler said: "Really, these things have been gone over time and time again."

"Of course," Killigen said, with just the right air of authority in his voice, "if you wish to insist upon my calling Mrs. Chester–Smith, I can do so."

The butler gulped a couple of times, then said, "Very well sir, step this way, please."

He led us out around the house to the north side.

Killigen said: "There's soft ground in the spaded flower bed. Doubtless there were tracks?"

"No footprints, sir," the butler said, "but the marks of the ladder, yes."

"We'll take a look at them," Barney Killigen said. "I presume they've been photographed?"

"Indeed, yes," the butler said.

We bent over the indentations in the soft, muddy soil pointed out to us by the butler. There were two of these indentations in the form of perfectly marked out–lines where the ends of two–by–fours had been pushed into the soil. They were spaced about eighteen inches apart. The one on the left flared out just a trifle to the east, the one on the right a trifle to the west. "Ah, yes," Killigen said, in that suave, courteous tone which indicated absolutely nothing of his thoughts. "And now where were the gems found? Right along this driveway?"

"Yes, sir. They were found scattered along here as though they'd been dropped in flight. Although they weren't exactly on the driveway, they were slightly to one side."

"On the right or the left?" Barney asked.

"Some on one side. Some on the other."

"I see. You couldn't point out the exact spot where the things were found, could you?"

"Some of them," the butler said. "Over here the diamond necklace given by Mr. and Mrs. C. William Pennybaker was lying in the grass. Over here was a platinum wrist watch, a gift from the groom's uncle, William Dewitt Huntley."

"Ah, yes," Killigen said, "the wrist watch. And what was the condition of the wrist watch? Was it running, or —"

"No, sir; it had evidently hit something rather solid when it was dropped. The crystal was broken, and I understand expensive repairs are necessary to put it in order. It's a dastardly outrage, if you're asking me, sir."

"Quite right," Killigen said, "and, at the same time, quite wrong."

"I beg your pardon, sir?"

"I meant to say," Killigen observed, "that it undoubtedly is an outrage, and that I'm not asking you."

The butler flushed, started to say something, then checked himself.

"And now," Killigen said, "we'll take a look at the room where the crime was committed."

"I beg your pardon, sir," the butler said, "but this has been gone over time and time again. Would you mind explaining the necessity of this visit?"

"Mind?" Barney Killigen exploded. "Of course I'd mind!"

"But it seems so unusual, sir. After the complete investigation, which —"

"Get Mrs. Chester–Smith at once," Barney Killigen said, fixing the butler with a cold eye.

"Mrs. Chester–Smith has left orders that she's not to be disturbed under any circumstances. She is already —"

"Get Mrs. Chester–Smith at once," Killigen repeated, "or I'll get her myself," and he strode toward the house.

The butler broke into a jog trot to keep up, explaining, expostulating, and apologizing; but Killigen was adamant. At length, the butler gave in.

"Very good, sir. If you'll be seated for just a moment, sir, I'll get Mrs. Chester–Smith."

He was back in a few minutes with a woman in the late forties, who regarded us as though we were some sort of insects, stuck with pins, and mounted on cards. Her facial expression was naturally haughty; her hands glinted as they moved. Diamonds sparkled from her earrings. She took to diamonds as naturally as a duck takes to water. Called on for a two word description, one would have said, "Diamonds and dignity" — and that would just about have covered the woman's character.

"I'm afraid," Killigen said, "I shall have to report your servant for insolence. He —"

"You'll do nothing of the sort," she interrupted. "Armstrong tells me that he has been most patient with you, and most considerate, and I have no reason to doubt his word. You police are assuming altogether too much authority. If you would put in half of the time trying to recover my property, which you have taken in snooping around the premises, you —"

"I *beg* your pardon," Barney Killigen interrupted, "but I'm not from the police."

"Not from the police!" she exclaimed.

"Why, certainly not," Killigen said. "I'm an attorney, and I certainly never intimated that I was from the police. I was afraid your butler might have thought I was passing myself off as an officer — which is one of the reasons I insisted he call you. I don't mind a servant being a bit cheeky, but when he presumes to confuse an honest criminal lawyer with a policeman, he's becoming too damned insolent."

The butler stared, agape.

Mrs. Chester–Smith said, in a voice filled with loathing, "A criminal lawyer?"

"But I certainly *thought* he was from the police, madam," the butler said.

"Come, come," Killigen remarked briskly; "you had absolutely no grounds for any such assumption."

"He started right in, ordering me around, just like the police do," the butler explained to Mrs. Chester–Smith.

"It's absolutely outrageous," she said. "I never heard anything like it. Whom do you represent, Mr. — er —"

"Killigen," Barney Killigen said. "Here's one of my cards."

"And whom do you represent, Mr. Killigen?"

"Estelle Whiting, the young woman who has been falsely accused of this crime."

Mrs. Chester–Smith's eyes flashed. Her face darkened. "Do I understand that you intend to try to acquit *that* woman?"

"Yes."

"Get out," she said chokingly, pointing an imperious finger in the direction of the door. "Out at once! Out of this house! Out!"

Killigen said affably: "And because I understand, Mrs. Chester–Smith, that you intend to absent yourself during the trial, so the common herd won't have an opportunity to gawk at your aristocratic features, I am herewith serving a subpoena upon you to be in court at the day and date therein designated, to testify as a witness on behalf of the defendant."

Barney Killigen whipped a folded oblong of paper from his pocket and pushed it into her hand. She dashed it to the floor, stamped on it. The butler moved ominously forward.

Barney Killigen squared himself to face the butler. "Of course," he said quietly, "if you want to start playing rough, Armstrong —"

Evidently Armstrong didn't. He looked at Mrs. Chester–Smith for instructions, and, receiving none, stood perfectly still, not wishing to retreat, yet afraid to go forward.

Barney Killigen said to Mrs. Dwight Chester–Smith: "The service of the subpoena was complete, Mrs. Chester–Smith, when I placed the document in your hands. Any disobedience will be a contempt of court. I feel quite certain you don't want *that* to happen. Come, Wiggy; we'll leave."

I was afraid the woman was going to burst a blood vessel before we reached the door.

"Scum! Shyster! Crook!" she screamed. "I'll have you disbarred. I'll — I'll —"

Barney Killigen held the door open for me.

"Fat people," he said calmly, and apparently apropos of nothing, "should never excite themselves. It's quite a strain on the heart. Promise me you won't ever get fat, Wiggy."

"I won't," I promised him, as we filed out.

And Barney Killigen, beating the butler to it by a fraction of a second, was the one to slam the door with such violence it shook the side of the building.

IV.

Barney Killigen sat tilted back in his swivel chair, his feet on the corner of the desk. A lighted cigarette was held in his fingers, but he wasn't smoking it; instead he was holding it where he could watch the smoke spiral upward. It was his theory that watching a thin stream of smoke spiraling upward was conducive to concentration. Formerly he had used an incense burner, but now he found cigarettes more convenient.

On the desk, in front of him, were three or four pieces of thin glass, slightly curved and broken, with irregular, jagged edges. The outer surface was coated with silver.

"What in the world," I said, as I stared at the broken glass, "are you doing with that?"

He looked up and grinned, that peculiar, boyish grin which indicated he was thoroughly enjoying life.

"I am engaged," he said, "in solving the burglary of Mrs. Dwight Chester–Smith's exclusive residence."

"You look like it," I told him. "I have some bad news. Do you want it now or later?"

"Now," he said, "and all in a lump. I'm just in the mood for bad news. I can shake it off as a dog shakes off raindrops. Give it to me in large doses, begin in the middle, and work simultaneously toward both ends. In other words, don't break it to me gently, hit me with a wallop."

"Jimmy Grayson," I said, "is an ex–convict."

"How do you know?"

"I picked it up from a friend of mine, who is in the Bureau of Identification."

"Male or female?" he asked sharply.

"Female," I said. "A stenographer. She wasn't betraying any particular confidence. The D. A.'s office is going to announce it in the newspapers."

"That's fine."

"What is?" I asked. "About his being a criminal?"

"No," Killigen said, "about your friend being a female. If it had been a male, I'd have either had to fire *you*, or shoot *him*. Either alternative would have been disagreeable."

"Why the violence?" I asked.

"Information is a two edged sword," he said. "Sometimes you're giving information when you think you're getting it. You can control your tongue with another woman, but you can't do it when you're talking to a man — not if you're sweet on him."

"Well," I said, "I'm not sweet on anybody. I'm heart–whole and fancy–free."

"Wonderful," he said, and his eyes were back on the curved fragments of glass on his desk, his thoughts evidently far away.

"Would you mind if I asked what that glass has to do with the burglary?" I inquired.

"I found these pieces of glass by the side of the driveway," he said. "I fancy there were more of them, but the butler was so irritatingly suspicious that I didn't have an opportunity to make any further investigation. I think we'll rush some want ads to the afternoon editions, Wiggy."

That was invariably a sign of Barney Killigen's cerebrations. He'd work around on a case for a while, playing with some angle no one else would ever consider as having any possible bearing on the case, and then suddenly he'd put want ads in the newspapers, asking for some of the weirdest things. Yet, by the time the case came up for trial, he usually had a plan of campaign laid out, so completely unconventional, so wildly unorthodox, that anyone who didn't know the mechanism of his chain lightning mind would have thought that only the most insane combination of coincidence would have made his solution possible.

"The first ad," he said, "will be for a live, very active, and untamed skunk, or polecat. You may offer a hundred dollars for a proper specimen."

My pencil simply refused to get near the paper. I found myself staring at him with wide eyes. Accustomed as I was to the vagaries of the man, this was the crowning climax. However, he seemed to see nothing unusual about either the request or my reception of it.

"Specify," he said, "that the skunk must be in good condition, very wild, and exceedingly active. In order to obtain the best results, the animal should be delivered under the influence of an anesthetic, but it must be specified that he will recover from the stupor, or the anesthetic, within at least two hours after delivery, and delivery must be made before ten o'clock tomorrow morning.

"Now then, we'll offer a prize of five hundred dollars to the artist's model having the most beautiful figure, who presents herself at two o'clock in the afternoon at the address mentioned in the ad. There are absolutely no strings attached to this offer. Five hundred dollars will be deposited with the newspaper, coincident with the filing of the ad. The newspaper will turn over the money to whichever contestant bears a certificate of award from the judges."

"Five hundred dollars?" I asked dryly.

"Yes," he said. "Make out a check, and I'll sign it."

"Have you," I inquired, "made any deposit during the last two days?"

"Deposit? No," he said. "Why?"

"I was thinking about the attitude of the bank in regard to the overdraft."

"Oh, forget it," he said. "I'll drop in and make a deposit one of these days. Don't take financial matters so seriously. We have Miss Ray for that. She does our worrying."

"And who," I asked, "is going to judge the artist's models?"

"Oh, yes," he told me, "get F. C. Underwood on the telephone."

"You know his address?" I asked.

"No, I don't," he said, "but I know he's a building contractor, and I know he's a close friend of Lame's. He probably isn't too busy right at present. Get him on the phone; I'll talk with him personally."

I found F. C. Underwood listed as a building contractor, and was satisfied that he answered the telephone in person, although he went through the motions of pretending to be a secretary, answering the first time in a high pitched tone of voice, saying, "Very well, I'll call Mr. Underwood," and then answering gruffly: "Hello, hello. Underwood speaking."

Barney Killigen took the telephone.

"Hello," he said, "this is counsel for Associated Bathing Suits, Inc. We're going to do something to increase the interest in swimming, not from the standpoint of featuring any particular make of suit, but simply to popularize swimming as a sport. In order to do this, we're going to try to bring people to the beaches, and, for that purpose, want to call their attention to the scenery which the beaches have to offer ... Yes, Mr. Underwood, don't be impatient; I'm coming to that. Give me a moment, please ... Briefly, we're offering a prize of five hundred dollars to — What's that? ... We want *you* to be one of the judges ... No, there are no strings tied to it, whatever. The money will be paid over to the person you and the other two judges name as the winner ... The other two judges? We haven't decided on those. I can assure you they'll be persons whom you'll find congenial ... Yes, it happens that one of my clients knew of you, and said he thought you were amply competent to judge ... No, no, nothing like that; but you're a man with an appreciative eye, and you know beauty when you see it ... Tell you what we'll do, Mr. Underwood. We'll let *you* select the other two judges. Suppose you give me their names right now.

"Milford? Never heard of him. What does he do? ... Oh, yes. Well, you see *he's* a building contractor, and *you're* a building contractor, Mr. Underwood. It would look a little better if you had someone who was in an entirely different profession ... How's that? A doctor? Well, with a doctor, there's always a feeling that his judgment is more anatomical than esthetic. We'd like someone who is in an entirely different branch of work from what you are. A baker, an undertaker, a detective, a — How's that? ... What's his name? ... How do you spell it? ... Oh, Lame. L–a–m–e; yes, Robert Lame. You say he's a detective? ... Yes, that'll be fine. He'll make an excellent second judge. Now, whom would you want for a third? ... Charles Sweeney, and he's in the real estate business. That'll be fine, Mr. Underwood. Now, the judging will take place at two o'clock tomorrow afternoon, two o'clock on the dot. I've rented a sample room in the Maplewood Hotel. The girls will be instructed to come there ... That's right, you'll award only one prize — five hundred dollars in cash ... Yes. Now, if you'll kindly ring up the other judges and make certain they can serve, then call me back and let me know. My number is Bayshore 69237 ... That's right; ask for Mr. Killigen."

Killigen hung up the telephone, and grinned at me.

"Now, what," I asked, "is the big idea?"

"Giving the girls a break," he said.

"You'd better talk to the cashier of the bank before you issue that check," I warned. "You know it's a felony to issue checks without funds in the bank."

"Phooey," he said. "There are enough loopholes in *that* law to drive a horse and buggy through. Besides, no one pays any attention to it these days, anyway. However, if you insist, I'll have a talk with him. Get him on the telephone."

I got the cashier. Barney Killigen turned loose his personality. Yes, he had a deposit which was coming through within two or three days, rather a substantial deposit, he couldn't tell the exact amount, somewhere between five thousand and ten thousand dollars. And, incidentally, he was issuing a five hundred dollar check — unless they made the check good, the fee wouldn't come through, and then the bank would lose the amount of its overdraft ... Oh, sure, he'd sign a note for it, but there'd be no need of going to all that bother, because he'd be down within a couple of days with a deposit. The fee's already in the bag ... Yes, definitely, before the first of the month.

He hung up, with a breezy nonchalance. "All right," he said, "that's settled. Now then, we need the skunk and the bathing beauties."

"I take it," I asked, "this whole thing is engineered for the purpose of getting Detective Lame at a certain place at a certain time?"

"You," he told me, "are getting rather observing. Now, here's something I'd like to have you do for me — that is, if you're game."

"What is it?" I asked.

"Drop around to Lame's bungalow. Give him any name which comes to your mind. Tell him you're going to enter the bathing beauty contest, put on by Associated Bathing Suits, Inc., and that you want to be certain you win the first prize."

"Say," I protested, "what are you talking about? A man like that will try to —"

"Sure, he will," Killigen said, "and you'll hand him a great line."

"Precisely what," I asked, "is the idea? Do you intend to enter *me* in that bathing beauty contest?"

He looked me over appraisingly, and said: "We'd be pretty certain to keep the five hundred dollars in the office, if I did, but I don't intend to subject you to that indignity. I just want to make certain that Lame appreciates the possibilities of the situation, and considers that bathing beauty contest an absolutely essential part of his life. Moreover, you'll plant the skunk in —"

The telephone rang. Barney Killigen scooped up the receiver, and said:

"Yes, Mr. Underwood ... They did, eh? ... Well, that's fine ... That's right ... Yes, I'm a lawyer. I handle a general practice. You'll notice an ad in the classified column tomorrow: 'Bathing beauties wanted, professional models. A five hundred dollar check for not more than ten hours' posing given to the lucky model.' ... That's right, professionals only. We want them to look well in bathing suits ... Why the devil should we care how you pick them? Just get us someone who looks like a million dollars in a bathing suit ... Use your own judgment. Have them stand on their heads and swivel their eyes, if you want them to ... All right, thank you. Good–bye."

Barney Killigen grinned across the desk at me. "Hook, line, and sinker," he said.

"And where do you want the wild skunk delivered?" I asked.

"To the office," he said, "in a box suitable for carrying, with holes bored for ventilation, and the owner must guarantee that the skunk is in a — er — quiescent state when delivered."

"Now, let's get this straight," I said. "All you want me to do is to call on Robert Lame, and tell him that I want him to pick me for the winner of the beauty contest?"

"Well," Killigen said, with a grin, "there's one other little thing you'll have to do."

"The skunk?" I asked.

"Yes. You'll take this quiescent, stupefied, slumbering skunk, and surreptitiously plant him in Lame's bungalow."

"Perhaps it's an apartment," I said.

"No," he told me, "it's a bungalow. I've looked him up. His wife is away, visiting her mother. He's there alone."

"What," I asked, "is the idea?"

"The idea," he said, "is multifarious — and nefarious. The whole case hinges on Lame. Lame identifies the defendants and their machine. Yet Lame can't swear the defendant, Grayson, ever touched a single gem. Lame was unconscious all the time Grayson was in the room. Now, much may happen while a man is unconscious. I can argue that point to the jury — and the jury won't listen. I need to clinch the point — drive it home — and a live skunk is the answer."

"I know almost as much as I did before," I said.

He nodded. "So many people don't," he remarked conversationally.

I gave up. "Now listen. I'll tell you exactly what I'll do, and that's all I'll do. I'll go to Lame's bungalow. I'll pull the bathing beauty line with him, but I *won't* go any farther. I won't let him date me. I won't even bother to kid the man along, and if he comes within two feet of me, I'll slap his damn face."

"And you'll plant the skunk?" he asked.

I sighed. After all, there was no resisting Barney Killigen. "All right," I said, "I'll plant the skunk."

V.

Barney Killigen always claimed you could get anything on earth by using an intelligently written want ad in the newspapers, and the "quiescent" skunk which I carried in the little black handbag, perforated with breathing holes to keep the air fresh, went a long way toward proving his contention. It had been supplied by a doctor, who had gone in for vivisection in a large way, lived out in the country, and was not at all averse to picking up the extra money — supplementing the rather meager income of a small practice. A faint odor of ether emanated from the bag, but none of the polecat smell was detectable.

I parked my car on the opposite side of the street, crossed over to the bungalow which had the number I wanted, and rang the bell. After a second or two, I heard the pound of masculine feet. The man who opened the door was shaving; lather was still on one side of his face. He looked at me, looked at the handbag in my right hand, and said: "No magazine subscriptions — and what do you want to work your way through college for, anyhow? You're too good looking to waste your time in a college."

He was the beefy type, with a good–natured grin, rather thick lips, black patent leather hair, slicked back smoothly, black, bushy eyebrows, and twinkling gray eyes. Looking him over, I just had an idea he was going to be a pretty tough customer to handle on cross–examination. I certainly hoped Barney Killigen had some idea of how he was going about that cross–examination.

I gave him a coquettish smile. "I'm glad you think I'm pretty."

His eyes became wary and watchful. "So what?" he asked, losing the banter in his voice.

"Just how pretty," I asked, "do you think I am? No, not just my face; look me over."

I swung around slowly, so he could get a good look.

He did.

"Well," he said, with an appreciation which he tried to keep out of his voice, "I'd say you were tops."

I laughed, and said: "I'm afraid a fortune teller would tell you that your head line dominated your heart line, Mr. Lame."

"Oh, you know who I am, then?"

"Of course," I said. "Why do you think I came here?"

"I'll bite," he said. "Why *did* you come here?"

"Dame Rumor hath it that you're judging a bathing beauty contest this afternoon, at two o'clock. I'm one of the applicants for first prize. May I come in?"

He hesitated a moment, while he put two and two together in that methodical mind of his. Then his grin lost all of its caution and threatened to engulf his ears. "Come on in," he said. "Come right on in!"

I went in and took a seat on the door side of the living room. He indicated his face, and said:

"You'll have to excuse me for a few minutes, while I get some lather off, and slip into a coat."

It was that simple. The skunk came out, an inert, slumbering polecat, which I slid in under a davenport with the edge of the handbag. Five minutes later, when Lame came out, I was glancing through a magazine.

He sniffed the air, and said:

"Something smells funny. What is it?"

"Ether," I told him.

"How did that smell get in here?"

"From the hospital," I said. "I just came from there. My sister was struck with an automobile, and has a broken leg. They had quite a time reducing the fracture. They used ether. I was standing by her, and got pretty well saturated with it."

"How's she coming?" he asked.

"She's going to be all right," I said, "but it's going to take money, and that's what I wanted to see you about. I need five hundred dollars in a hurry."

He licked his chops.

"There's five hundred bucks in it for the winner of that bathing beauty show this afternoon," I said. "I'm going to enter. What do you think of my chances?"

I decided to give him a glimpse of silk stocking, just to make the play look good — not too much, just a bit of a gesture.

He fell for it in a big way.

"Now wait a minute," I told him, as he lurched up out of his chair. "This is a business proposition. You and I understand each other. *I'm* talking with you now. *You're* doing the listening. I want that first prize. The contest is at two o'clock this afternoon. You see that I come out of there with the blue ribbon and the five hundred bucks, and, after that, *you* do the talking and *I'll* do the listening."

"The bird in the hand," he told me, "is worth two in the bush."

"It depends on the bird — and the bush," I said, picking up my empty handbag and starting for the door. "I just wanted to drop in and get acquainted."

"This," he protested, "is a hell of a way to get acquainted."

I smiled back over my shoulder, with my hand on the doorknob. "Isn't it?" I agreed, and stepped out into the bright sunlight.

VI.

That was all I ever knew of the mechanics of the thing. That was one thing about Barney Killigen: if anybody had to take chances, walking around the outside of the gates of State's prison, it was Barney Killigen who took 'em. You did what he told you, and you kept yourself in the clear; but, for the most part, you didn't ask questions, and, sometimes, you didn't particularly specialize on deductions — you just tagged along and played ball.

Barney Killigen was representing both James Grayson and Estelle Whiting by the time the preliminary hearings were called, and the D. A. indicated he was going to try them together. At any rate, so far as the preliminary examination was concerned.

Judge Tammerlane was the magistrate, and Judge Tammerlane was absolutely fair. He had a sense of humor, and I think he really enjoyed Barney Killigen's antics. He called the case of The People vs. Grayson and Whiting. Carl Purdue, one of the most aggressive trial deputies of the district attorney's office, announced that he was ready for the prosecution. Barney Killigen signified the defendants were ready, and the show started.

Mrs. Chester–Smith was there in response to our subpoena, and was mad as a wet hen. I think the deputy district attorney really wanted her there, but he didn't dare to antagonize so influential a person by hauling her into court as a common, ordinary witness. I think he was secretly pleased that we had done so.

The prosecution called Dwight Chester–Smith, II, to identify the diamond and emerald ring. He testified he was the bridegroom. He had been married the night of the robbery. The ring was one of the wedding presents given by a mutual friend. His uncle had given ten thousand dollars in one hundred dollar bills. The currency had been in an envelope, and the suggestion made by his uncle was that the money should be used to defray the expenses of the honeymoon. There had also been other presents, various and sundry pieces of jewelry in addition to huge quantities of linens and silver which would be of value in housekeeping. The jewelry, he explained, was given by the bride's relatives and his relatives. It was primarily for the bride. The day selected for the wedding had been her twenty–fifth birthday. She had thought it would be nice to be married on her birthday.

He was an innocuous little snob, and probably more to be pitied than blamed. He was the product of inherited wealth, an indulgent mother, and a silver spooned birth.

One by one, he identified articles of jewelry. Carl Purdue turned him over to Barney Killigen for cross examination. Barney Killigen, after seeming undecided whether to tear into him or to let him go, decided in favor of letting him go. The young man tripped off the witness stand with a self–conscious air of blatant virtue which made me want to kick him in the pants.

The butler took the stand. He identified various articles of jewelry as having been recovered the next morning in the grass, along the driveway.

"Why weren't they recovered before the next morning?" Barney Killigen asked on cross–examination.

"Because it seemed inconceivable that the thief should put such valuable jewelry in a pocket which had a hole in it," the butler said. "The police were looking for the car. They weren't particularly interested in looking where the car had been. It wasn't until the next morning, an hour or so after daylight, that these gems were dis–covered."

"Who discovered them?"

"I did."

"Where were they discovered?" Barney Killigen asked.

"In the driveway, just as I told you."

"On the driveway, or on the side of the driveway?"

"Well, to the side."

"Some were on one side, and some were on the other side, were they not?"

"That is correct."

"Now then," Killigen said, "assuming that the thief had put this very valuable property in a coat pocket, and that there was a hole in the coat pocket, the thief must have zig–zagged once or twice across the driveway in running to his car. Is that right?"

"The thief was under fire. Naturally, one would zigzag under those circum–stances."

"Have you ever been under fire?" Killigen asked.

"Me, sir?" the butler exclaimed indignantly.

"Yes, you," Killigen said.

"Certainly not."

"Well, I might put it another way." Barney Killigen grinned. "Have you ever been fired?"

"Objected to as incompetent, irrelevant, and immaterial, and not proper cross-examination," Carl Purdue shouted.

Judge Tammerlane suppressed a grin as he sustained the objection.

"Well, let's get back to this under fire business," Killigen said. "If you've never been under fire, how do you know that a person should zig–zag when he's being shot at?"

"From reading books."

"Textbooks on the subject of how to behave under fire," Killigen asked, "or fiction?"

"Fiction."

"Ah, yes. Detective stories?" Killigen inquired.

"Yes, sir," the butler said.

"And do these detective stories teach you any of the fine points of crime detection?"

"I think so. Yes, sir."

"Most interesting," Killigen said. "Now who discovered the imprints of the ladder under the window?"

"I did — that is, I pointed them out to the police."

"The police were with you at the time?"

"Yes."

Carl Purdue said: "One of my next witnesses will identify those ladder imprints if you're interested, Mr. Killigen. I'm mentioning it at this time so you won't waste time cross-examining this witness as to his recollection. A plaster cast of those imprints is to be a point of our case and we will introduce such a cast in evidence."

"Thank you," Killigen said. "That's all."

"I would not have presumed to call Mrs. Dwight Chester-Smith from her important engagements," Carl Purdue said, in unctuous, mealy mouthed tones, "but, inasmuch as she is here in court in response to a subpoena of the defendant, I wish to put her on the stand to establish certain preliminary matters. Mrs. Chester–Smith, will you come forward and be sworn?"

She marched down the aisle to the witness stand, oozing indignation from every pore. By her, Carl Purdue identified the various and sundry items of jewelry which had been found near the driveway and brought out the information that only the envelope containing the ten thousand dollars in one hundred dollar bills remained missing. That and the ring had been the only two things which the butler had failed to recover in his morning search.

Barney Killigen said, "No cross–examination," and the witness was excused.

Carl Purdue, with something of a flourish, announced, "My next witness is Robert Lame."

Lame took the stand with an air of smirking self-importance, but the man was smart and he was watching his testimony with a care equal to that of the deputy district attorney. He testified that he was a private detective, that he had been employed to act as guard for the wedding and birthday presents. He mentioned that he had just finished his supper of sandwiches, pie, and coffee, when a masked man, who he knew was Grayson, smashed in a pane of glass in the window with the barrel of a gun, turned the gun on him, raised the sash, and then knocked the witness unconscious. "The burglar," he explained, "had climbed a ladder which had silently been placed against the house." He told of regaining consciousness, of the flight of the burglars, of seeing the man and woman running away, taking the ladder with them. He testified he had been able to see four numbers of the license plate on their car, that he had called on the pair to halt, and then fired six shots from his revolver. He told of subsequently making an investigation, of finding where the ladder had been placed against the house, and described the indentations where the ends of the ladder had been imbedded.

The deputy district attorney introduced a plaster of Paris cast of these ladder marks, and Lame identified them, told of being present when the casts were made.

Carl Purdue turned him over to Barney Killigen for cross-examination.

"The man who held you up was masked?" Killigen asked.

"Yes."

"But you recognized him?"

"I won't say that I recognized him. No. But there were certain things about him which I noticed. Subsequently, when I saw the defendant, Jimmy Grayson, I realized that he and the man who had held me up had many points of similarity: the color of the hair, the slope of the shoulders, the shape of the neck, the size, weight, and voice. I take all of these things into consideration and say positively that Grayson was the one who held the gun on me."

"Now, how about the woman?" Killigen asked. "Do you absolutely identify her?"

"I'm not so positive of her identity as I am that of Grayson," Lame said, choosing his words cautiously, yet creating an impression of fairness which I knew was going to be deadly to the jury. "You must remember, Mr. Killigen, that I was looking down on her from a window. I didn't see her in the light of a room. On the other hand, she wasn't masked. I would say that the woman who accompanied Grayson as his accomplice in the robbery was about the same age, size, build, and complexion as the defendant, Estelle Whiting. I can't swear positively that it was she who was with Grayson."

"But you do swear positively that the burglar was Mr. Grayson?"

"Oh, yes."

"Now, you had just finished eating your midnight lunch?"

"Yes, that's right."

"Is it your custom to take lunch with you when you go to guard gifts at social functions such as this?"

"It is. Quite frequently more guests attend than the host plans on. In that event, there aren't many refreshments, and you can leave it to the servants to see that they don't suffer. The hostess frequently forgets the detective who is on guard. You can't summon the servants to have them tell her you're hungry, and you can't go to the kitchen yourself without leaving your station. I carry my lunch and eat when I'm hungry and have my coffee so it'll refresh me and keep me awake. People who don't like it, don't need to employ me."

"I see," Killigen said. "Now let's come back to the ladder. Let me call your attention to the plaster cast showing the marks made by the base of the ladder. Do you notice anything peculiar about them?"

"Nothing," Lame said.

"You're a detective?"

"Yes."

"And as such, you specialize on making deductions from clues?"

"Well, you might call it that, yes."

"And yet you see nothing strange about the imprints of this ladder?"

"No, certainly not. Those are the imprints of two two–by–fours which formed the uprights of the ladder. When the ladder was placed against the side of the building, and the defendant climbed up it, the two–by–fours were imbedded into the soft earth."

"Let's take another look at these," Barney Killigen said. "And in order to illustrate the point I have in mind, I'll take a carpenter's square. Now then, we'll place this square on one of the imprints made by this two–by–four. Now, do you notice anything peculiar about the imprints of the ladder?"

"Well," Lame said slowly, "the second imprint is an inch or two out of line with the square, but, of course, a man making a ladder doesn't have to make it just the way a carpenter would."

"I understand that," Barney Killigen said, "and, as I gather it from your testimony, the man and the woman who had robbed the house carried the ladder away with them, did they not?"

"That's right."

"Notwithstanding the fact that you were standing in the window shooting at them?"

"That's right. I didn't shoot at first, of course. I yelled at them to stop. I was groggy, punch drunk, and it took me a little while to get out my gun and — well, a man just doesn't start shooting at people without giving them every opportunity to submit to arrest."

"I understand that, and I think the jury will agree with you that you used most commendable restraint. But let's get back now to this ladder. You will note that when I put the carpenter's square on the other imprint made by the two–by–four, it's about the same distance out of true as this first imprint."

"Yes, sir."

"Now then, in making a ladder," Killigen said, "two stringers are placed in approximately parallel positions and crosspieces are nailed to them. Now, in the event those cross–pieces are nailed tightly to the two–by–fours, it's absolutely necessary for the two–by–fours to be squared, isn't it? In other words, for the two–by–fours to be on an angle, it would be necessary for the crosspieces to be nailed in such a way that they didn't rest tightly against the stringers."

"Yes, I guess that's right," Lame admitted.

"And that's impossible to do unless you've cut a recess in the two–by–fours for the crosspieces to rest in, and, under those circumstances, you'd have to cut each one of those rests at an angle, isn't that right?"

Lame seemed to be getting nervous.

"Yes, I suppose so."

Carl Purdue said: "After all, your honor, this cross-examination about the ladder isn't of any particular importance. A man doesn't have to be a carpenter in order to be a robber."

"Do you wish to object to it?" Killigen asked.

"No, no. Go ahead," Carl Purdue said, with a magnanimous wave of his hand. "I guess I can stand it, if the court can."

Judge Tammerlane said: "I think you had better confine your comments to the making of objections to testimony and arguments addressed to the court, Mr. Deputy District Attorney."

Purdue managed to make his facial expression that of one who has been wrongfully rebuked.

"Let's approach this problem of the ladder from another angle," Killigen said, and by this time, it was obvious to everyone in the courtroom that Lame was worried about questions concerning the ladder. "Let us suppose," Killigen went on, "that a man had stood in an upper window with a length of two–by–four scantling. Suppose that he had pushed that scantling down into the ground with all of his weight, then withdrawn it and moved it about eighteen inches to one side, but that he himself had not moved from his position in the window. Suppose he made a second imprint in the ground by the same method. Under those circumstances, his hands, holding one end of the scantling would have formed the center of a circle, and the two imprints in the ground would have been segments in the perimeter of such a circle, isn't that right?"

"I don't know what you're talking about," Lame said sullenly.

"I'll express it in another way," Killigen said, peering steadily at Lame. "If there hadn't been any ladder at all, Mr. Lame, but if you had decided that you were going to fake a holdup and had stood in the window and had pushed a length of two–by–four scantling into the ground in order to make it appear that a ladder had been placed at the window, those imprints would have been just at about the angle of these imprints shown in the plaster cast. Whereas, on the other hand, if the ladder had been placed against the side of the building; it would have been impossible for those two imprints to have been at that angle, isn't that right?"

"I don't think so," Lame said, his eyes furtive, his face flushed. "There was a ladder there all right, and a man standing on it. And if you're insinuating *I* faked this burglary, you're lying."

Barney Killigen calmly opened a box, took from it two of the curved fragments of silvered glass, and approached the private detective.

"I'll show you two pieces of glass, Mr. Lame, and ask you if you know what they are."

"No."

"Suppose I told you these were found by the side of the driveway of the Chester–Smith residence, at a point near where some of the jewelry had been recovered. Would that mean anything to you?"

"No."

"Suppose I further pointed out to you that these glass fragments constituted broken pieces from the glass container which goes on the inside of a Thermos bottle. Would you still say that you failed to appreciate their significance?"

Lame squirmed uneasily in the chair.

Carl Purdue said: "Your honor, I think this is improper cross–examination. It's argumentative and —"

"Overruled," Judge Tammerlane snapped. "I want to hear the witness answer that question."

"I don't know anything about them," Lame said.

Killigen was smiling affably. "I suppose, Lame, that when you saw an envelope containing one hundred bills each of one hundred dollar denomination, you saw an excellent opportunity to get away with ten thousand dollars. You knew it would be dangerous to take jewelry because, sooner or later, jewelry could be traced to you. You tried to figure out some method by which you could make it appear there'd been a holdup. You looked across to where they were building a garage and saw a long scantling which had evidently been used in scaffolding. You got that scantling, leaned it up against the side of the building, and returned to the room where the gifts were located. You watched your opportunity, impressed the end of the scantling deeply into the soft earth near the flower bed, and then tossed the scantling back toward the garage.

"You calmly walked over to the table where the gifts were on display, selected some of the most valuable gems, and tossed them out of the window in the general direction of the driveway. You removed the container from your Thermos bottle, cracked out the bottom half, and threw that out of the window. In the interior of that Thermos bottle, you stuffed the envelope containing the ten thousand dollars in currency and the ring which you wished to use to frame the defendant in this case. You already knew of the defendant and knew of his criminal record. You smashed the window with your gun barrel, fired six shots, then cracked yourself over the head so that you could show a bruise, and started yelling for help. Subsequently, you gave the police a description of the defendant. You didn't make it *too good* because you didn't want them to pick him up until you'd had an opportunity to plant that ring where he'd find it. You felt certain that if he found such a ring, not knowing anything about it, he'd accept it as a windfall. So you gave the police the first four numbers of the car you knew the defendant was driving and —"

"It's a lie," Lame screamed. "You can't prove it."

Barney Killigen looked him squarely in the eye. "Would you," he said, "be willing to let the deputy sheriff go to your house, unscrew the lid of the Thermos bottle which you have there, and investigate the contents?"

Lame fairly screamed, "I tell you this is a frame–up, a dirty frame–up!"

Barney Killigen smiled at Judge Tammerlane, walked back to his chair at the counsel table, and sat down.

"I have no further questions on cross–examination," he said.

Judge Tammerlane glanced at Carl Purdue and said: "Well, the court has questions, and I think the district attorney's office should have some."

Purdue said: "I'm going to ask the witness to remain in custody until deputy sheriffs can check up on that Thermos bottle."

Lame said sullenly: "It's a frame–up. I can't be responsible for all the stuff a man plants in my house."

"I presume," Barney Killigen said, with a smile, "that it's your idea the money has been planted in your Thermos bottle by the defendants, Lame?"

"You shut up," Lame yelled. "I've stood enough from you."

Judge Tammerlane said: "The court will take a thirty minute recess. During that time, the court will leave it to the sheriff to see that Robert Lame is kept under close surveillance."

It was a hectic half hour. Newspaper reporters took flashlight photographs of Barney Killigen in his pose of cross–examiner. Judge Tammerlane held a long, secret conference with the district attorney and the sheriff, and then the deputy sheriffs returned. They carried with them one Thermos bottle which was entirely empty, but when the glass container on the inside was removed, the lower half of it had been broken. In the interior of the Thermos bottle was a torn scrap of paper with just a bit of writing on it. It was as though someone had torn up an envelope, but a piece of that envelope had inadvertently been allowed to drop back into the lower part of the Thermos bottle, in the space opened up by the breaking of the glass container.

Handwriting experts proved that the paper was exactly the same as that in which the envelope, containing the bills, had been placed; that the bit of writing on the scrap of paper had been written by the man who had made the donation, and that the ink was of exactly the same chemical constituents as that which came from his fountain pen.

Judge Tammerlane released the defendants, and ordered Robert Lame into custody.

The police went to work on him to find out where the ten thousand dollars was hidden. They were ungentle in their methods.

We walked out of court in a blaze of glory. Estelle Whiting was kissing Barney Killigen, her mother was crying, and Jimmy Grayson seemed as one in a daze.

VII.

Miss Ray stared with bewildered eyes at the big roll of currency Barney Killigen tossed on her desk.

"Take it down and deposit it," he said.

"Where in the world did it come from?" she asked.

"Just a contribution made by a grateful client," Killigen said.

"Well, it's about time," she asserted, relief in her voice. "The bank was be—coming most insistent. They were particularly displeased with that last five hundred dollar check you put through, on the promise of making a prompt deposit."

"Banks are always displeased about something," Killigen said easily. "And, oh, yes, by the way, Miss Ray, your salary is due. Here it is."

He handed her two bills, one hundred dollar bill, and one fifty dollar bill.

"Come on in the office, Wiggy," he said to me.

I accompanied him to his private office. He opened his billfold and tossed me three hundred dollar bills.

"Here you are, Wiggy," he said, "another month's salary."

I stared at them for a moment, then held them under my nose.

"What's the matter?" he asked. "Don't they smell right?"

"I have rather sensitive nostrils," I told him.

"Good." He smiled. "And what does the bloodhound smell?"

"A very faint odor of coffee," I said, "and a very definite odor of polecat."

"It couldn't be your imagination?" Barney Killigen asked.

"No," I said.

"How's Miss Ray's sense of smell?" he inquired.

"She hasn't any."

"Well," he said, with a grin, "that will simplify matters. You'd probably better spend that money at your earliest opportunity, Wiggy."

"I will," I told him.

He opened the bottom drawer of the desk, pulled out his flask of whisky and two glasses.

"Well," he said, "we've got that case cleaned up."

"What happened to Estelle Whiting?" I asked.

"She got married," Killigen said. "Judge Tammerlane married them. You should have seen the old boy's face when he kissed the bride — I guess she gave him something to think about."

"She was giving you something to think about after the case was finished," I said.

"Yes," he observed, "she was grateful."

"Does Grayson have a job?"

"He can't get one around here," Killigen said easily; "his record's against him. He had one long enough to save up a little money, which he very foolishly put into making the down payment on an automobile. Then some detective told his employer about Grayson's criminal record, and the fat was in the fire, and Grayson out of a job."

I pressed the point, feeling that I already knew the answer. "Exactly what did he get married on?" I asked.

Killigen said: "Well, it's a peculiar thing, one of the wedding presents he received was an envelope with two thousand dollars in hundred dollar bills."

"Do you suppose," I asked, "that those bills smelled of coffee and polecat?"

"*I* wouldn't know," Killigen said, his eyebrows elevated. "*My* sense of smell isn't very acute. I would, however, say the money was clean."

"Slick and clean," I said.

He grinned.

"Of course," I went on, "putting two and two together, and knowing you as I do, I realize that *if* a person had been going out on a most important engagement — or one which he thought was most important — say, for instance, looking over a lot of feminine pulchritude in the altogether, and he discovered a skunk in his bungalow shortly before he was due to leave, he'd naturally have shut up the skunk in the kitchen, or whatever room in which he had discovered the animal, and would leave the windows open, hoping to get rid of the skunk, or at least to get rid of the odor."

"That's a natural enough deduction," Killigen admitted, smiling.

"And," I went on, "if someone had known to a virtual certainty that this man was going to be away during certain hours, judging said feminine pulchritude in the altogether, it would have been a relatively easy matter for such a person to have entered the house and found the Thermos bottle. At that, Lame was rather clever. He knew enough about crime to know that the most effective hiding place was one where no one would ever think of making a search."

Barney Killigen lighted a cigarette, smoked it for a couple of puffs, and then held it out to watch the smoke drift upward.

"Rather interesting reasoning, Wiggy," he said. "You wouldn't, by any chance, have thought of all that unless you happened to know me as well as you do, would you?"

I admitted, "I wouldn't."

"Excellent," he said. "You're the only one who knows me that well. And if poor people are going to be wrongly accused of crime, *someone* has to pay for defending them. But Estelle Whiting had no money with which to secure high priced legal services."

"Sort of a vicious circle," I suggested.

"Exactly," he agreed, "and when one gets in a vicious circle, the thing to do is to cut right across the middle."

"Is that what you did?" I asked.

"I," he said, "acted as a force of retributive readjustment. Dwight Chester–Smith, II, is a nincompoop, an innocuous nincompoop as yet, but a nincompoop, nevertheless. Too much money will eventually ruin him. He suffers from a surplus of unearned wealth. Estelle Whiting suffered from a shortage of earned wealth. I strove to rectify the situation."

"I see," I said. "And as for the law?"

"The spirit of the law was observed," he said. "I'm a great respecter of the law, but when the spirit of the law conflicts with the letter of the law, I'm a man of spirit rather than of letters. How was it you described this choke–a–horse roll of money?"

"Slick and clean," I said.

"Exactly," he agreed, grinning. "However, I'd prefer to say clean as a whistle. How about four fingers of good Scotch?"

"Two," I told him.

He grinned. "We'll compromise on three," he said.

And we did.

Take It or Leave It

I could tell there was some unusual activity in our office. A string of people kept marching back and forth past the door of the little cubicle in which I was supposed to be studying law. A procession of footsteps to and from old E.B. Jonathan's office proved incontestably that he was the focal point of the activity, and when activity centered around E.B., it meant the case which was breaking was one of major importance.

I tried to discipline my mind to follow the phraseology in which Blackstone had couched legal doctrines. But my mind was on the hubbub. The door of my little office opened and Cedric L. Boniface, looking plump, prosperous and smug surveyed me.

"I won't be able to discuss the doctrine of Mortmain with you this afternoon, Wennick," he said. "I'm leaving at once for Marlin."

"A case?" I asked.

"A murder case," he said, and went out.

Boniface was like that. He took himself very seriously indeed — the damned staffed shirt. If he had any inkling that in place of being a somewhat backward law student I was playing the game I was, he'd probably have needed a psychiatrist to calm him down.

He thought he was the big trial lawyer who was bustling about solving mysteries and getting innocent persons acquitted. He was the trial lawyer, all right. But I got the dope for him even if he didn't know it. However, what he didn't know wouldn't hurt him.

He'd been gone about five minutes when Mae Devers came into the office. "E.B. wants to see you, Pete," she said.

"When?" I asked.

"In about five minutes. As soon as he can get rid of Boniface."

"You," I said, "seem to know a lot of what's going on."

"Why not? I have an observing disposition."

My arm circled her waist. "You also," I said, "have a fine figure — if we're going to take a physical inventory."

"We're not," she said, laughing and pulling away. "At least not right now. I have work to do."

She blew me a kiss from the doorway, and I heard the swift click of her heels as she walked toward the outer office.

About five minutes after that, Boniface went striding self–importantly down the corridor, taking pleasure in his "great man" pretense. The outer door slammed, and Mae gave me a buzz on the intercom, and said, "E.B. wants you now, Pete."

I walked down the corridor into E.B. Jonathan's private office. He sat behind the desk, pouches hanging under his eyes, deep lines etched into his face. His head was as bald as a peeled onion.

His eyes met mine. "Sit down, Pete," he said.

When you looked into old E.B.'s eyes, you lost the feeling that you were dealing with an old man or a tired man. His eyes were bright and coldly efficient. There was no sentiment about E.B. He did things in his own way, and didn't give a damn for ethics. He wanted results, and he usually got them. And he saw to it that he was well paid for his efforts.

"Read the paper this morning?" he asked. "About the murder up in Marlin?"

"No."

"Well, Cromley Dalton," E.B. said in a tired, world–weary voice, "was the editor of the *Marlin Morning Star.* He was murdered around ten o'clock last night. There's a hot political situation up there with the city council and the mayor facing a recall election. I guess I don't have to tell you that excitement is at a fever pitch."

"Who's arrested?" I asked.

"The mayor, Layton Spred."

"The motive?" I asked.

"The *Marlin Morning Star* had been instrumental in getting the recall started. It had published a series of bitter personal attacks on the mayor. He'd threatened to shoot Dalton as he would a mad dog. Mayor Layton Spred is hot–tempered. Apparently he values personal honor and integrity very highly."

"Any further details?" I asked.

"Dalton went to call on Spred about ten o'clock last night. Dalton rang the doorbell and stood in front of the door. From where he was standing he could look through a diagonal window down the corridor. Spred, on the other hand, could have looked through the same window and seen Dalton.

"Evidently Spred, coming down the corridor, saw Dalton's face and pulled a gun from his hip pocket. Dalton didn't wait for him to get to the door. He started to run back toward the car where his two companions were waiting. Then, seeing that he couldn't make it, he swerved and ran around the end of the porch toward the back of the house. Spred ran out and dashed toward the porch, a gun in his hand.

"When the two men in the car saw him flourishing the gun and realized that Dalton had swung around toward the back of the house, they didn't wait to see what was going to happen. They sent the speedometer soaring and got away from there fast. But just before they passed beyond hearing range they heard shots.

"They notified the police. The police found Dalton's body lying just at the edge of the alley. He had been shot in the back. Death was instantaneous."

"What," I asked, "is Spred's story?"

"Spred says that someone rang his doorbell, and that he went to the door just in time to see a shadowy figure running through the darkness across the lawn and around toward the back of the house. He says he was afraid the man had been planting a bomb. He ran to the edge of the porch and called to him to halt.

"The intruder turned and shot twice at him, and Spred raised his gun and fired once. He says that at the sound of his shot, the man turned and resumed his flight running in the direction of the alley. Spred went back and called the police, reporting that someone had taken a shot at him. The neighbors heard three shots. When Spred was arrested, officers took his gun. It had been fired three times."

"That," I said, "doesn't make things look so good for Mr. Spred."

"And Spred," E.B. said, "is our client."

"What," I asked, "do you want me to do?"

"Boniface is going up to handle the case," E.B. said. "We've been retained by Millicent Spred, the mayor's daughter. The young woman is driving Boniface back to Marlin. Boniface will be registered at the Plaza Hotel. I have here a brief on appeal on which I desire his opinion. I'm sending you up on the three–ten train to deliver it. Ask him to telephone me what he thinks of it."

I nodded.

"That," E.B. Jonathan went on, "should make as good an excuse as any to get you on the ground. While you're there, you'll telephone me and tell me that it looks as though you could get a lot of practical knowledge being on the ground to help Boniface and watch what he does. That will account for your presence in town. Once you're there, get on the job just as soon as you can, and do your stuff."

"What," I asked, "do you want me to do?"

"I doubt," he said, "that they'll bring in a first–degree murder verdict against Spred. They might convict him of manslaughter. There are several elements of weakness in the prosecution's case. Boniface has, as a lawyer, one asset and only one — a rigid respectability. Behind the ethical screen which he will naturally provide for your activities, you shouldn't have much trouble making the case look so sick the prosecution will drop it."

"I'll see what I can do," I said. "You want me to take the three–ten?"

"Yes. Have Miss Devers give you seven hundred and fifty dollars expense money."

"Better make it two thousand," I said. "I don't know what I'll be running into. Or if I run short shall I drop in and ask Boniface to advance the balance?"

That shot told. "No, no," he said hastily. "You must never do anything like that. Boniface is highly ethical. He's the chairman of one of the important committees of the local bar association. It's only his ultra respectability that makes it possible for me to take advantage of the things you do. If Boniface ever found out, he'd quit. What's more, he'd be quite capable of making a stink about it."

I said, "But if I run out of expense money, I'll have to go to him."

He said testily, "Tell Miss Devers to give you two thousand. Damn it, Wennick. I find your resourcefulness invaluable, but at times you go too far. You might remember that before I picked you up here, you were a free–lance private detective drawing down damn few dollars a day — on rare days."

"Well," I said, "if you want to go into that, before you brought me into the firm, Boniface was losing cases with rhythmic regularity."

E.B. swung around in the swivel chair, and said, in a tone of finality, "I don't care to discuss it."

Marlin's Plaza Hotel was a pretentious affair. Boniface had the best suite in the house and was enjoying the role of being the high–priced city attorney imported to save the mayor's neck from the rope.

In the meantime, the town was buzzing with speculation and rumors, and the recall election was five days away.

The Free Press, the rival newspaper, was doing what it could for Spred. It had an editorial to the effect that Spred was undoubtedly justified in what he had done. It laid stress on the fact that the malicious campaign of character assassination which had been carried on by Cromley Dalton, followed up as it was by an impudent invasion of Spred's residence, certainly gave Spred every reason to believe that the dead man had been up to mischief, and had perhaps actually planted a bomb.

The newspaper gave me more details concerning the crime than I'd gotten from E.B. Jonathan. The two men who had driven out to Spred's place with Cromley Dalton were Preston Bode and Ray Mansfield, and there was considerable speculation as to the nature of the errand which had taken these three to Spred's residence.

Both Bode and Mansfield were members of the city council facing recall. Dalton was the editor of the paper which had been instrumental in bringing about that recall election. Rumor was rife that the two city councilmen had made some political deal with the opposition, and that the price demanded by Dalton for a cessation of his political attacks was the matter to be discussed at Spred's residence.

And there were some intimations the mayor was to be cynically and deliberately sacrificed on the altar of public opinion to save the political faces of all concerned.

I noticed that the editorial soft–pedaled the part of Spred's story which dealt with the two shots which had been fired at him. Two witnesses who lived nearby had testified positively to three shots, and only three. That made the three chambers in Spred's gun look rather bad for him combined with the fact that he had been standing up against the side of the house and the police could find no bullets buried in the wall anywhere or on the ground close to the house.

Even if the shots he'd claimed had been fired at him had gone wild a police search should have turned them up somewhere.

The betting was ten to one against Spred on the recall and three to one he'd be convicted of something — if not first–degree murder, then second–degree or manslaughter.

Boniface took the brief I gave him and said grumblingly, "I wonder how E.B. thinks I'll have time to read a brief with this case getting more complicated and explosive by the minute."

"A lot of excitement?"

"Yes," he said, shortly.

"I wonder if E.B. would let me stay up here and give you a hand," I said. "It should be a wonderful practical experience for me."

"There's nothing you could do, Wennick," he said. "You'd do more good for yourself by going back to your books and laying the foundations for a career of your own."

"I've nothing against books," I said. "But I like murder cases better when I've spent a week with Blackstone."

His silence was eloquent.

"Look," I said, "I don't want to butt in, but sometimes people have little lapses of memory. How do we know Mayor Spred's daughter didn't take that gun out to do some target practice with it without telling her father. She might have fired a couple of shots, and then forgotten all about it. If that's the case, it would account for the three exploded chambers. Don't you think it might be a good idea to ask her about it?"

"Certainly not," Boniface said with dignity. "If anything like that had happened, she would have told me."

"Perhaps she doesn't remember it. You should refresh her memory."

Boniface stared at me in righteous indignation.

"Don't you think you being just a little too much of a Southern gentleman in refusing to question Mayor Spred's daughter at all?" I asked.

Boniface said, "Pete Wennick, I am surprised. You'll never make an attorney until you have a more keen appreciation of professional ethics."

I saw there wasn't any use arguing with him, so I went out. From the doorway, I said, "I'll call E.B. and see if he'll let me stick around to watch. If he says 'yes,' can I help you in any way?"

"I don't know," Boniface said, "but I think not. To be perfectly frank with you, Wennick, I am very much disappointed in the way you are developing. If you are ever going to be of any practical assistance to me, you must progress more rapidly with your studies and learn to take the ethics of the profession more seriously."

I said, "Perhaps you're right at that, Mr. Boniface," and gently closed the door behind me.

II

Buildings were ablaze with lighted windows in Marlin as men sat late in their offices discussing the political situation, commenting on the murder and trying to turn a flip–flop in their political alignments so they could do business with the winners.

I found Preston Bode in his office. He looked tired and worried. He was that rare combination of a fat man and an inwardly lean man who is explosively energetic. He looked at my card, and said, "Your name's Peter Wennick, eh? Just what do you want?"

"A chance to talk," I said.

"Talk's cheap," he observed, shifting a cigar from one side of his mouth to the other, working his thick lips as he did so. Beneath the heavy jowls, I could see his jaw muscles tighten. A man with a powerful bite, a powerful grip, a powerful mind, a driving, obstinate, dangerous man.

"My talk," I said, "isn't going to be cheap." And I sat down.

He looked me over and said, "Out of Town?"

"Yes."

"Now get this straight, Wennick, I've been pestered to death with detectives and reporters. If it's about the Dalton murder, just start for the door. It's late, and I'm busy. I've been interviewed and questioned until I'm sick of it."

I lit a cigarette.

"Well?" he asked, at length.

"Personally," I said, "I like to gamble, and I always like the long shots."

"Meaning what?"

"Meaning," I said, "that they're offering one hundred dollars against ten dollars that you'll be kicked out of office on the recall election."

His heavy face turned florid, and his little eyes glinted in rage. "You," he said, "get to hell out of here."

"I was quoting facts. You shouldn't get touchy about facts."

"Get out!"

"Of course," I said, studying my cigarette, "I could go to the other crowd, and make my deal with them. But they'd want just as much for the concession as though they were already in office. With you it's different. Right now, the chances that you'll be elected are one in ten. Therefore, you should be willing to talk business on reasonable terms. Then if it's to my financial interest to see that you're returned to office, your chances might be a hell of a lot better than one in ten. It would pay you to give it some thought."

Slowly the florid color faded from his cheeks. I knew he was sparring for time and didn't crowd him any. After a minute, he said, "What's your game?"

"A new type of slot machine," I said.

I looked up at the ceiling and said noncommittally, "I know a lot about the psychology of selling slot machines, and I know a lot about politics. I sold the mayor of Henlotown to the voters the last election."

I saw suspicion flare into his eyes. "If you did that, how come you're wandering around with a slot machine racket? Why aren't you there grabbing gravy?"

"Some talk got started that could have led to trouble," I said. "Somebody had to take the brunt of it. If the mayor had taken it, it would have been a smear. I took it.

"Don't worry, brother, I'm getting mine for taking it, but the doctors have told me that for about a year I hadn't better be around the Henlotown climate. It's too high and dry."

Bode thought some more, then said, "You talk a lot — to strangers."

"You're not a stranger," I said. "What the hell do you suppose I've been doing the last couple of weeks?"

"What do you know about me?" he demanded belligerently.

I tried a shot in the dark. "More than your wife does," I said, and was pleased to see his eyes shift.

"What do you want?"

"Slot machines."

"It's out. The people won't stand for slot machines."

"I'll take care of the people. If I can make them stand for you, with the stink that's hanging to your coattails, I can make them stand for slot machines."

"You've got an over–confidence bug buzzing you, mister. Talk like that could get me mad."

"There you go again," I said, "refusing to face facts. Between you and me we may as well figure that a spade is a spade. When it comes to the taxpayers, we'll play the game differently. A spade will become a sturdy implement of rugged construction designed to be of inestimable benefit to the farmer, and the factory workers as well, symbolical of the rugged honesty of our esteemed contemporary and fellow townsman, Preston Bode, friend of the laboring man."

"Those are only words," he said. "You can't pull that friend–of–the–laboring–man racket in this town. The banks control it."

"Just a babe in the woods," I said.

"Who is?"

"You are. You talk simple."

"What's wrong with my statement?"

"Banks control finances," I said. "Labor controls votes."

"All right," he said savagely, "you try to court the labor votes and the bank puts financial screws on you, and you come out at the small end of the horn."

"You know how to handle that, don't you?"

"No, and neither do you."

"The ears of labor," I said, "listen for the loudest voice. Financial institutions have ears which are attuned to the faintest whisper. If you shouted to the labor and then quietly whispered to the bankers, and your words made sense, you'd go to town."

Bode started drumming nervously with the tips of his fingers on the edge of his desk. "Who thinks up the words that I shout and the words that I whisper?" he asked.

"That's easy. I do — if I get the concession."

"What kind of a concession do you want?"

I laughed, and said, "Don't pull that line. I told you what I wanted — slot machines."

"How much gravy for distribution?" he asked.

I said, "I've told you how much. I'm a gambler. I like to play the long shots. You're a long shot."

"You mean that if you show me how to beat this recall you want me to string along with slot machines for nothing."

"Oh," I said, "there'd be enough so you could keep yourself and friends in cigars. But I'd want you to remember that I was one of the early birds — up before breakfast to help you. If I deal myself in when things look pretty dark, I want to be in when they begin to look rosy."

Little blue puffs of cigar smoke drifted upward past his beefy neck. Abruptly he faced me and said, "I could use a good man."

"You're looking at one."

"This situation," he said, "isn't simple. You'd better get that straight before you start. The district attorney is out to make a killing by siding with the winner. A week ago he would probably have trailed along with the city administration. Now his head is full of maggots. He wants to be governor some day. He sees this as a good chance."

"How about the city police?" I asked.

"I control them," Bode said.

"You mean you did control them. They're ready to sell out if they can find a taker. You know that as well as I do."

"You," he said, "seem to know altogether too damn much for a stranger."

I said ominously, "I'm not a stranger, and I know a damn sight more than you think I do. Now then, do we trade or don't we?"

"I have two associates I'd like to consult," he said.

"How much time do you want?"

"Give me until ten–thirty tomorrow morning."

"Okay. But if you're going to play ball with me, we're going to have to work fast. That means I want to be all ready to go just as soon as you say the word."

"There'd be no percentage in moving slowly," he said. "I think the answer's going to be 'yes,' as far as that's concerned."

"If that's the case," I said, "we want to do something about that Dalton mess. It's being handled in the worst possible manner."

"How else are you going to handle it?"

"Lot's of ways," I said. "To begin with, you haven't done the cause very much good with your statement."

"What's wrong with my statement?"

"Everything."

"I told the truth."

"That," I said, "is not always wise. How deeply did you commit yourself?"

"What do you mean?"

"How much of your story can you change if you have to? Go ahead and give me the highlights of what you've told the officers."

Bode said belligerently, "I told them the truth. Dalton wanted to go out and see Spred. Ray Mansfield and I had a talk with him. We decide to drive him out."

"That story," I said, "isn't so hot. It isn't even lukewarm. It could be heated up by your enemies, though — in the wrong way."

"Why?"

"In the first place," I said, "Dalton was Spred's enemy. Spred was Dalton's enemy. What's more, you and Mansfield were in the other camp. I can't conceive of any reason why Dalton should want to go out and see Spred unless there had been a sellout. But if he did want to see Spred and had taken you two along, you certainly would have been the ones to go up and ring the doorbell.

"What's more, you'd have unquestionably telephoned Spred before you came out to prepare him for what was happening. Now then — suppose you give me the low down. If you do, I might be able to clear Spred, and that would change the political situation here overnight."

"You can't beat the rap on Spred. He's hooked this time. He killed him."

"How about his self–defense angle?"

"I wouldn't know about that. You see, we drove away."

"And you heard some shots?"

"Yes, about the time we got to the corner," Bode said.

"And you didn't go back?"

"No. We telephoned the police."

"And you," I said, "run the police."

"There's a chief," Bode pointed out, "but it's an appointive office."

"And I take it, that as is usual with cities of this size, the councilmen sort of divide up the work. One of them works with the tax department, one with the auditing department, and one with the police system."

"That's right."

"And you were the one who had charge of the police system?"

"Yes."

"Seems to me you could have used your position to put a sugar–coating on the pill."

"I couldn't. It was too hot. It was loaded with dynamite, I tell you. You've no idea of how intense the feeling is in this city."

I ground out my cigarette and said, "Well, I guess I don't want those slot machines after all."

"What are you talking about?"

"It's hopeless," I said, "I can't get you in office."

"Why not?"

"Because you won't come clean with me. You're a poor liar, considering all the practice you give yourself."

Bode said, "Now listen, I could tell you something which would change the whole complexion of this thing and make it look reasonable."

"I'm listening," I said.

"Ray Mansfield and I figured the fight wasn't doing the town any good," he said. "We went directly to Dalton and asked him what he wanted to call it off. He told us. He wanted eighty percent of the city printing, and Mayor Spred's scalp.

"He figured that Spred was inefficient and was giving the town a poor business administration. And he couldn't make peace without something to save his face. He said if Spred would quit, he would withdraw the recall business, and give us a list of a dozen men who would be satisfactory to him. We'd only have to agree to appoint any one of these men to fill Spred's unexpired term."

"And so you drove him out to Spred's place to put that proposition up to Layton Spred?"

"Yes. We figured there was a good chance Spred would do it, if it was put to him in the right way."

"Then why didn't you give him the right kind of sales' talk?"

"Because we didn't want Spred to know we were in back of it. We didn't want him to think the deal had been made. He'd have been sure we were selling him out. It was agreed that Dalton was to go in and put the proposition up to Spred. If Spred fell for it, or was dubious, Dalton was going to ring us in on the conversation.

"Otherwise, we were just going to sit in the car and Spred would never know we were waiting out there. Then Spred would tell us about it later and we'd try to sell him on the idea — as his friends."

"And what happened?" I asked.

"Dalton went to the front door and rang. He pushed his face against the diamond–shaped glass in the front of the door. He saw Spred coming down the corridor. Spred saw him. I don't know what Spred did that frightened Dalton, but I can guess.

"He started to run toward the car. Then he saw he couldn't make it, and swerved around the porch. Spred jerked the door open and didn't waste a second. He dashed along the porch. We could see that he was holding a revolver.

"We didn't want Spred to see us there. Dalton had already headed in the direction of the alley. There was nothing for us to do. We pulled out."

"And called the police?"

"I put through as anonymous call. I didn't want to figure in it. Later on, of course, I admitted my identity."

"And you really thought Dalton could sell Spred on quitting?"

"Yes. He was to resign on account of his health — after the recall had been dropped. Otherwise, he'd have been kicked out in the recall."

"Why didn't you point that out to him?"

"We wanted Dalton to break the ice. We didn't want Spred to think we'd sold him out."

"But you had, hadn't you?"

"Don't act dumb," he said savagely. "Of course we sold him out. Someone had to be the goat. It was better to toss him overboard than to have the whole damn ship sink."

"Whose proposition was it," I asked, "yours or Dalton's?"

"Mine," Bode admitted, "and I had to talk like hell to make it stick. Dalton had us on the run, and knew it."

"Well," I said, slowly, "that makes a lot more sense than the story you gave the press."

"But you see why we don't dare to tell the truth, Wennick."

"Yeah," I said. "And so I'll see you tomorrow morning at ten–thirty. In the meantime, where can I get some action?"

"What do you mean, action?" Bode asked.

"You know what I mean — gambling. I'm a stranger in town. I have no place to go."

"There isn't any place in town where you could sit in on a game," he protested. "This is a clean town. The police have —"

"Come on, Bode," I said. "You've got to do better than that. In the first place, you aren't fooling anyone, and in the second place, I'm a bad man for you to irritate right now."

He shifted his eyes and said, "Try three–eighteen Benson Avenue. Watch the crowd and get the set–up before you burn any bridges. And if you ever say I gave you the name of the place, I'll call you a liar. Do you get me?"

I said, "Okay, be seeing you tomorrow."

III

Judicious inquiry gave me the information I needed about how to get out to Spred's house. I bought a pocket flashlight in a drugstore, caught a bus, and had a fifteen minute ride from the center of town.

Layton Spred's residence was a product of bygone architecture. There were spacious grounds with a tennis court on one side and trees and hedges casting black splotches over the darkness of the lawn. The stars were staring down with that steady blaze of illumination which you'll only see in localities which are in the high, dry mountains or which border the desert.

I was able to get a pretty good idea of the lay of the land. I could see the wide veranda which ran around the south and west corner of the house. Evidently, Spred had run out the front door, dashed down this porch, and shot from the extreme end of it.

I decided to take a look around toward the back, where the body had been discovered, and debated for a moment whether to walk around the corner of the block keeping to the sidewalk and coming up the alley, or to vault the hedge. It was the part of prudence to keep out of the ground and go around the sidewalk.

It was shorter vaulting the hedge. I vaulted the hedge.

I was about half–way through the grounds, keeping to the denser darkness, and not taking my eyes from the huge pile of the dark house, when I became conscious of a shadow wavering across the lawn.

I stopped stock–still, wondering what had caused that sudden flickering. Had a light gone on in the house?

I stood perfectly still, waiting, listening, hearing and seeing nothing. But I was pretty sure that some nocturnal activity was going on in the grounds — an activity which might be connected with the matter I was investigating, and which it would be dangerous to ignore.

I was looking toward the house when I saw it again, a flicker of light across the grass. And this time a tree cast a definite shadow, enabling me to determine the direction of the source of illumination.

I swung about to face the alley near where the body had been discovered, and moved around the shrubbery until I had an unobstructed view.

A few seconds later, I caught the gleam of a flashlight, and saw a moving pencil of illumination flit across the lawn, hesitate for a moment as it passed over the edge of a flower bed, swung over to one side, and played for a moment at the base of the tree. Then it snuffed out into blackness.

I ran as fast as I could without stumbling in the darkness or running the risk of crashing headlong into a bush. By the time the flashlight came on again, I was crouched down in the shadows, keeping well out of sight. Then, in the ensuing interval of darkness, I closed the gap until I was within less than twenty feet of the tree over which the light had played before it had been switched off. Bent almost double, I crawled noiselessly through the shadows.

The next time the light came on I waited until the beam had swung in the other direction, then straightened, and strained my eyes to catch a glimpse of the figure using the flashlight. I stood motionless, watching, adjusting myself to a development which I had not anticipated. The figure which was outlined against the beam was a woman, and, as nearly as I could judge she was young and attractive.

The flashlight beam swung around again, now high, now low, and then went out for the third time.

I satisfied myself that the woman was alone, stepped out from behind the bush, and walked quietly along the grass. She was so intent on what she was doing, that she neither heard nor saw me. The flashlight came on again when I was within three feet of her.

"Looking for something?" I asked.

She screamed, and jumped back, then spun around facing me, and started doing something with her hands. I couldn't see just what, but I had no intention of taking chances. I covered the distance in two quick steps and circled her with my arms, holding her so that she couldn't move her hands.

She struggled fiercely but silently. She stamped at my instep, kicked up at me with her knee, and twisted furiously to get her arms loose. She was young, lithe, and as resilient as live rubber.

I said, "Take it easy, sister. If you'll act just a little more like a woman, I'll let you loose."

Her struggles subsided.

"I hate to do this," I said, "but I have to make sure you haven't a gun. Please understand that it's business and not affection."

I slid my hands along the outlines of her figure, patting the places where I thought she might have a gun concealed. I felt her stiffen indignantly, but she remained motionless.

"Sorry," I said, releasing my hold, "but I had to take precautions. Now, what are you doing here?"

"What," she countered, "are you doing here?"

"Looking around," I said.

"I'm looking around," she told me, "and unless you want to find yourself at police headquarters within the next thirty minutes, you'd better start talking now, and talk plenty fast."

I realized she had me. I had to tell her where I stood, but I wanted to make certain what I said wouldn't be something I'd regret later on.

"Look here," I said, "you don't think Layton Spred shot Dalton, do you?"

I heard her gasp. "The police say he did."

"Were the police here?" I asked.

"No, but the police have recovered the bullet, and it came from Mr. Spred's gun."

"That," I said, "makes it rather difficult, doesn't it?"

"Of course it does," she said.

"That," I told her, "is why I'm out here looking around."

"You mean you don't believe the police?"

"I don't believe Spred killed Dalton," I said, being pretty certain of my ground now.

"Who are you?"

"I'm an investigator from the city, and please don't turn that flashlight in my face, because I'd much prefer to remain entirely incognito."

"I'm sorry," she said simply, and stabbed the beam full in my face.

After a moment, the beam switched out, and she said, "I've never seen you before."

"Under those circumstances," I said, "perhaps you'll tell me who you are."

"I'm Edith Forbes, Layton Spred's secretary."

"Yes, you are!"

"But I am."

"Tell me something I can believe. If you were his secretary, you wouldn't be snooping out here in the grounds after everyone else in the house has gone to bed. You'd have gone into the house and talked with his daughter. You'd have told her what you had in mind, and the two of you would have been out here together."

"Not with that daughter," she said.

"What's wrong with her?"

"She's afraid I'm going to marry her father, and inherit half of the money."

"Is there money?" I asked.

"The stars," she said pointedly, "are unusually bright tonight, aren't they?"

"Just the stars?" I asked.

"And investigators from the city," she added.

I said, "We might help Mr. Spred, if we could quit swapping sarcastic comments long enough to get back to what we were discussing."

Edith Forbes said, "Well, if you're going to help him, you'll never do it working through Millicent. Do you know what that little fool did? Instead of hiring one of the local lawyers with political connections and a chance to get at least a hung jury, she went dashing down to the city and retained Jonathan and Boniface.

"I shouldn't have to tell you what that means. Everyone in town thinks she's sure her father is guilty, and that the case is just about hopeless. This man, Boniface, is a stuffed shirt. He won't be able to do anything with a local jury. God knows how he ever acquired the reputation he has."

"I take it," I said, "that Boniface has been questioning you. What did you tell him?"

"I told him that I thought his ability had been sadly overrated."

I chuckled at that, knowing how Cedric L. Boniface would take it. "I suppose," I said, "he didn't see the joke."

"It wasn't a joke," she said. "He didn't like it. He said, as he left the office, that he would advise his client to hire a new secretary."

"Makes it nice for you, doesn't it?" I chided, a trifle sardonically, before I realized that she was crying. "Come, come," I said, patting her lightly on the shoulder. "You've got to buck up. Giving way like this won't help to clear up the case, and get Spred out of jail."

I slid my arm around her waist, but she wouldn't take advantage of my shoulder as a resting place. She pushed me away and said, "I'm all right, and besides I'm not crying. I'm just a little nervous."

I said, "We're both nervous. What were you looking for out here?"

"Evidence," she said.

"Evidence," I said, "is a broad word."

She fished out a handkerchief.

"You must be looking for something, Miss Forbes," I said gently.

"I'm not," she said, "honestly. I'm just looking."

"Haven't the police searched the grounds pretty thoroughly?" I asked.

"I don't think so," she said. "I've a feeling the police are just going through motions. The case is so hot, and there are so many political risks involved in taking sides that the police are keeping right on the middle of the fence, carrying water on both shoulders."

"Look," I said, "the thing that makes the case so black against your boss is that three shells being fired from his gun. It looks as though he'd done all the shooting."

"Well, he didn't. He said someone fired at him out of the darkness and he could see the little spurts of flame which came from the muzzle of the gun when the shots were fired."

"I know," I said, "and if everyone on the jury knew him as well as you do, he'd probably be acquitted. But there are going to be people from both political camps on the jury. He'll have some friends who have no doubt as to his honesty. But there'll be others who have been influenced by the *Marlin Morning Star*. In their eyes he's the devil's chief deputy."

She said, "The way the *Star* has been lying about him is terrible. It's just been a malicious campaign of insinuations, innuendoes, and downright lies. I'm glad Dalton was killed!"

"I'm sure," I said, "there are lots of people who aren't shedding any tears over Dalton. But he seems to have been a pretty good publicity man. He got his stuff across. About two-thirds of the town thinks your boss is a crook."

Edith started to cry again then, and I said, "Now, take it easy. If you want to help him, you can't do it by roaming around with a flashlight in the dark and crying over the editorials Dalton ran in his newspaper. Do you know what would help him?"

"No," she asked, looking a little startled. "What would?"

"Well," I said slowly, "you'd better not stay out here any longer tonight, because I don't think you'll find anything. In fact, if you were found here, it might look bad for more than one reason. But if someone else did some searching, and should happen to find a gun lying on the grass or near the edge of the flower bed where it wasn't too conspicuous, and there were two discharged shells in the cylinder of that gun — well, it would be a cinch that your boss would be acquitted."

"Just a little thing like that?" she asked, and I could tell from the tone of her voice that she was doing a lot of thinking.

"A little thing like that," I said, "would change the whole picture. It would make it appear that Dalton had gone out to your boss's house intending to kill him, but had lost his nerve when he saw that Spred was armed, and had started to run. It would look as though he'd turned and fired two shots, at dangerously close range and Spred was forced to shoot back in self-defense.

"There'd be a big switch in public sentiment almost overnight. Your boss would be a martyr and a hero, and the recall election would fail and lots of things would happen, all over something as little and insignificant as a gun."

"What caliber gun?" Edith asked.

"It wouldn't make any difference," I said, "just so long as it was a gun."

"But how would that explain the fact that no bullets struck anywhere — not even against the side of the house?"

"It might mean that Dalton was so frightened he was shooting wild and missed the side of the house," I said. "It would give the lawyers something to argue about. And the weight of the evidence would certainly be in Mayor Spred's favor."

Edith Forbes nodded. "If there were only some way of accounting for those bullets not hitting the house we could get a hung jury, any way," she said. "I'm sure of that."

"Dalton might have been shooting up in the air in order to frighten him," I said.

"That's it," she said quickly. "The important thing is to convince the jury that Dalton fired first."

Her voice trailed away, and she stood still for a moment, staring at the ground. Abruptly, she asked, "What's your name?"

"Wennick," I said, "Pete Wennick."

"Mr. Wennick," she said, "I think you're wonderful. I'm awfully glad I met you tonight. I think perhaps it was fate. Do you have a car?"

"No," I said, "I came on a bus."

"Come on," she said, "I'll drive you back to town."

I tucked her arm through mine, and we walked to the long hedge which bordered the alley. She said, "You'll have to lift me over. I crawled through on my tummy when I got in, but —"

I scooped her up, lifted her over the hedge, and just before I dropped her on the other side, felt her arms around my neck, and the hot circle of her lips pressing against mine.

"You're wonderful," she said.

My blood pressure ran up seventy or eighty points, and I almost forgot to be careful about not leaving footprints when I came over the hedge. There was a lot about Edith Forbes I didn't know, but one thing I was sure — it wasn't the first time she'd ever kissed a man.

Her car was an inexpensive, new model convertible, and she was a good driver.

As we got out where the city lights were a little on the garish side I studied her profile carefully. She was chestnut–haired with a snug–fitting hat, a nose which turned up, and a mouth that I already knew about.

I was interested in thinking of possibilities which I hoped might materialize into a chain of events. I figured I could trust this girl, and if I was going to give stuffed–shirt Cedric Boniface very many breaks, I certainly needed someone I could trust.

Abruptly, she turned to me and said, "I'm going to an apartment. I want you to keep out of circulation for two hours, and then knock twice on the door."

"It will be after midnight, if I have to wait that long."

"That's all right," she said. "The door will be unlocked."

"Some girl's apartment?" I asked.

She hesitated for a moment, then said: "No, my boy friend."

"Oh–oh," I said.

"Now listen, what's your first name again?"

"Pete."

"All right Pete. Don't be like that. This boy is Carl Gail, and he's smart. He knows his way around. I think you'll like him. In any event, he can help us."

"Well, why not let me go on up and meet him. That way we'll be two hours to the good before we start? After all, we haven't unlimited time."

"No," she said, "I'm going to have to prepare him for this, and it will take a little time."

"Two hours," I said, "would give you time for a plane trip to Miami and back. Almost, anyway."

"We have things to do."

I started to ask some more questions, and then decided to keep quiet. She swung the car down a side street off the main boulevard and came to a district where old–fashioned residences stood elbow to elbow with tall apartment houses.

She said, "They keep the front door unlocked until one. You come in at twelve–thirty, climb the first flight of stairs, and walk back to apartment eighty–one. Just knock twice and go in. Don't let anyone see you."

I did a lot of thinking before I said, "Okay, Edith. It's your party."

"And you won't mind walking wherever you're going from here, will you? The center of town is straight down that street, and in about two blocks you'll come to a hotel where there is a taxi stand out in front. There's at least one cab there all the time. I'm sorry I can't drive you there, but seconds are precious, and we have things to do."

I said slowly, "You might tell your boy friend to remember that guns have numbers on them, and can be traced. It would look like hell if anything got traced back to you."

"Good Lord, Pete," she said, "I wasn't born yesterday."

"I'll be there at twelve–thirty," I said, and walked around to help her out of the car. She gave me a flash of legs, a quick smile, and was gone.

I walked down a street whistling a little tune, and beginning to think it was a pretty good world after all. It looked like Cedric Boniface might get the breaks he'd been counting on.

IV

Almost anything was apt to be behind the closed door of apartment 81. I had to open the door to find out. Of course, I was taking chances. Cedric L. Boniface was running no risks by wrapping himself in a cloak of professional ethics and staying in the best suite at the hotel, while he enjoyed himself looking up legal points in the law books. But I had to be out on the firing line.

I found the outer door of the apartment house open just as Edith Forbes had said it would be. I climbed the stairs, and walked noiselessly down the corridor. For thirty seconds I stood at the door of 81, listening.

Then I knocked twice, pushed the door open, and moved backwards a few steps just as a precautionary measure, in case I didn't like what I saw.

Lights were on in the apartment. Edith Forbes was seated facing the door. Near her, holding a glass of whiskey in his hand, was a thin guy with a dome–shaped forehead, bat ears and a scrawny neck.

"Come in, Pete," Edith Forbes said.

I walked on in, grinning sheepishly. "One never knows what's on the other side of a door in a strange house," I said.

Edith said, "This is Carl Gail about whom I told you." Her voice sounded dispirited.

The skinny guy put down the glass, strode across to the middle of the room, and wrapped cold, bony fingers around my hand.

I pumped his arm up and down for a second, walked to the couch, seated myself, and looked meaningly at the whiskey glass by the side of Gail's chair.

"Drink?" he asked.

"Yes," I said.

He went out to the kitchenette, and after a moment, called out, "Do you want a chaser, Wennick?"

"Just a whiskey on the rocks," I said.

I looked across at Edith Forbes. She wouldn't meet my eyes. I could see she'd been crying.

Gail came back with the drink. "Don't you want one, Edith?" he asked.

I motioned a salute to them over the rim of the glass, and tossed it off. Gail sat down. No one seemed inclined to say very much. I took a package of cigarettes from my pocket, picked one out, and said, "Who does the talking?"

No one said anything for a second. Then Edith Forbes started to say something, and when she did, Gail interrupted her to say hastily, "I do the talking — what there is of it."

I lit the cigarette and settled back against the cushions.

"Your idea," Gail said to me, "is lousy."

I raised my eyebrows. "My idea?"

"Yes. Trying to get Edith to plant a gun out there at Mayor Spred's place. I'm surprised you'd make a suggestion like that. Planting evidence in a murder case is a damned serious offense —"

"Now wait a minute," I interrupted. "Somebody's got the cart before the horse, and the buggy turned backwards. What the hell are you talking about?"

"You know," he said. "What you told Edith to do."

"I didn't tell her to do anything."

"Didn't you tell her to get a gun, fire two shots from it, and plant it?"

"I certainly did nothing of the sort," I said indignantly. "What the hell do you think I am? I mentioned to Edith that if the police hadn't searched the place closely they should do so because they might find a gun with two exploded chambers. She said she knew Mr. Spred was incapable of telling a lie, and I was inclined to take her word for it. Therefore, I think there's a gun out there."

"And you didn't want her to plant one?" he asked.

"Good Lord, no! Of course not!"

Edith Forbes looked up, and started to say something. Then she seemed to think better of it, and lowered her tear–swollen eyes.

I warmed to my subject. "I can't look any farther into a brick wall than the next man," I said. "But if Spred is telling the truth there's bound to be a gun like that out there somewhere. Neighbors heard three shots. They heard them distinctly. It was a calm, still night. There isn't any chance they could be mistaken about the number.

"Spred says someone fired two shots at him. Now, of course, it might be that someone was lying in wait for him out in the shrubbery and that Dalton didn't fire at all. I'd say the chances were about one in a thousand it happened that way."

"Make it one in a million," Gail said.

"Okay, we'll make it one in a million. Now then, if Spred's telling the truth and Dalton shot at him, the gun must have been dropped by Dalton about the time he was shot, or he might have flung it away after he fired the two shots and turned to run."

Gail said slowly, "Spred isn't telling the truth."

Edith Forbes looked up indignantly. "He is! He is, Carl, and you know it."

Gail didn't say anything to her. He kept his eyes on me, large, brown, thought-ful eyes. "Edith," he said, "is crazy about Layton Spred. She's worked for him ever since she got out of school. She doesn't realize that no matter how square a shooter a man may be to those who are working with him, he has to protect himself and his friends when it comes to a murder rap."

"You know him well?" I asked.

"Of course I know him well. I've been at his house for dinner with Edith half a dozen times."

"Pardon me for getting personal," I asked, "but as Edith's boy friend?"

"Naturally. Oh, don't look at me like that. Hell, there's nothing between Edith and her boss. She's just a hero worshipper. He's old enough to be her grandfather, and everything's on the up and up."

"I see," I said.

"I had dinner there three nights ago," Gail said, "and he was very friendly and went out of his way to make me feel he was glad to see me, and so did Millicent, his daughter. Edith doesn't like her, but for the life of me I can't see why."

Edith Forbes said, vindictively, "She's a scheming little witch. Of course, she was nice to you, Carl, because she hopes you'll marry me. She's afraid I'll marry her father."

Gail's laugh was scornful. "Don't be such a fool," he said. "She tries her best to be nice to you, but you snap her head off every time she opens her mouth."

I saw color mounting Edith Forbe's cheeks, so I said, "Well, I just dropped in to say 'hello' and meet you. I still think it would be a good idea to have the police search the place pretty thoroughly. But don't get any ideas through your head about me wanting to have Edith plant a gun."

"Well," he said dubiously, "I'm glad you feel that way about it, because it would have put Edith in a hell of a spot."

I got up and shook hands with him.

"That's the last thing I'd want to do," I said.

Edith Forbes waited until I was almost at the door before she asked:

"What are you going to do now?"

"Just look the city over a bit," I said. "I'll probably be turning in in another hour or so."

"You're going to do some investigating?"

"Oh, I'll drift around and keep my eyes and ears open," I said.

She gravely handed me a leather key container. "That's what I thought," she said. "You're going to need a car. Take mine."

"No, thanks," I said. "I wouldn't think of it. I'll get along all right. You'll need to get home and —"

"I am home," she said.

I didn't want to make a bum guess on what she seemed to be implying. Carl Gail saw the look on my face, and laughed. "She means she has an apartment in this same building," he said, "down on the lower floor. Her car stays out front. So you don't need to worry about using it.

"Go ahead and take it, drive around as much as you want to, and bring it back here by eight o'clock in the morning. Edith won't even miss it."

"You don't need to bring it back," she said. "I hardly use it except on weekends. Carl uses it most of the time, and if you're working to help Mr. Spred, Carl can walk."

"Sure, I'll walk," he said, slipping a long thin arm around Edith's shoulders. "Don't stay angry with me, honey. I'm just as anxious as Mr. Wennick is to help Spred clear himself, if he's not guilty. I just didn't want to have you get into serious trouble with the law." Carl Gail nodded at me. "She'll feel a lot better if you'll use the car, Wennick!"

"All right," I said, to smooth things over. "I'll use the car and thanks a lot, Edith. I'll have it back by three o'clock in the morning."

"You'd better keep it until tomorrow," she said. "You'll find taxis hard to get in this city. They don't cruise around much. You have to find a taxi stand or else telephone."

"Okay, folks," I said. "Thanks."

I walked down the corridor and did a lot of thinking. I was still thinking when I hit the sidewalk. It looked as though Boniface might not get the breaks after all, unless I wanted to stick my own neck out. And that I didn't feel like doing under the circumstances.

Guns can be traced, and it would never do for me to plant a gun which had a big city background. And I couldn't afford to take a chance trying to dig up a gun inside of Marlin. I didn't know the town well enough.

I decided I'd drift down to the address Preston Bode had given me, and get an earful. I was sort of marking time until ten–thirty in the morning.

I eased myself into Edith Forbe's convertible, turned on the ignition, and moved slowly away from the curb, getting the feel of the car.

I'd gone about two blocks, when the left front tire went *ker–thunk, thumpity–thump!*

I got out and looked at the flat tire. If there were garages open that would send a man to fix a flat at that time of night, I'd have needed a crystal ball to locate them. I could have walked away and left the car at the curb, but ...

I peeled off my coat and started looking around for tools, and when I went to pull out the jack, I saw something that glittered in the reflections of the street light.

I gave a low whistle, took a handkerchief from my pocket so I wouldn't leave any fingerprints, and picked up the gun. It was a thirty–eight caliber, blue–steel. I broke open the cylinder.

There it was, just like the doctor ordered, two shells fired.

I wanted to do a little thinking, so I climbed into the back seat and sat holding the gun on my handkerchief. I fished out one of the live shells and looked at it. It was a blank! Another surprise awaited me. The other three live shells were ball cartridges.

I examined the manufacturer's mark on all of the shells and saw that the blank had been made by one company, the ball cartridges by another. As might have been expected, the two discharged shells were of the same make as the live blank.

That made it very simple.

I got out of the car, turned back to face the apartment house, and lifted my hat in a salute of silent respect.

Carl Gail's girl friend had said he knew the ropes and knew his way around. I'll say he did! And the beauty of it was, Edith Forbes probably didn't know anything about it. He'd simply excused himself for an hour or so, gone out and picked up the gun, planted two exploded blank cartridges, one unexploded blank cartridge, and three ball cartridges. He'd put it under the front seat of the car where the tools were, and stuck a tack in the top of the left front tire.

After that, all he needed to do was to see that I took the car. The rest worked out like clockwork. If anyone ever claimed he'd given me the gun, he could deny it under oath with no danger of facing a reprimand for perjury and complicity in planting false evidence and a prison term of four or five years.

I jacked up the car, put the spare on the left front wheel, and drove out to within two blocks of Layton Spred's house. By this time, I knew the ropes pretty well. I didn't try to gild the lily in any way.

I stood by the hedge in the alley, picked a likely–looking flower bed, made certain none of my fingerprints were on the gun, and tossed it over.

I returned the car to the curb in front of the apartment house, went to my room, and slept the dreamless sleep of the pure in heart.

In the morning, I found a telephone booth in a large restaurant, and called police headquarters.

I didn't do anything as crude as suggest to the police they'd find the gun if they looked around Layton Spred's grounds. I said, "There's something I think you should know. Cromley Dalton went out to Spred's place in connection with a payoff. Dalton had one hundred thousand dollars in greenbacks he was going to slip to Layton Spred. If something happened to him and you didn't find the money, you'd better go back and take another look."

I slammed the receiver back into place.

I didn't give a damn who controlled the police force. No cop was going to take a chance that a package containing one hundred thousand dollars in cold cash might fall into the hands of someone who didn't know what to do with it.

Ten–thirty found me at Preston Bode's office. His secretary said I was expected, and to go right on in.

When I pushed open the door of the private office, I got a shock. Two men were with Bode. One of them was Carl Gail. The other was a tall fidgety man in the late fifties who looked frightened to death.

Bode said, "Good morning," to me, and then to the tall man, "Meet Mr. Mansfield, Mr. Wennick. And shake hands with Mr. Gail."

I shook hands with Mansfield and turned around to face Gail, wondering what he was going to say.

All he did was wrap his cold, thin fingers around my hand, and acknowledge the introduction with a nod.

I sat down and sparred for time while I was getting out a cigarette. I looked across at Preston Bode, but my mind wasn't where my eyes were. My attention was concentrated on Carl Gail, whom I could still see out of the side of my eye.

Gail wasn't avoiding me in the least. He seemed no more than just naturally curious.

Bode said, "Gentlemen, Wennick has a proposition to make us."

"Haven't you outlined it to them?" I asked.

"Not in detail," Bode said. "I just touched on the high spots."

I was seized with a desire to do no more talking than was necessary.

"The high spots," I said, lighting my cigarette, "are all there is to it. I want slot machines. I could go to the opposition and talk terms. Those terms would be just about the same as they will be after the opposition has been elected to office. You people stand a slim chance of getting in, so I'm talking with you on a ten to one basis. After I get the concession, I'll do my best to keep you in office."

"How much?" Preston Bode asked.

"Five percent of the gross take," I said.

He snorted, "We could get fifty."

"Five percent is one tenth of fifty percent," I said. "You're a ten to one shot."

Mansfield said in a harsh, treble voice, "We didn't come here to be insulted."

Bode turned to him angrily. "The hell you didn't. I don't give a damn on the take on the slot machines. The thing that interests me is that Wennick can put us across with the voters. He's put other mayors in office. He knows his way around with voters. He has some ideas on mob psychology which sound all right to me. He can wrap ideas up in words when he wants to, and the words sound like maple syrup on buttered hot cakes. He understands politics, and we need someone who knows how a political machine should operate."

"It's all right by me," Gail said. "If he can put the ticket across, in the face of the stuff we've got to fight, I'd be willing to give him the town."

Mansfield tightened his lips. He was a sturdily built man with heavy black eyebrows that met above the bridge of his nose, and a jaw that seemed only a little less massive than the ones I'd seen on gorillas in the zoo.

"I don't like it," he said.

"Don't like what?" Bode demanded.

"Don't like anything about it. I started following your advice, and it keeps getting me in deeper and deeper. I want to quit. That's all I want. I want peace. I don't care about graft. I don't care about —"

"Shut up," Bode said. "You're in no position to quit now."

"I just want you to count me out. I don't want to have anything more to do with any of this business."

Bode said to Gail, "Don't pay any attention to him, Carl. He'll see reason when he hears what Wennick has to say."

Gail nodded. "I'd like to know something of Wennick's plan for handling this political situation."

"He says he can get Spred acquitted," Bode said, "and make him something of a martyr."

Mansfield cracked his knuckles, and said, "That's too dangerous to fool around with. Gentlemen, the more we get tied up with Spred's case, the more we are damned in the eyes of the public. My advice is to throw Spred overboard, denounce him in no unmistakable terms, take everything which has gone sour during the last two years, and dump it on Spred's shoulders."

"You can't do that," I said. "If anything has gone sour, you either got your cut or you were suckers. With the *Star* beating the reform drums, the people aren't going to like crooks."

"Wennick's right," Gail said, through a cloud of cigarette smoke. "The minute we go before the voters trying to show that Spred victimized us and we didn't know what was going on, we make ourselves the laughing–stock of the city."

"Let's hear some more," Bode said.

"Before I do any talking," I said, "I always like to know whom I'm talking to. As I understand it, Mr. Mansfield is one of the councilmen."

"That's right."

"And who is Mr. Gail?"

Bode's eyes met mine. "Mr. Gail," he said, "is Mr. Gail."

"So I gathered," I said dryly.

"I am vouching for Mr. Gail," said Bode.

I looked across at Gail and said, "There's something vaguely familiar about your face. Haven't I seen you before somewhere?"

Gail looked me over with the sudden interested curiosity of one who is trying to place a familiar face. He studied my features, pursed his lips, looked reminiscent for a moment, and then slowly shook his head.

"I've never seen you before in my life," he said. "I never forget a face and I wouldn't be apt to begin with yours."

"Then it must have been a case of mistaken identity," I said. "Well, gentlemen, you can take it or leave it. My best guess is, that the way to handle this thing is to get Spred acquitted."

"Would we need a fall guy?" Gail asked.

"Why not make Dalton the fall guy?" I asked.

"How?" Bode asked.

"By making it appear that Spred shot him in self–defense."

"It's too late to do anything like that now," Bode said.

"I'm not so certain," Gail said, studying the tip of his cigarette.

The telephone rang several times, sharply, insistently. Bode frowned and said, "Damn that girl. I told her I wasn't to be interrupted, no matter what happened."

He jerked the receiver from the telephone, and said, "Evelyn, what the hell's the matter? I told you I wasn't to be —"

His voice trailed away into silence. I saw his face show a quick flicker of surprise, then set in the wooden lines of a man who is betting aces–up in a poker game and is worried about them. They're too big to lay down, and not big enough to put much faith in.

He did lots of listening and no talking. After the receiver had stopped making noise in his ear, he said, "I'll think it over and call you back. I'm busy now. Goodbye."

He dropped the receiver into place, and looked around at us as though debating whether he should say anything. Finally, he said, "That was police headquarters giving me a first confidential report. The boys made another search of Spred's grounds this morning. Down in a flower bed where it had escaped observation before, they found Dalton's gun. Two shells had been fired.

"It looks as though they were blanks. Four shells hadn't been fired — one blank and three bullets. You see what that means? Dalton figured Spred was bluffing with all of his talk about shooting him down like a dog. He was going to show Spred up. So he either fired straight at him to give him the fright of his life, or fired the blanks at his feet to make him dance."

Ray Mansfield wiped his forehead with his handkerchief.

Carl Gail was eying him narrowly. His face became cold, and hard as granite. I saw the skin grow white across his knuckles as his hands gripped the arm of the chair.

"How," he asked, "did the police happen to go out there to look?"

"Some guy telephoned in that Dalton had dropped a wad of pay off money."

"And the cops went out without saying anything to you?" Gail asked.

Bode fidgeted. "Well," he said, "the call came in early this morning and —"

"Nuts," Gail interrupted. "If the dough had been there, they were going to give you a double–cross. That shows how much control you have over the police department."

"Boys," I said, "you can see for yourselves what it all adds up to. Mayor Spred is certain to be acquitted now. Don't you think it would be wise for me to handle it so you can get a coat of whitewash?"

It was Gail who spoke. "No," he said. "We don't."

I tried to keep the surprise out of my face and knew that I failed. Hell, he could have hit me in the face with a wet towel, and I wouldn't have felt any more surprised.

Bode almost fell out of his chair. "What's that?" he asked.

Gail ground out the end of his cigarette in an ash tray. "I said no," he said simply.

Mansfield fidgeted around in the chair. "As far as I'm concerned, that's exactly the way I feel about it. I just want out of this. I want to quit."

"Carl, what's eating you?" Bode said to Gail. "This man can —"

"You asked me, didn't you?" Gail said, without raising his voice,

"Sure, I asked you. But I thought your answer was going to make sense."

"You have it," Gail said. "It does."

Bode looked imploringly up at me. "Now listen, Wennick, let's not have any hard feelings over this. I think there's been a bit of a misunderstanding. Would you mind leaving us alone while we talk it over?"

"Not in the least," I said, and then turned to face Gail. "Your young friend has the reputation of knowing his way around. He thinks that with the finding of that gun, Spred's acquittal is certain, and that you don't need to make any concessions in order to beat the recall election. That, gentlemen, is what I call chiseling, and I have one treatment for chiselers. I hope I don't have to use it. Good morning."

VI

I walked out into the sunlight as dazed as an addle–brained boxer who has stopped one with his chin just when he thinks the other man's knees are buckling. I had one little chore I wanted to do.

I called a taxi and went into Spred's office. Edith Forbes was in the reception room, pounding away on a typewriter. She looked up as I opened the door and smiled when she saw who it was.

"Hello," I said, "How's chances for a talk?"

"Swell."

"You and I," I said, "have a few things to go over."

"I know," she said. "I've been expecting you. You've no idea how cheap I felt when Carl Gail turned us down. I thought I could surely depend on him. But instead of that he had this virtuous attitude and — but you were splendid, Pete. You went out and did it all by yourself, didn't you?"

I looked at her the way a banker eyes an applicant for a promissory note. "Yes," I said. "All by myself without any help from anyone."

Her hand closed over mine impulsively. "Oh, Pete," she said, "I'm so glad!"

"How," I asked, "did you hear about it?"

"One of the girls at the *Free Press* rang up to tell me about it. She said it's thrown the district attorney into a stew. He doesn't know what to do now."

"No," I said, "he wouldn't. How long was your boy friend gone last night?"

"What do you mean?"

"After you saw him the first time he went out, didn't he?"

"No," she said, looking at me blankly.

"Are you sure?"

"Yes."

"Were you there all the time?"

"Well not all the time. I went in and talked with him, and then when I saw how he was, I went out in a rage and went down to my apartment. I came back after a while and pleaded with him."

"How long were you gone?"

"Oh, I don't know. Fifteen or twenty minutes perhaps."

"He was there when you left?"

"Yes, of course."

"And when you got back?"

"He was still there."

"What was he doing when you returned?"

"Why, playing the radio and smoking."

I heaved a sigh, and said, "That boy friend of yours is a fast worker. How long have you known him?"

"Oh, almost a year."

"What does he do for a living?"

"He's a promoter," she said.

I nodded. "I'll say he's a promoter."

"Listen, Pete, you don't need to pay any attention to him. I know one thing. He'll keep his mouth shut."

"Yes," I said, "he seems to be rather close-mouthed. I sat in on a conference with him about half an hour ago, and he'd said he'd never seen me before in his life."

She stared at me incredulously. "He said what?"

"That he'd never seen me before in his life."

She stared at me for a minute, and then slow comprehension appeared in her eyes. "Oh," she said, "that's wonderful!"

"What," I asked, "is wonderful about it?"

"Carl," she said. "He's taking that way to let you know he's standing by you. Can't you see? He wants you to know that he'll never repeat that conversation which took place last night."

The telephone rang. She picked up the receiver, and said, "Yes? Why, yes, he is. Very well, hold the phone please."

She looked up at me and said, "Were you expecting a call, Pete?"

I shook my head.

"It's Mr. Boniface. He says that he wants to talk with you."

Now, how the devil did old stuffed shirt Boniface know where I was? I took the telephone, said, "Hello," and heard Boniface's voice sounding as mournful as winter wind howling around the eaves of a deserted house — and just about as cold.

"Wennick," he said. "I'm in my suite in the hotel. You will please come up here immediately."

"I'm busy now," I said.

"Not too busy to come here," he said. "I don't mind telling you that I am standing between you and a most serious charge. Only my personal influence has kept the situation in hand thus far. I feel certain that anyone who has had the privilege of working with such a strictly ethical attorney as E.B. Jonathan could never be guilty of the things of which you are accused. But, nevertheless, I must admit the evidence is —"

"Who's doing the accusing?" I asked.

"The police," he said.

"All right," I told him, "I'm coming up."

I hung up the telephone. Edith Forbes looked at me with eyes that were filled with gratitude. "Pete," she breathed softly, "I can never thank you enough, and you can bet that Mr. Spred will never forget what you did as long as he lives. Very few men would have had the courage —"

I patted her shoulder, and said, "Better wait and see how it works out. We aren't exactly out of the woods yet. Keep your ear to the ground and find out everything you can. I'll be seeing you."

I was doing lots of thinking on my way to the hotel, and I did a lot more when I opened the door of Boniface's suite and found an officer in a captain's uniform, a plain clothes man, and a guy who had young hoodlum stamped all over him standing on opposite sides of Cedric L. Boniface, who looked as though he was just about to give birth to kittens.

I didn't say anything in greeting, just waited for Boniface to say something. But before he could the kid who looked like a juvenile trouble–maker turned watery eyes in my direction, stretched out a yellow–stained forefinger, and said, "That's the guy."

There was an instant of silence, one of those dramatic silences which seemed to call for the accused to do something dramatic, like taking poison or sobbing out a confession. But all I did was to sit down in one of the overstuffed chairs, take out a cigarette, light it, blow out the match, and nod.

"Unquestionably, I am the guy," I said. "Now, what's it all about?"

The police captain started to speak, but Boniface interrupted him. "Let me handle this, please."

When the captain yielded the floor, Boniface turned to me in his most pompous manner, and said, "Wennick, do you know the nature of the charge against you?"

"I've waded through three books of Blackstone," I said. "I think the reading has probably broadened my mental powers. But telepathy is a bit advanced, and I don't know of a judge who would permit you to base a case on it."

He said, "The occasion hardly calls for levity, still less for sarcasm. Were you aware, Wennick, that the police had discovered a gun out at Spred's house?"

"I heard something about it," I said.

"Where?"

"I was in a conference with some people, and the police telephoned."

Boniface waved aside my explanation as if he didn't think it was worth a moment's consideration.

"Wennick," he said, "this young man was picked up by the police this morning." He pointed to the young punk. "Admittedly he is a vagrant. His purpose in the neighborhood is open to question, to say the least. But the fact remains that around one o'clock this morning he was in the vicinity of Spred's residence.

"While he was there, he saw a car drive down the alley and stop. Because he thought it was a police prowl car, he hid in back of the hedge which borders Spred's grounds. He was, therefore, a witness to what happened. Do you know what happened — or shall I tell you?"

I blew a smoke ring at the ceiling, and said, "By all means, tell me."

"Very well," Boniface said. "This young man saw you vault over the hedge, walk to a flower garden, take a gun from your pocket, wipe it carefully to make certain you were leaving no finger prints, plant it in the garden, and return to the car. He had the presence of mind to get the license number of the automobile. It was one which belonged to Edith Forbes, the secretary of Layton Spred.

"An investigation discloses that you were driving that car last night. His description, however, fits you so perfectly, that as soon as I talked with him, I knew that he must have seen you, and that you must have been the man who was on the grounds.

"Now, Wennick, I implore you, for the sake of our office, for the sake of our client, and your own career, please make some explanation that will hold water. If you were just there looking for evidence, and perhaps you picked something up and put it in a handkerchief instead of dropping it —"

The punk kid was way ahead of Boniface, "He can't make that stick," he protested. "No matter what he claims. He wasn't picking anything up. I tell you, he took it out of his pocket and put it down, and even dusted off his hands with his handkerchief."

"You," I said, "have good eyes."

"You bet I have good eyes," he said, "particularly at night. But don't worry, there was enough light for me to see everything. I saw the kind of clothes you were wearing, the way you wear your hat tilted to one side, the swing to your shoulders, the —"

"Forget it," I said. "If you say you saw me climb over the hedge and put a gun in that flower bed, you're a damn liar."

Cedric Boniface heaved a sigh of relief. "Wennick," he said, "I was hoping you could say that."

"Well, I can say it all right, and what's more, I can make it stick."

The police captain said, "Don't think you're going to just pull that kind of stuff and get away with it. You're going to answer a lot of questions, and you're going to answer them right. Now, you had Edith's car last night. Where do you go?"

I looked at him, and said, "Who wants to know?"

He turned to the plain–clothes man. "We'll take him down to headquarters and question him there. We can do a lot better with a temporary detention cell at the end of the corridor. Maybe it won't be so temporary."

Boniface ran around like a mother hen chaperoning a chick under her wing when a hawk approaches. He put a fatherly hand on my shoulder. "Don't be like that, Wennick," he said. "Can't you realize that these gentlemen represent law and order? Don't you know that this attitude of insolent independence will get you nowhere?"

"For Pete's sake," I said, shaking off his hand. "Can't you ever get over being so damned pompous always?"

Boniface's jaw sagged. His face flushed a purplish red. "You damned up–start!" he said. "You have no right to speak to me that way —"

VII

Cedric Boniface broke off as the door opened and Preston Bode entered the room without the formality of knocking. Behind him was Carl Gail, and Ray Mansfield, who gave the impression of being in the party but not of it. His hang–dog manner, nervously twitching fingers, and downcast, shifty eyes all showed his wish to be somewhere else.

"Who are these men?" Boniface asked.

The captain got to his feet, and saluted. "Preston Bode," he said, "is the police commissioner. Ray Mansfield is councilman." He didn't say what Gail was.

Bode pushed a cigar up at an aggressive angle, surveyed Boniface, and said, "I know all about you. You're Cedric Boniface. You're Spred's lawyer. And I'm commencing to find out a hell of a lot about this guy, Wennick. He's the guy who does the dirty work. Well, this time he's done just a little too much of it."

"Now, what the devil are you talking about?" I asked Bode.

"You know damn well what I'm talking about. You planted that gun, and there's no use denying it."

"Now listen," I told him. "I'm commencing to get tired of this. But just in case you want to wash a little dirty linen in public, kindly remember that your political future depends on Layton Spred's acquittal, and you're the one who controls the police force."

"Well, I don't control the district attorney," Bode said. "And if you think I'd overlook my sworn duty in order to make political capital, you're crazy. I wouldn't condone crime no matter what depended on it. If you were my own brother, I'd adopt a fair, impartial attitude."

I looked at Gail and felt myself frowning thoughtfully. "You," I told him, "sure as hell do get around."

He didn't say anything.

Boniface said, "Really, gentlemen, I must call your attention to the fact that this is my suite in the hotel. I asked Mr. Wennick to come here so he could be confronted with witnesses and make any explanation which he could. I hardly intended to have the matter become a question of —"

"Never mind what you intended," Bode said. "We're running this town, and you're in a pretty tough spot yourself."

"I am?" Boniface exclaimed.

"You sure are."

"Why, I don't know what you're talking about," Boniface said. "Are you presuming to question my ethics, Sir?"

"Forget it," Bode said. "You're representing Spred. Wennick is your man. Wennick goes out and pulls a fast one. Don't tell me you weren't in on it."

As the full implication of the charge crashed home to Boniface, he sat down abruptly, all the color draining from his face.

I turned to the young punk. "You got the license number of that automobile?" I asked.

"Of course," he said.

"And you saw me jump over the hedge?"

"That's right."

"You," I told him, "are a damn liar. I parked the car two blocks from the place, and threw the gun over the hedge. I never left the alley."

"That's an admission," Bode shouted. "He's admitted now that he planted the gun. That's a confession."

"Sure, it's a confession," I said. "There's no law against tossing a gun into a flower bed. Wake up, you dumb hicks, and don't waste so much time trying to stampede me by getting a punk stool pigeon to bring in a perjured accusation. Of course, I took that gun out and threw it over the hedge. Now, I'll tell you some more things about that gun.

"I went up to Gail's apartment last night. I didn't say anything, but I knew it had been suggested to him that it would be a swell idea to plant a gun with a couple of exploded shells out there on Spred's grounds. He pretended to be indignant about the whole idea, but insisted that I take Edith Forbe's car. When I started to drive the car, I found I had a flat tire. And when I went to get at the tools, I found this gun.

"I figured that Gail had been a lot smarter than I'd given him credit for. He didn't want to get his fingers dirty, messing around with the thing, but he fixed it so that I could take the responsibility if I wanted to.

"I'm willing to admit that threw me all off the track. However, events of the last few hours have put me right back on the track.

"Now, let me ask you something. Why do you suppose I was wandering around here leaving myself wide open, asking someone to furnish a gun to toss into Spred's flower patch?"

"Because you were desperate and trying to get Spred acquitted," Bode said. "You admitted that yourself."

"Nuts," I said. "Let's do a little constructive detective work here instead of talking just for face exercise. Let's suppose that Layton Spred is telling the truth about what happened. People have been known to do that, you know. In that event someone framed him. Someone wanted to get Spred to fire a shot in the darkness.

"They knew the best way to do that was to get two shots fired out of the darkness at him. But in order to account for those two shots, they had to plant two empty cylinders in Spred's gun. That means it was someone who had access to the house. The daughter was out. Spred was a bachelor and didn't do any entertaining in his home. His secretary had the run of the place. Therefore, it looked as though she was nominated.

"I contacted her by accident. I wanted to see if she had a gun with two exploded shells in the cylinder. So I put on a nice act for her. She led me to her boy friend. The thing was handled so smoothly that it took me in. I fell for it, hook, line, and sinker. I figured Edith Forbes and her boy friend must be innocent, that they had gone out of their way to give me some evidence to plant. I believed them but I couldn't tip my hand by not doing my share, so I took the gun out and planted it.

"Recently, I've realized that what I thought was clever planning was just an accident. The car actually did have a flat tire, and Carl Gail had been using Edith Forbes' car. He'd used it the night of the murder. He had to put the gun he'd used some place where it wouldn't be found. Under the front seat on top of the tools looked like a good place. He didn't expect to be searched, but he wasn't taking any chances.

"Figure out for yourselves what happened. Cromley Dalton would never on earth have driven out to Spred's house with Bode and Mansfield. He'd never on earth have left Bode and Mansfield in the car and gone up to talk with Layton Spred himself. Nor would Bode and Mansfield have let him.

"What happened is a damn sight more apt to run like this. Dalton was conducting a hammer and tongs campaign. Bode and Mansfield had been running the police department. Carl Gail had been their contact man with the underworld, collecting the pay–off money. Cromley Dalton got the dope on the play. He was getting evidence that couldn't be contradicted. Gail and Bode decided they were going to kill him. They made Mansfield come in on it. He didn't want to.

"Gail managed to get Spred's gun when he was out there at dinner. They fired a couple of shells and saved the bullets, leaving the empty cartridges in the gun. They ambushed Dalton, shot him from behind, drove out and planted his body by the alley at Spred's house, rang Spred's doorbell, and when he came to the door, started to run toward the back.

"Naturally, Spred, being a hot–headed southerner, did just what they expected he would do — pulled a gun from his pocket and ran around the porch. Gail fired two blank cartridges. Spred rose to the bait, raised his gun, and fired wild into the darkness, and that was all they needed. Bode and Mansfield notified the police.

"It took Gail to plant the empty shells in Spred's gun, Bode to switch bullets at the police post mortem, substituting a bullet fired from Spred's gun in place of the one that had been taken from the body. That's the only way the facts make sense."

Bode said, "You're crazy. In addition to that, you're a damn liar. Furthermore, you're going to be arrested for defamation of character, for compounding a felony —"

I pushed him aside and walked over to where Mansfield was sitting. I grabbed him by the necktie, jerked him over to the edge of the chair, put my palm under his chin, and pushed his head up so he had to look me in the eyes.

"The trail is forking for you right now, Mansfield," I said. "Take the side which leads toward law and order, and you'll probably get off with a life sentence as having been an unwilling accomplice. Try to back these crooks up, and you'll be climbing the thirteen steps to the gallows. You know what they'll do when it comes to a showdown. They'll sell you out and make you the patsy!"

Bode lunged for me and said, "Captain Jones, arrest him."

I clipped Bode on the jaw. Gail came for me. I caught him in the pit of the stomach with the ball of my foot. The police captain scrambled toward me.

"Go on, Mansfield," I said. "Speak up. It's true, isn't it?"

Mansfield gulped twice, and said, "It's true," just as the captain's hand came down hard on my shoulder.

I said, "Okay, Captain Jones, you heard that confession. Mr. Boniface has heard it. Your police commissioner is a murderer. There's going to be a new police com–missioner. Now's the time for you to reach your decision. Are you going to stay with a sinking ship, or are you going to take the transfer?"

Mansfield said, "My God, I never did want to do it! I haven't been able to sleep since."

A shot rang out behind me. The back of the chair just behind Mansfield's head dissolved into splinters.

I whirled around. Bode had recovered from my punch and had a gun in his hand. "You damn squealer," he yelled at Mansfield, and raised the gun again.

I think he intended to escape — if he had any definite plans. But he clearly intended to give Mansfield a one–way ticket before he left.

I looked across at Boniface. He was nearest to Bode. "Grab him," I cried.

Boniface stood there as white and as useless as a hunk of dough.

I went for Bode.

I saw the business end of his gun looking like the entrance to a subway, pointed directly at my forehead. I went forward in a football tackle, trying to hit him low just below the knees.

I knew I wasn't going to make it from the time I left the ground, and so did Bode. There was a sneer on his face as he depressed the muzzle of the gun, drawing a bead on me just as a quail hunter takes a bead on a flying bird.

Suddenly a shot rang out.

I hit the floor and was surprised as hell to find I could still get up. Bode was staggering around the room, his right arm limp and nerveless at his side. Captain Jones had made his choice — with a big forty–five.

I decided I might as well be nonchalant and started dusting off the knees of my trousers. I'd have lit a cigarette, only I knew my hand would have trembled so I couldn't have held the match.

Boniface dropped back into his chair and was saying, "A fine way to bring a case to law! A fine way!"

I felt something puffing at my coat, looked down and saw that Ray Mansfield was on his knees.

"Don't let them!" he pleaded. "You're the only one who can straighten this thing out. They told me if I squealed they'd pin all of it on me."

"Better keep your mind on your work," I told Captain Jones. "Bode's shifting that gun to his left hand."

The captain took care of that.

Mansfield went on yammering.

The police captain said, "I'm leaving it up to you to square me with the public. You're a witness that I didn't let Bode keep me from doing my duty. I acted."

"Me, too," the plain–clothes man interrupted. "Don't leave me out of this."

I reached for my cigarette case then, and said, "I seem to be important as hell around here. Jones, you'd better put handcuffs on Gail while he's out. He's the brains of the outfit."

V

We sat in old E.B. Jonathan's private office, and from the way Cedric Boniface had told the story, you'd have thought I should have gone into the law library and committed hari–kari.

"It was," he concluded, "the most disgraceful exhibition of crude, vulgar violence I have ever seen. I warn you, Mr. Jonathan, that such tactics will result in the loss of our professional reputation. I am willing to admit that the case was solved, but only because I kept my head sufficiently to realize the full import of the statements made by the witnesses.

"The damning thing, the incredible thing, is that Peter Wennick, a man in our employ, should have actually gone out to the scene of the crime and planted evidence. If he had found that gun and thought it had any significance he should have reported it to the police. I demand that Wennick be discharged. We cannot afford to jeopardize our reputation."

Old E.B. looked at me sternly over the tops of his bifocals. "Wennick," he said, "you have heard the charges made by my junior partner. Because of your zeal, I am not going to let you out. But I warn you that if anything of this sort happens in the future, you will be discharged without so much as a day's notice. Do you under— stand?"

"I understand," I said.

Cedric Boniface got up and stalked pompously from the office. At the door he turned and said, "This is against my better judgment. If you keep him on, you will have to assume full responsibility."

Jonathan said, "I am not in the habit of delegating to others either my responsibilities, or my authority, Mr. Boniface."

Boniface was too dignified to slam the door, but his coat tails were eloquent as he stepped into the corridor and gently but firmly closed the door behind him.

Jonathan looked at me, and said, "Nice going, Wennick. But you should have kept Boniface from knowing."

"I couldn't," I said. "They went to Boniface with their own story, and he called me to his room. The thing started breaking all over the carpet. What the hell could I do?"

"I'm sure I don't know," Jonathan said. "But don't let it happen again. Incidentally, Miss Devers has something for you. You'll find her waiting in your office."

I didn't have any dignity to uphold, so I slammed the door as I walked out.

Mae Devers, looking as trim as an airplane stewardess, was perched on a corner of my desk, one shapely leg kicking gently back and forth.

"What ho, Counselor!" she said. "Why the frown?"

I said, "The frown becomes a grin. E.B. said you had something for me."

"I have," she said, and pushed out a tinted oblong of paper. "A check in your favor for a couple of thousand dollars drawn on E.B.'s private account. Naturally, he doesn't want Boniface to know he's giving you a bonus."

I pushed the check to one side and said, "He told me you had something for me."

She laughed and tried to duck.

"You wouldn't want to make E.B. Jonathan a liar, would you?" I asked.

"You win," she told me, and gave me her lips.

Flight Into Disaster

Only once before had the woman in the club car ever known panic — not merely fear but the real panic which paralyzes the senses.

That had been in the mountains when she had tried to take a short cut to camp. When she realized she was lost there was a sudden overpowering desire to run. What was left of her sanity warned her, but panic made her feel that only by flight could she escape the menace of the unknown. The silent mountains, the somber woods, had suddenly become enemies, leering in hostility. Only by running did she feel she could escape — by running — the very worst thing she could have done.

Now, surrounded by the luxury of a crack transcontinental train, she again experienced that same panic. Once more there was that overpowering desire to run. Someone had searched her compartment while she had been at dinner. She knew it was a man. He had tried to leave things just as he had found them, but there were little things that a woman would have noticed that the man didn't even see. Her plaid coat, which had been hung in the little steel closet so that the back was to the door, had been turned so the buttons were toward the door. A little thing, but a significant thing which had been the first to catch her attention, leaving her, for the moment, cold and numb. Now, seated in the club car, she strove to maintain an attitude of outward calm by critically inspecting her hands. Actually she was taking stock of the men who were in the car.

Her problem was complicated by the fact that she was a compactly formed young woman, with smooth lines, clear eyes, a complete quota of curves, and under ordinary circumstances, a latent smile always quivering at the corners of her mouth. It was, therefore, only natural that every male animal in the club car sat up and took notice.

The fat man across the aisle who held a magazine in his pudgy hands was not reading. He sat like a Buddha, motionless, his half-closed, lazy-lidded eyes fixed upon some imaginary horizon far beyond the confines of the car — yet she felt those eyes were taking a surreptitious interest in everything she did. There was something sinister about him, from the big diamond on the middle finger of his right hand to the rather ornate twenty-five-dollar cravat which begged for attention above the bulging expanse of his vest.

Then there was the man in the chair on her right. He hadn't spoken to her but she knew that he was going to, waiting only for an opportunity to make his remark sound like the casual comment of a fellow passenger.

He was in his late twenties, bronzed by exposure, steely-blue of eye. His mouth held the firmness of a man who has learned to command first himself and then others. The train lurched. The man's hand reached for the glass on the little stand between them. He glanced apprehensively at her skirt.

"Sorry," he said.

"It didn't spill," she replied almost automatically.

"I'll lower the danger point," he said, raising the glass to his lips. "Going all the way through? I'm getting off at six o'clock in a cold Wyoming morning."

For a moment her panic–numbed brain failed to appreciate the full significance of his remark, then she experienced a sudden surge of relief. Here, then, was one man whom she could trust. She knew that the man who had searched her baggage hadn't found what he wanted because she had it with her, neatly folded, fastened to the bottom of her left foot by strong adhesive tape. Therefore the enemy would stay on the train as long as she was on it, waiting, watching, growing more and more desperate, until at last, perhaps in the dead of night, he would ... She knew only too well that he would stop at nothing. One murder had already been committed.

But now she had found one person whom she could trust, a man who had no interest in the thing she was hiding, a man who might well be a possible protector.

He seemed mildly surprised at her sudden friendliness.

"I didn't know this train stopped anywhere at that ungodly hour," she ventured, smiling.

"A flag stop," he explained. Across the aisle the fat man had not moved a muscle, yet she felt absolutely certain that those glittering eyes were concentrating on her and that he was listening as well as watching.

"You live in Wyoming?" she asked.

"I did as a boy. Now I'm going back. I lived and worked on my uncle's cattle ranch. He died and left it to me. At first I thought I'd sell it. It would bring a small fortune. But now I'm tired of the big cities, I'm going back to live on the ranch."

"Won't it be frightfully lonely?"

"At times."

She wanted to cling to him now, dreading the time when she would have to go back to her compartment.

She felt the trainmen must have a master key which could open even a bolted door — in the event of sickness, or if a passenger rang for help. There *must* be a master key which would manipulate even a bolted door. And if trainmen had such a key, the man who had searched her compartment would have one.

Frank Hardwick, before he died, had warned her. "Remember," he had said, "they're everywhere. They're watching you when you don't know you're being watched. When you think you're running away and into safety, you'll simply be rushing into a carefully laid trap."

She hoped there was no trace of the inner tension within her as she smiled at the man on her right. "Do tell me about the cattle business," she said ...

All night she had crouched in her compartment, watching the door, waiting for that first flicker of telltale motion which would show the doorknob was being turned. Then she would scream, pound on the walls of the compartment, make sufficient commotion to spread an alarm.

Nothing had happened. Probably that was the way "they" had planned it. They'd let her spend one sleepless night, then when fatigue had numbed her senses ...

The train abruptly slowed. She glanced at her wristwatch, saw that it was 5:55, and knew the train was stopping for the man who had inherited the cattle ranch. Howard Kane was the name he had given her after she had encouraged him to tell her all about himself. Howard Kane, twenty–eight, unmarried, presumably wealthy, his mind scarred by battle experiences, seeking the healing quality of the big, silent places, the one man on the train whom she knew she could trust.

There was a quiet competency about him, one felt he could handle any situation — and now he was getting off the train.

Suddenly a thought gripped her — "They" would hardly be expecting her to take the initiative. "They" always kept the initiative — that was why they always seemed so damnably efficient, so utterly invincible.

They chose the time, the place and the manner — give them that advantage, and ...

There wasn't time to reason the thing out. She jerked open the door of the little closet, whipped out her plaid coat, turned the fur collar up around her neck, and, as the train eased to a creaking stop, opened the door of her compartment and thrust out a cautious head.

The corridor was deserted.

She could hear the vestibule door being opened at the far end of the Pullman.

She ran to the opposite end of the car, fumbled for a moment with the fastenings of the vestibule door on the side next to the double track, then got it open and raised the platform.

Cold morning air, tanged with high elevation, rushed in to meet her, dispelling the train atmosphere, stealing the warmth from her garments.

The train started to move. She scrambled down the stairs, jumped for the graveled roadbed by the side of the track.

The train gathered speed. Dark, silent cars whizzed past her with continuing acceleration until the noise of the wheels became a mere hum. The steel rails readjusted themselves to the cold morning air, giving cracking sounds of protest. Overhead, stars blazed in steady brilliance. To the east was the first trace of daylight.

She looked for a town. There was none.

She could make out the faint outlines of a loading corral and cattle chute. Somewhere behind her was a road. An automobile was standing on this road, the motor running. Headlights sent twin cones of illumination knifing the darkness, etching into brilliance the stunted sagebrush shivering nervously under the impact of a cold north wind.

Two men were talking. A door slammed. She started running frantically.

"Wait!" she called. "Wait for me!"

Back on the train the fat man, fully dressed and shaved, contemplated the open vestibule door, then padded back to the recently vacated compartment and walked in.

He didn't even bother to search the baggage that had been left behind. Instead he sat down in the chair, held a telegraph blank against a magazine, and wrote out his message:

THE BUNGLING SEARCH TRICK DID THE JOB. SHE'S LEFT THE TRAIN. IT ONLY REMAINS TO CLOSE THE TRAP. I'LL GET OFF AT THE FIRST PLACE WHERE I CAN RENT A PLANE AND CONTACT THE SHERIFF.

Ten minutes later the fat man found the porter. "I find the elevation bothering me," he said. "I'm going to have to leave the train. Get the conductor."

"You won't get no lower by gettin' off," the porter said.

"No, but I'll get bracing fresh air and a doctor who'll give me a heart stimulant. I've been this way before. Get the conductor."

This time the porter saw the twenty–dollar bill in the fat man's fingers.

Seated between the two men in the warm interior of the car, she sought to concoct a convincing story.

Howard Kane said, by way of introduction, "This is Buck Doxey. I'm afraid I didn't catch your name last night."

"Nell Lindsay," she said quickly.

Buck Doxey, granite–faced, kept one hand on the steering wheel while he doffed a five–gallon hat. "Pleased to meet yuh, ma'am."

She sensed his cold hostility, his tight–lipped disapproval.

Howard Kane gently prodded for an explanation.

"It was a simple case of cause and effect," she said, laughing nervously. "It was so stuffy in the car I didn't sleep at all.

"So," she went on quickly, "I decided that I'd get out for a breath of fresh air. When the train slowed and I looked at my wristwatch I knew it was your stop and ... Well, I expected the train would be there for at least a few minutes. I couldn't find a porter to get the vestibule open, so I did it myself, and jumped down to the ground. That was where I made my mistake."

"Go on," he said.

"At a station you step down to a platform that's level with the tracks. But here I jumped onto a slanting shoulder of gravel, and sprawled flat. When I got up, the step of the car was so far above me ... Well, you have to wear skirts to understand what I mean."

Kane nodded gravely. Buck turned his head and gave Kane a quartering glance.

She said, "I guess I could have made it at that if I'd had sense enough to pull my skirt all the way up to the hips, but I couldn't make it on that first try and there wasn't time for a second one. The train started to move. Good heavens, they must have just *thrown* you off!"

"I'm traveling light," Kane said.

"Well," she told him, "that's the story. Now just what do I do?"

"Why, you accept our hospitality, of course."

"I couldn't ... couldn't wait here for the next train?"

"Nothing stops here except to discharge passengers coming from a division point," he said.

"But there's a ... station there. Isn't there someone on duty?"

"Only when cattle are being shipped," Buck Doxey explained. "This is a loading point."

"Oh."

She settled back against the seat, and was conscious of a reassuring masculine friendship on her right side, a cold detachment on her left side.

"I suppose it's horribly ravenous of me, but do we get to the ranch for breakfast?"

"I'm afraid not," Kane said. "It's slow going. Only sixty feet of the road is paved."

"Sixty feet?"

"That's right. We cross the main transcontinental highway about five miles north of here."

"What *do* we do about breakfast?"

"Well," Kane said, "in the trunk of the car there's a coffee pot and a canteen of water. I'm quite certain Buck brought along a few eggs and some ham ..."

"You mean you stop right out here in the open and cook?"

"When yuh stop here, you're in the open, ma'am," Buck said and somehow made it seem his words were in answer to some unjustified criticism.

She gave him her best smile. "Would it be impertinent to ask when?"

"In this next coulee ... right here ... right now."

The road slanted down to a dry wash that ran east and west. The perpendicular north bank broke the force of the north wind. Buck attested to the lack of traffic on the road by stopping the car squarely in the ruts.

They watched the sun rise over the plateau country, and ate breakfast. She hoped that Buck Doxey's cold disapproval wouldn't communicate itself to Howard Kane.

When Buck produced a battered dishpan, she said, "As the only woman present I claim the right to do the dishes."

"Women," Buck said, "are ..." and abruptly checked himself.

She laughingly pushed him aside and rolled up her sleeves. "Where's the soap?"

As she was finishing the last dish she heard the motor of the low–flying plane.

All three looked up.

The plane, which had been following the badly rutted road, banked into a sharp turn.

"Sure givin' us the once–over," Buck said, his eyes steady on Kane's face. "One of 'em has binoculars and he's as watchful as a cattle buyer at a loading chute. Don't yuh think it's about time we find out what we've got into, Boss?"

"I suppose it is," Kane said. Before her startled mind could counter his action, Buck Doxey picked up the purse which she had left lying on the running–board of the car.

She flew toward him.

Doxey's bronzed, steel fingers wrapped around her wet wrist. "Take it easy, ma'am," he said. "Take it easy."

He pushed her back, found her driving license. "The real name," he drawled, "seems to be Jane Marlow."

"Anything else?" Kane asked.

"Gobs of money, lipstick, keys and … Gosh, what a bankroll."

She went for him blindly.

Doxey said, "Now, ma'am, I'm goin' to have to spank yuh if yuh keep on like this."

The plane circled, its occupants obviously interested in the scene on the ground below.

"Now — here's something else," Doxey said, taking out a folded newspaper clipping.

She suddenly went limp. There was no use in further pretense.

Doxey read aloud, " 'Following the report of an autopsy surgeon, police, who had never been entirely satisfied that the unexplained death of Frank Hardwick was actually a suicide, are searching for his attractive secretary, Jane Marlow. The young woman reportedly had dinner with Hardwick in a downtown restaurant the night of his death.

" 'Hardwick, after leaving Miss Marlow, according to her story, went directly to the apartment of Eva Ingram, a strikingly beautiful model who has, however, convinced police that she was dining out. Within a matter of minutes after entering the Ingram apartment, Hardwick either jumped or fell from the eighth story window.

" 'With the finding of a witness who says Frank Hardwick was accompanied at least as far as the apartment door by a young woman whose description answers that of Jane Marlow, and evidence indicating several thousand dollars was removed from a concealed floor safe in Hardwick's office, police are anxious once more to question Miss Marlow. So far their efforts have definitely not been crowned with success.'

"And here's a picture of this young lady," Buck said, "with some more stuff under it.

" 'Jane Marlow, secretary of scientist who jumped from apartment window to his death, is now sought by police after witness claims to have seen her arguing angrily with Frank Hardwick when latter was ringing bell at front door of apartment house from which Hardwick fell or jumped to sidewalk.' "

Overhead, the plane suddenly ceased its circling and took off in a straight line to the north.

As the car proceeded northward, Buck put on speed, deftly avoiding the bad places in the road.

Jane Marlow, who had lapsed into hopeless silence, tried one more last desperate attempt when they crossed the paved road. "Please," she said, "let me out here. I'll catch a ride back to Los Angeles and report to the police."

Kane's eyes asked a silent question of the driver.

"Nope," Buck said decisively. "That plane was the sheriff's scout plane. He'll expect us to hold you. I don't crave to have no more trouble over women."

"All right," Jane said in a last burst of desperation, "I'll tell you the whole story. Then I'll leave it to your patriotism. I was secretary to Frank Hardwick. He was working on something that had to do with cosmic rays."

"I know," Doxey interrupted sarcastically. "And he dictated his secret formula to you."

"Don't be silly," she said, "but he *did* know that he was in danger. He told me that if anything happened to him, to take something, which he gave me, to a certain individual."

"Just keep on talking," Buck said. "Tell us about the money."

Her eyes were desperate. "Mr. Hardwick had a concealed floor safe in the office. He left reserve cash there for emergencies. He gave me the combination, told me that if anything happened to him, I was to go to that safe, take the money and deliver it and a certain paper to a certain scientist in Boston."

Buck's smile of skepticism was certain to influence Kane even more than words.

"Frank Hardwick never jumped out of any window," she went on. "They were waiting for him, and they threw him out."

"Or," Buck said, "a certain young lady became jealous, followed him, got him near an open window and then gave a sudden, unexpected shove. It *has* been done, you know."

"And people *have* told the truth," she blazed, "I don't enjoy what I'm doing. I consider it a duty to my country — and I'll probably be murdered, just as Frank Hardwick was."

"Now listen," Kane said. "Nice little girls don't jump off trains before daylight in the morning and tell the kind of stories you're telling. You got off that train because you were running away from someone.

She turned to Kane. "I was hoping that *you* would understand."

"He understands," Buck said, and laughed.

After that she was silent ...

Overhead, from time to time, the plane came circling back. Once it was gone for nearly forty–five minutes and she dared to hope they had thrown it off the track, but later she realized it had only gone to refuel and then it was back above them once more.

It was nearly nine when Buck turned off the rutted road and headed toward a group of unpainted, squat, log cabins which seemed to be bracing themselves against the cold wind while waiting for the winter snow. Back of the buildings were timbered mountains.

The pilot of the plane had evidently spotted the ranch long ago. Hardly had Buck turned off the road than the plane came circling in for a landing.

Jane Marlow had to lean against the cold wind as she walked from the car to the porch of the cabin. Howard Kane held the door open for her, and she found herself inside a cold room which fairly reeked of masculine tenancy, with a paper–littered desk, guns, deer and elk horns.

Within a matter of seconds she heard the pound of steps on the porch, the door was flung open, and the fat man and a companion stood on the threshold.

"Well, Jane," the fat man said, "you gave us quite a chase, didn't you?" He turned to the others.

"Reckon I'd better introduce myself, boys." He reached in his pocket, then took out a wallet and tossed it carelessly on the desk.

"I'm John Findlay of the FBI," he said,

"That's a lie," she said. "Can't you understand? This man is an enemy. Those credentials are forged."

"Well, ma'am," the other newcomer said, stepping forward, "there ain't nothing wrong with my credentials. I'm the sheriff here, and I'm taking you into custody."

He took her purse, said, "You just might have a gun in here."

He opened the purse. Findlay leaned over to look, said, "It's all there."

"Come on, Miss Marlow," the sheriff said, "You're going back in that plane."

"That plane of yours holds three people?" Findlay asked.

The sheriff looked appraisingly at the fat man. "Not us three."

"I can fly the crate," Findlay said. "I'll take the prisoner in, lock her up and then fly back for you and ..."

"No, no, no!" Jane Marlow screamed. "Don't you see, can't you realize, this man isn't an officer. I'd never get there. He ..."

"Shut up," the sheriff said.

"Sheriff, please! You're being victimized. Call up the FBI and you'll find out that ..."

"I've already called up the Los Angeles office of the FBI," the sheriff said.

Kane's brows leveled. "Was that because you were suspicious, Sheriff?"

"Findlay himself suggested it."

Jane was incredulous. "You mean they told you that ...?"

"They vouched for him in every way," the sheriff said. "They told me he'd been sent after Jane Marlow, and to give him every assistance. Now I've got to lock you up ..."

"She's my responsibility, Sheriff," Findlay said.

The sheriff frowned, then said, "Okay, I'll fly back and send a deputy out with a car."

"Very well," Findlay agreed. "I'll see that she stays put."

Jane Marlow said desperately, "I presume that when Mr. Findlay told you to call the FBI office in Los Angeles, he gave you the number so you wouldn't have to waste time getting it through an operator, didn't he?"

"Why not?" the sheriff said, smiling good–humoredly. "He'd be a hell of an FBI man if he didn't know his own telephone number."

The fat man fished a cigar from his pocket. Biting off the end and scraping a match into flame, he winked at the sheriff.

Howard Kane said to Findlay, "Mind if I ask a question?"

"Hell no. Go right ahead."

"I'd like to know something of the facts in this case. If you've been working on the case you'd know ..."

"Sure thing," Findlay agreed, getting his cigar burning evenly. "She worked for Hardwick, who was having an affair with a model. We followed him to the model's apartment. They had a quarrel. Hardwick's supposed to have jumped out of the window. She went to his office and took five thousand dollars out of the safe. The money's in her purse."

"So she was jealous?"

"Jealous and greedy. Don't forget she got five grand out of the safe."

"I was following my employer's specific instructions in everything I did," Jane said.

Findlay grinned.

"What's more," she blazed, "Frank Hardwick wasn't having any affair with that model. He was lured to her apartment. It was a trap and he walked right in."

Findlay said, "Yeah. The key we found in his vest pocket fitted the apartment door. He must have found it on the street and was returning it to the owner as an act of gallantry."

The sheriff laughed.

Howard Kane glanced speculatively at the very young woman. "She doesn't look like a criminal."

"Oh, thank you!" she blazed.

Findlay's glance was patronizing. "How many criminals have you seen, buddy?"

Doxey rolled a cigarette. His eyes narrowed against the smoke as he squatted down cowboy fashion on the backs of his high–heeled riding boots. "Ain't no question but what she's the one who jimmied the safe, is there?"

"The money's in her purse," Findlay said.

"Any accomplices?" Buck asked.

"No. It was a combination of jealousy and greed." Findlay glanced inquiringly at the sheriff.

"I'll fly in and send that car out," the sheriff said.

"Mind if I fly in with yuh and ride back with the deputy, Sheriff?" Buck asked eagerly. "I'd like to see this country from the air once. There's a paved road other side of that big mountain where the ranger has his station. I'd like to look down on it. Some day they'll connect us up. Now it's an hour's ride by horse ..."

"Sure," the sheriff agreed. "Glad to have you."

"Just give me time enough to throw a saddle on a horse," Doxey said. "Kane might want to ride out and look the ranch over. Yuh won't mind, Sheriff?"

"Make it snappy," the sheriff said.

Buck Doxey went to the barn and after a few minutes returned leading a dilapidated–looking range pony saddled and bridled. He casually dropped the reins in front of the ranch "office," and called inside:

"Ready any time you are, Sheriff."

They started for the airplane. Buck stopped at the car to get a map from the glove compartment, then hurried to join the sheriff. The propeller of the plane gave a half–turn, stopped, gave another half–turn; the motor sputtered, then roared into action. A moment later the plane became the focal point of a trailing dust cloud, then raised and swept over the squat log buildings in a climbing turn and headed south.

Jane Marlow and Kane watched it through the window until it became but a speck.

Howard Kane said, "Now, Mr. Findlay, I'd like to ask you a few questions."

"Sure, go right ahead."

"You impressed the sheriff very cleverly," Kane said, "but I'd like to have you explain ..."

"Now that it's too late," Jane Marlow blazed indignantly. "You've let him ..."

Kane motioned her to silence. "Don't you see, Miss Marlow, I had to get rid of the sheriff. He represents the law, right or wrong. But if this man is an imposter, I can protect you against him."

Findlay's hand moved with such rapidity that the big diamond made a streak of glittering light.

"Okay, wise guy," he said. "Try protecting her against this."

Kane rushed the gun.

Sheer surprise slowed Findlay's reaction time. Kane's fist flashed out in a swift arc, just before the gun roared.

The fat man moved with amazing speed. He rolled with the punch, spun completely around on his heel and jumped back, the automatic held to his body, his eyes glittering with rage.

"Get 'em up," he said.

The cold animosity of his tone showed that this time there would be no hesitancy.

Slowly Kane's hands came up.

"Turn around," Findlay said. "Move over by that window. Press your face against the wall. Give me your right hand, Kane. Now the left hand."

A smooth leather thong, which had been deftly knotted into a slipknot, was jerked tight, then knotted into a quick half hitch.

The girl, taking advantage of Findlay's preoccupation, flung herself on him.

The bulk of Findlay's big shoulders absorbed the onslaught without making him even shift the position of his feet. He jerked the leather thong into a last knot, turned and struck the girl in the pit of the stomach.

She wobbled about for a moment on rubber legs, then fell to the floor.

"Now, young lady," Findlay said, "you've caused me a hell of a lot of trouble. I'll just take the thing you're carrying in your left shoe. I could tell from the way you were limping there was something ..."

He jerked off the shoe, looked inside, seemed puzzled, then suddenly grabbed the girl's stockinged foot.

She kicked and tried to scream, but the wind had been knocked out of her.

Findlay reached casual hands up to the top of her stocking, jerked it loose without bothering to unfasten the garters, pulled the adhesive tape off the bottom of the girl's foot, ran out to the car, and jumped in.

"Well, what do you know!" he exclaimed. "The damn yokel took the keys with him ... So there's a paved road on the other side of the mountains, is there?

"Come on, horse, I guess there's a trail we can find. If we can't they'll never locate us in all that timber."

Moving swiftly, the fat man ran over to where the horse was standing on three legs, drowsing in the sunlight.

Findlay gathered up the reins, thrust one foot in the stirrup, grabbed the saddle, front and rear, and swung himself awkwardly into position.

Jane heard a shrill animal squeal of rage. The sleepy–looking horse, transformed into a bundle of dynamite, heaved himself into the air, ears laid back along his neck.

The fat man, grabbing the horn of the saddle, clung with frenzied desperation.

"Well," Kane asked, "are you going to untie me, or just stand there gawking?"

She ran to him then, frantically tugging at the knot.

The second his hands were freed Kane went into action.

Findlay, half out of the saddle, clung drunkenly to the pitching horse for a moment, then went into the air, turned half over and came down with a jar that shook the earth.

Kane emerged from the cabin holding a rifle.

"All right, Findlay, it's my turn now," Kane said. "Don't make a move for that gun."

The shaken Findlay seemed to have trouble orienting himself. He turned dazedly toward the sound of the voice, clawed for his gun.

Kane, aiming the rifle carefully, shot it out of his hand.

"Now, ma'am," Kane said, "if you want to get that paper out of his pocket ..."

She ran to Findlay, her feet fairly flying over the ground despite the fact that she was wearing only one shoe and the other foot had neither shoe nor stocking ...

Shortly before noon Jane Marlow decided to invade the sacred precincts of Buck Doxey's thoroughly masculine kitchen to prepare lunch. Howard Kane showed his respect for Findlay's resourcefulness by keeping him covered despite the man's bound wrists.

"Buck is going to hate me for this," she said. "Not that he doesn't hate me enough already — and I don't know why."

"Buck's soured on women," Kane explained. "I tried to tip you off. He was engaged to a girl in Cheyenne. No one knows exactly what happened, but they split up. I think she's as miserable as he is, but neither one will make the first move. But for heaven's sake don't try to rearrange his kitchen according to ideas of feminine efficiency. Just open a can of something and make coffee."

Findlay said, "I don't suppose there's any use trying to make a deal with you two."

Kane scornfully sighted along the gun by way of answer.

Jane, opening drawers in the kitchen, trying to locate the utensils, inadvertently stumbled on Buck Doxey's private heartache. A drawer containing letters, and the photograph of a girl.

The photograph had been torn into several pieces, and then laboriously pasted together and covered with Cellophane.

The front of the picture was inscribed: "To Buck with all my heart, Pearl."

Jane felt a surge of guilt at even having opened the drawer, but feminine curiosity caused her to hesitate long enough before closing it to notice Pearl's return address in the upper left–hand corner of one of the envelopes addressed to Buck Doxey ...

It was as they were finishing lunch that they heard the roar of the plane.

They went to the door to watch it turn into the teeth of the cold north wind, settle to a landing, then taxi up to the low log buildings.

The sheriff and Buck Doxey started running toward the cabins, and it was solace to Jane Marlow's pride to see the look of almost comic relief on the face of the sheriff as he saw Kane with the rifle and Findlay with bound wrists.

Jane heard the last part of Doxey's hurried explanation to Kane.

"Wouldn't trust a woman that far but her story held together and his didn't. I thought you'd understand what I was doing. I flew in with the sheriff just so I could call the FBI in Los Angeles. What do you know? Findlay is a badly wanted enemy spy. They want him bad as ... How did *you* make out?"

Kane grinned. "I decided to give Findlay a private third–degree. He answered my questions with a gun. If it hadn't been for that horse ..."

Buck's face broke into a grin. "He fell for that one?"

"Fell for it, and off it," Kane said.

"If he hadn't been a fool tenderfoot he'd have noticed that I led the horse out from the corral instead of riding him over. Old Fox is a rodeo horse, one of the best bucking broncs in Wyoming. Perfectly gentle until he feels it's time to do his stuff, and then he gives everything he has until he hears the ten–second whistle. I sort of figured Findlay might try something before I could sell the sheriff a bill of goods and get back."

It had been sheer impulse which caused Jane Marlow to leave the train early in the morning.

It was also sheer impulse which caused her to violate the law by forging Pearl's name to a telegram as she went through Cheyenne.

The telegram was addressed to Buck Doxey, care of the Forest Ranger Station and read:

BUCK I AM SO PROUD OF YOU PEARL.

Having started the message on its way, Jane looked up Pearl and casually told her of the torn picture which had been so laboriously pasted together.

Half an hour later Jane was once more speeding East aboard the sleek streamliner, wondering whether her efforts on behalf of Cupid had earned her the undying enmity of two people, or had perhaps been successful.

When she reached Omaha two telegrams were delivered. One was from Howard Kane and read simply:

YOU WERE SO RIGHT. IT GETS TERRIBLY LONELY AT TIMES. HOLD A DINNER DATE OPEN FOR TONIGHT. YOU NEED A BODYGUARD ON YOUR MISSION AND I AM FLYING TO CHICAGO TO MEET YOU AT TRAIN AND DISCUSS THE WYOMING CLIMATE AS A PERMANENT PLACE OF RESIDENCE.

LOVE, HOWARD

The second telegram was the big surprise. It read:

I GUESS I HAD IT COMING. PEARL AND I BOTH SEND LOVE. I GUESS I JUST NEVER REALIZED WOMEN ARE LIKE THAT.

YOURS HUMBLY, BUCK DOXEY

Bibliography

"Snowy Ducks for Cover." First published in *Dime Detective*, November 1931 (Vol. I, #1); copyright © 1931 by Erle Stanley Gardner, renewed 1959.

"The Corkscrew Kid." First published in *Black Aces*, January 1932 (Vol. I, #1); copyright © 1932 by Erle Stanley Gardner, renewed 1960.

"The Danger Zone." First published in *Argosy*, November 15, 1932; copyright © 1932 by Erle Stanley Gardner, renewed 1960.

"A Logical Ending." First published in *Detective Fiction Weekly*, April 29, 1933; copyright © 1933 by Erle Stanley Gardner, renewed 1961.

"Restless Pearls." First published in *All Detective*, November 1933; copyright © 1933 by Erle Stanley Gardner, renewed 1961.

"Time for Murder." First published in *Dime Detective*, January 15, 1933; copyright © 1933 by Erle Stanley Gardner, renewed 1961.

"Hard as Nails." First published in *Dime Detective*, January 15, 1935; copyright © 1935 by Erle Stanley Gardner, renewed 1963.

"Complete Designs." First published in *Short Stories*, July 25, 1936; copyright © 1936 by Erle Stanley Gardner, renewed 1964.

"Barney Killigen." First published in *Clues*, December 1938; copyright © 1938 by Erle Stanley Gardner, renewed 1966.

"Take It or Leave It." First published in *Black Mask*, March 1939; copyright © 1939 by Erle Stanley Gardner, renewed 1967.

"Flight Into Disaster." First published in *This Week Magazine* as a two–part serial, May 11 and May 18, 1952; copyright © 1952 by Erle Stanley Gardner, renewed 1970.

CRIPPEN & LANDRU, PUBLISHERS

P. O. Box 9315
Norfolk, VA 23505
E-mail: info@crippenlandru.com; toll-free 877 622-6656
Web: www.crippenlandru.com

Crippen & Landru publishes first edition short-story collections by important detective and mystery writers. The following books are currently in print in our regular series; see our website for full details:

Who Killed Father Christmas? by Patricia Moyes. Signed, unnumbered cloth overrun copies, $30.00. Trade softcover, $16.00.

My Mother, The Detective by James Yaffe. Trade softcover, $15.00.

In Kensington Gardens Once . . . by H.R.F. Keating. Trade softcover, $12.00.

The Ripper of Storyville by Edward D. Hoch. Trade softcover. $17.00.

Renowned Be Thy Grave by P.M. Carlson. Trade softcover, $16.00.

Carpenter and Quincannon by Bill Pronzini. Trade softcover, $16.00.

Not Safe After Dark and Other Stories by Peter Robinson. Trade softcover, $17.00.

All Creatures Dark and Dangerous by Doug Allyn. Trade softcover, $16.00.

Famous Blue Raincoat by Ed Gorman. Signed, unnumbered cloth overrun copies, $30.00. Trade softcover, $17.00.

McCone and Friends by Marcia Muller. Trade softcover, $16.00.

Challenge the Widow Maker by Clark Howard. Trade softcover, $16.00.

The Velvet Touch: Nick Velvet Stories by Edward D. Hoch. Trade softcover, $16.00.

Fortune's World by Michael Collins. Trade softcover, $16.00.

Long Live the Dead by Hugh B. Cave. Trade softcover, $16.00.

Tales Out of School by Carolyn Wheat. Trade softcover, $16.00.

Stakeout on Page Street by Joe Gores. Trade softcover, $16.00.

The Celestial Buffet by Susan Dunlap. Trade softcover, $16.00.

Kisses of Death by Max Allan Collins. Trade softcover, $17.00.

The Old Spies Club and Other Intrigues of Rand by Edward D. Hoch. Signed, unnumbered cloth overrun copies, $32.00. Trade softcover, $17.00.

Adam and Eve on a Raft by Ron Goulart. Signed, unnumbered cloth overrun copies, $32.00. Trade softcover, $17.00.

The Sedgemoor Strangler by Peter Lovesey. Trade softcover, $17.00.

The Reluctant Detective by Michael Z. Lewin. Signed, numbered clothbound, $42.00. Trade softcover, $17.00.

Nine Sons by Wendy Hornsby. Trade softcover, $16.00.

The Curious Conspiracy by Michael Gilbert. Signed, numbered clothbound, $42.00. Trade softcover, $17.00.

The 13 Culprits by Georges Simenon, translated by Peter Schulman. Trade softcover, $16.00.

The Dark Snow by Brendan DuBois. Signed, unnumbered cloth overrun copies, $32.00. Trade softcover, $17.00.

Jo Gar's Casebook by Raoul Whitfield, edited by Keith Alan Deutsch [Published with Black Mask Press]. Trade softcover, $20.00.

Come Into My Parlor by Hugh B. Cave. Trade softcover, $17.00.

The Iron Angel and Other Tales of the Gypsy Sleuth by Edward D. Hoch. Signed, numbered clothbound, $42.00. Trade softcover, $17.00.

Cuddy – Plus One by Jeremiah Healy. Trade softcover, $18.00.

Problems Solved by Bill Pronzini and Barry N. Malzberg. Signed, numbered clothbound, $42.00. Trade softcover, $16.00.

A Killing Climate by Eric Wright. Signed, numbered clothbound, $42.00. Trade softcover, $17.00.

Lucky Dip by Liza Cody. Signed, numbered clothbound, $42.00. Trade softcover, $17.00.

Kill the Umpire: The Calls of Ed Gorgon by Jon L. Breen. Signed, numbered clothbound, $42.00. Trade softcover, $17.00.

Suitable for Hanging by Margaret Maron. Signed, unnumbered cloth overrun copies, $32.00 Trade softcover, $17.00.

Murders and Other Confusions: The Chronicles of Susanna, Lady Appleton, Sixteenth-Century Gentlewoman, Herbalist, and Sleuth by Kathy Lynn Emerson. Signed, numbered clothbound, $42.00. Trade softcover, $17.00.

Byline: Mickey Spillane by Mickey Spillane, edited by Max Allan Collins and Lynn F. Myers, Jr. Signed, numbered clothbound, $48.00. Trade softcover, $20.00.

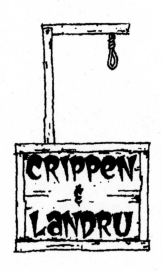

CRIPPEN & LANDRU LOST CLASSICS

Crippen & Landru is proud to publish a series of *new* short-story collections by great authors who specialized in traditional mysteries. Each book collects stories from crumbling pages of old pulp, digest, and slick magazines, and most of the stories have been "lost" since their first publication. Each volume is published in cloth and trade softcover. The following books are in print:

Peter Godfrey, *The Newtonian Egg and Other Cases of Rolf le Roux*, introduction by Ronald Godfrey

Craig Rice, *Murder, Mystery and Malone*, edited by Jeffrey A. Marks

Charles B. Child, *The Sleuth of Baghdad: The Inspector Chafik Stories*

Stuart Palmer, *Hildegarde Withers: Uncollected Riddles*, introduction by Mrs. Stuart Palmer

Christianna Brand, *The Spotted Cat and Other Mysteries from the Casebook of Inspector Cockrill*, edited by Tony Medawar

William Campbell Gault, *Marksman and Other Stories*, edited by Bill Pronzini; afterword by Shelley Gault

Gerald Kersh, *Karmesin: The World's Greatest Crook — Or Most Outrageous Liar*, edited by Paul Duncan

C. Daly King, *The Complete Curious Mr. Tarrant*, introduction by Edward D. Hoch

Helen McCloy, *The Pleasant Assassin and Other Cases of Dr. Basil Willing*, introduction by B.S. Pike

William L. DeAndrea, *Murder – All Kinds*, introduction by Jane Haddam

Anthony Berkeley, *The Avenging Chance and Other Mysteries from Roger Sheringham's Casebook*, edited by Tony Medawar and Arthur Robinson

Joseph Commings, *Banner Deadlines: The Impossible Files of Senator Brooks U. Banner*, edited by Robert Adey; memoir by Edward D. Hoch

Erle Stanley Gardner, *The Danger Zone and Other Stories*, edited by Bill Pronzini

T.S. Stribling, *Dr. Poggioli: Criminologist*, edited by Arthur Vidro

Margaret Millar, *The Couple Next Door: Collected Short Mysteries*, edited by Tom Nolan

Gladys Mitchell, *Sleuth's Alchemy: Cases of Mrs. Bradley and Others*, edited by Nicholas Fuller

FORTHCOMING LOST CLASSICS

Phillip S. Warne/Howard W. Macy, *Who Was Guilty? Two Dime Novels*, edited by Marlena Bremseth

Rafael Sabatini, *The Evidence of the Sword*, edited by Jesse Knight

Michael Collins, *Slot-Machine Kelly*, introduction by Robert J. Randisi

Julian Symons, *Francis Quarles: Detective*, edited by John Cooper; afterword by Kathleen Symons

Lloyd Biggle, Jr., *The Grandfather Rastin Mysteries*, introduction by Kenneth Biggle

Max Brand, *Masquerade: Nine Crime Stories*, edited by William F. Nolan, Jr.

Hugh Pentecost, *The Battles of Jericho*, introduction by S.T. Karnick

Erle Stanley Gardner, *The Casebook of Sidney Zoom*, edited by Bill Pronzini

Mignon G. Eberhart, *Something Simple in Black and Other Mysteries*, edited by Rick Cypert and Kirby McCauley

Victor Canning, *The Minerva Club, The Department of Patterns and Other Stories*, edited by John Higgins

Elizabeth Ferrars, *The Casebook of Jonas P. Jonas and Others*, edited by John Cooper

FORTHCOMING TITLES IN THE REGULAR SERIES

The Confessions of Owen Keane by Terence Faherty

The Adventure of the Murdered Moths and Other Radio Mysteries by
Ellery Queen

Murder – Ancient and Modern by Edward Marston

Murder! 'Orrible Murder! by Amy Myers

*More Things Impossible: The Second Casebook of Dr. Sam
Hawthorne* by Edward D. Hoch

14 Slayers by Paul Cain, edited by Max Allan Collins and Lynn F.
Myers, Jr. Published with Black Mask Press

Tough As Nails by Frederick Nebel, edited by Rob Preston.
Published with Black Mask Press

The Mankiller of Poojeegai and Other Mysteries by Walter
Satterthwait

A Pocketful of Noses: Stories of One Ganelon or Another by James
Powell

You'll Die Laughing by Norbert Davis, edited by Bill Pronzini.
Published with Black Mask Press

Hoch's Ladies by Edward D. Hoch

Quintet: The Cases of Chase and Delacroix, by Richard A.Lupoff

SUBSCRIPTIONS

Crippen & Landru offers discounts to individuals and institutions who
place Subscriptions for its forthcoming publications, either the
Regular Series or the Lost Classics or (preferably) both. Collectors
can thereby guarantee receiving limited editions in the Regular Series,
and readers won't miss any favorite stories. Subscribers receive a
specially commissioned story in a deluxe edition as a gift at the end
of the year. Please write or e-mail for more details.

Lost Classics